DEEP WATERS

ALSO BY

ALSO BY LINDA REID

FICTION

As Y S Pascal:

Renegades (The Zygan Emprise Trilogy, Book 1)
Redemption (The Zygan Emprise Trilogy, Book 2)
Rebirth (The Zygan Emprise Trilogy, Book 3)

NONFICTION

As Yolanda Reid Chassiakos

Collaboration Across the Disciplines in Health Care
New Leadership for Today's Health Care Professionals

PRAISE FOR AWARD WINNING SAMMY GREENE SERIES

DEAD AIR:

"*Dead Air* is a medical thriller on steroids. an antibody for boredom, the Rx-read you've got to fill."

- John Driver, Broadway playwright, director
& author of *Hunger of the Beast*

"*Dead Air* is a truly enjoyable, fast-paced, intriguing mystery with an appealing protagonist. Sammy Greene is inquisitive, feisty, imaginative, and stubborn, all the qualities needed to be a successful amateur sleuth. Plus she's 5 feet tall, has unruly red hair, and spouts Yiddish—what's not to love?"

- Rabbi Ilene Schneider, author of
Chanukah Guilt

"Sammy Greene, our sleuth for all seasons, is needed now as never before. Long may she live, to expose the truths we need to face."

- Kerry McKernon, Washington,
DC radio personality

"The announcer's booth is the perfect setting for this fast-paced and lively medical thriller.I found myself back in my early days behind the microphone when every disembodied voice on the line could be the source of something sinister. *Dead Air* is an incredible read. Well done!

> **- Barbara Whitesides, award-winning national radio news anchor, talk-show host and writer**

DEVIL WIND:

"Bristling with suspense, *Devil Wind* sizzles with the heat of high-level corruption, lowdown murder, and scorching desert winds howling down Los Angeles canyons and ratcheting up the excitement. Part Raymond Chandler, part Michael Connelly, this combustible tale is perfect beach reading."

> **- Gayle Lynds, New York Times best-selling author of *The Book of Spies***

"The whirlwind of a mystery pits the forces of justice- led by a quirky overnight radio personality- against the forces of evil from L.A.'s gritty streets, its drug-fueled cocktail parties, and its corridors of power. Taking a scalpel to crime, corruption, and hypocrisy, the authors of *Devil Wind*, both doctors, expose the frayed nervous system of Los Angeles at the turn of the twenty-first century, when the suffocating power of the Santa Ana winds blew into the soul of the city."

> **- Donald Bain, author of the Murder She Wrote mystery series**

DEEP WATERS:

"*DEEP WATERS* is that rare thing—a stylish adventure that weaves together fascinating historical detail, terrific characters and real suspense. A great read!"

> **- Dennis Palumbo, author of the Daniel Rinaldi Mystery Series**

"*Deep Waters*, the third in the wonderful Sammy Greene series, is a tightly plotted thriller that rivals Daniel da Silva and Dan Brown. Bravo!

> **- Spencer Grin, JD, PhD, Publisher of the Saturday Review**

"A white-knuckle, lip-chewing historical thriller that's simply exhilarating. Sammy Greene is my kind of hero — a female Indiana Jones who's bold and street-smart. If you're looking to plunge yourself into exotic mystery and globe-trotting suspense, *Deep Water* is just the ticket."

> **- John Ling, USA Bestselling Author of the Raines & Shaw series**

DEEP WATERS

BY DEBORAH SHLIAN
& LINDA REID

This book is dedicated to survivors of Greek history
Anastasios Hasiakos, George A. Hasiakos and Anastasia Hasiakou,
and E.G. and Effie Stassinopoulos

AUTHORS' NOTE

In November, 2018, divers discovered what is believed to be a missing piece of the Antikythera mechanism, an ancient analog computer, in the remains of a 2000-year-old shipwreck off the scenic Greek island. The encrusted cogwheel sported a drawing of Taurus the Bull. Ancient shipwrecks and their sunken treasures abound in the azure Aegean Sea and the Mediterranean shores. Deep Waters, our latest Sammy Greene thriller, may be fiction, but it is based on a vivid reality of Greek and Roman sailors daring to tackle the mighty seas—in which victory over Poseidon was not always assured.

Tourists who visit Greece enjoy its beautiful landscapes and beaches, delicious cuisine, and warm and friendly people, who embrace visitors with "Καλώς Ορίσατε", Welcome to Greece! Though most Greeks speak some English, it is helpful to have a little background about Greece's history and its heroes to help guide the path through an exploration of ruins and museums. But, for radio talk-show host and reporter Sammy Greene, who lands in Greece and stumbles on ancient and modern mysteries and murder, the warning signs all point to danger:

Enjoy her latest adventures!

Sincerely,
Deborah Shlian and Linda (Stassinopoulos) Reid

GUIDE FOR READERS
OF DEEP WATERS:

Hypatia—Hypatia was a Hellenistic philosopher, astronomer, and mathematician. She lived in Alexandria, Egypt, during the prominence of the Byzantine Roman Empire, and was renowned as a great scientist and teacher. She may have edited Ptolemy's "Almagest". She constructed astrolabes and hydrometers. She followed the Hellenistic religion, but was tolerant to Christianity, and taught Christian students. In 415 AD, she was kidnapped by a mob of Christian monks, and dragged through the streets until she died. The shocked empire named her a "martyr for philosophy".

Antikythera Device—The Antikythera Mechanism is an ancient Hellenic analog computer and orrery, which predicts the positions of the constellations and stars and was used for navigation, astrology, and calendaring. The mechanism has over 30 bronze gears. It was discovered in 1902 off the coast of the Greek island Antikythera, south of the Peloponnese.

Makronissos—Makronissos is a long island off the east coast of the Greek peninsula of Attica, which is also known as the "Island of Exile". The island was used as a military prison during the Greek Civil War from 1945-1949, as well as during the junta that ruled Greece from 1967-1973. The island is currently uninhabited—most of the time.

Elgin marbles—The Elgin Marbles originated from the Parthenon, and were designed and sculpted by Phidias, and included extended portions of the Parthenon frieze. They were removed by Thomas Bruce, 7th Earl of Elgin in the early 19th century and taken to Britain for "safekeeping", and are currently on display in the British Museum.

Palimpsest—A palimpsest is a manuscript or piece of writing from which the original text has been scraped or washed off so that the pages can be used for another text or document. It typically still bears traces of the original erased work.

Codex—A codex is an ancient manuscript constructed as a book. It can be made of sheets of paper or papyrus, and can contain scripture or classical literature or annals.

Solidus—A Roman coin that is typically solid gold.

Panaghia—Panaghia is one of the titles for Mary, Mother of Jesus Christ, commonly used in the Easter Orthodox faith.

Alto-Relievo (high relief)—a type of bas-relief wherein the sculpture projects at least half or more of its circumference from the background, and can have parts entirely disengaged, thus approximating sculpture in the round.

Mount Athos—Mount Athos is a mountain in northeastern Greece, and a center of Eastern Orthodox monasticism. It hosts 20 monasteries, and is commonly known in Greek as the "Holy Mountain". Monks from Greece, Romania, Moldova, Georgia, Bulgaria, Serbia, and Russia come to Athos, which is governed, like the Vatican, as an autonomous polity. Access to Mount Athos is forbidden to women; and has welcomed male dignitaries such as Prince Charles and Vladimir Putin.

Skete—A Skete is a community of monks that allows for both isolation and communal services, in which monks can avoid distraction as they pray to God. A middle ground for monks who wish to avoid complete isolation, and share resources.

DEEP WATERS

AND IN THOSE DAYS there appeared in Alexandria a female philosopher, a pagan named Hypatia, and she was devoted at all times to magic, astrolabes and instruments of music, and she beguiled many people through Satanic wiles. And the governor of the city honored her exceedingly; for she had beguiled him through her magic. And he ceased attending church as had been his custom. … a multitude of believers in God arose under the guidance of Peter the magistrate — now this Peter was a perfect believer in all respects in Jesus Christ — and they proceeded to seek for the pagan woman who had beguiled the people of the city and the prefect through her enchantments. And when they learnt the place where she was, they proceeded to her and found her seated on a chair; and having made her descend they dragged her along till they brought her to the great church, named Caesarion…And they tore off her clothing and dragged her through the streets of the city till she died. And they carried her to a place named Cinaron, and they burned her body with fire. And all the people surrounded the patriarch Cyril and named him "the new Theophilus"; for he had destroyed the last remains of idolatry in the city.

—By John, Bishop of Nikiu, from his *Chronicle* 84.87-103

PROLOGUE

Greece, 415 CE

"Hypatia is dead! Murder!" Breathless, the messenger raced into the tiny shrine at the rear of the Parthenon where a crowd of gray-haired clerics had gathered.

One of the elders held up a hand. "Explain, my son."

"Christos' worshipers are rising up from Kriti to Korinthos," he gasped. "Many of our followers have been massacred, burned alive!"

"It is true then. We are done." A tall curate, veins throbbing in his scrawny neck, turned on his brethren with bitter reproach. "We should have acted back when Theodosius banned the Delphic Oracle."

Another cleric shook his balding head. "There was still hope that Julian's acolytes would prevail, and that co-existence would be possible in Byzantium. Hypatia herself had been given sanctuary in Alexandria."

The tall priest nodded toward the shrine's doorway to the temple's atrium; the view through the opening was filled by the skirt of Phidias' enormous gold statue of the goddess Athena. "Zeus is being mortally wounded by the disciples of the cross. I now fear for our patroness."

A wide-eyed middle-aged priest, as ashen as his habit, cried, "They will rend Athena into pieces!"

The young man wiped sweat from his brow with the sleeve of his dirt-caked robe. "Do not doubt they will seize her gold even as they will bathe the Acropolis in our blood, and

1

denounce us as infidels and unbelievers. We must not wait for the slaughter."

The bald cleric pursed his lips. "Thanks to the scholars of Heron we are prepared to safe-keep Athena. Though I never truly believed this day would come. Philippos?"

Everyone turned to the most senior of the clerics. His expression somber, Philippos continued to stroke his long gray beard for several minutes before clearing his throat. "Καιρόανήκω". *It is time.*

CHAPTER ONE

Greece, November, 1997

S ammy Greene gripped the rail of the bucking Hellenic
Cultural Ministry research vessel Θησαυρός (Thesaurus) as
a large swell crested over its anchored bow, drenching her and
plastering her curly red hair like a cap against her ears.
"*A brokh!*" she cursed in Yiddish learned at the knee of her
Bubbe Rose.

Poor Ollie must be on a roller coaster ride in the depths below.

Clinging to the rusty railing, Sammy squinted through the
mist at the churning waters beyond. The distance lines for the
dive team were being lashed by the whitecaps; the sound
reminded her of a twirling jump rope slapping the brick
pavement of the Lower East Side alley where she and her
friends used to play during the hot summer evenings years ago.
*Would the nylon cords be strong enough to survive the rough seas
and lead Ollie and the others up to safety?*

"May God's hand protect them!" cried Father Mihalis in
Greek, his soaked black robes dripping a trail of water onto the
polished tips of his ebon shoes. A foot taller than Sammy, the
imposing, bearded Orthodox priest almost knocked her over as
he staggered to keep his balance.

Loukas Doxiadis, dismissing the priest's supplication to
God, stubbed out his cigarette, threw it over the side of the
Thesaurus, and ran a sinewy hand through his long black hair.
The young graduate student from the renowned Athens
University winked at Sammy, adding in English, "You know,

3

Father Mihalis, our ancestors might insist it is Poseidon who is quite angry with us for disturbing his lair."

His comb-over long lost to the tempest, Professor Andreas Roussos lurched towards them, twisted the edge of his pencil-thin mustache and wagged a minatory finger at his protégé, Doxiadis. Apparently, even the less faithful were expected to offer the clergy respect.

Not religious herself, Sammy had been just as willing to blame a displeased Poseidon as a vengeful God for the nausea-inducing storm. But Ollie, her cameraman, must have been trying to hedge his bets when he'd let go of the ship's ladder and fallen supine into the sea two hours earlier. Sammy was certain she'd caught the diver's free hand touching his mask, left chest, right chest, and heart—the Gentile sign of the cross—as the grey eddies enveloped him and drew him into the deep.

Professor Roussos propped himself against the railing and shook his head. "Only six Beaufort today," he said, describing the wind speed of twenty-five knots. "The Aegean was not so calm when the *Apocalypsi* capsized." He pronounced the sunken vessel's name in Greek, with the accent on the syllable 'ca'.

Only? Sammy scoffed, willing her stomach to stay "below decks". Experienced sailors might consider the weather simply a strong breeze, but the scopolamine patch her sometime boyfriend Reed Wyndham had prescribed for motion sickness was no match for this Six Flags spin. Growing up in her landlocked New York neighborhood, she'd rarely had an opportunity to *see* the open sea, much less bounce around in it. Thank goodness Oliver "Ollie" Haines was seasoned underwater and hadn't expected *her* to don scuba gear. Rational or not, Sammy's feelings echoed those of the ancient Greeks about Poseidon - there was something sinister about probing Davy Jones' locker. *Godspeed, Ollie, godspeed.*

"Focus there, at Makronissos." Doxiadis stretched his arm out toward the bleak island five kilometers to the northeast. "Not down at the lines."

A nod. *Do I look as green as I feel?* Despite the graduate student's helpful advice, Sammy found her eyes drawn back to the swirling waters that teased the divers' black umbilical cords flapping against the side of the *Thesaurus*. Shivering, she pulled the hood of her windbreaker over her sodden curls and gazed out at the fog-enshrouded land mass several miles in the distance. According to Professor Roussos, the *Apocalypsi* had lain undiscovered off the coast of Makronissos Island for centuries. Maybe Doxiadis was right. Disturbing its grave now had angered the gods.

Angering the gods. She was good at that. Why else would CNN have sent her to produce a minor feature five thousand miles from the network's offices in Washington? An ancient shipwreck might captivate viewers of the Discovery Channel, but the kind of investigative reporting she'd hoped to score after graduation was in the political arena, not the classical one.

It *was* politics that led to this assignment, according to Vito, assignment editor for Barry Kane's *Up Front DC*. He'd hinted that Sammy's aggressiveness pursuing congressional fraud and corruption had begun to ruffle some powerful feathers among her Washington targets. "Look Sammy, you're less than a year out of college. If you want a permanent gig here, you gotta take it slow. Let things cool off for a while. In fact, speaking of cool, I've got a cool feature piece for you. Should help you raise your stock a bit when you get back."

A week later, Sammy met Ollie at Athens' Hellenikon Airport. They'd grabbed a taxi to the port of Lavrium near Poseidon's temple at Cape Sounion and connected with the team of Greek archaeologists, professors, divers, and maritime engineers who were tasked to research a lost chapter of human history. But now, having lost the battle to stay dry, she started focusing on staying upright. *Sure, guys, the discovery was exciting, but shouldn't you have waited to go back out until the weather cleared?*

When another dose of spray splashed onto Sammy's windbreaker, Professor Roussos suggested Sammy follow him back down to the cabin where his colleagues were busy sorting through already-salvaged artifacts. "It is more comfortable downstairs. I can show you what we have discovered, and why these finds are so important for our work."

With nothing she else could do on deck, Sammy agreed, glancing at her Timex for the fifth time since Ollie had let himself fall into Poseidon's arms. *Worrying about Ollie wasn't helping anyone.* "Yes, thanks," she said to the Professor. "I'm right behind you."

CHAPTER TWO

The same day

Far beneath the surface, there was barely a hint of turbulence. Bringing up the rear of the dive team, Oliver Haines couldn't help thinking that Sammy was missing a rare treat. Too bad the kid had no sea legs. She'd groused about this assignment from the moment their they'd left Athens' airport.

For his part, the English free-lancer was delighted that CNN had called. The Beeb and Sky still paid Nam-level wages. Pre-inflation. And, on the heels of that bloody gig in the Balkans that had almost cost him his life, he needed respite. What could be better than a chance to dust off his scuba gear and test his new underwater video equipment? The crystalline Aegean was one of the most beautiful places on the planet. In the past few minutes, he'd already caught graceful electric blue damselfish, spiral tubeworms, and elegant starfish on film.

Given the cool temperature of the water, he was glad the dive team leader had insisted he borrow the extra crushed neoprene drysuit on board—even if it was a bit snug. With so little time to practice, he hoped he would remember instructions for inflation and deflation.

Cautiously, he added air to the suit to eliminate the squeeze and used his buoyancy control vest to descend. As he vented air, he drifted downward until he reached twenty meters. He ignored the dusky groupers and saddled seabreams brushing past to focus his Nikonos video camera along the trail of debris left when the ancient ship ran aground, captivated by the knowledge that the last time the mariners of this vessel had been on dry land, Constantinople was the center of the Byzantine Empire, and the cradle of Christianity in the "New Rome". His scuba gear was like a time machine that would give him—and his viewers—a glimpse of a remarkable past.

While Father Mihalis remained on the upper deck, Sammy and Loukas trailed Professor Roussos down a narrow set of steep stairs into the stuffy cabin.

"Father Mihalis must think he'll get better reception to heaven up there," Loukas muttered as they entered a narrow stateroom where several scientists, dressed in medical scrubs and wearing latex gloves, were carefully rearranging tagged artifacts on a tarp covered table.

Ignoring the comment, Professor Roussos explained that the research vessel had been aptly named. "Thesauru translates to English as Treasure. And we are blessed to have found the motherlode."

Sammy pulled out a notebook and pen from her jacket pocket and jotted down Thesaurus/treasure, and the names and professions of two archaeologists and a maritime engineer as Professor Roussos introduced them. The rest of the recovery team, the scientists they'd met that morning, he said, were napping. Apparently, they'd been staffing round-the-clock shifts for the past two weeks, trying to finish their work before the onset of winter rains.

"Last summer," Roussos began explaining in accented English, "a German couple on a sailing holiday went diving off Makronissos Island—50 kilometers from Athens—and found several pieces of broken pottery wedged in seaweed in the silt." He indicated a few shards on the table. "Because Makronissos has been deserted for a long time, there hasn't been any significant scientific exploration of the area. I immediately petitioned the government to authorize further study. Afraid of looters, the Ministry of Mercantile Marine declared the area off limits to tourists and gave their blessing to our expedition."

"Speaking of blessings, is Father Mihalis part of your team?" Sammy asked.

"Government and religion are bedfellows here in Greece. Ministry oversight includes representatives of the Greek Orthodox Church. Who better to protect our sacred history, yes? Father Mihalis is the protopresbyter at St. Therapon Cathedral in Zografou, Athens—not far from our University. The senior priest," he stated proudly.

Sammy returned his smile. "So how did you make the leap from a few pieces of pottery to a shipwreck?" she asked, intrigued.

"Every historian dreams of such a discovery." Roussos couldn't hide his pleasure at the notion. "The shelf where the *touristes* found the pottery is about twenty meters deep. About sixty-five feet," he explained. "One hundred meters out, three hundred feet, it falls away to almost a thousand feet. So it was possible that a ship could run aground on the shelf, then sink.

"It took weeks using sonar and a remote controlled exploration vehicle, but we finally located the actual site of the wreck. I had hoped to find an intact ship at that depth, but, alas, most of the wood had been devoured by shipworms. Only bronze struts and rusted bolts were left. And of course, some of the pottery. Claude here," he said, indicating the older of the two archaeologists busy at the table, "determined that the pottery design was similar to artifacts from the Severan Dynasty. *N'est-ce pas?*"

Sammy almost lost her footing again as the ship rocked from side to side. "How old?" she asked, trying to focus on something other than her persistent seasickness. And Ollie's absence.

"That's what we're trying to determine now." Roussos said.

The French archaeologist nodded, adding a few words in accented English. "*Troisième* century AD, *c'est possible*."

Roussos pointed to several ceramic fragments laid out before them. "These are the newest, but we've already recovered at least twenty fragmentary jars scattered near the ship and on the shallower shelf that are being reconstructed at the Hellenic Archaeological museum. These amphorae were used to transport wine and oil. Look. Tall, narrow proportions, lack of neck, low rim, small ring handles at the shoulders, and bands of ridging near the rim and base. These kind of jars circulated widely across the Mediterranean from at least the third to the eighth centuries."

Amazing! "So it was some kind of trading ship?"

"That's my theory. I'd date it around the seventh century based on the healthy trading economy of the period, but *others* disagree."

A throaty grunt came from the far corner of the cabin where another of the scientists was hunched over a collection of rusted struts. Rising to face them, the plump middle-aged man was just a few inches taller than Sammy. He had a permanently furrowed brow and bushy eyebrows overhanging wire-rimmed glasses.

"Professor Lambros and I work together at Athens University," Roussos said, his tone gaining an edge. "Harris, this is Sammy Greene from CNN. She's come to do a story on my—our finds."

Harris Lambros' dark brows formed a skeptical V as he scrutinized Sammy. "Are you a student of Greek history?"

"Afraid not, but I'm here to learn," she replied, dismissing the man's condescension with her sweetest smile. Her nausea rising with each wave's crest, she'd say anything necessary to get her story and return post-haste to solid ground.

"Well, despite what *my esteemed colleague* insists, I believe the amphorae carried cargo from a Roman trireme. To

Constantinople if we track the journey from Piraeus, the Port of Athens. That could make it fourth or fifth century, not seventh."

Sammy added that to her notes.

"A trireme is a warship," Roussos injected. "Harris doesn't accept the common knowledge that the trireme never sank because it contained such little ballast. That's why there's never been one found."

"Up to now," Lambros replied, his eyes narrowing.

If this was the first such discovery, Sammy realized, what a coup that would be for the diminutive professor....Lambros. No doubt though, from Professor Roussos would not be happy to be outshined by someone at least a decade younger. An embarrassing career setback for the expedition's lead archaeologist. Sammy felt am unwelcome chill. Three years ago, when she was a student at Vermont's Ellsford University, an academic clash had led to a professor's murder and almost cost Sammy her life. Academic conflicts could be deadly.

Sammy held her breath, expecting a snide retort or worse from Roussos. Instead, he burst out laughing. "Such is the joy of the academy. We shall have spirited debates for the next many months about all the treasures we have found. *Eh*, Harris?"

For over thirty minutes Ollie had filmed the divers combing through the shelf's soft bottom for artifacts and debris from the sunken ship. The strong currents had slowed their progress, but they'd managed to collect several netfuls of broken pottery.

Unfortunately, tedious scenes of divers hunting for vases were hardly likely to get decent airplay on the network. Especially after video of the wreck itself, shot from a sonar-guided remote explorer had already aired to much fanfare. With only one day allotted to his own shoot, it might have to be up to Sammy to find a way to punch up the heat level for the B-roll he'd recorded. Otherwise, their piece would end up as weekend filler on a slow news day.

Ollie checked his gauges, satisfied that he could remain at twenty meters for another ten minutes before beginning his rise to the surface. Let the diving team do their job; he needed to do his. Get film segments that would pop off the screen.

He signaled one of the team with a thumbs-up indicating he was about to start his ascent, then turned in the opposite direction away from the mooring line, aiming towards the location of the shipwreck. A few more shots would spice up his stock. The siren call from the murky depths of Amphitrite, Poseidon's beautiful wife, was too tempting to resist.

Struggling to hold his camera steady, Ollie let the swift current carry him closer to the edge of the shelf. As he neared the drop-off, he was battered by a rush of ice-cold flow which threw him back onto the shelf's sea floor. *Christ*, he thought. *Downwelling*. One of his worst nightmares, he'd only encountered it once before – a dive off Sydney years ago when he was a lot younger and fitter. He'd spilled off the Great Barrier Reef, riding helpless down an underwater waterfall deeper towards the bottom. Ollie scoured his memory for the steps to recover. Buffeted again and again by the water's force, he fought to ascend against the current. He knew he was using precious air, but he had no choice. With excruciating slowness, he inched his way back to the mooring line.

Just as he grasped hold of it again, one of his fins got caught in a protruding bronze strut. He bent to dislodge it with the same hand that held his camera when he noticed something embedded in a small rock nearby, its visibility hampered by the current stirring the silt. Closer inspection suggested it too was made of some kind of metal. Bronze? Aiming his camera, he adjusted the lens until a three-inch wheel came into clear focus. There was writing on it...ancient Greek?

This could be something significant. Excited, Ollie clipped the camera to the D ring on his BC, let go of the rope using his wedged fin as leverage and scooped up the rock with both hands. His fingers clutched the wheel and gently lifted it from the silt. Ollie saw that a toothed gear had adhered to the wheel's back. The thin rusted metal from both pieces reflected the light from his torch into his eyes, momentarily blinding him. He quickly stashed his find in his vest pocket, then felt a tug behind him.

A trail of bubbles...

Ollie swiveled to see one of the dive team hovering. He'd barely registered the names and faces of the team members when he'd been introduced yesterday, but in any case, the tight-fitting masks they all wore distorted their features, making identification of his companion difficult. An extra pair of hands was very welcome to help him extricate his trapped fin so he could head back up to the ship. Ollie couldn't wait to show Sammy and the team the treasure he'd discovered.

With only minutes of bottom time remaining, Ollie grabbed the rope and gestured at his jammed fin. To his surprise, the diver made no move to help, but continued to float beyond arm's length above.

His anxiety growing, Ollie tried a distress signal, waving his hand quickly over his head. Still no reaction from the diver. He struggled to free himself from the strut. Couldn't the bloody fool see he was in trouble?

Frustrated, but aware that he needed to hurry, Ollie turned away to focus on his predicament. Hyperventilating with the effort, he knew he was expending his air supply too quickly, yet didn't dare release the mooring line to use both hands. The strong downwelling could push him farther toward the bottom, making it impossible to return to the surface in time.

Ollie forced himself not to panic. There! He'd managed to unclip the fin from his boot. Giddy with relief, he inhaled one deep breath before checking the gauge on his air tank. Bloody hell! Less than one hundred psi of compressed air remained. Shit, he'd used up too much trying to get free!

He lifted his head. Even at seventy feet down he could see rays of sun angling down from the shimmering surface. The trip up, with appropriate safety stops to decompress, should take four to nine minutes. With little reserve in the tank, Ollie no longer had the luxury of making a slow ascent. Unless...

Desperate, he twisted to face the diver who still hovered nearby, his hands tucked in his weightbelt like a nonchalant American gunslinger. Simulating a throat slitting motion, Ollie made the universal sign signifying that he was nearly out of air, and with it, an appeal to share the diver's oxygen.

For a moment, the diver seemed to back off, then, as if reconsidering, swam hurriedly toward him. Grateful, and hungry for air, Ollie reached out for the diver's spare regulator, only to have his own hose ripped from his lips. *What the hell?* Ollie sucked in a mouthful of seawater and lost his grip on the mooring line. Choking and disoriented, he was in no position to fight when the diver reached into his vest pocket, grabbed the wheel and gear, and unbuckled his weightbelt, launching him toward the surface like a projectile.

In his final moments of consciousness, Ollie suspected that someone must have tampered with his BC vest. But he never had time to wonder why.

CHAPTER THREE

"*Voitheia*! *Voitheia*!" echoed through the stateroom.

No one needed to translate the call for help for Sammy. Arguments were quickly dropped as the professors, led by Sammy, hurried up the narrow stairs.

Two of the divers, back on deck and relieved of their tanks, were pointing at something in the water off the port bow of the *Thesaurus*. They shouted at two others in a motorized rubber raft who were making their way toward a large black object bobbing in the waves.

"God in heaven, it's a body!" Father Mihalis cried out in Greek.

Forcing herself on unsteady legs to find a sightline at the rail, Sammy watched with growing dread as the rescuers pulled what was now clearly a man in a neoprene drysuit into the dinghy and unclipped his air tank.

"Ollie!" Sammy recognized her cameraman the moment they'd laid him supine on the deck and pulled off his mask. Even from where she stood on the research vessel, she could see that Ollie's face was a dark shade of purple, with gobs of red foam bubbling from the corners of his mouth. Shaking, Sammy observed the rescuers unlatch his camera, tear off his drysuit, and begin CPR. Father Mihalis blocked her view as he rushed to the feet of the unconscious man and began reciting last rites.

"C'mon, Ollie," Sammy whispered, hugging herself to ward off the bitter cold that now engulfed her. "C'mon."

The captain placed an oxygen mask over Ollie's mouth while the rescuers continued rotating through several rounds of chest compressions. The first officer raced up carrying a small yellow plastic suitcase and opened it to reveal an Automated External Defibrillator.

"Breathe," Sammy urged, feeling helpless.

Loukas put a comforting arm on her shoulders, and sighed. "Even a decompression chamber would be of no use now, I fear," he said.

Once a rescuer had attached the AED's pads, the first officer shouted "clear", warning everyone to stand back. Ollie's body jerked as the jolt raced through his lifeless body.

"Again!" the officer cried, and Ollie's arms and legs danced before returning to the stillness of demise. Several more rounds of AED jolts alternated with CPR did not return a pulse or heartbeat to Ollie's immobile form. Finally, the officer shook his head.

Sighing, the captain turned and nodded at the somber priest and pronounced, "He is gone".

Father Mihalis echoed the news. "*Aionia i mnimi*," he began to chant. *May his memory be eternal.*

CNN Studios, Washington, DC

Three days later, Sammy was back at her desk. "Jet lag" was her excuse for her bloodshot eyes framed by dark circles. Those penetrating green eyes, like everyone else's in the newsroom, were now glued to the monitors on which CNN anchors were breathlessly detailing breaking news of a massacre in Luxor.

"Egyptian police say over thirty-three tourists were killed and many more wounded today. So far, eight Americans are identified among the dead. Reports indicate the Jihad Talaat al-Fath terrorist group may be behind the attack. Egyptian President Mubarak has announced he will replace of his Minister of the Interior and will address the Egyptian people in less than an hour. We'll take you live now to Cairo and to correspondent Reza Isfahani…"

Sammy turned away from the TV. Death, death, and more death. In her twenty-three years, Sammy had already seen more than her share - her mother's suicide, the murders at Ellsford, and now Ollie. Fighting a recurring wave of nausea, she rested her head on her scribble-filled blotter, hiding welling tears. She'd flown back from Greece as soon as the medical examiner in Lavrium had completed the autopsy and announced his results. Oliver Haines had died of asphyxiation and rapid decompression, drowning in his own blood. A sad, fatal accident.

Though she'd only met the cameraman two days before the shoot, Sammy had been impressed by his adventurous spirit and passion for journalism. The moment she'd landed back at Dulles airport, she'd rushed to the network offices, hoping to convince Vito and the producers not to kill their story. Greek authorities had promised to release Ollie's camera as soon as they filed their official report. If the film had survived, she'd argued, she could salvage the piece and give Ollie his last bow on the air.

The suits hadn't ruled out that possibility entirely. But Sammy knew the wave of tragedy that had just crashed onto the Middle East would wash away the opportunity. *I'm so sorry, Ollie.* The news spotlight was now on Egypt. No one in charge in DC or Atlanta would be eager to spend valuable airtime on an ancient shipwreck—or its final victim.

CHAPTER FOUR

Greece, April, 2003 (six years later)

"*Aionia i mnimi, Aionia i mnimi.*" Eternal is his memory.
Gus Pappajohn patted Eleni Kapsis' hand as the priest prayed for the soul of her husband George. Like his sister, Pappajohn was widowed. His beloved wife Effie had succumbed to cancer almost a decade earlier. The damp handkerchief clutched in Eleni's palm re-triggered the pain of his bereavement. *If only our losses could be wiped away like tears.*

The funeral was merely the beginning. Knowing how difficult the weeks and months ahead would be for Eleni, Pappajohn had caught the first flight out of Boston the minute she'd called with news of George's passing. The ex-police chief planned to travel to Crete with George and Eleni this summer; their excursion to Northern Greece and Mt. Olympus last year had been fueled by laughter and fun. Eleni had even teased her brother that she'd find him a female companion among George's many friends for their seaside August vacation this year. Instead, George's devastating heart attack brought Pappajohn prematurely to Greece in the chill of late spring. *Heart attacks are never planned.*

Gazing at his sister's bowed, gray-streaked head, Pappajohn felt another wave of sadness. George is—*was*—a wonderful man who'd made Eleni so happy. After her first husband died, Eleni vowed never to marry again. Then, six years ago, while vacationing in Athens, she'd met George, who'd wooed her with a charm and energy that belied his seventy years. He'd finally

18

persuaded her to take one more chance on love, allowing the childless widow to become a mother to his children and grand-children. It was a role she'd treasured—to be both a wife and a *yiayia Grandma*.

Pappajohn was delighted to witness his sister's new-found joy. He'd liked George the moment they'd met and had given the golden couple his blessing, dancing at their wedding and wishing them years of happiness.

Why could there not have been more years? He brushed away a solitary tear while the priest intoned: "Who hast trampled down death by death and overthrown the Devil and hast bestowed life upon Thy world: do Thou Thyself, O Lord, grant rest to the soul of Thy departed servant, *Yeorgios Kapsis*, in a place of brightness, a place of verdure, a place of repose, whence all sickness, sorrow and sighing have fled away."

As the polished mahogany casket was slowly lowered into the gravesite, Pappajohn surveyed the somber crowd gathered to honor their departed father, grandfather, cousin, and friend. Several of the young adults coming to pay respects had journeyed hours to this mountain village of Gravia where George had spent much of his life, first as a student, and then as the town's revered high school professor, their *kathigitis*.

"For Thou art the Resurrection, and the Life, and the Repose of Thy departed servant *Yeorgios Kapsis*." While the priest continued with the Litany of St. John Chrysostom, Pappajohn offered his own silent prayer that the love of Eleni's new family would lessen the pain of her loss.

"O Christ our God, and unto Thee we ascribe glory, together with Thy Father, Who is from everlasting, and Thine All-Holy, and Good and Life-Giving Spirit, now and ever, and unto ages of ages."

"Amen." The sea of mourners murmured, as the first shovels of dirt sprinkled onto the flowers adorning the casket, muddying their colors with the brown cloak of death.

"*Aionia i Mnimi…*"

George's eldest son, Anastasios, nicknamed Tasos, invited mourners to the family's ancestral home down the road from the church for the traditional "mercy meal". Hours later, Eleni allowed herself a sigh of relief, seasoned with more than a twinge of sadness, as the last of the guests exited the century-old stone house. George's love of learning had inspired so many of his students. *How kind of them to share their memories and gratitude. But I am so very, very tired.*

Closing the weather-beaten wooden door, Eleni surveyed the tiny front room, imagining a teenaged George and his brothers and sisters huddled near the fireplace on the far wall during the frigid winters, studying tattered books by the light of oil lamps, and hoping one day to fulfill dreams of attending a teacher's college in German-occupied Athens.

George had told her how, nearly frostbitten, he'd trudged through winter snow for twelve hours each autumn to attend high school fifty kilometers away from his family, and renting a cot for the academic year in a drafty cellar of a wind-battered cottage by the sea.

Life had only gotten worse during the four-year Greek Civil War after the defeat of the Nazi occupiers in World War II. Draftees from families like George's, identified as leaning left-wing, were soon feared to be "Communist sympathizers" who wanted Greece to join the Eastern Bloc. Not trusted by Athens' right-wing government to fight on the front lines, George and his compatriots were shipped to the infamous Island of Exile, Makronissos. There, they joined thousands of imprisoned political prisoners confined in concentration camps, where they were starved and brutalized for almost four years.

The thought of how her husband must have suffered brought Eleni fresh tears. At the sound of laughter from the next room, she dried her eyes and entered the kitchen where her extended family were almost finished cleaning up. Modern appliances had not been installed in this century-old cabin, so Tasos' buxom wife Daphne stood washing dishes at the sink, and their son, eleven-year-old Georgie, was busy drying the chipped Italian china. Maria, Tasos' fourteen year old daughter, was arranging leftovers in a rickety icebox while listening to music on her iPod.

"What's so funny?" Eleni asked.

They pointed towards the corner. Pappajohn had fallen asleep in a rocking chair, his salt-and-pepper mustache flapping as he snored.

Smiling, Eleni whispered in English, "Jet lag."

Everyone understood.

The back door opened and Tasos staggered in, carrying a load of firewood. "Still gets cold up here even in late spring," he complained in Greek as he set his stack on the floor. The husky policeman eyed his daughter's tank-top and low-cut blue jeans. "How can you wear that in this weather?"

Daphne met Tasos' eyes and shrugged. "Without discomfort, no winnings."

Maria removed the earpiece from her iPod. "Baba, can you take us to the Inn of Gravias tomorrow? I want to take a picture of our family name on the memorial."

The girl's request surprised Eleni. The national monument rested where George's great-great grandfather Anastasios had joined rebel leader Odysseas Androutsos and a hundred other men to hold off Ottoman Empire soldiers during a crucial battle for Greek Independence in 1821. *A Greek Alamo. For a teenager like Maria, even the notorious Greek Junta, which re-settled Exile Island with a new wave of political prisoners in 1967, must seem like ancient history.*

"Yeah, let's go. I can use my new digital camera," piped in young Georgie.

Tasos held up a hand. "No sightseeing tomorrow, kids. I'm back on duty Friday, so I'll need everyone here to help me pack up Pappou's things to take back to Athens." He paused, turning to Maria. "Though I think Pappou may still have your great-grandfather Anastasios' broken sword in his valise downstairs. Why don't we go look?"

Maria shivered. "No way. Spiders."

Impulsively, Eleni slipped off her apron and patted her granddaughter's hand. "I'll go get it," she said, gritting her teeth. She didn't relish the notion of entering the stuffy cellar any more than Maria, but she knew that sorting through Grandpa George's memorabilia was a task she'd have to face sooner or later. And it was better to do it with her sturdy and dependable stepson Tasos nearby.

Grandpa George's dusty old leather valise held a wealth of treasured memories of a full lifetime. So many that, long after the rest of the family had retired for the night, Eleni, Georgie, and Tasos found themselves perusing dozens of papers, photos and books he'd packed away.

Eleni carefully removed George's folded olive-green military uniform. Underneath were several yellowed black and white snapshots of her husband and his imprisoned army buddies. She allowed herself a sad smile as she studied the thin young man in the photo. The George she'd known and married had an ample paunch unable to handle the tight fit and those brass buttons.

"From the exile," said Tasos, referring to the internment camp on Makronissos.

Eleni nodded. Though her husband rarely spoke about his years as a political prisoner on that deserted rock, the scars on his back told the story of multiple beatings by his guards. *A terrible stain on Greek history.*

"Eureka!" Tasos reached into the valise. Fishing around, he pulled out the tarnished sword he'd promised the kids. "*Voilà!*"

The ornate metal had oxidized to a musty green, but the sword still spoke of majesty and patriotic fervor. Eleni noticed that its tip was missing. *Perhaps it had remained in a vanquished Ottoman soldier's bone.*

"Wait a minute. There's something else here." Reaching in again, Tasos pulled out a piece of metal, rusted and chipped. He studied it, frowning. "Looks like some kind of a dial." Tasos held it up to the light as Georgie and Eleni moved closer. "There's writing on it."

"It's Pappou's writing," Georgie insisted.

Eleni shook her head. "Can't tell. I don't have my reading glasses."

"There seem to be letters wrapped around it, but you're right, my boy," Tasos said, turning it over. "These scratches here. Says *Makronissos 1948.*"

"Is it from the prison?" Georgie asked.

"Maybe," said Tasos, squinting at the disk. "I think there's something else etched here, too." He squinted to read the tiny lettering under the date. "*Ka, kai, kairos.*"

Eleni was puzzled. "*Kairos?* Weather? Part of a thermometer?"

Tasos shrugged. "*Kairos* also means time. Maybe it's a piece of an old clock."

"Let me take a picture," Georgie said, holding up his camera.

Tasos rubbed the dial on his soft shirt and posed it for the digital shot. "Why don't I have Daphne's cousin, the archaeology professor, look at it when we get back to the city? He might be able to tell us. Who knows—it could actually be worth something."

Eleni yawned, overwhelmed by fatigue from the stress of the day. "Why not," she agreed, placing an arm around her grandson's shoulders. "We've got nothing to lose. Uncle Gus could even help you sell it on that new Internet site he was talking about—e-Bay."

CHAPTER FIVE

May 2003 (Two weeks later)
Los Angeles

As the national news droned on radio station KACL's monitor, Jim Lodge flicked on his intercom. "Hey, Sammy, how about we play 'Don't Let the Sun Go Down On Me.'? That's how I went out the first time I got fired."

Sammy crinkled her freckled nose at her long-time producer on the other side of the glass. Exiled to a small, progressive radio station near Hollywood after losing her job at CNN, Sammy was grateful for Jim's mentoring and friendship. A scarecrow with long gray hair and a three-day salt-and-pepper scruff, Jim was one of the few radio veterans who'd managed to weather the ups and downs of the business without selling his soul—or curbing his acerbic tongue. They'd made a good team over the last three years—the aging hippie and the New Yawk fireball. *I couldn't imagine hitting New York's airwaves without him by my side.*

"With all due respect to Elton John—*and* the seventies," Sammy intercommed back, "those lyrics are too much of a double-entendre for "My Generation". And, hey, I'm glad we're leaving. I wouldn't want to be on the same station as Fred Feral's syndicated dreck. Radio USA is a step up, remember." Radio USA *was* a start-up, but at least it was going to be, Sammy told herself, a *national* radio network. A *liberal* radio network.

"How many markets have they booked again?" Jim chided. "Podunk, Bakersfield? Any place in the top thirty?"

Sammy wasn't buying his pessimism. "They've just signed Berkeley. Signal should reach all of the Bay Area. That's not bad. Washington DC. That's a big one. And Boston." Sammy felt a twinge in her chest the moment she mentioned the city where her *very* ex-boyfriend, Reed Wyndham, now lived. Not wanting to dwell on their break-up, she quickly added, "St. Pete, Indianapolis—"

"You know LA, New York, and Chicago are the gold rings, right?"

Gold rings. Another uninvited twinge. "We'll get them. After all, we'll be doing the show from Queens. We have to get something in Metro New York by September." The progressive talk network wasn't launching until Labor Day - plenty of time to add more syndicate outlets. "Americans need an alternative to that right-wing blowhard Fred Feral and his cronies. We're in the right place at the right time."

"Or the left place," chuckled Jim as he pointed a finger at Sammy. "Five seconds."

Sammy clicked on her mic and turned up her pot. "Sammy Greene on the LA Scene with good news and bad news. The good news, Truthseekers, is that this coming fall, Jim and I are taking our message nationwide. That's right. We'll be doing afternoon drive at Radio USA, a brand new radio network that's a voice for progress."

She winked at Jim. "Believe me, we've got an important job to do. Two years after our country was attacked in New York and Washington, we're mired in a war against a missing dictator who had absolutely nothing to do with 9/11. If there was ever a time to balance the debate, to get our country back on track – and out of 'Eye-Rack'—this is it, team. Radio USA will spread the word—*and* stop the insanity!

"Unfortunately, we don't have an outlet in LA. You loyal LA listeners who've been seeking the truth and fighting corruption with us could be out in the cold unless a local station comes through. Send your emails to KACL and ask them – no, demand - that they pick us up in September. We guarantee you won't regret your efforts, although crooked politicians, fraudulent hucksters, and rapacious corporations might. Fight the Power, power up Radio USA! Eleven after."

Sammy clicked off her mic and signaled Jim to run the block of commercials. Jim aimed his thumb at the two men in gray suits pacing stiffly outside Sammy's glass booth. "Looks like the Donald and the Dick out there won't be upset to see you go."

Sammy smiled broadly at the new owners of the Canyon City station and gave them a flat palms-out wave. "Don't worry," she whispered back to Jim, "it's a trick I learned from my friend, Gus Pappajohn, the retired cop. That gesture really means F.U. in Greek."

Jim laughed. "By the way, it's real nice of Officer Gus to invite you to spend a few weeks with his family in Greece. Sure there's no room in your suitcase for me?"

"Not this summer," she said, turning serious. "His sister Eleni's husband just passed and Gus thought she'd cheer up seeing me again. I visited her a lot when I was at college in New England. And it'll give me a chance to—"

"Five seconds." Jim gave her the next cue.

Mic on, Sammy continued. "Sammy Greene on the LA Scene. Bad news, Part II. Loyal Truthseekers, tonight is our last show on this station. KACL's new owners" — she paused to bestow the two men outside with another palm-out wave through her booth window — "think a conservative like Fred Feral is the tsunami of radio's future. Personally, if you ask me, I'd like to see Fred do a belly flop in the Gulf of Mexico, but then that tsunami would put New Orleans under water.

And there wouldn't be enough Oxycontin in the world to clean up that mess.

"So, it's going to be up to you all to carry the flame of activism we lit in LA. Just don't do it during Devil Wind season, okay? I see the phones lighting up — how about we let our new owners hear what you have to say — G-rated please," she added as she hit the first button.

By the end of the show, the owners and KACL listeners had heard a mouthful from angry callers decrying Sammy's termination and wishing Sammy and Jim well.

"See?" she told Jim as she helped him pack up his CDs after they'd signed off the air. "Ready-made demographic waiting for us on Radio USA."

"Must be fun being an optimist. Think you'll miss LA?"

"Sure. We did good things here."

"Can't argue with that. Still, New York City. Blech." He shook his head. "Nice to get back to your roots, I guess."

She nodded, turning away.

"Sometimes," added Jim, after a beat.

She was hoping Jim wouldn't try to comfort her after hearing the news in this morning's email. Too late. Why had she shared Reed's message with him at all?

"He's a damn fool, Dr. Wyndham, you know—"

Sammy turned to Jim and held up a hand. "It's a fresh start. Good to shed your skin once in a while and move on."

Toughen up, buttercup. After all, Reed got the job offer at Mass General three — four—months ago. She could've accepted his marriage proposal and followed him to Boston. And a tenure-track faculty post in cardiology at Harvard Medical School. Reed's lifelong dream come true.

His dream. *Why couldn't he understand that I needed to follow my dreams, too?* The offer from the nascent Radio USA network in the number one broadcast market made Sammy realize she still wasn't ready to move back to New England and make the kind of personal commitment Reed demanded. They'd parted friends, but today's email announcing his engagement to a woman he'd met only a month earlier hit Sammy square in the gut. *Will I ever be able to reconcile my career and love?*

Imagine. She'd even thought about visiting Reed in Boston in August after getting settled in New York. Logan Airport was only an hour's flight from LaGuardia, and her weekends would be free. After today's news, however, she had to admit the truth once and for all. It was over. For good.

Forcing a smile, she looked up at Jim and asked, "Where're you going for Memorial Day?"

"The Grand Ole Opry."

"*The* Grand Ole Opry? In Tennessee?" Sammy's jaw dropped. "I didn't know they played Heavy Metal."

"Ha, ha. Actually, my brother Harvey's lead guitar for his band 'Just Us Folk'. Acoustic, of course. Thought I'd hang with him in Nashville and save a month's rent."

"That's our Jim." Sammy gave him a warm hug, then picked up her linen satchel with a sigh. "Well, then, see you in…the City." She nodded at the door to the sales office. "Let's say good-bye to the people who'll remember us after next week."

CHAPTER SIX

Athens, Greece
Monday June 2, 2003

Kiki Matsas couldn't be more excited. In a society where men were still dominant, she'd already made headlines as the first woman associate director of Athens' renowned Hellenic Archaeological Museum. The news tabloids had proclaimed her a modern day Aphrodite whose stylish beauty was complemented by the intelligence and political skills of a Maggie Thatcher. In the six years since she'd graduated from Oxford with her PhD, the thirty-two year old Athenian had climbed the unstable academic ladder to her ground-breaking museum leadership post — with future ascension to the Directorship very much on the table. Director Nikos Tountas was approaching the mandatory civil service retirement age of sixty-five.

Kiki's ambition and efforts had brought new resources to what had become a struggling enterprise, dependent primarily on government largesse. The tall, slim brunette had induced some of the wealthiest businessmen in Greece, contributors to her father's campaigns in the conservative New Conservative Party, into donating millions of euros and dollars to the museum. To date, the widely circulated left-wing newspaper *Free Press* had been unable to prove that Kiki had either seduced or blackmailed the donors, and grumpily acceded that the donations might have been inspired by national pride and facilitated by a superb saleswoman.

In a short time, the Hellenic Archaeological Museum collection had grown to include an impressive A-list of Greek artifacts from prehistory to late antiquities. Kiki was an outspoken bearer of the mantle to return the Elgin Marbles from London back to Athens, and recently she'd filed a lawsuit to retrieve a stolen sculpture that somehow had found its way into California's Getty Museum. But the *Apocalypsi* and its treasures would be the jewels in her crown.

The *Thesaurus* deep sea recovery expedition had worked for two years salvaging what they could from the ghost ship. Over the last six years, scores of archaeologists, scientists, and professors from around the world had spent months sifting through the ship's debris, trying to glean clues from the salvaged finds. Among the discoveries that Kiki had claimed for her museum were the dials, wheels, and gears from a navigation device that appeared to be a more modern version of the famed Antikythera mechanism. Museum staff had dived into the arduous task of analyzing, restoring, polishing, and studying this remarkable ancient analogue computer. Kiki had arranged for the salvaged device to greet visitors to the Hellenic Archaeological Museum's upcoming *Apocalypsi* exhibit opening, before Professor Roussos' keynote speech.

Thesaurus archaeologists Professor Andreas Roussos and his protégé, Assistant Professor Loukas Doxiadis, had focused their efforts on the dented bronze struts and plates that had weathered the one and a half millennia on the seabed. Some had been identified as part of the ship itself. Roussos and Doxiadis and their students had taken the remaining recovered pieces and painstakingly reconstructed a bronze "skeleton" that formed the frame of an *alto-relievo* sculpture over thirty feet in length. Its wooden core had not survived. However, the bronze structure suggested that the statue's model had been a woman, her body decorated by the few flakes of gold still glittering on the strut remnants on the muddy sea floor. Completed at last, the reconstructed skeleton would make its debut the day after tomorrow before a modern Athenian oligarchy of famous politicians, entrepreneurs, and glitterati at the exhibit's launch gala.

For now, the waterlogged "shy bride" was "cloistered" under an enormous tarp at the south end of the museum's enclosed atrium. Kiki had instructed the museum staff to arrange the other artifacts in a scatter pattern that would guide the guests and visitors towards the giant central display. Amphorae and other pottery lined the red carpet, secreted in temperature-controlled glass cases that allowed viewing without the invasive effects of polluted air and curious fingers. The reconstructed *Apocalypsi* device recovered by the divers shone under its glass enclosure, its rusty gears and dials polished by the museum staff to better display the etched constellations and phases of the sun and moon. Years of delicate and diligent work by scientists at the Athens University and her museum had finally resulted in this majestic exhibition—*her* majestic exhibition.

Kiki signed onto the PC at her desk and clicked open the file she'd dubbed "Panaghia". Within seconds, a three-dimensional design rendering of the reconstructed statue filled the screen. Roussos and Doxiadis were convinced that the *Apocalypsi* sculpture had been of The Virgin Mary and baby Jesus, with their features cast in ephemeral silver, ivory, or gold. The shape of the struts and a few surviving bronze plates formed was clearly that of a woman, with feminine breasts and the curves of a flowing skirt. Roussos theorized that the statue had been ordered by Emperor Justinian of Constantinople and was to be nested in the new Hagia Sophia Cathedral rebuilt by Isidore and Anthemius in the sixth century AD. *Had Mary's journey been ravaged by the brutal north wind storms of the Aegean Sea? Or had Balkan or Persian invaders or pirates led to the Apocalypsi's capsizing and the theft of Mary's precious metals?*

"She could never hold a candle to you, *chryssoula*." A deep voice and the odor of musk and garlic.

Kiki smiled as she gently peeled off the hands grasping her waist from behind. "Sacrilege, Harris. I'd worry about vengeful ears, yes?" When she turned to face Professor Lambros, however, her smile was genuine.

Lambros leaned in, not turning his cheek. "Your ex always was a Philistine. I prefer the French approach," he added as he indulged in the intimate kiss. Breathlessly: "And I'll wager you do, too."

Blushing, Kiki raised a hand and eased him away. "It's over, Harris. You do have some attractive gifts." She tapped his temple, and allowed herself a quick glance down to his feet. "But I am not so continental that I can overlook your dalliances with your students, your neighbors," she paused, "or your 'escorts'. Besides, I think your one true love is in your mirror, my love."

Lambros' bushy eyebrows met in the center of his forehead, but he managed a chuckle, and a genial, "Your loss." His eyes fell on the model displayed on Kiki's monitor, and the frown deepened.

"You're determined to unveil this sculpture at the gala as the Virgin Mary and Jesus?" Lambros asked.

Kiki sighed. "I know you're no fan of Roussos, but he leads a team of experts who all agree. A merchant ship left Piraeus harbor on its way to Byzantine settlements in Anatolia. It carried wares to fill the palaces of the Roman outposts in the East Aegean and this statue of Mary Parthenos to grace the Cathedral of Constantinople." Kiki pointed to the head of the frame visible on the screen. "This is where the halo would have been attached."

"Mary Parthenos?" Lambros sneered. "Then where are the arms to hold the Christ child? They were never found in the wreck."

Kiki clicked open another file. "Roussos' team thinks the curved plates they found here form a piece of the arm." She pointed to a filled-in rendering of the statue with arms enfolding the infant son of God. "It all fits."

Lambros reached in his pocket and opened his palm to reveal a gold coin, its edges worn. "And what if Roussos and his team of so-called experts are wrong? All I need is a bit more time to study the collection."

"You're still stuck on one solidus?" Kiki's voice expressed exasperation over what had become an ongoing argument about the Roman coin. "Harris, we've talked about your theories. You're a historian. You know far better than me that just because those coins were reintroduced by Constantine centuries earlier doesn't mean a seventh century seaman wouldn't carry them. Don't you still keep a stash of drachmas in a drawer?" She pulled out an Altoids box from her desk and opened it to reveal some coins from Greece's pre-euro currency among thumbtacks and paper clips.

"An average seaman wouldn't carry such an expensive coin. But a fifth-century soldier might have been paid with them."

Kiki shook her head. "Okay, if you're so convinced this was a Roman warship and the soldiers were paid with solidari, why didn't we find a horde of similar coins?"

Lambros shrugged. "Missing evidence is the bane of my profession."

"That's not good enough." Kiki snapped. "Listen, Harris, this gala is more important to me than your need to upstage a colleague. You've had years to find something more than one bronze coin to back up your theory." She pressed a bright red manicured fingernail against his chest. "Not only will the rich and famous of Greece be here, but I've invited some of the top collectors and curators from around the world. After tomorrow, no one will deny me the directorship of this museum when Tountas retires." She tapped her finger for emphasis. "No one."

It was Lambros' turn to step back and raise a hand. But he'd broken into a grin, "Do you know how beautiful you look right now?"

"Yes." Kiki turned her head to look over Lambros' shoulder. "Ah, our Curator of Religious Artifacts." She smiled at the dark-haired man standing in the doorway, pointedly ignoring his disapproving expression. "Alex, dear, please let our friend Professor Lambros into the event hall...so he can tilt at windmills."

The silence in the deserted hallway was only broken by the two men's footsteps echoing off the marble floors and walls. Most of the museum employees followed the long-standing Greek motto of 'working to live, rather than living to work' and had gone home soon after the three P.M. closing time for dinner and siesta. The truly dedicated stayed until five, or at most, six. It was nearly seven.

Lambros himself would have been among the revelers a few years ago. Now he was relieved that the museum was almost empty except for Kiki and her irritating ex-husband, the 'Curator of Religious Artifacts'. As they walked, Lambros stole a glance at the glum archaeologist. Why Kiki had fallen for this pale, bookish student at Oxford was a mystery. His only passion seemed to be his studies of ancient and modern Western religions. No wonder Kiki had sought affection in another man's arms.

Alex paused at the double doors to the darkened exhibit hall. "You want to reexamine the statue?"

The frigid tone made Lambros wonder if the museum curator had uncovered the identity of 'the other man'?

"Roussos' folly?" Lambros smirked. "The Virgin Mary indeed."

His back to Lambros, Alex punched his code into the keypad lock and opened the doors to wave the professor in. "You don't agree?"

"Not by two hundred years. I believe the sculpture's intended host was much more likely to be Julian than Justinian."

Alex's face registered surprise as he flipped the bank of switches that turned on the lights. "Julian? The Apostate?"

Lambros looked up at the slender curator and nodded. "Or his followers. Fourth or fifth century at most. Of course, you're probably toeing the company line that the *Apocalypsi* foundered around the seventh century."

The men stepped into the cavernous chamber. "I'm a disciple of history," Alex said, "not of politics. Show me substantial proof that counters Roussos' thesis and I shall give it due consideration."

Lambros rested his briefcase on top of the glass case. Inside it shielded the multiple dials from the navigation device that had survived the shipwreck. Lambros opened the case and removed his Nikon digital camera. "Soon, Alex, soon. I just need a few more photos, a few more missing pieces. Then Roussos' reputation will be in ashes."

Alex eyed the rusted dials, nodding. "Professor Doxiadis admitted the other day that there could be more to this compass than was recovered."

Lambros scoffed. "Compass." He pointed the camera at the spotlit display. "Did you read my files?"

Alex shook his head. "You know how busy we've been with the opening. Be patient. After tomorrow, I should be happy to hear your theory — and study your proof." Alex took a few steps toward the door. "I'll be back in an hour to close up." At the door, he paused and added, "Professor Roussos is a Goliath in his field. You'd best be certain your slingshot has good aim, Professor David."

Lambros chuckled as he started snapping pictures. "The gods are on my side."

On the other side of the staff door, the figure who'd been listening from the shadows of the deserted hallway tiptoed out of the museum through the rear exit, unseen into the night.

CHAPTER SEVEN

Tuesday, June 3, 2003

T asos turned on his squad car's blue light and triple-parked on Akadimias Avenue to let out his relatives mere steps from the main entrance to Athens' National and Kapodistrian University. Daphne gave her husband a warm kiss before following Eleni and Pappajohn out onto the sidewalk.

As the trio made their way towards the antiquated Schliemann Building, Pappajohn scowled at the multicolored graffiti defacing its stucco façade.

His sister shrugged. "You've been away too long, Kosta," she chided her brother, using his Greek nickname. "Graffiti's considered an attractive urban art form these days."

"I'd call it something else," Pappajohn grumbled as he tailed the women inside.

"Cousin Harris' office is in the basement." Daphne pointed to the ancient looking elevator. "You want to take the lift?"

Pappajohn shook his head. He hadn't been away long enough to believe that elevators in Greece no longer took unscheduled rest breaks in-between floors. "Stairs. I need the exercise."

Eleni's wry smile suggested she wasn't fooled by his excuse.

Ignoring her, Pappajohn wiped the perspiration from his brow with his sleeve before taking the lead down the long flight. Pushing through a pair of scratched glass doors, the group entered a dark and musty subterranean corridor. As they traveled down the empty hallway, Pappajohn noted the cracked cement walls and chipped plaster with disgust. Couldn't the Greek government find the funds to improve the appearance of one of the oldest and best universities in the country? Scattered stubs of cigarettes littering the corners only managed to further aggravate his overly sensitive stomach. Why should he be surprised by the flagrant disregard for several prominently posted 'No Smoking' signs? This *was* the Greece Pappajohn remembered. A place where no one followed the rules.

Daphne stopped in front of a half-open doorway near the end of the hall. "Harris' office," she announced, though the name Professor Haralambos Lambros, PhD on the door had long faded.

They entered a tiny, windowless room smelling of mildew and stale smoke, illuminated only by a flimsy overhead fluorescent light fixture that flickered on and off and cast an eerie glow on the cluttered space. Hardly an appropriate office for a full professor, Pappajohn thought.

"Yia 'sas, hello!" came a disembodied voice from behind a stack of books and papers piled high on an old wooden desk. A second later, the diminutive Lambros emerged, squishing his half-smoked cigarette in a flowing ashtray in the corner and extending both arms to greet his visitors.

Daphne shared the traditional double-cheek air-kiss with her cousin and turned to introduce her guests. "My mother-in-law, Eleni, and her brother, Gus — Kostas — Pappaioannou. From America. A policeman, like my Tasos."

"Retired," Pappajohn said in Greek.

Lambros shook his hand, took Eleni's hand in both of his. "I am so sorry for your loss." He removed a ream of yellowed papers from two rickety-looking chairs for Eleni and Daphne and a splintered stool for Pappajohn who noticed that Lambros had no desk chair. "Sit," Lambros said, making a perch for himself at the edge of his desk by throwing one journal halfway across the room. The force of his toss surprised Pappajohn.

"More of Roussos' rubbish," Lambros said without further explanation.

Once they had all settled gingerly onto their seats, Lambros asked Daphne how he could help.

"As Tasos told you, we found something in his father's old trunk we thought you might be interested in." She reached inside her purse and produced a cloth wrapped object. "Maybe some kind of wheel or dial."

Lambros hopped off the desk and accepted it from Daphne, carefully removing the cloth to reveal the rusty metal dial.

"Makronissos 1948 — that's my father-in-law's writing. He was a political prisoner on the island during the Civil War," Daphne explained. "Rings of letters. They look old. There's lettering on the other side that says *Kairos*. Could it be some kind of thermometer?"

For just a split second Pappajohn thought he caught a look of sheer surprise from Lambros, but the professor's expression turned neutral before Pappajohn could be sure.

Pushing his wire rim glasses onto his forehead for closer inspection, Lambros turned the piece in all directions, rotating it this way and that, and holding it above his head in the flickering fluorescent light, his bushy eyebrows bunched together in total concentration. After several minutes, he laid it over some photographs on his desk with a deep sigh. "I'm afraid I don't know. It may very well be from the Greek Civil War. But I'd need to study it further." He turned to Daphne. "If you don't mind."

"Keep it," she said. "Our dear George is gone. It is of no use to us any more."

Lambros expressed his understanding with a somber nod. "I can't be certain, but I don't believe it has much value. I hope Tasos won't be too disappointed."

Daphne shrugged. "It's okay. He just bought a new batch of lottery tickets. We're bound to win something someday." Daphne stood up and leaned over to give her cousin another kiss on each cheek. Pappajohn and Eleni shook hands, politely avoiding a more intimate greeting once again.

"We'll see you tomorrow, Cousin," Daphne said at the door.

"Tomorrow?" Lambros asked.

To Pappajohn, the professor's attention seemed far away. *What was Lambros thinking?*

"Ah yes," Lambros responded after a beat. "The opening of the *Apocalypsi* exhibition. Where I shall slay the false idols." He smiled at Eleni and Pappajohn. "I hope you will both come, too. It should prove to be a most interesting evening."

Moments after his guests had departed, Lambros peered into the corridor to be sure none of his colleagues were around before shutting his office door and turning the lock. He could barely contain himself as he rushed back to his desk and opened a drawer where he kept a pair of cotton gloves. He slipped them on and carefully picked up the dial. With the light touch afforded a fragile Faberge egg, he held the corroded metal up to the light, this time using a magnifying lens to study the sequence of oddly-shaped letters etched in concentric circles around the dial on one side and the barely visible word etched into the other.

Kairos.

Yes! It all made sense now.

Eleni had said her husband had found the gear on Makronissos. The island close to where the *Apocalypsi* had foundered. For so long Lambros had been combing the evidence for more tangible proof of his own theory. Finally the gods were with him, dropping this dial into his lap. If only he'd known of its existence sooner, or had more time to study and analyze the dial's message, but with the exhibition opening tomorrow night, he really had no choice.

Damn that Roussos. Lambros had spent too many years listening to that jerk pontificate about his fictional history of the *Apocalypsi*, while refusing to consider alternate theories for the vessel's aborted mission. His former mentor had become the major impediment to Lambros' own research, ultimately forcing Lambros to keep his real work a secret. Roussos' frequent biting suggestions that Lambros seek a position at another university, or, better yet, as a tour guide on a Pullman bus for American tourists, had inflamed him. But cuckolding the old man hadn't brought Lambros any vengeful satisfaction. Instead, Roussos' young wife had started barraging him with amorous phone calls. Her infatuation had become another albatross around his neck and a source of displeasure for Kiki.

Lambros laid the dial gently on his desk and reached under the pile of scattered photos for a black and white snapshot of two bronze dials blown up to approximately the same size as the one Daphne had brought in today. Each acquisition represented years of dabbling in the notorious global black market in Greek antiquities, a venture that had bankrupted him literally and emotionally. He'd sold everything but the roof over his head to purchase the first item from a shady businessman with a muscled and menacing bodyguard. The second fully drained thousands of euros from his most generous EU grants earmarked for his ongoing study of sixth and seventh century Byzantine manuscripts. Ironically, it was what he'd discovered in those ancient manuscripts that had shaped his theory over these past six years, turning his search for more evidence into an obsession and leading him to cross even his own fuzzy ethical lines in his quest.

Holding the photo near the dial on his desk, he compared the structures. Of course, he'd need to put all three together, but for the moment, he felt sure they were part of the same mechanism. His camera could provide 10x digital close-ups of the markings, as well as copies of the deciphered writing under the Biblical texts.

He booted up his desktop computer and clicked on the folder MINERVA, bypassing the subfiles labeled MONASTIRAKI and MASADA, for a file he'd labeled MAKRONISSOS. Scrolling past notes on scanned photos and documents of Cicero (*Posidonius*), Lactanius (*Divinarum Institutionum Libri VII*); Claudian (*In sphaeram Archimedes*); John, Bishop of Nikiu (*Chronicle*); Conon of Samos (*Parapegma*); and Proclus (*Commentary on the first book of Euclid's Elements of Geometry*), he typed in the date and a few short sentences: *Found another one. Plan to return to Makronissos soon after tomorrow's presentation.*

Anxious to remove the dial away from prying eyes, he carefully hid it along with the black and white snapshot in his briefcase under his camera. It was time. This little wheel, coupled with the Biblical palimpsest, the museum photos, and the two dials he'd been studying, meant Roussos wouldn't have a leg to stand on. No doubt Kiki would be furious. He'd promised not to spoil her evening. On the other hand, he could honestly predict that his revelations tomorrow would advance her career faster than she'd ever hoped. By the end of the night, Lambros was convinced he'd be celebrating with Kiki between her red silk sheets. She'd understand and applaud — that revealing the truth trumped everything — politics, religion, even her ambition.

Lambros opened his locked desk drawer and removed a tin of pipe tobacco from the back. Prying off the top, he brushed aside the drachmas, francs, and marks he'd amassed and checked to make sure the index card onto which he'd taped his safe deposit box key was there under the gold solidus. On his way to the gala, he'd place this new find at the National Bank of Greece. But first he needed to make a call.

After replacing the can in the desk and locking the drawer, Lambros pulled his mobile phone from of his pocket and flipped it open, scrolling down a list of earlier calls. Finding the number, he initiated the call and waited for an answer.

"We have to talk."

CHAPTER EIGHT

Wednesday, June 4, 2003

*I*t's all about being in the right place at the right time...
Sammy looked up from her Sky Magazine and rested her eyes on the clouds out of her porthole. *If only "Finding the One" was as simple as the author of the article asserted.* Like Bubbe Rose would've said *narrischkeit.* Nonsense. Though Sammy had adored the woman who raised her after her mother died, her late grandmother would not have been the best resource for marital advice, having agreed to an arranged marriage in her late teens. And Sammy's father was definitely not someone whose counsel she'd seek on the subject. After turning California "state's evidence", Jeffrey Greene was now building a lucrative business as a life coach in Miami with wife number four, who, at age twenty-eight, was a year younger than Sammy. A life coach!

The jet banked to the left as the loudspeaker crackled. "Good evening, this is Captain Oberlander speaking. We're leveling off at thirty-three thousand feet. Flight time to Athens will be eight hours and thirty-five minutes. We're expecting good weather most of the trip, but just to be safe, please keep your seat belts fastened. If you look out the starboard side you'll see us passing Boston..."

Boston.

Where her old friend Gus Pappajohn was living with his daughter Ana and grandson Teddy. In many ways, Pappajohn had been more of a father to Sammy than self-absorbed Jeffrey

Greene. She and Gus had been through a lot together — solving a tragic mystery at Ellsford University and then saving thousands in Los Angeles. Gus was the first person she'd phoned about Reed's engagement to someone he'd just met.

Sammy peered out the window, digesting the irony that Reed lived in Boston now – the newest Assistant Professor of Cardiology at Harvard Medical School. *Had he been 'the one'? The one that got away? Why, why hadn't I said 'yes' when he asked me to join him? There were plenty of radio and TV stations in Boston where I could have applied for a job. And the Boston Globe was one of the country's best papers.* Had she used her "career" in LA as an excuse to…to what? Preserve her freedom? Avoid getting hurt? Guarantee she'd die bitter and alone?

Listen to me, madela. If you ever need a helping hand, you'll find it at the end of your arm.

Remembering one of her grandmother's favorite expressions, Sammy chuckled. Rose was never one to wallow in self-pity. And pity-parties weren't Sammy's style either. She watched her fingers close into a tight fist. Onward.

It was only when the TV monitor showed the 747 flying over Nova Scotia that Sammy felt her neck muscles relax. She leaned back in her seat and smiled, recalling Gus' sales pitch that handsome young men from all over Europe congregated on the Greek shores as soon as the weather turned warm. Gus was right — she needed to get away, to make a fresh start. What better place than the clear azure waters of the Mediterranean, he had asked. Especially with him and his sister there as guides? She knew Gus meant well, but meeting a new partner was the last thing she was up for now. The latest Michael Chabon novel she'd brought along would be quite enough company for this trip, thanks.

Of course, Gus didn't know that Sammy's last trip to Greece years ago had ended with Ollie's tragic death. Still, how could she turn down the invitation? Eleni — and Gus —

needed her. And, perhaps she could get away for a few days and head to that port city—Lavrium, was it?—and see if anything was left of Ollie's camera and tape.

Sammy flipped the magazine's glossy page to reveal a banner photo of the ancient Parthenon framed by a cloudless blue sky. The article, 'Greece's Ancient and Modern Treasures', highlighted Athens' renowned Hellenic Archaeological Museum and its Bronze Age exhibits which included statues and artifacts recently reclaimed from museums in Chicago and LA. New York will be reclaiming me soon, Sammy mused. *It is time for me to go home.*

Wednesday evening, June 4, 2003

"Isn't that Jules Dassin?" Eleni nudged Pappajohn while Tasos drove his Citroen patrol car onto the curb and turned off the engine. "Melina Mercouri's husband. There, behind the photographers."

Pappajohn squinted to catch a glimpse of the elderly man stepping from the limousine across the street. A long row of limos snaked around the cobblestone streets of Plaka at the base of the Acropolis. Even with Tasos' "creative parking skills", they were still a half block from the Hellenic Archaeological Museum. "Wouldn't surprise me," he mumbled in English. "Judging by all the security, we'll be seeing a lot of VIPs tonight."

Tasos nodded, adding, "And paparazzi."

At eight P.M. the sun had just begun to drift toward the horizon, casting shadows that provided cover for the numerous security guards, discreetly clad in "civvies", who'd been hired for the museum's *Apocalypsi* gala. Lambros had hinted that in addition to the President and Prime Minister of Greece, the guest list included the ambassadors of a number of EU and G-12 countries, including the United States. With the Olympics only a year away, ensuring safety for these illustrious visitors was paramount.

"Wow, Aristotle Vandis," Daphne said as they all stepped from the car. A short, stocky man with horn-rimmed glasses and a gray-haired buzz-cut was being escorted from his limo and through a gauntlet of reporters and cameramen by a tuxedoed museum employee.

"Doesn't he own Attica Airlines?" Eleni asked her step-daughter.

"Yes and several shipping lines, too," Daphne said. "A billionaire."

Leaning over Pappajohn, Tasos said in a low voice, "My father, God rest his soul, would have scorned all this pomp and circumstance. But, since I'm not on duty for once, I'm going to enjoy myself."

The wave of paparazzi started flashing light bulbs again as the next guest appeared. "Who's that?" Pappajohn wondered, eyeing the glamorous woman in her curve-hugging sparkling gown.

"Sara Nida, one of our hottest singing stars," Tasos said. Catching his wife's sharp look, he added, "She has a wonderful voice."

"Harry will meet us inside," Daphne announced with a hint of coolness. "The speeches aren't scheduled until nine."

The foursome took their place in the long receiving line behind two bearded clerics in long black robes who introduced themselves as Bishop Theosophos and Father Mihalis. Following Greek tradition, Tasos and Daphne each kissed the priests' extended hands in greeting. Nodding, Eleni and Pappajohn followed suit.

"The News was right. Anyone and everyone is invited tonight," Tasos remarked when the two men had moved ahead.

"Well, I guess I'm anyone," Pappajohn joked, feeling stiff and uncomfortable in his rented tux. He was sure Tasos felt the same. Neither was used to wearing these penguin suits. Daphne, on the other hand, had spent all afternoon primping. Pappajohn didn't think it was just to honor her cousin. The handsome middle-aged man in the photographer's circle whose tux definitely seemed tailored had caught Daphne's full attention.

"Jean Dumas," Daphne said to Eleni. "The Parisian art dealer. His new lady's a model."

"Rich bachelor," grumbled Tasos, as Pappajohn and his sister chuckled.

Pappajohn was pleased to see Eleni smiling. Much too rare in the weeks since George's passing. Glad he'd convinced her to come this evening after all. Except for the short run to the university yesterday and George's forty day memorial last Sunday, she hadn't budged from home. He considered the tux and the small talk tonight a worthwhile sacrifice. And with Sammy arriving tomorrow morning, Eleni's spirits would certainly get an added boost.

"Could this queue go any slower?" Tasos complained. "I'm starving."

"I'm not spending all evening at the hors d'oeuvres table again," Daphne said.

"I'll keep him company," Pappajohn offered.

Eleni patted her brother's tight cummerbund. "Go easy or you'll pop that thing."

Wednesday night, June 13, 2003

The statuesque brunette smiling from the glossy magazine page in Sammy's lap clearly possessed confidence and charm. And, Sammy read as she turned the page, a PhD from Oxford. Angeliki Matsas. Nickname: Kiki. Beauty *and* brains. According to the article, Kiki was urging tourists to visit the new exhibit due to be launched tonight at her Hellenic Archaeological Museum. A slew of Greek, European, and international notables were invited to celebrate the viewing of artifacts rescued from the sunken vessel *Apocalypsi* by the *Thesaurus* research expedition.

Apocalypsi!

Sammy did a double take. That was *our* shipwreck! Its discovery had been a short-lived sensation six years ago. CNN had sent her overseas to cover it, but, after Ollie's accidental drowning, the story had died along with the cameraman. In the world of 24/7 news, terrorism always trumped treasure.

Sammy folded a corner on the page she'd been reading and slipped the magazine into the pocket of the seat in front of her. Leaning down, she reached into her tote bag and pulled out a tattered spiral notebook filled with notes from some of her old stories.

Flipping through, she located the page where she'd jotted down names of the *Thesaurus* expedition. An odd mix on that treasure hunt, as she recalled. Religion and science. Father Mihalis, the black-robed Greek Orthodox priest who'd ended up praying over Ollie's body. And Loukas Doxiadis, the handsome graduate student who'd offered her a comforting shoulder when her colleague's death re-awakened childhood memories of her mother's suicide. Sammy had been just seven years old when she'd come home from school—*too late*—to find her mother lifeless. Her long-buried sadness had floated to the surface once more.

"The Greek Orthodox religion has all the flaws of a human product," Loukas had whispered, "but its promise of eternal life offers hope and solace. As scientists, we must remain skeptics. Nevertheless, I see no harm in allowing yourself the comfort that you will see your mother again in heaven someday."

"Unfortunately, heaven is not a certainty in the Jewish faith," she had admitted. "*Olam Ha-ba* could portend an afterlife, or a resting place for souls awaiting the return of the Messiah. *Gan Eden*, is the return to the Garden of Eden."

At that point, she'd let her tears flow. "Me? I was banished from Gan Eden as a child…"

Now Sammy turned her head to peek out the porthole window, blue sky above fluffy clouds beyond the glass fogged by moistness on her cheeks. She wiped away the droplets, closed her eyes for a moment, then opened them to continue reading. Despite the fact that she'd written the names of the various archaeologists and maritime engineers from around the European Union on the team, she couldn't picture them all. Only the two sparring Greek professors were truly memorable. Expedition leader, Andreas Roussos, with his pencil thin mustache and haughty mien, and the diminutive, assertive Harris Lambros with the imposing 'unibrow'.

'Trading ship versus warship' read Sammy's notes. 'Seventh versus fifth century'. The two men may have been colleagues, but it seemed clear at the time that their careers — and egos — hinged on who was right.

Retrieving the airline magazine, Sammy flipped to the bookmarked page and perused the article again. Nowhere did the magazine mention either Roussos or Lambros. Still, Sammy wondered whose theory had won out in the end.

"The distinguished looking chap with the silver hair is Nikos Tountas, the museum's Director," Daphne coached as the receiving line surged forward.

"And that lovely woman next to him?" Pappajohn asked.

Daphne hesitated before answering. "Angeliki Matsas, the Associate Director."

"She looks so young," Eleni said. "She must be very good."

"Harris said so," Tasos whispered to Pappajohn, dodging another icy glare from his wife.

"I wish *I* could afford a dress like that," Daphne said.

"Stunning," Eleni agreed.

"And those diamond earrings. Family heirlooms, I think. Her father was the Speaker of the Hellenic Parliament."

"Glad there's plenty of security around," Pappajohn muttered, "Prime hunting ground for a nimble-fingered thief."

Tasos leaned towards him and spoke softly in English. "Reminds me of a joke. A robber pulls out his gun to rob a man and says 'Give me your money!'. The man protests, 'Do you know who I am? I am a former Prime Minister!' 'Oh, I am so sorry,' the robber says, 'I did not know. Then give me MY money!'"

"You are so fortunate," Tasos said to Pappajohn as the others chuckled, "to live in a country where government is ethical and the politicians serve the people and not themselves."

Before Pappajohn or Eleni could respond, the group reached the head of the line and were greeted with a polite handshake by Director Tountas, "Welcome to the Hellenic Archaeological Museum."

"You must admit my theory is correct," Lambros whispered to Alex as they ambled from the exhibit hall towards the museum lobby.

Alex forced a smile. "I told you. I haven't had time to review your files. In any case, I still believe there's a better time and place than tonight for your revelations. If only for Kiki's sake."

Lambros shook his head. "*I* am not faint-of-heart. Roussos has to be taken down and I intend to do so with my proof — right after his presentation." His fingers stroked the disk on key drive in his suit pocket. "My photos will be irrefutable. A literal *Apocalypsi* — an uncovering. And Kiki will have more publicity than she ever dreamed. As the Americans say, a win-win."

"Knowing Kiki, you'd be wise not to tally the bill without the hotelier," Alex warned, using the Greek version of 'don't count your chickens before they hatch'.

But Lambros wasn't listening. He'd shot ahead, waving to a group of guests entering at the museum entrance.

"Tasos, Daphne!"

Pappajohn felt the spasm in Kiki's fingers as Lambros reached the group, leaning in on tiptoe to kiss his cousin and her husband. "Thanks for joining us tonight. You won't regret it," he gushed.

Pappajohn released Kiki's hand and shared a look of fellowship. Guess he wasn't the only one who found the professor annoying.

"Ya'sou," Lambros greeted in Greek. "Kiki has prepared a feast for both the stomach and the mind tonight. And I," he added loudly, "shall be serving the dessert." He glanced towards the door, his expression turning to disappointment when he saw Kiki's focus had returned to greeting the incoming guests. "The crème de la crème of Europe is here tonight, my friends," he said, "so let me lead you to the reception hall for introductions."

"And the appetizers," Tasos said, as his wife gave him a nudge.

Pappajohn, grinning, eyed his sister, happy to see her return the smile. Perhaps the night wouldn't be a disaster after all.

CHAPTER NINE

Too rough.

The sudden rocking terrified Sammy. Back and forth, up and down, her stomach roiled. She held on for dear life.

Desperate to remain calm, she sensed something terribly wrong. Where was she? Why was a life preserver slung on the rail?

Confused, she blinked at the letters stamped along its rim. ΘΗΣΑΥΡΟΣ.

Of course. *Thesaurus.* The Greek research vessel.

Leaning over the side of the ship, Sammy scanned the turbulent sea surface for some sign of her missing cameraman. The pitching and yawing heightened her nausea, but, determined, Sammy kept her eyes glued on the churning waters.

Ollie, where are you? Should've been back up from the dive by now.

We've angered the gods.

Far in the murky distance, she spotted something in the water. Focusing, she realized it was... a body! *Ollie!*

Sammy opened her mouth to scream just as a huge swell surged over the *Thesaurus'* bow and washed her into the frigid surf below.

Can't swim!

Crashing waves sucked her under.

Help!

Flailing, Sammy glimpsed a robed figure out of reach on the ship. Chanting in Greek. *"Aionia h mnimi!"*

No, I'm not dead!

But the figure didn't seem to hear.

No, I'm not dead!

Sammy's lungs felt as though they'd burst as she was dragged downward.

Bubbe Rose! What do I do?

Sammy, madela, how many times have I told you "do not meet troubles half-way. You can do what you need to do."

Fight, Sammy, Fight! Survive!

Submerged in icy blackness, Sammy forced herself to kick upward again and again, until at last, she drew a breath of air, and then another. Reveling in the pure joy of each deep inhalation, she lay back and floated on the jostling surface, eyes shut tight, letting her racing heartbeat slow.

"Sorry for that folks," announced a professional voice. "Some unexpected chop. We're heading up to thirty-nine thousand feet where we hope your flight will be much smoother. Just in case, we'll be keeping that seat belt light on 'til we're over Ireland."

"You okay?"

Sammy felt a gentle pat on her arm and blinked. Her seatmate, a gray-haired woman nestled under a pair of blankets, peered at her with concern. "I was worried about you, dear. You were mumbling about drowning."

Sammy offered up a weak smile. "Thanks. I'm okay. Bad dream."

The woman nodded. "No matter how many times I fly, I'm white knuckles the minute there's a little rough patch. Here." She handed her a napkin she'd secreted in her seat pouch. "Let me help. Turbulence knocked your drink all over you."

"Thank you." The toppled glass of water had soaked the magazine in her lap, the melting ice cubes still drenching Kiki Matsas' proud face.

"I must introduce you," Lambros insisted as he led Pappajohn towards a tall, well-coiffed man who sported a tailored tux, and a convincing air of distinction. "Ambassador Richard Davenport, from Washington, yes? Gus Pappajohn, my American cousin."

"From the Hub, actually. The City Upon a Hill," Davenport returned with a smile.

Shaking hands, Pappajohn noticed the ambassador's tie clip. "Harvard alum?"

"Right. And I'm guessing from your accent that you hail from Boston too. Dorchester?"

"Couldn't afford Beacon Hill on a cop's salary," Pappajohn said. "Or all this. Quite a shindig," he added, tilting his head at the crowds surrounding the buffet table.

"My second event tonight." The Ambassador's voice was a shade weary. "Took a bullet for the Crimson and gave a Yale faculty contingent a tour of Athens this afternoon."

Pappajohn chuckled, more at the expression of confusion on Lambros' face. "Very nice to meet you, too."

"McAllister!" the Ambassador greeted a pale blond man approaching from the entrance. "My counterpart from the UK," he explained to Pappajohn. "Enjoy your stay in Athens. And have a safe trip home," he said, nodding, as he hurryied off in pursuit of his colleague.

"You would think England and America were still one country." Lambros shrugged. "I am not an Anglophile, my friend. See that old chap over there?" He pointed to a white-haired man brandishing an intricately carved cane who was deep in conversation with a youthful, well-toned, dark-haired companion. "Hugh Wellington, one of the richest men in

England and an expert dealer in ancient art. He is a great-great-grandson of Lord Elgin — the larcenous genes run deep."

"You're referring to the Elgin Marbles?" Pappajohn asked.

"Of course. In the early nineteenth century, Lord Elgin weaseled a pass from our Ottoman occupiers to 'transport' the Parthenon Friezes from Athens to the British museum. For 'safekeeping'" Lambros snickered. "I'll wager that Wellington's here tonight to check out the latest wave of cultural artifacts he and his agents will steal off to Britain at a ridiculously low price."

Pappajohn took a moment to glance over at the buffet table where Eleni, Tasos, and Daphne were sampling *tiropites* and *spanakopites,* flaky cheese and spinach pies. When his gaze returned to Lambros he was surprised to see the professor frowning. "Anything wrong?"

"I'm not sure, but that young man Wellington is talking to, Mr. Muscles — I've seen him before." Lambros scratched his chin. "Not around Wellington. Somewhere else. Monastiraki, I think." Lambros clapped Pappajohn on the back. "Tell you what, Cousin. Why don't you go and get something to eat with Daphne? I'll catch up with you in a few minutes, eh?"

Pappajohn nodded politely and set off for the appetizers. He watched Lambros make a beeline for the art dealer and 'Mr. Muscles' before turning his attention towards his relatives and the tasty tapas on the other side of the reception hall.

Wending his way through the crowd, Pappajohn marveled at the Babel of languages overheard from the enthusiastic guests. It was one of the things he loved about Europe — its multifaceted diversity. The auburn-haired woman speaking German to a rapt audience of scholars and reporters reminded him of Hillary Clinton. No doubt, Angela — with a hard 'g' — was a politician, too. That stylish French playboy was engaged in a chat with, of all people, a full-bearded Greek Orthodox priest. Pappajohn's French wasn't strong, but he did think he heard a few words that, even more surprisingly, sounded like, "eight million in Swiss francs".

A turbaned Sikh was discussing Aristotle's Metaphysics with an African diplomat and a Dutch professor who sported a Phi Beta Kappa key on his tuxedo lapel. Bypassing a crowd of fans and photographers that had encircled the pop singer, Sara Something, Pappajohn observed she'd lathered herself in make-up and bling. Even the obvious traces of Botox couldn't hide the fact that, close-up, she looked nearer to Pappajohn's age than to her younger audience's.

"You have to try this." Eleni handed her brother a piece of moussaka on a napkin. "Even better than mine."

Pappajohn had to agree. It *was* delicious. "But yours is still the best," he insisted with kind diplomacy after a few more bites. "How's the stargazing, Daphne?"

"I ate a shrimp right next to the Prime Minister! Bishop Theosophos gave us all his blessing. And I actually spoke to Aristotle Vandis. Told him I'd flown on Attica Airlines," she related proudly.

Tasos rolled his eyes. "*Everyone* in Greece has flown on Attica Airlines."

Pappajohn couldn't resist a smile as his eyes scanned the room, searching for Lambros. He finally spotted him in a far corner of the hall, away from other guests, and, it seemed, from the animated gestures, arguing with the same trim, dark-haired man who'd just been talking with the art dealer.

The murmur of the crowd dimmed as two men exited from the locked doors of the exhibit display hall, their heads together in deep conversation. "Professor Roussos," whispered Daphne as the tall bespectacled man moved ahead of his thin, bearded companion and allowed the display doors to lock behind him. "He looks angry. The younger professor, Doxiadis, I think. Used to be Roussos' graduate student, Harris said. Now up for tenure."

Heading towards Kiki and Tountas in the lobby, Roussos was intercepted by Lambros within earshot of the buffet. "Eh, Rousso, have you and your…valet sharpened your wits for the gladiators' arena tonight?"

Pappajohn saw Roussos grit his teeth before he replied, "I won't play your games, Lambre. And I don't fear your pen or your sword. You should. You're only a danger to yourself."

Without saying another word, Roussos strode off, followed by Doxiadis, leaving Lambros standing alone, looking, per Pappajohn, more than a little foolish. Academicians. The ex-campus police chief recalled the all-too-familiar Henry Kissinger quote: "University politics are so vicious precisely because the stakes are so small".

Daphne sighed. "Even as a boy, Harris was a fighter. Always coming home with a bloody nose. He never listened when we warned him to be careful. That someday he might really get hurt."

CHAPTER TEN

L ambros dropped his cigarette stub onto the concrete when he felt it burn his fingers. A dreadful habit, to be sure, but the nicotine provided a soothing antidote to Roussos' biting assault. *Be patient,* Alex had said. He'd been patient enough. In the fading twilight, his digital watch blinked nine o'clock. Let that pompous ass Roussos believe he'd had the last word. Daphne's dial was the final key he'd been seeking. In a few minutes, he'd disprove every claim Roussos had made about the *Apocalypsi's* mission. Revenge would be sweet.

The receiving line from the front entrance had thinned out, but Lambros thought it best to avoid Kiki or Alex until after his victory. Instead, he walked over to a locked side entrance. Marked 'Staff Only' in Greek, it led to the museum's private offices behind the exhibit areas. Affecting nonchalance, he nodded at the security guard ambling by and quickly punched in Kiki's code in the door's OmniLock. *Eh Rousso, if you only had my skills at observation.*

Predictably, the office wing was deserted, with the museum staff out front greeting and mingling with guests. Reaching the half-open rear door of the darkened main exhibit hall, Lambros thought he observed a flicker of light inside. He peered in, but only saw the rising moon throwing shadows along the distant rows of display cases filled with *Apocalypsi* artifacts. In less than a half hour they would all be spotlit, the subject of awed scrutiny by invited faculty and guests.

Good. Everything seemed to be in place — podium right in front of the door, the covered statue of Roussos' "Virgin Mary" to the left and the chairs and projector beyond. Lambros strode over to the rolling table that held the laptop and projector for the presentations. He pressed the computer button to jog it from sleep mode, and, retrieving his compact USB disk-on-key flash drive from his pocket, slipped it into the slot to upload his file into the GALA directory. As he waited for the file to load, a soft tap, like a faint footfall, made him swivel around to scan the shadows. *Nothing there. Stay calm.*

Lambros slowly rotated his neck to stretch taut muscles. Good, all done. He opened the directory to the folder 'GALA'. Scrolling past Roussos' PowerPoint icon, 'PANAGHIA', with a snort, he opened his own uploaded folder, 'MINERVA'. Clicking on it, he scrolled down the subfile list and rested the cursor on his PowerPoint, double clicking. A quick review — all there. Soon the name Lambros would be on everybody's lips.

Above the noise of the gala crowd outside, he heard the sound again, louder and closer. *What the hell?* About to turn, Lambros felt something hard pressed against his back.

"Don't move. That's a knife you feel, Harris."

Recognizing the voice, Lambros froze. "Is this a joke?"

"Hardly. Hand over that drive."

Incredulous: "Why?"

"You cannot guess?"

"I shared my discovery with you."

"Your mistake. And now I'm afraid I must prevent you from sharing it with the world."

The increased pressure of the knife underscored the terrifying implication of the words. "You're going to stab me in the back?" Lambros gasped.

"No, takes too long. And too much blood."

Before he could respond, Lambros felt a huge explosion of pain as a sharp point was jammed in his spinal cord and up into his brain.

After staging the professor's small body for maximal dramatic reveal, the killer removed Lambros' cell phone and flash drive, then deleted his PowerPoint and files from the museum computer.

The buzz of conversation diminished as lights in the reception hall dimmed and shone to the rhythm of a soft chime.

"Ladies and gentlemen, please take your seats." Speaking into a hand held microphone, Kiki urged her guests towards the artifact display room where the presentations were due to start.

"Nine thirty," Pappajohn said, looking at his watch. "Fashionably late. Typical for Greece. Shall we head in?" He reached for Eleni's elbow.

"I could just stay here," Tasos joked, resting his plate reluctantly on the edge of the buffet table.

Daphne's frown suggested otherwise. Sighing, he followed his family toward the exhibit area.

Pappajohn looked around at the visitors amassing at the door. "Where's Harris?" he asked Daphne.

"Haven't seen him for a while. Probably going out for a smoke to cool down before the show. We'll save him a seat inside."

Eleni's eyes widened as they entered the brilliantly lighted exhibit hall. "How beautiful."

Gazing at the extraordinary number of displayed artifacts lining both sides of the long room, Pappajohn had to agree. At the far end, rows of chairs faced a podium and large screen. To the right of the screen a massive tarp-covered structure was guarded by a circle of gold stanchions tied together with velvet burgundy cords.

"*Paithia*! Look at this!" Tasos waved his family over to a nearby display and pointed to a polished mechanical device with multiple gears labeled ἀστρολάβος ναυσιπλοίας / navigation astrolabe. "These dials look a lot like the one Baba found at Markonissos," he whispered. "With all the rust gone."

Pappajohn stood on tiptoe to peer over his shoulder. Tasos was right. The three polished dials positioned between the gears of the mechanism had been restored to a gleaming shine, but otherwise they did resemble the one they'd brought to Professor Lambros yesterday. *Damn. I knew Lambros thought the piece was valuable.*

"I never ceased to be amazed at the ancients' accuracy in observing our universe," came a voice behind him. Turning, he faced Roussos' dark-haired companion who seemed to be studying the exhibit. "The location of the sun and moon could be predicted for each season," Doxiadis said, indicating the designs on the middle dial. "Of course, today, with our telescopes and satellites, we can calculate the orbits of every planet in our galaxy."

"Professor Doxiadis, right?" Daphne extended a hand. "You work with my cousin and Professor Roussos."

"Assistant Professor, really, for now. Professor Roussos was my PhD advisor. Who is your cousin?"

"Harris Lambros."

Doxiadis broke into a wide grin. "How can I not know Harris? He was on my thesis committee. An outstanding researcher and scientist. Made me work very hard for my PhD," he added with a wink. "For which I shall always be grateful."

Bishop Theosophos and Father Mihalis strode by, chatting with the Greek President. Doxiadis waited until the trio was out of earshot before saying, "And then, there's the antithesis of science, religion."

"Science and faith are not enemies, son," Professor Roussos chided, joining the group. He clapped his protégée on the back.

"We may not be able to prove the existence of God, but neither can we prove his absence."

"That seems to be your job, Alex," Doxiadis jibed as the Curator of Religious Artifacts appeared next to them. He nodded at Daphne, "Alex Matsas, the museum's lead religious scholar. Daphne here is the cousin of Harris Lambros."

"Thank you for coming," Alex said. "Though I'm afraid our exhibition tonight will focus on the physical, not the metaphysical."

"Friends, friends, we're running late," Kiki came over and took Roussos' arm. "Let me escort you to the podium, Andreas," she said, leading him toward the dais where museum Director Tountas and the Greek Prime Minister had joined the Greek Orthodox clerics.

"Strange bedfellows, politics and religion. Alas, I have little respect for either," Doxiadis added as he took off for a row near the front.

"And I have great respect for the power of both," Alex said. Nodding, he added, "If you'll excuse me, I must go help Kiki."

"We might as well sit down ourselves," Pappajohn suggested as Alex strode towards the podium.

Daphne looked around with an anxious expression. "Harris should've been back by now."

"Probably needed to smoke a whole *pack* of cigarettes," Tasos joked, choosing a row near the back. "We can save him a seat here. Come on."

Frowning, Daphne sat, placing her purse in the seat between her and Eleni. "I can't believe he's not here yet." She continued to crouch up to scan the room while everyone took their places in the audience.

"Sit down," Tasos whispered as Kiki stepped up to the dais and tapped the microphone.

Except for a spotlight on the podium, the room had grown dark.

"Ladies and gentlemen, welcome to the Hellenic Archaeo-logical Museum. I'm Associate Director Angeliki Matsas. On behalf of Director Nikos Tountas and the Hellenic Archaeological Commission, I'd like to welcome you, our esteemed guests, to the unveiling of the 'Treasures of the *Apocalypsi*'."

The audience burst into a round of applause. Kiki stood, nodding and smiling, until the applause faded, then continued, "To lead us through this journey of discovery, the Aristotle Vandis Endowed Chair Professor of Archaeology, Andreas Roussos."

Roussos emerged from the shadows and stepped up to shake Kiki's hand. He cleared his throat as she stepped behind him to take a post next to the tarp. "Good evening. Thank you all for affording me this great honor and opportunity. Mr. Director. Mr. Prime Minister."

Roussos waved a finger at the screen and watched as his first PowerPoint slide appeared. "Haghia Sophia, the renowned temple and nucleus of Orthodoxy." The slide clicked to show a profile drawing. "On 23 February 532, Emperor Justinian the First decided to build this magnificent basilica, larger and more majestic than its predecessors." The slides continued to follow the lecture. "Using the framework of Heron of Alexandria, he tasked Isidore of Miletus and Anthemius of Tralles with the construction. Under its central dome, the largest heretofore constructed, we believe that the last emperor of the Justinian dynasty, Flavius Mauricius Tiberius commissioned, at the end of the sixth century, the sculpting in Athens of a towering statue of Haghia Panaghia, the Virgin Mary and the baby Jesus."

The slide now showed a model of the statue, eliciting "oohs" and "aahs" from the audience.

"Unfortunately, this statue never found its home in the Patriarchate. We believe that Panaghia foundered in a storm on its way to Constantinople at the dawn of the seventh century sinking with the ill-fated schooner *Apocalypsi* in the rocky waters near Makronissos Island, perhaps one of the first victims of the devastating Byzantine-Sasanian War of 602.

"Tonight, after seven years of intensive recovery, study, and reconstruction, we're proud to be able to rescue Panaghia from her watery grave and present her to you at Athens' renowned temple of historical research, the Hellenic Archaeological Museum."

Roussos waved his hand again and the screen rose. Overhead lights came on, revealing the entire tarp covered structure. "Ladies and Gentlemen, I introduce to you the Virgin Mary, Haghia Panaghia."

Kiki and Alex had each taken one end of the tarp and begun rolling it off the bronze struts of the supine skeleton. The "oohs and aahs" grew louder as slowly the statue was revealed: first its enormous feet, then the trunk, followed by silk pants visible inside the bronze pelvis and rib cage.

A sudden cry pierced the room. More screams and gasps. A few tall guests in front of Eleni stood for a better view. Daphne jumped to her feet. Tasos and Pappajohn did the same.

"What's happening?" Eleni asked.

Kiki and Alex had stopped rolling up the tarp and were ripping it off, exposing the entire statue.

"Is that...?" Pappajohn couldn't believe his eyes. Inside the enormous structure lay a diminutive tuxedoed body. Pappajohn was too far away to see the lifeless eyes staring at the ceiling, and the sharp features frozen in horror.

But Daphne knew. "*The-eh mou*, my God!" she wailed. "It's Harris! Harris is dead!"

CHAPTER ELEVEN

O nly a handful of people could see the dead man lying under the tarp, but Daphne's cries were enough to trigger total chaos. Panicked guests began pushing their way to the rear exits, stumbling over those whose agility could not match their alarm. Government security agents from Greece's Ministry of Public Order and Citizen Protection abandoned any goals of promoting order, surrounded the Greek Prime Minister and the other VIPs in the front rows, and, guided by Director Tountas, ushered them out through the staff door Kiki had opened behind the display. Off to one side, Alex had pulled out his phone and was trying to alert the police, shouting to be heard over the clamor of the escaping crowd and the static bursts and chatter from the guards' walkie-talkies.

Tasos, ever the dutiful officer, jumped on the dais, grabbed the microphone and pleaded with everyone to remain calm. "Stay where you are. Please. The authorities are on their way." To the remaining guards-for-hire, he barked in Greek: "Lock down the museum. Make sure no one leaves the premises."

Within ten minutes, a pair of Tasos' Hellenic Police colleagues on patrol arrived rolling out Greek-lettered red and white crime scene tape. As they began encircling the skeletal statue and Professor Lambros' body, Tasos directed dazed museum staff to guide the rest of the gala guests back into the reception area.

Pappajohn joined Eleni in the reception hall, bookending a devastated Daphne. Staggering between them, Daphne's eyes were streaming with tears. "Look after her," Pappajohn instructed his sister, settling them both in a corner of the lobby. As an ex-cop, he'd seen more than his share of high profile murders and hoped never to see another. "I'll see if I can help with the investigation," he added as Eleni cradled Daphne in her arms.

Back in the exhibit hall, Tasos was on his knees, leaning over the body, studying the scene. In an eerie funereal tableau, Lambros' arms were folded across his chest. A first aid kit lay open by his head.

"Find something?" Pappajohn asked.

Tasos slipped on a pair of latex gloves and gently lifted Lambros hands. "Perhaps." He indicated a primitive looking knife lying underneath. Reaching down, Tasos drew up an intricately designed three by six inch implement made of bronze with an iron blade. It contained a spoon, fork, spatula and small toothpick.

Pappajohn noted what appeared to be dried blood on the retractable spike. "Murder weapon?"

"That's my guess," Tasos agreed, standing. "We must wait for the medical examiner to move him, but I see no injury in the front."

A fellow officer pointed to some purple stains under Lambros neck. "Not much blood either. Entry wound's probably in the back, low velocity."

Pappajohn squinted at the weapon. "If I didn't know better, I'd say that thing was a Swiss Army knife."

"Roman, actually." Kiki seemed to have appeared out of nowhere. "World's first army knife. Likely eighteen hundred years before its modern counterpart."

Pappajohn peered over her shoulder at the locked display cases. "Was it part of the *Apocalypsi* collection?"

Kiki seemed to hesitate, her face, a tight grimace. "Yes, I believe so."

"Who had access to the exhibit here?" Pappajohn asked, slipping easily back into interrogation mode. "Any security cameras?"

Ignoring him, Kiki glared at Tasos. "I hope you don't expect my guests to stay here all night. This is already a disaster."

"They'll stay until Christmas if they have to," interjected a raspy voice. Pappajohn turned to face a middle-aged woman in a starched blue shirt with a mane of curly black hair that fell to her shoulders. She held up a wallet ID with the seal of the E.K.A.M, *Eidiki Katastaltiki Antitromokratiki Monada,* the Special Suppressive Anti-Terrorist Unit.

"Captain Despina Katsoulis," she announced. "Everyone. Do not touch anything without my permission. The Δ.E.E.should be here in fifteen minutes."

"*Diefthynsi Eglimatologikon Erevnon,* The Forensic Division," Tasos explained to Pappajohn. He placed the knife in a plastic bag and handed it to Captain Katsoulis. "We think this is the murder weapon."

"Did you not hear me?" the Captain scolded, her strong jaw set in a determined scowl. Grabbing the bag, she demanded, "who's in charge here?"

Kiki waved Director Tountas over from the door and turned to the Captain with icy politeness. "Obviously, *you* are."

Sleep was out of the question, Sammy finally admitted, envious of her seatmate snoring peacefully. The nightmare visions of losing Ollie again had jolted her into a state of anxious alertness. Lifting her window shade halfway to peek out, she only saw the barest hint of dawn across the darkened horizon. Three more hours to go.

She couldn't seem to concentrate on Chabon's "Yiddish Policemen's Union". The rubber chicken offered by the flight attendant now lay like a lump in her queasy stomach. Another round of turbulence and Sammy couldn't vouch for its remaining there. Cramped and overtired, she wished her solicitous neighbor would open her eyes. Escaping from the window seat for a stroll up and down the aisles would be a welcome respite for even a few minutes.

As the woman's snoring grew louder, Sammy yawned and reopened her book. Back to homicide detective Meyer Landsman and his investigation. Homicide belonged in the pages of a gripping novel, not in real life. *When I get to Greece it'll be for a few weeks of fun. I'll have nothing more to do with death and murder.*

Captain Katsoulis ordered everyone away from the crime scene until her Forensics Team arrived. As the guests gathered at the far end of the exhibit hall, she told Pappajohn that she didn't need help from an ex-Boston cop—or his patrolman nephew. "My team is perfectly capable of handling the situation."

Pappajohn held his tongue. He was a fish out of water here. No point in tangling with this woman who clearly needed to assert her authority. It was only when she waved over three men carrying video equipment that he couldn't resist a word of advice. "If I were you, I wouldn't let the press in here yet." To Pappajohn, news reporters, even good ones like Sammy, were, how did would she say it, *tsoris*. Trouble.

Katsoulis turned to Pappajohn with a frown. "Press? No, these are my men. We're filming interrogations of the suspects."

"Without their lawyers? The Boston DA would have had my badge."

"This is not America," Katsoulis snapped. "We follow the French system of laws. Here everyone is potentially guilty. One has to prove one's innocence." Her eyes narrowed. "In fact, I think we'll begin with you and your nephew. Maybe a little too eager to dip your hands into this tragedy, no?"

The gall of this woman. *Tsoris* in uniform. "Of course," Pappajohn forced the words through clenched teeth. "We have nothing to hide."

The SMS message traveled the thousand kilometers from Athens to Jerusalem in seconds on the GSM network. "The light extinguished, eternal life through Heaven's Gate." The agile fingers then deleted all the messages, snapped the mobile phone shut, and slipped it back into the tuxedo pocket. It would not do to have these secrets discovered by the police.

CHAPTER TWELVE

Thursday, June 5th

Pappajohn stifled a yawn as he checked his watch. Four A.M. might be well past closing time in the States, but in Athens the night was still young. Tavernas and dance clubs in the surrounding streets of Plaka were typically packed with reveling customers who wouldn't be venturing home before dawn.

Here in the museum lobby, however, the gala was clearly over. The forensics team was busy sifting through the rubbish bins, bagging champagne glasses and half-eaten crudités for, Pappajohn surmised, DNA testing. He hoped they planned to test the Roman knife as well. With so many potential suspects, this was going to be a tough case to crack. Large crowd, everyone milling about. Anyone intent on killing Lambros could have slipped away and done the deed before he — or she — was missed.

Pappajohn looked around the atrium. A few guests still waiting to be questioned ignored signs banning all phones and danced around the reception hall to maintain erratic cell reception. Surprisingly, everyone heeded the 'no smoking' signs. Most of the remaining visitors sat glumly in folding chairs, attempting to nap. Eleni and Daphne had both succumbed to fatigue. Pappajohn welcomed hearing his sister's rhythmic breathing on a nearby bench as she cradled her daughter-in-law in her lap. Poor Daphne had cried herself to sleep.

Despite her blowhard threats, Katsoulis had yielded to Kiki's pressure and started the interrogations with the VIP guests. Nary a politician, ambassador, or pop star was left in the thinning crowd. The gilded-robed clerics had also been given permission to leave. Never hurt to be on the good side of the Man Upstairs.

The academics had been next. Professor Roussos had launched an indignant protest at the inconvenience of waiting three hours to defend his innocence. Pappajohn wondered if the real reason for Roussos' distress was the fact that his colleague's dying tonight had stolen his thunder. Loukas Doxiadis had sat quietly listening to his mentor's rant, stroking his trim beard, while most of the other faculty were speculating about who would fill Lambros' shoes in his competitive university department. Pappajohn pulled out the BlackBerry his current boss Keith Mackay had given him and typed in a few notes to jog his memory later.

Scanning the room, Pappajohn noted the absence of Hugh Wellington, the English art dealer Lambros had dissed. A sigh. Even if you're not a man of God, money'll sure get you on the VIP list. Funny, Wellington's companion, 'Mr. Muscles', whom Lambros had trapped in a "spirited" discussion a few hours ago, wasn't as lucky. Sitting on a marble bench in a quiet corner of the hall, he was skimming a tattered copy of Der Spiegel. Or not. His roving eyes met Pappajohn's eyes with a steely gaze.

Perhaps, Pappajohn considered, it would do him good to stretch a bit. Take a stroll over towards his fellow observer. Dust off his detective skills and try to determine what had engaged the thirty-something man and Lambros so intently earlier in the evening. You never know. 'Muscles' might be more likely to open up to a civilian about Lambros' demons, and drop a few clues about the poor professor's murder.

"Wie geht's?" ventured Pappajohn with a rueful smile as he sat down on the other end of 'Muscles'' bench. "Gus Pappajohn. Unfortunately, that's all the Deutsch I sprechen."

'Muscles' folded the magazine closed, but didn't return the smile. "No problem. I went to high school in Brooklyn," he said, traces of the New York accent spicing his fluent response. "Ilan Einav. I'll try to translate your South Boston burr." A chuckle. "Itching to get sprung from here, aren't you?"

"Yesterday. But I don't have the kind of pull your friend Wellington did." Pappajohn made the money gesture with three fingers. "Why are *you* still here?"

"'Cause neither do I. Salaried, just like all the rest of us." He waved an arm at the waiting guests. "Museum curators make even less money than professors." Ilan's eyes narrowed for a moment, as he seemed to study Pappajohn.

Pappajohn expected the curator to continue chatting, but the man merely returned a polite smile. Interesting. Most people welcome the opportunity to spill their thoughts. Back to fishing. "So you work for this place then?"

"No. The Jerusalem Museum. They sent me to review the *Apocalypsi* finds and see if it was productive to arrange a tour. Don't think that's going to happen in the near future now."

"Yeah, no kidding." Pappajohn shrugged. "It's sad." A long pause. *Okay, let's try again.* "I hear Wellington's one of the biggest art dealers around. Maybe he'll have some other options for your museum."

To Pappajohn, Ilan's nod seemed just a second too late. "Could be. Wellington's loan of his Japanese screens collection was a sellout for six months and we couldn't have gotten the Byzantine medallion without his, uh, intervention. He's been a good friend to the world of art."

Pappajohn leaned back against the marble wall. "Unlike Professor Lambros, eh?"

Ilan didn't blink. "Lambros was a scientist, not a business-man," he sighed. "Today, one needs to be a little of both." Flashing another polite smile, Ilan re-opened his magazine and focused his gaze on the article he'd been reading.

Pappajohn peeked at the photo on one half page which was filled with a familiar visage. That Hillary Clinton-like politician they'd seen hours ago topping the headline, "Ein aufgehender Stern".

"Mr. Einav?" One of Katsoulis' officers stood by the open door to her interrogation room.

"Well, I'm up." Ilan stood and handed the magazine to Pappajohn. "You seem intrigued, take it, it's yours. And I'll put in a good word for you with the powers that be. Maybe you'll even get to give your statement before sunrise."

As Ilan entered the interrogation room, Alex Matsas exited, heading straight for Pappajohn. "Our deepest apologies." His deep voice had a trace of British in the Greek accent that Pappajohn hadn't noticed when he'd been introduced earlier as a Hellenic Museum curator.

"Beg pardon?"

"This was supposed to be an evening of enlightenment for our guests, not harassment."

"As an ex-cop, I've found it damned enlightening," Pappa-john said with a measure of sarcasm. "Makes me value the Anglo-Saxon system of justice."

"I studied religious history at Oxford, not law, but I'd have to agree." Alex rubbed his neck. "Alas, we Greeks are a suspicious lot, especially after surviving centuries of Ottoman conquest. Tragically, we've always been masters at destroying ourselves. Professor Lambros, may God forgive him," Alex whispered, under his breath, "was the most adept of all."

Pappajohn raised an eyebrow. "Did you know him well?"

"Only professionally." Alex did not seem inclined to elaborate.

Pappajohn switched gears. "Any thoughts about who might've done this?"

"As I told Captain Katsoulis, I'm afraid Harris had more than his share of enemies." Alex tilted his head toward Daphne's sleeping figure a few yards away. "His cousin?"

"Yes."

"My condolences to her and the family." Alex hesitated for a moment before adding, "Harris wanted to show me something he'd discovered. When things settle down, I'd fancy our reclaiming copies of his papers to review."

"Good luck with that. At this rate," Pappajohn pointed at the conference room door, "an investigation could take months."

"Indeed. My apologies once again on behalf of our museum. I feel a bit guilty going home, except that I have to be back by ten A.M. to help Kiki and Director Tountas inventory the exhibit. At least the traffic to Geraka at this hour should be light." Alex extended a hand to Pappajohn. "I hope they call you in soon."

Pappajohn returned the firm handshake. "Geraka? That's close to the new airport, isn't it?"

"Ten minutes or so via the Attiki Odos, the new super-highway."

Checking the time, Pappajohn realized Sammy would arrive in a few hours. By the time he had his turn, they'd never make it to the airport even if Tasos drove the patrol car at warp speed with blue lights flashing. He fished a slip of paper from his pocket. "Could I ask for a big favor? I'm expecting a good friend to arrive this morning around eight-thirty. I was supposed to pick her up, but —"

"Of course. I will go. Least I can do after what we've put you through."

"Wonderful. Let's trade phone numbers just in case she finally takes my advice not to talk to strangers."

Thursday, June 5th

At six-thirty A.M., the Athens University was still clothed in enough darkness to mask the figure who crept into the basement level of the Schliemann Building. At the end of the unlit corridor, he tugged on a pair of latex gloves before reaching into his jacket pocket for a penknife. Within moments he'd jiggled open the locked door to Professor Lambros' office. Once inside, he flipped on the overhead fluorescent fixture, illuminating the windowless room.

Knowing exactly what he was after, he wasted no time searching through the loose articles, papers, and books piled high on the professor's old wooden desk. Housekeeping, such as it was, started their rounds at seven, and he needed to be long gone by then. First, he crouched under the desk and disconnected the compact PC from the cables attaching it to the CRT monitor above. Glad he had decided to go bigger than a rucksack. The unwieldy computer barely fit into his gymnasium bag. Sitting in Lambros' lumpy chair, he jimmied open the locked middle desk drawer and removed a pipe tobacco tin secreted in the back. Prying off the top, he pushed aside the short stack of old and foreign currency until his fingers brushed against what he'd been looking for. Lambros' safety deposit box key was taped to the middle of a yellowed index card. Smiling, he pulled it out and noted the name of the National Bank of Greece and the box number scrawled alongside the key.

Was that a door closing down the hall?

He pocketed the index card and key, stuffed the tin back in the drawer and eased it shut. Turning off the overhead light, he opened the door and peeked around to check the hallway.

No one.

He picked up the gym bag, and, pulling the door shut, slipped into the hallway, tiptoeing to the nearby stairwell before scrambling upstairs. The bank would be open at eight and he'd need to be at the front of the queue.

CHAPTER THIRTEEN

Thursday, June 5ᵗʰ

The flight attendant's hand on her shoulder startled Sammy. "Sorry, miss. You'll have to move your seat into the upright position. We'll be landing in Athens soon."

Momentarily disoriented, Sammy looked around. Her seatmate smiled at her. "You fell asleep again."

Sammy nodded. At least this time it had been a dreamless nap.

The 747 banked sharply in a series of turns. Sammy raised her window shade to face the rising sun. Below, mountains appeared as brown hills with polka dots of green bushes and trees. Lapping at the coves were acres of crystal blue water, its warm azure tint so much prettier than the gray waters of the Hudson River and the cold Atlantic. White houses with orange tile roofs lined the bases and sides of the hills and covered the flatlands like a tsunami of civilization advancing unchecked towards the mountain peaks. Warm and welcoming, the country seemed so different at the dawn of summer. Her last approach six years ago had been through dark storm clouds battering turbulent coasts with curtains of rain, an omen for the tragedy of Ollie's death.

Sammy gasped when the plane skimmed over the top of an IKEA store, then made a perfect landing at the Eleftherios Venizelos Airport in Spata.

The brand new airport was a pleasant surprise. Unlike the crowded and dingy Hellenikon Airport Sammy remembered, this facility was a gleaming beauty, ready and proud to greet guests for the Olympics next June. Gone were the rattling diesel-spewing shuttle buses that used to ferry passengers from the tarmac to the grimy main terminal and customs. Now Sammy walked off the jetway and down a brightly-lit, sparkling-clean corridor and picked up a free cart to collect her luggage. Uniformed employees smiled and greeted her in English, wishing her a pleasant stay in Greece.

With nothing to declare, Sammy was waved through customs with a cursory passport check. Automatic doors whooshed open to usher her into a large modern hallway lined with retail stores, pharmacies, and car rental outlets that would put American malls to shame.

Sammy said goodbye to her seatmate who was off to visit a cousin in Corinth. Hoping to spot Gus or Eleni, Sammy peered through the crowds waiting for the arriving passengers, but all she witnessed was a sea of unfamiliar faces. Chauffeurs in uniform held up placards, but none of the signs read 'Greene'. Well, their flight *had* arrived twenty minutes early. Nothing to do but wait.

Thirty minutes later Tasos emerged from the interrogation room looking like a whipped dog — or a wet cat, as they say in Greece. He'd slipped off his rented tuxedo jacket and rolled up the sleeves of his now sweat-stained shirt.

"What the hell happened in there?" Pappajohn asked.

Tasos shook his head. "Katsoulis is looking for a scapegoat and I'm it." He told Pappajohn that Katsoulis had criticized his well-intentioned efforts to take over the scene before the homicide team arrived, reminding him he was merely a patrol officer. "She even accused me of contaminating the case because Daphne is Harris' cousin."

"Nonsense." Pappajohn felt the characteristic burn he experienced in his gut whenever he was upset. An antacid would be welcome now, but the bottle was sitting on the kitchen counter at Eleni's. He laid a comforting arm on Tasos' shoulder. "You did what you had to do. Captain Katsoulis should be grateful you were there to keep things under control."

Tasos managed a thin smile as he cast a worried eye at his sleeping wife. "Well, she's not. While we focused on the body, apparently someone got to the computer and projector and deleted Harris' presentation. I never even thought about that."

"You weren't on duty and you still aren't. Just take care of Daphne and —"

"Konstantinos Pappaioannou."

Acknowledging his Greek name, Pappajohn pocketed his BlackBerry and waved to the police stenographer standing by the conference room door. "Go sit with your family," he told Tasos. "Hopefully, this won't take too long."

As soon as Pappajohn was escorted into the room, Katsoulis pointed to an empty chair facing the video cameras. "Please, have a seat," she said in English, her voice sounding hoarse.

Whatever anger and resentment Pappajohn had been harboring toward this woman on Tasos's behalf evaporated the moment he heard the strain and saw the weary set of the captain's shoulders. The ex-cop recognized not only fatigue, but frustration that came from being handed such a difficult, high-profile murder case.

Katsoulis opened her notebook. "You speak Greek, yes?" she asked..

Pappajohn nodded. "Some. The diaspora in Boston is a close community. And we had a few Greek boys on the police force. But, my English is better. "

Nodding, Katsoulis continued in English. "So you are an ex-policeman?"

"Yes. Retired after I was injured in a drug bust gone sideways." Seeing her confused expression, Pappajohn added,

"Uh, that went awry. That didn't go well. I consult for Pueblo Systems now. It's a computer firm in Cambridge."

Katsoulis looked up. "Computers?"

Pappajohn raised a hand. "Tasos told me about the missing file. Deleted doesn't mean gone. Recovering files is our specialty."

. "Then I shall call on you and your company. This is beyond the scope of our tech team and I don't trust the security experts the US has sent us to prepare for next year's Olympics." Captain Katsoulis leaned in and whispered, "Seeah."

Uncertain at first, her meaning finally hit Pappajohn. "Ah, C-I-A." He tried not to smile. Apparently American anti-terrorist teams on loan for next year's Olympics — the first in Greece since the modern games began in the late nineteenth century — were rubbing the local *gendarmes* the wrong way.

Pappajohn spotted the intrusive camera's red light. "Have you checked the security cameras in the exhibit hall yet? Hopefully they've recorded whoever tampered with the file. Maybe even the murder." He sat forward in his chair and met Katsoulis' gaze.

Katsoulis looked down, rubbing her temples. "One camera, only, aimed at the dais and the statue. You cannot see the projector or the computer. Until the crowd entered and the lights were turned on, the video shows nothing but darkness and flickering shadows." She faced Pappajohn, adding, "The museum was trying to save money. If the system had been set up to record sound, I might have been able to narrow down the list of suspects."

Pappajohn folded his arms. "Let's be honest with each other, Despina," he said, using the captain's first name to forge a bond. "You know that neither Tasos nor I should be on that list. Think about it. Lambros was family. Even if we had motive and means, would we not have chosen a less public opportunity? You're wasting your time with us here."

"I give you the point," Katsoulis chuckled. "In truth, I was hoping to tap your expertise as a detective. I should wager that your experienced eyes are better than the best security cameras."

Not immune to flattery, Pappajohn pulled out his Black-Berry and began to share some of his observations of the evening.

At eight A.M., having stashed the gym bag in his Smart Car's boot, the university thief stood second in line in front of the main entrance of the National Bank of Greece on Kotzia Square. His briefcase was nestled under his left arm. In his right hand, he held a rose he'd snipped from a garden down the street next to his parked car. Thank God for the inspiration to have Lambros followed over the past week. Acquiring the Kairos dial meant the professor was moving much closer to inferring the truth. As soon as Lambros had left the bank, the thief had opened a new account with a safety deposit box at the same branch.

When the bank doors opened at ten after eight, he strode confidently into the main hall and headed for the desk of the female assistant manager whose friendship he'd deliberately cultivated over the past week's visits — just enough playful banter to earn her trust. With a warm smile, he handed her the rose and mentioned that he needed to remove a few things from his safety deposit box. "Perhaps after my trip, sweet Soula, we can get together over a Nescafé?" He reached into his pocket for his wallet, and opened it to take out his identification.

Blushing, the blonde twenty-something raised a hand and giggled. "Don't worry. I know you. Yes. When you return." She scribbled her phone number on a Post-it note and slipped it to him as she got up from her desk. Not bothering to check the the box key was his, she led him to the bank vault and punched in the entrance code, opening the door. "Thank you for the beautiful rose," she added, smiling and squeezing his hand before letting him walk unaccompanied into the vault.

"I won't be long," he said as she shut the door to give him privacy. A quick glance at his watch prodded him to hurry.

Placing his briefcase on the table in the middle of the narrow room, he slipped on a pair of latex gloves. Although he couldn't imagine a scenario in which fingerprints might be an issue, he was an exceedingly careful man. Mistakes were for fools like Lambros. Turning to the rows of metal boxes, he searched until he located the number he'd memorized. As expected, Lambros' key fit perfectly.

Sliding the safety deposit box from its bin, he carried it over to the table and lifted the top. Inside, on a soft cotton cloth resting under a few black and white family photographs, a paper-clipped stack of bills in drachmas and a tattered, yellowed copy of the New Testament, lay three ancient dials with attached gears, two of which he'd helped Lambros purchase. He secreted both of those dials in his briefcase and gently removed the third — inscribed with the word *Kairos* — out of the box.

He took a moment to admire this rusted masterpiece, fearing what could happen if it fell into wrong hands. Paired with the Zodiac dial he'd stolen from the museum, the *Kairos* dial could unleash a revivalist wave of heresy that would drown the Word of Christ, struggling once again in this modern world. That's why he had to stop Lambros once and for all.

Carefully he placed the third dial in his briefcase. Then he covered the contents of the safety deposit box with the cloth, pocketed the stolen key, and, with a self-satisfied smile, buzzed himself out of the vault.

CHAPTER FOURTEEN

As nine A.M. neared, Sammy watched employees of the retail outlets lining the airport's ground floor open their doors for business. Passengers from her flight had already been swept away by enthusiastic friends and relatives. The next wave of arrivals, a flight from Asia, were just trickling through the automatic doors.

Sammy began to worry. It wasn't like Gus to be late. He'd promised to bring Eleni to meet her plane as well. Granted, a strong tailwind had pushed up her arrival time, but now it was long past the hour they'd agreed to meet. She flipped open her cell phone, on the off chance that it might work here in Greece. No luck. No signal.

Sammy scrolled down her phone's contact list to pull up Eleni's number in Athens. Maybe she could find a pay phone and use a credit card or get some Euros from an ATM that she could break into change. After stopping a ·few passers-by who just shook their heads at her limited Greek, one hip-looking teen pointed to a flashing red neon G a few doors down the mall. G for Germanos turned out to be an electronics store much like a Radio Shack. The impressive selection of inexpensive burner cell phones solved Sammy's communication problem.

Within moments the handsome young Greek cashier who spoke fluent English helped her activate her new pay-as-you-go mobile telephone. "Sammy?" he asked after studying her Visa card. "Isn't that a man's name?"

Before she could roll her eyes, another voice behind her echoed, "Sammy. Sammy Greene?"

Sammy jumped. She spun around to face a slender man she guessed to be in his early thirties. His khaki slacks and pale blue shirt seemed newly pressed. He was clean shaven and his dark hair was wet — as if he'd recently stepped out of the shower. A couple of inches shorter than her ex-boyfriend Reed's six feet, he still towered over five-foot Sammy. He offered neither a smile nor a handshake.

"And you are?"

"Alexander — Alex Matsas." He grabbed her suitcase. "Kostas has been detained. He asked me to pick you up."

"Kostas? You mean Gus?" Sammy wasn't used to the Greek version of Pappajohn's name. "Detained? Where? Why?"

"Come," he said, starting for the exit, "I'll explain on the route."

Sammy retrieved her new purchase from the counter and called after him. "Wait a second. How do I know Gus really sent you?"

Alex stopped walking and faced her. His serious expression had morphed into a bemused grin. "Besides the fact that he told me you have lovely red hair, he thought you'd probably be difficult. Said you were always a pain in the *tookas*."

That made Sammy smile. As a student reporter, she'd crossed swords with Ellsford University's Greek-American Chief of Police. They'd eventually built a friendship of opposites, in which he'd often chide her in what she called his pidgin Yiddish. "The word is *toochus*," she advised Alex, as she once had her old friend. "Soft h."

Alex nodded and headed for the terminal doors. Outside it was blistering — a dry and dusty heat that reminded Sammy of the Southern California desert. Despite the lack of humidity here, several of her natural red curls soon clung to her forehead like a glistening valance as she rushed to keep up.

Dodging speeding taxis vying for arriving tourists, Sammy followed Alex across the street to the short term parking lot and its automated pay stations. Alex processed the parking stub and set off again past a sea of parked cars. He finally stopped in front of a tiny brown coupe that resembled a snub-nosed sedan with its rear half missing and rested the suitcase on the pavement. "Here we are."

"I don't think my bag will fit in that, uh—"

"Smart Car," he said when she started to laugh. "Very handy for parking in town. And maneuvering in Athens traffic. And with petrol at one-fifty a liter, very affordable."

With surprising ease, Alex wedged her suitcase behind the passenger seat and stepped aside for Sammy to enter. She folded her tiny frame into her seat. "Well, *I'm* a perfect fit." she admitted, searching for her seat belt.

"Probably fell under the seat." Alex slid into the driver's side, started the engine, and shifted into reverse.

The car jerked and whined as he backed out of the space and headed for the car park exit. By the time Sammy managed to buckle up, Alex had merged onto the airport spur of the Attiki Odos superhighway going south at a hundred and ten kilometers an hour.

He expertly navigated the miniature automobile through busy morning traffic, weaving in and out of lanes like a fearless Manhattan cabbie. Sammy caught her breath at a few close calls. Lucky the cars on the road were smaller than in the States — she'd hate to have a run-in with a Hummer in this sardine can. She was amazed at the oblivious and clearly gutsy workmen standing perilously close on the highway's median. Alex explained that they were finishing a train line to downtown Athens in preparation for the upcoming Olympics.

After a few kilometers, the freeway ended, and, to Sammy's relief, Alex slowed to blend in, joining the traffic entering a four lane divided highway bracketed by service roads. Most of the scenery along the route was industrial: factories, warehouses and some retail box stores. Few people walked outside the buildings, though Sammy did spy a group of gypsies selling bamboo furniture from an empty lot next to the gravel shoulder.

"Very overpriced," was Alex's only comment.

Bored with the industrial scenery, Sammy turned her attention to her companion. She studied Alex's classical Greek profile: the wavy dark brown hair, high forehead, square jaw, long, angular nose and, most of all, his large, intelligent eyes. A solid seven. Not very talkative, though. Maybe Alex was uncomfortable speaking English or just shy. Unlike Sammy, who couldn't abide silence. As a radio host, dead air was her nemesis.

"You said you'd tell me what happened to Gus?" she ventured. "Is he okay?"

"He's fine." Alex maneuvered around cross-traffic to avoid a passing motorcyclist whose long braid flapped in the wind, then braked to miss a young man carrying large boxes across the road. "Kostas is helping the police at the museum, " Alex said, shifting up a gear. "We had an unfortunate incident."

At the next busy intersection, Alex flicked the right turn signal and slowly turned the corner, his eyes glued on the traffic light on the dusty median while pedestrians crossed and jaywalked in all directions.

"No right on red here?" Sammy wondered aloud as she watched a motor scooter with two unhelmeted riders drive up alongside and stop in front of their car to wait for the green.

Alex shook his head. "Our streets are dangerous enough without inviting total chaos."

"No helmet laws either, I see."

"Yes, we have helmet laws," Alex said with a hint of a smile.

When the light changed, Alex veered right onto a crowded two lane road. Sammy caught a sign announcing they'd reached the town of Vari. The scooter had already shot several car-lengths ahead. And Alex was silent once again. Sammy gave conversation another try.

"What museum? What happened?"

"The Hellenic Archaeological Museum in Plaka."

Sammy sat at full attention. "Is that the one near the Acropolis?"

"Yes."

"No kidding. I just read about it on the plane. There was supposed to be a big gala last night. The woman in the article, Kiki something, was opening a new exhibit of artifacts from the ship *Apocalypsi*."

"Angeliki Matsas."

A bell went off. *Alex Matsas.* "Wait a minute. Matsas. Are you and Kiki....?"

"Divorced." The tone was dismissive. Clearly not a subject Alex wanted to pursue. Instead he offered, "I'm the Curator of Religious Artifacts at the museum."

Sammy tried a different tack. "So the *Thesaurus* expedition was a success."

Alex raised an eyebrow. "How do you know the name of the expedition? Are you a student of archeology?"

"No. I worked for CNN. My boss sent me here six years ago to cover a story on the *Apocalypsi* discovery."

"I don't recall seeing you on CNN," Alex said, his brow furrowed.

"I was a producer. I worked behind the scenes."

"My preference as well."

Catching a glimpse of the aquamarine sea on their horizon, Sammy sighed.

Alex glanced at her. "Something wrong?"

Sammy shook her head. Back to the present. "There was a terrible accident. My cameraman died during a dive."

"Oh. I am sorry."

"So am I." She cleared her throat. "Our story never aired, but I always wondered which of the two professors' theories about the ship won out."

Alex raised the other eyebrow.

Sammy reached into her purse and pulled out her notebook. "Here," she said, flipping to the page where she'd listed names. "Roussos or Lambros. I assume, as curator at that museum, you must know."

Alex sucked in a breath. "Actually, I'm afraid the incident at the museum last night...."

"Yes?"

"Professor Lambros was killed."

Sammy was shocked. "Oh my God. What happened?"

"Sorry, I'm not able to share the details, but I can tell you that —."

"Hey!" Sammy felt her head and neck snap back against the headrest as Alex floored the accelerator.

A motorcyclist wearing a large black helmet and dark visor that barely covered his dark beard had zoomed up next to the driver's side window, shouting in Greek. Sammy saw a blur of motion and a flicker of light. The sun's reflection on glass perhaps?

With the flash that followed she knew the flash was reflecting metal. A gun!

Sammy gasped as Alex swerved the Smart car sharply right and rocketed ahead, jumping the curb, barely missing an elderly woman waiting for a bus.

At that same moment, something shattered the rear window. Sammy heard the cyclist shake his fist and cry out, "*Thanatos stous airetikous!*"

"Duck!" Alex shouted, taking his right hand off the gearshift to push Sammy's head down. "Bullets!"

From her crouched position, Sammy heard at least two more shots, both of which ricocheted off the driver's side mirror.

"*Ghamo to!*" Alex cursed as the Smart Car skidded on the turn.

Sammy recognized the curse as one of the few Greek words she'd learned from Pappajohn. Watching Alex's feet, she could see that he never touched the brakes when he turned on Vouliagmenis Boulevard, then made a quick U-turn to aim back towards the coastal highway ahead. Her heart raced, her breath came in ragged bursts. Peeking into her side mirror, she could see the motorcycle and its helmeted driver still on their tail, his long hair flapping in the wind. Another shot caromed off her now cracked mirror. She ducked down again, willing herself to emulate Alex's controlled breathing.

Alex turned onto a side street lined by double-parked cars. Barely missing pedestrian shoppers, the Smart car flew down the narrow alley, dodging garbage bins and empty boxes, then back onto another cramped lane past a "No Entry" red and white sign.

"Wrong way!" Sammy shouted.

Alex slammed on his brakes inches from an opposing car and squeezed between two parked cars onto the sidewalk to continue going south. The "right way" driver waved his flat palm out of the window after they'd swung back onto the road, yelling what sounded to Sammy like "*Malaka!*"

Alex didn't bother looking back, as he reached the coastal highway once again and hung a right. Sammy lifted her head just enough up to see a crowd of pedestrians watching the spectacle and blocking the motorcycle from giving chase. Alex drove a few yards out of sight, made a quick left over the grassy median and crossed another curb onto the parking lot of a beach side nightclub, stopping behind a large parked tourist bus.

From their idling perch, Sammy and Alex watched the motorcyclist race past on the coastal highway heading towards downtown.

"We'll stay here a few minutes." Alex shut off the engine. "Let him find easier prey." He glanced at Sammy's trembling hands. "Are you okay?"

"Are you serious?!" Sammy pointed to her bullet cracked side mirror. "Is this how they welcome tourists to Greece nowadays?!"

Sucking in a deep breath, Alex said, "Of course not. These types of ambushes usually target our politicians. The terrorist organization *17 November* killed a British attaché in Athens three years ago. But, Greece is a country of many passions."

"*Meshuga*. Maybe I should just go back to the airport! What was that man shouting?"

Alex ran a hand through his thick brown hair. "Literally, you jerk. But the word is better translated as 'arsehole'."

Sammy shook her head. "No, I meant the bike guy."

Alex looked at his hands, hesitating. "Death to the Heretics."

"So why shoot at us? He certainly doesn't know me and I assume he doesn't know you."

Alex sighed. "Greece is a very modern country, but her roots remain buried in ancient traditions. And rivalries. Even innocent bystanders like us sometimes get hurt." A deep breath. "Rarely. Very rarely. You should feel safe."

"What I felt was 'closer to God' back there," Sammy said. "And I'm not religious."

She quickly scanned the surroundings. No sign of the sniper. The peaceful azure waters of the adjacent bay lay beyond an open air dance club to her left. On the right, busy tram lines, and then the divided coastal highway framed contemporary buildings that resembled a modest French Riviera. Pedestrians, many sporting micro-minis and stylish short shorts, crowded the streets in this upscale neighborhood, stopping to shop at ground level retail stores and breakfast at the many open sidewalk cafés. Unlike in neighboring Turkey, which was experiencing a renaissance of religious-secular conflict, there were no burka-clad women among the fashionable strollers. "What about Muslim fundamentalists?" Sammy ventured.

Alex shook his head. "Fundamentalists are not exclusively Muslim."

Sammy fought a shiver. "Well, it's over. I hope. You did an incredible job back there. You saved my—our lives."

A wan smile. "Wasn't just me." Alex's index finger pointed towards the sky.

Sammy grinned. "Then Mad Max there really did have the wrong target."

As Alex started the engine and turned back onto the highway, Sammy studied his profile, trying to scope out this quiet museum employee who'd just morphed into James Bond before her eyes. "Tell me, how'd *you* stay so calm? I was terrified. Can't imagine it's part of your job description."

"Two years in the Greek army, two months in Iraq. Desert Storm. Calm is safer."

"You volunteered?"

"Not exactly. All men in Greece have to serve. In my day, it was for two to three years. Now it's only a year. The EU has an international force, so few Greeks are in Iraq this time round." He gave Sammy a wink. "With our 'ambitious' Turkish neighbor, we have a greater need for soldiers closer to home."

Sammy nodded. Gus had once told her that tensions between Christian Greece and Muslim Turkey stretched over centuries of Ottoman occupation through the Greek War of Independence in 1821. Gus himself had lost several relatives in the massive ethnic cleansing and expulsion of Greeks from western Turkey in 1922, an event that he called "The Catastrophe."

Clearing his throat, Alex shifted the Smart Car into first gear. "I believe it's now safe for us to go. Though I shall take a roundabout route just in case."

"Shouldn't we stop at a police atation and report what happened?" Sammy suggested.

Alex hesitated again. "If you want to spend the next few hours standing in a virtual sauna in a winding queue. I promised your friend Kostas I'd bring you to the museum right away, and he'll be worried if I don't. Tell you what. His nephew is a police officer and should be there, too. We can ask him for advice."

"I just don't want to see anybody else get hurt."

Alex nodded. "Believe me. Neither do I."

On the drive back to the museum, Alex considered his explanation to Sammy — that the shooting had been some kind of mistake. He wished it were so, but he knew better. He *was* the intended target. What he wasn't yet sure of was *why*. And that was a question for which he'd now have to find some answers. *Before* reaching out to the police.

CHAPTER FIFTEEN

"Gus!" Sammy rushed to greet a visibly weary Pappajohn the moment he dragged himself out of the interview room. "I've been practicing '*Kalimera, Kostas*' for days, but I can see it's not a good morning. Are you alright?"

Pappajohn opened his arms for a bear hug before pulling back. "I'm fine, but…"

Sammy nodded at her escort, who set down her suitcase behind her. "Alex told me about Professor Lambros. That's awful. I'm so sorry." Observing that Pappajohn was dressed in evening clothes, she added, "How'd you get mixed up in this?"

"Dr. Lambros was a cousin of Eleni's new family. He invited us all to attend the gala. Eleni'd planned to come with me to the airport this morning."

Sammy scanned the atrium.

Pappajohn shook his head. "It's been a long night. I sent them all home to get some rest. Eleni's anxious to see you, but I'm afraid it'll have to wait until I'm done here." He studied Sammy. "How about you? Are you tired? Need some coffee?"

"No thanks. Believe it or not, I slept on the plane," Sammy said. She turned her head for a quick wink at Alex. "I've got enough adrenaline to keep me up all day." *No point in sharing what happened on the ride over yet. Better to find that officer Alex mentioned and not scare Gus.*

A group of uniformed police officers were carrying sealed boxes towards the lobby where two soldiers holding MG3s stood guard. "Don't tell me you're a suspect," Sammy asked, raising an eyebrow.

"Not anymore." Pappajohn gestured toward the chamber from which loud voices were heard arguing in Greek. "Captain Katsoulis is a tough broad. She didn't want outside help. Especially from an American. But when I told her I do IT work with Keith MacKay's company in Boston, she let me call in the tech cavalry. Turns out some files on Lambros' computer were deleted. I've been online with Keith overnight trying to see what we can salvage."

"You think the killer took the time to erase them?" Alex asked.

"Could be," Pappajohn deflected. He smiled at Alex. "*Efharisto* for picking up Sammy." A glance at his watch. "Ten-thirty. I'm so sorry. Tell Kiki your delay was my fault."

Alex returned a rueful smile. "She'll find something else to blame me for." A firm handshake for Pappajohn. "It was my pleasure. Sammy? Nice to have met you."

The two-handed handshake surprised Sammy. *Hmm. Nice.* Sammy's gaze followed Alex until he entered a side door that read "Prosopiko". *Employees Only?*

She turned back to Pappajohn with a sigh, "You have any suspects?"

Pappajohn tapped the pocket holding his BlackBerry. "No standouts, but lots of possibilities."

"Anything from the museum computer?"

"The victim's file was deleted." Pappajohn shrugged. "Guess it's going to be up to Keith to see if he can pull a rabbit out of Lambros' data."

To Sammy, the woman striding down the hallway was every bit as beautiful as her photo in *Sky Magazine*. If Kiki Matsas hadn't been sporting a gorgeous evening gown, no one would guess she'd been up all night.

Breezing by Sammy and Pappajohn, Kiki pushed open the door to the interview room and leaned in. "Captain, there are television trucks surrounding the museum. I can't hold off the press any longer. ERT-TV has pounced on the American Ambassador and Lord Wellington has already given a full interview to the BBC."

"This should be interesting," Pappajohn whispered.

From where she stood, Sammy could see a middle-aged woman she guessed to be Captain Katsoulis rise to face Kiki toe-to-toe. Katsoulis pointed an index finger at the assistant director. "This is a murder investigation, not a reality show, Madame. Police business trumps public relations."

Kiki was unfazed. "The E.K.A.M. could benefit from a dose of public relations, Captain. Considering all the misinformation that your unit's obsessive avoidance of the media has triggered. The tabloids are hyping terrorists around every corner during the Olympic games." Kiki shook her head. "Hunkering down is a dangerous strategy. You run your investigation, but let me make sure the right message goes out to the vultures over there."

"She's got a point," Sammy whispered to Pappajohn. "It's a new world. 'If it bleeds, it leads.' If CNN taught me one thing, no matter what, you gotta get ahead of it."

Pappajohn sighed, "Alright. You know better than me." He nodded for them to walk over to the two women. "Despina, may I introduce you to my friend Sammy Greene? She worked for CNN and —"

"CNN? How did *you* get in here?" Kiki demanded. "I told the guards to keep out the press. This is —"

"I met the victim on the *Thesaurus* expedition," interrupted Sammy.

Confusion blossomed on Pappajohn's face. "You met Lambros? When?"

"Six years ago," Sammy said to Pappajohn. "I'll explain later." To Katsoulis: "But right now, Ms. Matsas is right. Give them something good to put on the air. And you'll buy yourself the time you need to do your job."

Katsoulis narrowed her eyes and glared at Sammy, before waving a hand and saying to Kiki, "*Ghamo to.* Go." Kiki sped off towards the lobby. Katsoulis turned back to Sammy. "You, you come in, Kostas' friend. The *Thesaurus*? Explain later? No. I think you need to explain now."

Pappajohn followed them. "If you don't mind, Despina, I'd like to sit in on this one. I have a few questions of my own."

For the next twenty minutes, Kiki stood on the front marble steps of the grand museum, framed by two massive, ornate columns, lobbing questions from the press about the "ongoing investigation". "Yes, the loss of Professor Lambros is heartbreaking... Top government law enforcement resources have been brought to bear... Fortunately, the priceless artifacts from the momentous *Apocalypsi* discovery have not been damaged or destroyed... No, there is not yet an official cause of death... Yes, Professor Roussos' long-awaited presentation will be rescheduled — perhaps as soon as the following month... In fact, the Professor has kindly agreed to hold an exclusive press conference prior to the rescheduled opening and will be available to answer all your questions about the capsized trade ship and its treasure..."

A few yards away, Katsoulis wasted no time in grilling Sammy.

"So," the Captain said, pacing back and forth in the interview room. "You met Lambros six years ago on the *Thesaurus*. Why were you there?"

"CNN sent me to do a feature story," Sammy replied from her seat. "The *Apocalypsi* had just been discovered and the Greek government had mounted a high-profile recovery and research expedition. Some of the items reportedly found looked like pieces from the Antikythera device. You know, that ancient compass that could predict eclipses."

"Yes, of course. The Antikythera mechanism has been labeled by archaeologists as 'the first computer'."

"Yeah. Right after that, the Greek government invited news organizations to cover the expedition. To be right there as the buried treasures were uncovered after a millennium, my assignment editor said. How could I turn that down? Two days later, I was trying to keep my balance on that *furshlugginer* rocking boat while Professor Lambros was sparring with his colleagues about the discoveries." Sammy shrugged. "That's all I can tell you. We didn't have much time to talk."

"I understand," Katsoulis acknowledged. "But your impressions of the man might be helpful for my investigation. So far, most of my witnesses have described him as stubborn and argumentative. Though such individuals tend to have more enemies than friends, no one has been willing to ID anyone who might want him dead." She stopped her pacing to face Sammy. "What did *you* think of Lambros?"

"Well, whoever told you he was argumentative was right. I remember that very well. He and Professor Roussos did not see eye to eye on the origin of the sunken ship or its cargo." Sammy leaned over to reach into her tote and retrieved the old notebook she'd brought with her. Flipping to the wrinkled page, she read: "Roussos — trade ship early seventh century. Lambros — warship, fifth century. Serious infighting between two academics."

Pappajohn wrinkled his brow. "Enough to make Roussos a murder suspect?"

"Seemed like whoever had the correct theory, well, it'd be a career-maker, but —." Sammy shook her head. "I know, Gus, neither of us can forget what happened at Ellsford University. Still, I didn't get *that* vibe. In fact, I thought such spirited exchanges were kind of the Greek way. Was Lambros up for tenure?"

"No," said Katsoulis. "He has been," she shuffled some records on the table, "at the University for over twenty years. Permanent. Promoted to full Professor nine years ago." Back to Sammy: "So you observed the two disagreeing about the ship. Then what?"

"Then all hell broke loose on deck." Sammy chewed on her lower lip. "Ollie..." Her voice trailed off as she looked away.

A raised eyebrow from Katsoulis. "Ollie?"

"Oliver Haines. My cameraman. He was, um, trying to get some underwater B-roll of the wreck and his oxygen malfunctioned. By the time he floated to the surface, we couldn't save him." Sammy shook her head, remembering. "It was awful."

"I'm so sorry, Sammy," Pappajohn said. "You never told me."

"You had your own worries at the time. Ana had gone off the grid. You'd gone out to California again to search for her. Remember?"

"Yes." Pappajohn let out a long exhalation as if to signify how could he forget. Sammy knew he didn't want to relive the details. Especially now that he had his daughter and grandson safely back home in Boston.

Katsoulis was still frowning. "This Ollie. Was he English?"

"Yes?" Sammy replied. "Why?"

"My husband Spiros had a partner who was promoted to Assistant Chief of Police in Lavrio—"

"Lavrio. I think that's the port where they brought Ollie and his things!" Sammy blurted out. "After —"

Katsoulis sighed. "A sad accident. Spiros said that the *Apocalypsi* had claimed yet another victim."

"You think your husband could help us get back Ollie's camera?" Sammy asked. "CNN killed the story and never bothered to follow up. If some of Ollie's last work by the shipwreck can be salvaged, I bet we could donate it to the museum for the *Apocalypsi* exhibit."

"No. Impossible." Katsoulis said. Seeing Sammy's surprise, she added, "Spiros died four years ago. Bomb squad. *17 November* terrorism." Her gaze grew cold. "We finally got the anarchists last year. They are on trial now." Sadness crept into her face. "But my son remains without a father. He is only thirteen."

"Oh," Sammy said, "I didn't realize. I'm so sorry." She glanced at Pappajohn, whose eyes were glistening.

Pappajohn opened his mouth to speak, but Katsoulis was already 'back to business'. She signaled to the videographer to stop taping and slid a pad and pencil towards Sammy. "Write down your observations and sign it, please." An afterthought. "I can make a call or two to Lavrio— but after this investigation is over, not before."

A few moments later, the door swung open.

Sammy put down her pencil and looked up to see a visibly agitated Alex step into the room.

"Excuse me Captain."

Katsoulis threw up her hands. "I said no interruptions!"

Alex flinched, but didn't back down. "I'm afraid this is a emergency. I was finishing my inventory of the exhibit items. We've been robbed."

"You told me nothing was stolen," Katsoulis barked.

Alex raised a hand. "I didn't see it on first pass. I do apologize. But it's missing. There were four in our display. Now there are only three."

Pappajohn spun around in his chair. "Three what?"

"Dials. For the *Apocalypsi* device. In the display case. The large dial with the Zodiac symbols at the rear of the mechanism. It's gone."

Katsoulis shook her head. "First a murder, now a theft." Cursing in Greek. "I just sent the forensic team back to the station. We'll need a full set of prints on the display case."

"Can I help?" Pappajohn asked.

"Yes. When your friend is finished with her statement you can take her home." Katsoulis waved to the videographer to follow her and Alex out the door.

CHAPTER SIXTEEN

Thirty minutes passed before Tasos' cruiser pulled up to the sidewalk across from the museum entrance.

"Thanks for coming to pick us up," Pappajohn said. He nodded at Sammy, "My friend from America, Sammy Greene."

Sammy extended a hand and smiled. "*Ya'sou* and *Ef-efharisto*. Did I get it right?"

"*Nai*. That means 'yes'."

Pappajohn held open the rear door for Sammy to slide in and joined Tasos in the shotgun seat. "How is Daphne holding up?"

Tasos started the engine and shrugged. "*Etsi-ketsi*. So-so." He gunned the engine and aimed the car towards the highway to the southern suburbs of Moschato. "Eleni is letting her sleep and fixing food for her and the children." He turned to his passengers. "You are both invited for lunch, of course."

"Eleni's delicious cooking is nectar for my taste buds," Pappajohn admitted, "but can we make a detour first?"

"Sure," Tasos said. "For why?"

"You know the dial we took to Harris' the other day? The one you found in your father's trunk from Makronissos?"

Tasos nodded.

"Well, remember the three dials we saw in the display case last night? They looked like yours."

Another nod.

"There were supposed to be four, not three in the case. One's missing. Alex — one of the curators we met at the gala —

thinks it was stolen overnight." Pappajohn shook his head. "I blame the museum for not having a security camera aimed at each case with such treasures. One camera for a whole room. Pfft."

"You think the murderer stole it?" Tasos asked.

"That would be my guess," Pappajohn said. He directed Tasos to turn to the north. "Can you take us back to Lambros' office at the University? I'd like to see if your dial is still there. And we may find some other evidence or clues among the chaos."

"So who do you suspect?" interjected Sammy, as Tasos turned onto the new route. "You mentioned the other professor. Roussos."

Pappajohn pulled out his BlackBerry. To Sammy: "Keith MacKay keeps me outfitted with the latest tech." He scrolled down his notes. "Roussos, for sure. Tenure isn't the only motive for an academic battle. Ambition and fame can play. Kiki Matsas and her boss Tountas are in that column. And money would be on the list for them, too. The French art dealer and the Jerusalem curator had an eye on business as well as art. And Lord Wellington is a renowned art dealer. His grandfather was the Elgin Marbles black sheep."

"One dial is worth killing for?" Tasos asked. "Greece is full of ancient artifacts for those who want to make a deal in the black market."

"Good point," agreed Pappajohn. "Unless it was a deal gone bad."

"Unlikely," Tasos continued, "Stabbings are not the typical currency for those who dabble in illegal trade. The knife is a weapon of passion. Of jealousy. Of revenge." A pointed glance.

Pappajohn raised an eyebrow. "Someone in particular?"

Tasos paused. "Well, since Harris himself is dead, I'd suggest Kiki's former husband. The Curator of Religious Artifacts. Alex Matsas."

"No!" Sammy blurted out from the back seat.

"I had him on my list," Pappajohn said, "but only because he was at the gala. Honestly, he doesn't seem to fit the type. First impression, anyway."

"Daphne told me Harris had bragged about dating Kiki Matsas. And the affair started even before their divorce. If it was *my* wife…!"

Pappajohn sighed and retyped Alex's name on his BlackBerry.

As Tasos drove into the university parking lot, Sammy only responded with an "Oh".

Back in her office, Kiki was fuming. She'd just left her press conference, reassuring the world that she had everything under control — and now this. Theft of a priceless artifact on top of murder. With last night's debacle, how could Director Tountas see her as a capable replacement after his upcoming retirement? She'd worked so hard and given up so much to come so close. And yet, before her, ashes.

"What?" snapped Kiki, as Alex peeked into her office.

"You did what you could," he said. "You know how much a new security system costs."

Kiki grumbled, "Tountas the Miser wanted us to get the *Apocalypsi* revenue up front before he'd even consider the investment. I should have pushed harder." She pursed her lips. "We'd be celebrating today. And Harris would still be alive."

A wince crossed Alex's face before he reached out to pat her hand. "There's nothing we can do now. What's done is done."

"Well," she glared at Alex, "Some will certainly be happy he's gone."

"But not you."

Kiki ignored the obvious sarcasm. "He and I? Please. Not the best fit." She shook her head. "But I will miss the friendship."

She peered into Alex's hazel eyes. "You of all people should understand that."

Alex forced a smile. "More than you know, Kiki." He reached into his back pocket and pulled out a paper. "Some good news," he said, unfolding it. "Finished the audit. Nothing else missing. Just the one dial and Lambros' computer file titled MINERVA.

"I thought the files were deleted?"

"The folder's in the desktop rubbish bin, but it's empty. Police techs will see if they can pull something from the hard disk. And Captain Katsoulis told me she uploaded a copy of all the hard disk contents to Sgt. Pappaioannou's colleague in Boston through a virtual private network. She hopes they can recover the contents somehow."

Kiki scoffed "Good luck with that." Her eyes narrowed. "You know, Harris emailed me a few files earlier this week. I think the folder was titled MINERVA"

"He emailed material to me, too. Haven't had time to review it though."

Kiki sat down at her desk, booted up her computer, then scrolled through her emails until she found Lambros' files. "Yes, MINERVA. I looked at the first subfolder. Here we go, 'MASADA'. Full of conspiracy ramblings about art thefts from two archaeological museums — Eretz Israel and the Israel Jerusalem. Didn't get to the rest." She clicked on the file. "Come, see."

Alex leaned in to glance over her shoulder. The screen filled with several jpegs, each a photo of Middle Eastern artifacts. Another attachment contained news stories from Western and Eastern Europe, Israel, and Russia, and yet another included a couple of police reports. Kiki clicked back to the directory. "Okay, here's a subfolder he titled MONASTIRAKI, another called MAKRONISSOS, and, yes, a PowerPoint titled Minerva by itself."

"Let's check the PowerPoint," Alex said. "He was hoping to show it last night."

Shaking her head, Kiki clicked open the presentation and started scrolling through the first five slides. "This is a screed. All he's doing is countering Roussos' theory. Here we go. Slide six. Fifth century, Julian the Apostate, Julian dynasty." She continued scrolling. "There's that solidus again. Did he show it to you?"

Alex nodded.

"Some photos of amphorae. The last slide is half-finished. Just the title and an illustration of a trireme. Athena's Rescue." She looked at Alex. "You think he's suggesting the goddess rescued the shipwrecked sailors? Some of them might have swum to the island, but the Θησαυρός team never found any bones on Makronissos."

Alex shrugged. "I honestly don't know. A lot to digest. We'd probably need to study the material in the other folders. The techs sure have their work cut out for them."

"You're not expecting that we give these files to that harridan Katsoulis?" Kiki's face darkened. She had no doubt the Captain would relish the chance to make her own reputation *and* ruin Kiki's.

"Well..."

Kiki shook her head. "That's my Alex. Always Mr. Goody Two-Shoes."

"What did *you* have in mind?"

Desperate to maintain some level of control over the process, Kiki thought for a moment. If spun the right way, breaking this information herself might just make up for last night's fiasco. "Why not wait until after we've had a chance to go over it all ourselves?" she suggested. "The police aren't experts in archaeology." She moved a little closer to Alex knowing he'd find a whiff of her perfume hard to resist as in the past.

A sigh. "I suppose… It is intriguing…"

Sensing Alex's resolve slipping, Kiki produced an electric-white smile. "Pull up a chair, *agapi mou*, and let's get started." She paused as he stood rubbing his chin. "What?"

"You're right. We may be experts in archaeology, but we could use an expert, too — in police work. Like Pappaioannou. He's not only an ex-cop but he works in IT. What if we consult with him about what we suss out before we go to Katsoulis?"

"You don't think he'll run straight to the shrew?"

Alex shook his head "Not if it's not the right thing to do. Sammy called him a *mensch*."

Kiki raised an eyebrow. "Sammy?"

"From CNN. The one who…"

"Ah, yes. The cute little redhead. The one I should thank." Waving a hand, Kiki turned her head to hide a knowing grin.

Sammy and Pappajohn were waiting outside when Tasos returned from the main office of the College of Humanities on the ground floor of the Schliemann Building.

"Did you get the key?" asked Pappajohn.

"Badge still carries some weight. At least until Captain Katsoulis decides to join us. I expect she and her forensic team will be here soon."

As they all walked down the marble stairs to Lambros' basement office, Tasos said to Pappajohn. "I'm not surprised no one found the missing dial at the museum. If you're right and whoever killed Lambros also stole the dial, that person could easily have taken it before we even entered the artifact display room. Remember, the VIPs were escorted out the back door, bypassing the guards at the front entrance. The perpetrator could've gone out the same way."

"Where does the back door lead?" asked Sammy.

"Museum offices."

"Anybody there see anything?"

"Captain Katsoulis told me all the staff were in the reception hall schmoozing with the gala guests." Pappajohn wrinkled his brow. "You're right, Tasos. Out the back door is definitely a possibility or the perp could have circled around and entered the gala area without being seen and gone out the emergency exit. Which," he grumbled, "should have been wired with an alarm, too."

"Albanian crime has spurred us to upgrade our security," Tasos admitted, "but we are not yet a fortress like the United States."

Arriving at the office, they stopped to check the area. The scuffed marble tiles in the dank hallway led to a row of offices, most of which were unlit. Sammy noted an unkempt bulletin board across from Lambros' office with faded Greek and Roman lettering. *Dep rtm t of Arch logy.*

Tasos handed each a pair of latex gloves he'd borrowed from the first aid kit in his trunk. "Don't want to leave any fresh prints."

Pappajohn squinted at the door handle on Lambros' office. "Tasos, come look here. Scratches?" He pointed to the lock with a gloved finger.

"You think someone broke in?" Tasos peered at the lock. He pulled out his Sanyo mobile. "I'll take a picture before we enter."

"With your phone?" Sammy raised an eyebrow. "We're not getting that model til next year."

Tasos snapped the photo. "The EU is no longer just the Common Market, but - how you say - a 'hot one'." He winked, before turning to unlock the door.

Sammy stepped in, tiptoeing over scattered papers littering the dusty tile floor.

"Looks pretty clean," Tasos said. "For Harris."

Pappajohn shrugged. "If there was a break-in, I'll bet the burglar wore gloves, too." He gazed around the room, pointing out the disrupted dust patterns, indicating that each corner had been explored. "Doubt they'll get any usable prints in here. Except ours from a couple of days ago."

"The monitor is still here, but the computer was taken," said Tasos, indicating the dust-free rectangular space and dangling wires under Lambros' otherwise messy desk which still supported a bulky CRT. "Have you heard anything from your tech friend in Boston about the missing file?"

Pappajohn shook his head. "Not yet. They're working on the drive 24/7, but Keith said it could take days."

"Days are better than weeks," Tasos muttered. "We cannot get DNA analyses in less than a month here. And for a King's ransom."

"There's this new TV show called CSI," Sammy offered, "and they get their results in their own lab in hours."

"Yes," said Tasos, his half-smile acknowledging Sammy's obvious attempt at levity. "I have seen the Las Vegas version. You Americans, you are good at fantasy and special effects, yes?"

Pappajohn chuckled as he flipped through the papers on Lambros' chair and bookshelves. "Have to give the man credit, though. He has a very comprehensive collection of his own publications as well as related literature in his field. Looks like they go back at least thirty years."

"Any things missing?" Tasos asked.

"How could we tell?" retorted Sammy, as she pored over a pile of tattered books stacked on the floor of the dimly lit room. A gasp, when the pages of the tome she opened launched two silverfish towards the floor.

"Actually," said Pappajohn, "We may have a hint. I can't find any papers from the past six years." To Sammy: "That's when you all were on the Thesaurus. Six years ago, right?"

"Yeah."

"A few photos here," Pappajohn said, as he began searching through a shoebox of black and white pictures and old Polaroids resting on the windowsill. He held up a couple featuring Lambros. "Harris sure scowled a lot, didn't he?"

Tasos chuckled. "Monsieur Charisma." He scanned the room again. "You know, I don't see his camera. A Nikon. It was here the other day when we visited."

Pappajohn stopped what he was doing to look around, then walked over to the desk.

"You're frowning, Gus," Sammy said. "Find something?"

"Not sure." Pappajohn bent over for a closer inspection of the middle desk drawer. "Same kind of scratches here on the lock. Nothing on the other drawers. As if our thief knew what he was after. Taso, take a photo."

Tasos snapped the picture, then reached over to pull on the drawer. It opened easily. "It's unlocked."

"What's in there?" asked Sammy.

"Just some old coins. Mostly drachmas, shekels, and francs. More family and conference stuff," said Pappajohn. "I don't see a dial. There's a photo of some kind of manuscript kind of stuck to a commencement photo." He gently peeled off the stuck picture and narrowed his eyes. "Are these class notes? I can't seem to understand this Greek."

Tasos and Sammy inched over to look.

"No, I think that is *katharevousa*," explained Tasos. "The formal Ecclesiastical dialect. A bridge between Ancient and Modern Greek. I can recognize some of the words, but not most of them. They stopped teaching *katharevousa* during Prime Minister Pappandreou's tenure. I was in the Lycée then." He squinted at the ornate writing. "It says something about Athena's legacy, but I can't make out most of the words. Maybe I can ask the priest at the funeral tomorrow to clarify it for us."

Pappajohn nodded. He lifted an empty manila folder lying atop Lambros' desk. "I'll put it here for safekeeping along with the picture of the manuscript. Sammy, can you squeeze this into your tote?"

As Sammy curled the folder into her bag, Tasos pulled out a tin box from the back of the desk drawer. "Let's see what's in this."

He handed it to Pappajohn who opened it with a disappointed expression. "No dial in here either. I wonder if that's what the thief was after. Certainly there was something on the desktop computer he wanted."

"Was your dial like the one stolen from the museum?" Sammy asked Tasos.

"A little bit. It was an old rusty wheel with some Greek letters and words. My son Georgie took a picture, but Harris told us it was worthless. My father, may God forgive his soul, had picked it up on a nearby island during the Greek Civil War."

"Whoa. Gus, you never told me Greece had a Civil War. I mean past the ancient City-States era, of course," said Sammy.

Tasos explained. "Yes. We had the misfortune of straddling both sides after World War II, geographically and politically. Leftist guerillas who resisted the Nazi occupation wanted Greece to side with the Soviet Union. That did not please the conservative parties who favored the West or the Marshall Plan. Four years' war. It was a long…" His voice cracked. "And very painful time in our history. Brother against brother." To Pappajohn: "Find something?"

Pappajohn was still checking the tin. "There's some foreign currency here. Looks like francs and marks, and a few euros." He turned to Tasos. "Know anything about his finances?"

"Not sure what it means, but Harris sold his Porsche a few months ago. He used to call it his…" Tasos hesitated, eyeing Sammy, "his, um, courting car. He must've needed money if he gave that baby up."

"Well, couldn't that be a lead?" Sammy suggested. "Follow the money."

Pappajohn nodded. "I suppose we could start in his apartment. Try to locate some kind of accounting ledger or his bank book. Maybe whoever broke into the office *was* looking for your dial and didn't find it because Lambros had taken it home."

Tasos shrugged. "Daphne has a key. We can stop by this afternoon."

"Good," Pappajohn said. "Now assuming the dial wasn't here when this person broke in, can you think of any other place where he might have stashed it?"

Tasos tilted his head in thought. "Actually I think Harris has a safety deposit box," he said. "I remember Daphne saying that as his closest relative she'd have to go there to pick up his things. He is — was — no longer married and he has no children." He checked his watch. "It's almost two. We won't make it to the bank today. Let's have lunch at home and get the key to Harris' flat. We can go there after siesta."

Sammy followed Tasos and Pappajohn into the hallway. Tasos jiggled the keys to Lambros office, ensuring that the door was locked.

"*Eh*! What are you doing there?"

The three whirled around to face an irritated looking Roussos.

Pappajohn stepped forward and offered his hand. "Professor Roussos, good to see you again. Kostas Pappaioannou." He indicated Tasos. "Tasos Kapsis. Tasos and I met you last night at the museum gala. And this", he said, gesturing towards Sammy, "is my friend Sammy Greene. She's visiting from America."

Roussos acknowledged all three with a curt nod.

"We were so looking forward to your presentation," added Tasos, as Sammy zipped the top of her tote bag shut.

"Not as much as I was," Roussos said. "Didn't expect to be upstaged." A frown. "What are you doing at Lambros' office?"

"My wife is Harris' cousin," Tasos started to explain. "She…"

"My sympathies," Roussos interrupted, though his tone had an edge of sarcasm.

"We need to find Harris' will before we make funeral arrangements. Figured it might be here, Daphne thought one of her keys could get us in." A dramatic sigh as he jiggled the key ring. "Unfortunately, I haven't gotten one of these to work."

A deep voice approaching from the end of the hallway called out. "Everything all right, Professor?"

"Yes, Louka," Roussos said as Doxiadis reached the group. He pointed to Tasos. "Harris' cousin here wanted to check for a will in the office, but apparently none of the keys he brought fit."

Pappajohn stepped over to shake Doxiadis' hand. "Good to see you again. The gala."

"Of course." Doxiadis shook hands with Pappajohn and Tasos before turning to face Sammy. "I know we didn't meet last night, but you look very familiar."

Sammy studied the bearded thirty-something for a few seconds. "Wait a second. I know. Though if my memory serves me, the last time you had long black hair."

Doxiadis ran one hand through his gray-streaked, stylish coif. "When was that?"

"Six years ago," Sammy prompted. "We met on the *Thesaurus.*"

"Yes, yes. Of course. CNN." He extended a hand for a firm shake.

"I never thanked you enough for your kind words when my cameraman, Ollie, passed. I am truly grateful," said Sammy.

Doxiadis nodded. "No worries. We archaeologists quickly come to appreciate both the value and the fragility of human existence. That's why so many religions offer hope for reincarnation or an afterlife. I do hope that Professor Lambros' next act is one that honors his scientific contributions."

Roussos scoffed. "Really, Louka, you no longer have an obligation to flatter Harris' memory. One can say that his true reward was to escape the humiliation of seeing his theories disproven by our research."

"Is there something we can help you with here?" Doxiadis stepped in, nodding at Lambros' door. "We might be able to get you a key from the main office after lunch." He gave Sammy a warm smile.

"No, no! Thank you," said Tasos. "We'll just get the will from his attorney. My wife wants to be sure we respect his final wishes. *Efharisto*."

"Speaking of your wife, Taso, we're going to be late for lunch ourselves," Pappajohn interjected, patting Tasos on the shoulder. "Professors, thank you, but we'd better be on our way."

CHAPTER SEVENTEEN

The moment Sammy stepped into Tasos' apartment she was enveloped by welcoming arms. Eleni and Daphne ran over to greet her and offer the traditional Greek hug and double-cheeked kiss. Maria stopped texting on her flip phone and looked up with a smile and a wave. Georgie tossed his Nintendo Game Boy onto the couch and strode to the door, extending his hand for a grown-up shake.

Despite their sorrow at the loss of Eleni's husband, and now Daphne's cousin, everyone's pleasure at meeting their new guest seemed genuine. Sammy quickly felt like she was part of their extended family — a legacy she'd missed as an only child. Bubbe Rose had been nurturing, when raising Sammy after her mother's death, but never effusively warm. A survivor of the Holocaust, Rose had made certain that her granddaughter developed the necessary life skills and independence that now marked Sammy's character.

The dinner table had already been set for the mid-afternoon meal. Sammy was guided to a chair between Eleni and Pappajohn for a chance to "catch up". She patted Eleni's hand and whispered her condolences for the death of her husband George.

Eleni nodded, "May he rest in peace." A sigh. "He so wanted to meet you."

"And I him," Sammy admitted. "He must have been a wonderful man — and lucky to have you."

Daphne leaned over Sammy's shoulder and ladled steaming lentil soup into Sammy's bowl. "My recipe. Yiorgos and Tasos loved my lentil soup."

"Hey, I'm *still* here," Tasos complained. "And hungry. Daphne and Eleni are the best cooks. Wait til you taste her *youvetsi*."

Maria rolled her eyes. "Meat. Meat. Always meat. It's so hard to be a vegan in this family."

Daphne chided her daughter as she ladled out a larger bowl of lentils for her. "It's so hard to make sure you get enough to eat."

"I *never* get enough to eat," complained Georgie.

Pappajohn chuckled. "And he's not a teenager yet."

After diving into the main course of lamb and orzo, the conversation turned to the events of the previous evening and the subsequent investigation.

Pappajohn and Tasos filled the curious diners in on the news about the missing museum dial, Kiki's press conference, Katsoulis' forensic team, and their expedition to Harris' office.

"We were almost caught in the leeks by the snobbish professor," Tasos bragged. "But I told Roussos we were looking for Harris' will."

"In the leeks?" Sammy asked.

"Greek expression," Pappajohn said. "Caught red-handed. Stealing vegetables."

"I wouldn't mind some vegetables now," Maria interrupted.

"We can go to the greengrocer after siesta," Daphne promised. " I'll make a salad for supper." To her husband. "Quick thinking. I'm sure Harris' will will be in the bank safety box. He always had to be sure things would go his way." A sigh. "Stubborn as a mule, but I shall miss him so…"

"You are right, my sugar. We will all go to the bank tomorrow," Tasos agreed. "I'm hoping our dial will be in there too. Or at his flat. Do you still have the spare he gave us?"

Daphne nodded. "Honestly, his plants did better when I watered them than when *he* was there." She pursed her lips. "We'll have to adopt them when the police are done. So Pappou Yiorgos' dial wasn't in his office?"

"No. Harris' computer was gone, too. All we found at his office were a couple of photos of a manuscript in *katharevousa*. I was hoping to ask Father Mihalis about it after the funeral. Is everything all set with the church?"

"Yes, the service will start at six in the afternoon. Father Mihalis invited Bishop Theosophos to perform the service. I've ordered the wreaths and Eleni was kind to pay for the casket with her credit card. We will have to get cash from the bank tomorrow for Bishop Theosophos."

"Did she mean six in the evening?" Sammy asked Eleni.

"No, days are divided differently here," she said. "Midday starts at noon and goes until six. Afternoon is six to nine or ten, and then it's night. You get used to it. In any case, during the summer, the sun doesn't set until after nine. Summer in Athens is like summer in Boston. Speaking of Boston, Gus, Teddy called. He wanted to tell you he won first place in his school science fair."

Remembering how close Pappajohn had been to losing his daughter Ana and grandson Teddy in Los Angeles three years ago, Sammy was glad to see her friend break into a grin. She gave him a thumbs up.

As they tackled their sweet *galaktoboureko* dessert, Daphne motioned towards the hallway to the rear of the flat. "Kosta is in the room with Georgie. Sammy, we've set up a cot for you in the room with Maria and Eleni."

Sammy looked at Pappajohn, "I thought we were going to Harris' apartment after lunch?"

"At my age, I'll be a better detective with an hour or two of sleep. And, listen Georgie, I know *you* never close your eyes, but mute that Game Boy music." A grimace. "Please."

CHAPTER EIGHTEEN

Thursday, June 5ᵗʰ

It was six in the evening — no, the afternoon—when Tasos, Pappajohn, and Sammy hopped into the police cruiser for the forty-minute trek through crosstown traffic to Lambros' apartment in the University Village of Zografou.

Sammy enjoyed the forced leisurely drive on serpentine narrow streets among honking cars and zig-zagging motorcycles. The tour gave her a chance to see Athens' bustling shops, restaurants and open air cafés, as well as the flourishing multi-hued political graffiti that seemed to cover almost every wall that didn't sport flyers or posters. Even the balconies of the National Polytechnic University's ramshackle dormitory towers were decorated with urban artists' *oeuvres*. Eleni was right. Just as with summers in New England, the sun here was still high in the sky. Six P.M. really did feel like afternoon.

Tasos parked the car on the sidewalk across from the St. Therapon Cathedral on barely two-lane Dimokratias 'Boulevard'. Sammy had counted at least ten churches on their trip. It seemed as if there was one on nearly every block. Were there any synagogues in Athens, she wondered.

Dodging fearless mopeds, they dashed across the narrow street and approached the entrance to Lambros' flat which was on the third floor of a six-story apartment building. Tasos key admitted them into a marble-floored lobby. At the rear, two steps led to the thick metal door of an elevator. When the lit cage arrived on their level, Tasos manually opened the door and motioned for Pappajohn and Sammy to squeeze into the small rectangular space. "I think we can all fit in the lift," he ventured.

"This feels smaller than a Port-a-Potty," Sammy grumbled as the elevator lurched up, jostling them up to Lambros' story. She noted that, unlike in the US, the elevator started counting floors at zero. So Lambros' apartment was really on the fourth floor.

The moment the elevator came to a jiggly stop, Tasos pushed the manual door, holding it for them to exit. He led them to Lambros apartment and was about to insert his key when an elderly woman in a faded housecoat peeked through the half-open door of the opposite apartment and shouted in Greek.

Sammy gave up trying to catch any recognizable words in their exchange, but was relieved when Tasos unlocked Lambros' apartment and led them inside.

The neighbor's door slammed as Tasos laughed. "Thought we were burglars," he explained to Sammy.

"The good news," Pappajohn remarked, "is that Nosy Nellie said she hadn't heard anybody coming to Lambros' since he left yesterday afternoon. We should have a clean scene."

Tasos scanned the living room which was as messy as his cousin's office. "Not very." His eyes landed on several scraggly houseplants stretching for light by the curtained window. "Daphne used to try to clean when Harris went to a conference, but says it was a lost cause, even in a place so small." A deep breath. "Well, let's start searching."

Pappajohn and Sammy each accepted a pair of latex gloves from Tasos who warned them to leave everything as they found it. "Just in case Katsoulis decides to send a forensic team."

"I would expect nothing less from that woman," Pappajohn posited.

Tasos snickered. "Okay, Sammy, you take the bathroom; Kosta, take the bedroom. Harris might keep his bank book by his bed. I'll check this room for our dial."

"Nothing in the bathroom except poor housekeeping," Sammy announced to Tasos after a quick search. "More hair gel than I've ever owned. Medicine cabinet had a bottle of Xanax that also contains some little blue pills."

"Ha!" exclaimed Tasos. "No, no, I meant the camera. It's here in his kitchen cupboard."

Sammy ran to the pantry which was lit by a ray of sunlight from the kitchen window. "Good job. Digital?"

Tasos nodded, pushing the Nikon's button to review any pictures Lambros might have taken. "Here are some of Daphne and the kids in Crete two years go," he said, scrolling through a number of family shots. "This one seems to be Harris on the ferry to Mt. Athos. Whoa," he exclaimed, "these are nice pictures of Kiki."

Sammy peeked over his arm to see a photo of Kiki in a string bikini on the beach of what she surmised was a classic Greek island.

"Mykonos," said Tasos. "Daphne and I used to party there — before the kids."

"TMI, Tasos," Sammy whispered. "Anything there related to our case?"

"Let me see." Tasos reluctantly scrolled through the rest of the photos. "Here. These look like photos of my dial. See." He magnified the photo with his fingers. "The writing says *Kairos*."

"Finished the bedroom." Pappajohn came back into the living/dining area. "A copy of Playboy under his bed. A Bible and a Bulgarian-Greek dictionary in his nightstand drawer. I found this black and white photo of a couple of dials in the bottom of one of his bureau drawers under his Tighty Whities. It's a snapshot of two dials and some gears, but neither looks exactly like the one you brought him, Tasos. Did you find it anywhere?"

Tasos shook his head. "No, just Harris' camera. He took photos of our dial, too."

Pappajohn peeked at the viewer.

"And here are a couple more that look like they're in a display case. There's the one with the sun and the moon phases and a big one in the back with what look like constellations. He must have shot them at the museum. Alex said the Zodiac dial had been stolen." He sighed. "We'll need some expert help studying all of these."

"Should we take the camera?" asked Sammy.

"No." Pappajohn took the camera from Tasos, turned if to OFF and flipped a switch to open its side. "Thought so. It has a secure digital card. Tasos, give me your fancy phone. I can slip the memory card into it and copy the photos we want onto your RAM."

Shrugging, Tasos handed over the mobile and continued his search of the apartment as Pappajohn tried to upload the stored pictures.

"No sign of the will, but," Tasos held up a beige card, "the name and address of his attorney. An office in Plaka, near the Acropolis," he added for Sammy's benefit.

The usual sounds of motorcycles revving and cars honking from the street below became screeching tires, brakes, and shifting gears. Tasos ran to the living room window and peeked beyond the curtains down to Dimokratias Boulevard.

"*Ghamo to!* It's the forensics team! They must have finished up at the museum and they've come here and — *chestikame*, that's Katsoulis' car driving up!" He pivoted towards Pappajohn. "You done?"

Pappajohn shook his head. "I need five more minutes. Maybe she'll walk slowly."

"Wait, I have an idea," Sammy said. "Tasos, you finish searching, and I'll run to that awful elevator and call it up here. It stays on the upper floor if you hold the entry door open, right?"

"Yes," Tasos grinned. "Go."

While Sammy kept the elevator door ajar on floor number three, she could hear agitated voices through the gap in the adjacent stairwell. If the lift didn't arrive on the ground floor soon, they'd start climbing up.

She breathed a sigh of relief when Pappajohn and Tasos exited the apartment and Tasos locked the door. They'd left the camera behind, but Pappajohn carried two of the struggling plants while Tasos held another. As they squeezed into the elevator, Pappajohn advised her to hide her gloves.

Tasos whispered, "Katsoulis will understand how much Harris wanted us to save his plants."

Sammy shoved the latex gloves into her jeans pocket.

The moment the elevator inched reached the lobby, Katsoulis tugged open its door. A second of shock.

"You again!" the Captain scolded Tasos.

Pappajohn held out the pots. "Couldn't leave these to die."

Katsoulis gave him a grudging nod. "I hope you all didn't touch anything else."

"Of course not," Tasos countered. "If I found something, you'd be the first to know."

She waved over two of the forensics team. "Make sure these plants are clean before our horticulturists leave the premises."

Stepping into the elevator, Katsoulis turned to face Pappajohn.

"Kosta, anything from your Boston friend? Lambros' office computer is missing. Now I'm even more anxious to know what was in that deleted file."

"I'll call Keith as soon as we get home. I have your number, and, believe me, I'll use it."

The motorcyclist stopped his bike at an Esso station two blocks north on Dimokratias Boulevard. He removed his helmet and shook loose his long hair. As the attendant filled up the tank, the bearded rider flipped open his phone and speed-dialed his contact. Walking a few steps away from the pumps, he whispered in Greek, "Followed them from Moschato to Zografou, but had to hightail it out. Police and forensics are all around there now. I'll see if I can catch them again outside the perimeter."

He slammed the phone shut when he heard the cursing from his contact.

CHAPTER NINETEEN

"Give me those dishes so you can use the table," said Daphne as Eleni handed her a wobbly stack.

Maria pulled off the tablecloth and walked it over to the kitchen door to shake out the crumbs.

"Done," said Pappajohn as he followed Georgie into the dining area. "I printed out the pictures of all the dials." He laid them out side to side on the polished wood surface.

"You need light," insisted Daphne. She turned up the wattage on the chandelier. "Much better."

"I need my glasses," Pappajohn countered. "The etchings are so small."

Tasos, Sammy, Pappajohn, and Georgie leaned over the photos, studying the details from the magnified printouts.

"Can I have my phone back?" Tasos grumbled.

Pappajohn fished it from his trousers pocket. "Here. Pictures are still on it. I just copied them on your son's computer." A pause. "By the way, did your cousin have a mobile phone? I didn't see one at the museum."

Tasos shrugged. "Neither did I, but I can check with the forensics team tomorrow morning."

Eleni stepped in to cover dish duty as Daphne brought three cups of tea to the table. "Not tomorrow. I left a message with Harris' lawyer that we'll stop by before we check the safety deposit box at the bank."

Tasos nodded. "We need to see his financial records, too." He glanced at the picture of the *Kairos* gear - the one he'd given to Lambros. "We should have kept Baba's dial."

"*Kairos* can mean weather or time," Pappajohn explained to Sammy. "Depending on the context."

"Why are these letters on the other side written in a circle?"

Pappajohn shook his head and shrugged. "Not sure."

Sammy pointed to a photo of another dial with Greek letters. "Are these words? Can you read them?"

Pappajohn frowned. "No. Taso, *katharevousa?*"

Tasos squinted at the picture and shook his head. "I don't think so."

"I know, Baba!" cried Georgie, "They're numbers."

Tasos held the photo up to the light. "You know, son, I think you're right."

"Of course," said Pappajohn, catching Sammy's puzzled expression. "The ancient Greeks didn't use Arabic numbers. A was 1, B was 2, ⊠ was 3, and so on."

"I only count up to twelve," said Georgie.

"Twelve?" Sammy pondered. "Hours, months, degrees, eggs, children, bagels…could be anything…"

Pappajohn was about to respond when his mobile phone jangled in his pocket. He pulled it out and flipped it open. "*Embros?*" His ears reddened. "Oh, hello, Despina…yes, yes, all of us…thank you…No, we didn't see it either…just the camera…OTE, of course…" Pappajohn covered the mouthpiece, "No phone, so she'll check with OTE, the Greek AT&T, for call records." Back to his phone. "No, sorry…nothing. Can you track a GPS?…Oh, okay." Pappajohn shook his head. "I'll call my colleague Keith and let you know…Great, what did the Medical Examiner say?…Uh, huh. Pithy? Pith…like a frog?" He grimaced. "Damn. At least it was quick." A sigh. "Damn." Softer. "Thank you. I'll give you a call when…tomorrow? Yes, the funeral. All right, see you then. *Geia.*"

Pappajohn stared at all the photos for a few more moments without speaking, then pointed to the picture of the *katharevousa* document. "Father Mihalis may be able to help us with this one. But for the rest of these shots, we need an expert in ancient or Byzantine Greek. I expect we'll see him at the funeral tomorrow, too, but just to be sure, let me give him a call."

He pressed the button to dial the number and nodded. "Hello, Alex?"

CHAPTER TWENTY

Friday, June 6th

T he attorney stubbed out his cigarette in an already full ashtray and looked up from the document on his desk.

"Straightforward, really," he continued in Greek. "As the only living heir, Daphne, the flat in Zografou and its contents, a 1998 Fiat Uno and the contents of his safe deposit box all go to you." He lit another cigarette, and took a deep puff. "The computer in his office belongs to the university, but I'm sure they will let you have his papers."

Daphne blew her runny nose in a ragged tissue. "Wish he hadn't sold his Porsche. I loved that car."

Tasos stepped in. "We planned to go to his bank today. Can we also get his bank records?"

The lawyer raised a hand. "No problem. I'll call Panos and arrange for copies. Give me a few days on the apartment title and the car, okay?" He blew out a puff of smoke. "Next week."

Tasos and Daphne said their goodbyes and headed back to the lobby where Pappajohn and Sammy were waiting.

"Ten-thirty. Lucky us. Only took an hour. Off to the bank," said Tasos, checking his watch.

Pappajohn sighed. "I'm afraid we'll have to take a detour. Captain Katsoulis called. She wants to see us all at the Police Station. Now."

The line barely moved. At a few minutes before two P.M., Sammy, Pappajohn, Daphne and Eleni were standing in a winding queue for the Athens National Bank's Services Desk that now appeared to have completely stalled.

"This is ridiculous," Daphne complained. "The bank closes in a few minutes; we have to go home and pick up the children. I wanted to be at the church by five to make sure the wreaths were delivered and everything was all set."

"Nothing in Greece works on a schedule," Eleni explained to Sammy. To Daphne: "We won't lose our spot, don't worry."

"If that nasty old captain hadn't made us go to the police station and get fingerprinted, we'd have been done by now! Does she actually think we're suspects?" Daphne fumed.

"No, in fact, it's to rule us out. Your prints and our prints are likely to be all over Harris' home and office," explained Pappajohn. "And I wouldn't say she's exactly *old*," he added.

Daphne produced an indulgent smirk. "Where is Tasos?" She searched around for her husband. "If they call us and he's not here..."

"Lambros!"

"Great timing," said Pappajohn. He turned to the sound of the page and pointed across the lobby. Tasos stood near a gold-plated door, laughing with a petite man dressed in a stylish three-piece suit.

The group walked over to join him.

"Eh, come and meet Panos, my classmate from the Peiramatiko Lyceum. High school. We were best mates for the last two years." Tasos clapped his slim friend on the back, dislodging his thick glasses. "Number one in our class. Carried the flag every 25th March." To Sammy: "That honor is given to the best student in the class."

"Ah, *now* I understand," said Daphne, with a sly smile. "He did your homework and you kept the bullies at bay."

"A fair trade," Panos acknowledged. "We both made it out alive." He handed Tasos a manila envelope. "Lambros' bank records."

Tasos gave the envelope to Pappajohn to put in his leather briefcase.

Panos pulled out a jangling ring of keys and selected one to open the golden door. "Come with me. Your cousin's safety deposit box should be ready."

Inside the bank vault, Panos pulled the out the box and laid it on the table in the middle of the room. Opening the lid, he slid the box toward Daphne and invited her to remove the contents.

As they peeked inside the open box, Daphne's and Tasos' expressions slowly morphed from eager curiosity to disappointment. Daphne shook her head.

"I was truly hoping we'd find the dial from our cellar at least..." Tasos mumbled.

"When was the last time Professor Lambros accessed the box?" Pappajohn asked Panos in Greek.

"I'll have to check, but I think Tuesday. My assistant Soula keeps the log," Panos explained.

"Can you get us a printout," Pappajohn said. To Tasos: "Might give us a clue as to what he did with the dial."

Panos laughed. "I wish. Our logs are still on paper. I'll ask my assistant manager Soula to write up a list of his visits in the last year if you want."

Pappajohn smiled. "Thank you. That'd be great. We shouldn't be too long here ourselves."

Nodding, Panos slipped out of the chamber. Pappajohn turned back to the deflated couple.

With a dramatic sigh, Tasos lifted a fragile copy of the New Testament out of the box and handed it to Pappajohn. "We already have a Bible."

Pappajohn nodded and slipped the heavy yellowed book into his briefcase as Tasos removed the paper-clip from a stack of Greek drachmas, the country's former currency, and spread them out.

"Wow," Sammy marveled, "look at all the 100,000 and 50,000 bills. That's a fortune!"

Tasos' expression was sour. "Not really. They're all from the last twenty years. Worth virtually nothing today with inflation."

"Maybe Harris thought they'd be valuable collectors' items after we moved to the Euro," Daphne suggested.

"Worth less than a thousand Euros all together, I'd say." Tasos swept the money into Daphne's purse. "We could splurge on another trip to Mykonos."

Daphne nudged him with an elbow. "Didn't you promise to take Georgie to Disneyland Paris? And Maria and I could go shopping on the 'Sans Eliseh'."

"That wasn't exactly what I had in mind," grumbled Tasos, turning back to the box.

"What about these?" Sammy interrupted, pointing to several black and white photographs. "Valuable?"

"Oh, my, yes," Daphne's voice cracked. "This one." She held it up for the others to see.

A sigh from Tasos.

"Who are they?" Sammy asked, noting the smiling faces of two teen-aged girls in dated dresses.

"My mother and Harris' mother, my Aunt Sophia, as young women." Daphne blinked back tears. "This is worth more to me than any other treasure."

Tasos' second sigh projected resignation, as Panos reentered the chamber holding a lined piece of paper filled with neat Greek handwriting and handed it to Pappajohn.

Pappajohn scanned the paper, commenting, "He's been in and out a lot in the past year. But, the only time this month was Tuesday, not long after we stopped by his office." He pursed his lips and shook his head. "If he dropped the dial off, it should still be here. So, I guess he didn't. We'll have to keep looking." To Panos: "Thank you."

Tasos clapped Panos on the back. "Yes, thank you, my friend. We're all finished. We should not be disappointed to inherit only memories." He placed a comforting arm over his teary wife's shoulders. "Let's go home and pick up the kids for the service."

CHAPTER TWENTY-ONE

The temperature had passed the forty degree Celsius mark when Sammy and Pappajohn, along with Lambros' relatives, stepped out of the bank's revolving door and into the bright afternoon sunshine. The sizzling afternoon heat had not discouraged Athenians from venturing outdoors. Traffic on the busy avenue yielded a cacophony of horns, squealing tires and ineffective car and motorcycle mufflers.

Before joining Daphne at the bank, Tasos had managed to squeeze his police car between two Fiats straddling the median strip three blocks away, so the group began trudging uphill in uncomfortable silence, wending their way on the narrow cracked sidewalk in single file. Amidst the vehicle noise, none of them noticed that one motorcycle, its long-haired driver sporting an opaque black helmet, leather jacket, and jeans, was following them at a discreet distance.

Tasos turned a corner and, grinning, pointed to the parked police vehicle ahead. Happy to dive into the car and its air conditioned interior, the group also missed seeing the cyclist spy the blue lights on the car's roof and accelerate off in the opposite direction.

As the mourners made their way up the cobblestone path to the cemetery, Pappajohn regretted having brought his briefcase along on such a hot afternoon. At least he should have left the heavy Bible in the car. But Tasos had assured him Father Mihalis could translate some of the writing in the document photo from

Lambros' office and Pappajohn wanted him to weigh in on the Bible as well. Lambros had not impressed him as a particularly religious man.

Sweat dotted Pappajohn's polo shirt. If only the funeral had been at Father Mihalis' church, St. Therapon, a quick walk from the street. But St. Therapon had no cemetery, so it had to be the ninety hectare cemetery and chapel up on the hill of Zografou. Thank goodness the Greeks yielded to the triple-digit afternoon temperatures and didn't demand suits and ties for warm weather funerals, especially during a heat wave.

Sammy had offered to help carry the case, but Pappajohn refused. He wasn't about to admit that both his body and soul were weary. A second funeral in a little over a month. He passed the gauntlet of flowered wreaths balanced on stands lining the path to the church door. Slightly less than a decade since his own dear Effie had died and his mind flashed to the moments he had made a similar painful walk to St. Sophia's in Boston with Eleni at his side. Now she took his arm in hers and he welcomed the opportunity to lean just a little on his sister once again.

Daphne and Tasos were at the chapel door, greeting friends and extended family with hugs and double-cheek kisses. Their son Georgie looked serious as he handed out memorial flyers with invitations for the guests to share a wake after the ceremony at a nearby outdoor cafe. Maria, all teenager, was dressed in a demure frock, but her eyes were glued to a handsome altar boy who had stopped to chat and escort her into the church. Pappajohn remembered when his own daughter Ana had been that age. If only the boys who responded to her youthful charm had been altar boys instead of street hooligans.

Pappajohn spotted Professor Roussos and his younger colleague among the crowd. Nice of Roussos to honor Lambros, despite their academic conflicts. Of course, the museum contingent was expected. Tountas, Kiki, and Alex were standing together at the fringe of the group. But, a couple of surprises. 'Muscles' with the New York accent — what was his name, Ilan Einav— had come. And, Pappajohn had not bet on seeing Captain Katsoulis attend in mufti, her blue and white uniform exchanged for a very attractive black dress. She was leaning on a eucalyptus trunk, enjoying a cigarette, but her eagle-eyes gave her police background away. Pappajohn watched her scan the attendees, nodding when her eyes rested on his. Was that a hint of a smile?

Eleni guided Papajohn to his seat next to Tasos in front of the altar. He'd hoped to find a rear pew, so like Katsoulis, he could continue to observe the mourners during the service. Through the arched doorway to the altar beyond, Pappajohn did notice the priest from the gala, Father Mihalis, in black with a white collar, talking to a resplendent Bishop Theosophos and an ornately garbed priest, likely local to this church. They were interrupted by an agitated monk, clad in robes and a hood, who pulled Father Mihalis off to the side and out of view, allowing the Bishop and chapel priest to begin rinsing their hands over a gilded font in preparation for the service.

Minutes later, the monk exited through a side door amidst the icons in the altar wall and strode down the aisle to their right. As the last of the mourners took their seats, the church's priest stepped down from the altar and raised his hands for the congregation to rise.

Patting Eleni's hand, Pappajohn willed his knees to help him stand up without a grunt as the service began.

"Aionia h mnimi!"

With the pews filling, Sammy opted to stand in the rear of the small chapel, allowing older and younger attendees to sit for the service. Besides, she hated the idea of an open casket ceremony. Too many memories of her mother's funeral.

The other reason she didn't mind hanging in the back was the fact that she was wearing a bright green cotton sundress. Although it certainly complemented her red hair and green eyes, it was hardly appropriate garb for the occasion. But then, she hadn't packed for a funeral.

Scanning the crowd, Sammy observed Kiki greeting mourners as if she were the hostess of another gala. Looking elegant as usual, Kiki was dressed in a simple short black dress and heels. Remarkable, Sammy thought. Everything Kiki did seemed to call attention to herself. She was smiling ear to ear as she shook hands with a TV reporter and his cameraman from the government station ERT-TV. No doubt the Associate Director had invited the media to stir up publicity for the museum's exhibit. A touch relieved, Sammy didn't spot Alex anywhere near his ex, nor among Lambros' colleagues seated in the middle of the church.

As the priest and the altar boys began a slow walk down the aisle, clouds of incense sprayed over the parishioners. Sammy smelled the bitter smoke approaching and fought to avoid a loud cough. She inched toward the open door, holding her breath, slipping outside before the chalice got closer.

A few deep breaths and Sammy was ready to return to the service when she heard male voices arguing in the distance. The miked cantor's singing being piped to the speakers outside the chapel made it impossible to tell what was being said. A high row of bushes obscured her view, so Sammy crept closer. The two men had their backs to her. One dressed in a hooded monk's robe was gesticulating wildly, repeatedly dislodging the man-purse slung over his shoulder. Sammy couldn't see his face, but saw the fingers of his right hand fold into a fist more than once. The argument grew louder, but the Greek words were incomprehensible. However, Sammy did recognize the familiar dismissive Greek palm wave as the monk stomped off towards the cemetery section. Throwing up his hands, the second man turned back towards the service. Alex! Why *had* Alex been arguing with a monk?

Not wanting to be caught snooping, Sammy tiptoed toward the street, praying that Alex would opt for the pathway closer to the church and not the sidewalk on which she was hiding. She let out a soft exhalation as she watched him approach the chapel steps.

Just then the crowd began trickling out to join pallbearers and priests on their march to the gravesite. Alex merged into the solemn group walking along the same route the hooded monk had taken. Feigning nonchalance, Sammy sidled up to Pappajohn and offered, again without success, to carry his briefcase. Her eyes never lost sight of Alex who whispered in Kiki's ear and then shook his head. Sammy experienced an unwelcomed twinge as she watched what appeared to be a natural intimacy. Even more curious about their relationship, she wondered whether Kiki was also involved in that mysterious argument with the monk.

Once the mourners reached the gravesite, the priest continued the service with the Trisagion. "Final committal prayers," explained Pappajohn. The priest poured a bottle of oil and red wine over the coffin in the form of a cross and placed sand in the coffin, again in the form of a cross, before the coffin was to be lowered into the grave.

Daphne's sobs reminded Sammy of how Bubbe Rose had reacted at her mother's funeral. Sammy couldn't bear the echo of such grief and stepped back, seeking solace in a moment alone. *Maybe it was better to keep relationships at arm's length than to face unbearable loss.* Like her father had done, over and over. Like she had done with her ex-boyfriend Reed.

The sun was low on the horizon as Sammy strolled along the cobblestone lane amidst the headstones and crypts a few yards away from Lambros' gravesite. The crowded cemetery had consumed one side of the Athenian hill. There were only a few pine and eucalyptus trees to add a touch of green to the gray and white marble landscape. Arriving at the top of a small slope near a fork in the path, she paused. The same agitated monk was approaching one of the crypts below. From her angle she could see him remove a small brown-wrapped package the size of a CD from his 'murse' before entering the crypt.

Sammy secreted herself behind a pine tree with a better view and waited. Seconds later, the monk exited the crypt without the package and sped off in the opposite direction. Damn. Shadows of impending twilight had hidden his face, though Sammy thought she had seen something dark above his neck. A beard maybe?

"Sammy!"

Hearing the familiar voice, Sammy looked over at the other path where Pappajohn stood next to Captain Katsoulis. He waved and yelled "It's over. Let's go!"

Sammy waved back, hoping to stall Pappajohn, but he'd already set off toward her. The last thing she needed was her friend or that tough lady cop chiding her for playing amateur detective. Later, when the two professionals weren't watching, she'd return to find out what the man had hidden in the crypt.

Once the monk had deposited his package, he sent an SMS message to his contact, alerting him that it needed to be picked up ASAP.

CHAPTER TWENTY-TWO

I t was dusk by the time the party ambled down the cobblestone street from the church to the open-air taverna for the wake. The outdoor café sported a wooden sign of a beret-wearing man, arms raised, clad in a blue kilt, white tights, and pom-pommed shoes. "The Dancing Evzone" had set up several rows of tables on the patio, laden with white paper "tablecloths", baskets of fresh-baked thickly-sliced bread and jugs of red house wine. A dozen rickety wooden chairs surrounded each table, their narrow rush seats ensuring that broad-*tushed* lingerers would soon feel discomfort and move on.

The younger contingent laid claim to their own "children's table", and, Sammy chuckled, so did the academics, save for Professor Roussos, who had distinguished himself from his junior colleagues by wearing a suit and tie and aiming for the seats next to Tountas and Kiki. Roussos' protégé, Loukas Doxiadis followed his mentor and sat next to Kiki on the other side.

Waving at Doxiadis, Sammy took a seat at the end of the 'VIP' table beside Pappajohn, and, realizing she was famished, reached out for a slice from the pristine loaf set near her plate. The bread was warm, tasty, and almost melted in her mouth. *Better not try a second slice or I'll eat the whole thing. And I won't be able to fit in these narrow chairs.*

Fortunately, a tall young man wearing a stained apron had arrived, balancing several plates of Greek salad with radiant vegetables topped by oregano and a slab of feta cheese. After dealing the salads around the table, the waiter pulled out a folded piece of paper and stubby pencil from his apron pocket and asked for entrée orders at the opposite end. Kiki immediately chose grilled fish, no butter. Professor Roussos opted for *paithakia*, translated as lamb chops on the shared menus. Director Tountas ordered spaghetti with ground beef sauce and Father Mihalis went for the chicken *souvlaki (kabob)*. Tasos asked for a big plate of *pastitsio,* Greek lasagna, but Daphne struggled to decide between the lamb roast and the veal cutlet. With everyone distracted by the delicious sounding menu choices, Sammy realized she might have a few minutes to slip away without arousing suspicion. She was determined to follow up on the shadowy figure she'd spied at the funeral.

Sammy tapped Pappajohn on the shoulder. "Restroom. Be right back." Except for what looked like an extended family staffing the busy kitchen, there was no one inside the restaurant when she entered. A grizzled chef was hacking a roasted lamb with a cleaver. "Toilet?" she asked. He nodded to his right. Sammy thanked him and hurried down a dimly-lit hallway toward the back of the building. A stack of boxes, some holding bones and carcasses discarded during and after dinner preparations lined her path, providing a bloody landscape to compliment the odor of charred meat and unflushed plumbing.

Passing a half-hinged door with an eroded design of a fedora-wearing man smoking a cigar, Sammy aimed for the next portal which featured a full-skirted female posing with a cigarette holder. The "fire exit" just beyond the ladies' room was propped open with a wooden wine crate. Sammy approached. Careful to avoid a hinge squeak, she tiptoed over the crate and out into the dark alley behind the taverna.

From where she stood she could see Pappajohn and Eleni's heads in an animated culinary debate, spotlighted by the citronella torches next to the wake party's table. Even if they looked her way, it would be difficult to make out her figure as she sidled next to the building and across the alley into an adjacent street.

Stopping to orient herself at a pedestrian-crowded corner, Sammy set off toward the nearby cemetery where Lambros had been laid to rest. Her commitment to LA Fitness came in handy as she sprinted up the hill without panting. The cemetery gates were still unlocked and, even though it was past nine P.M., the office door a few yards away was slightly ajar, and the lights, though dim, were on. Inside the foyer, Sammy could see two seemingly agitated figures gesturing, but couldn't make out what they were saying. From the shadows, she noticed the person whose back was to the door had a pony tail and wore a dark shirt and jeans. When he or she stepped to the right, the light fell for a split second on the other figure's face. Clearly a man. And although Sammy couldn't be sure, he did resemble Alex. *And Alex hadn't been at the taverna...*

To avoid being seen, Sammy crouched down as she passed by, creeping along the unlit stone path, trying to stay in the shadows cast by the moonlight-bathed eucalyptus and pine trees. She hopped over the fallen twigs that yesterday's north winds had blown onto the path. The cemetery, so full of visitors an hour before, was otherwise deserted now, and Sammy could hear her heart beating as she continued up the path towards the crypt.

A crackle startled her. She turned quickly to check if she'd been followed, but there was no one in the darkness. A sliver of moonlight spotlit a rolling pine cone from a large fir she had just passed. *Stay calm*, she whispered, hoping to slow her pounding heartbeat.

A few more steps and she spied the ornate crypt ahead. The heavy double doors had gilded handles with no locks. Sammy took a moment to admire the sculpted marble portico that invited guests to honor ΣΩΤΗΡΗΣ ΧΑΤΖΗΜΑΝΟΛΗΣ,

1917-1999. After a slow deep breath, she pushed open the doors and entered a small chamber whose wall to wall icons were lit only by the flickering flames of a few oil lamps and votive candles. The monk's package was nowhere in sight. At the far end was a gold-framed black and white photo of a puffed-up, bald-headed man Sammy guessed to be somewhere in his seventies. She studied the picture for a minute, thinking, *Hubris. Pride goeth even after a fall.*

Loud knocking and bumping from behind made Sammy spin around. A faint shadow moved between the gap of the closed gilded doors. "Who's there?" Sammy rushed to the entrance of the crypt, only to find that she could neither push nor pull the doors more than a centimeter or so. Through the gap, she could see the shadow of someone threading a thick branch between both outside handles. Though she tried to break its resistance, Sammy's muscles weren't strong enough to fracture the hardened wood. Realizing she was was locked inside, she began to scream.

"No! Help! Help!" Sammy banged on the doors to no avail. What was the Greek word that had struck fear into her heart back when they'd found Ollie? Voy-a? "*Voy-a! Voy-a!*" she cried.

No answer. Only the ghosts could hear her in this deserted corner. How stupid she'd been to come alone. Pappajohn would worry when she didn't return to the restaurant, but even if he looked for her, he'd never think to come back here. Panicked, she pressed her face near the tiny gap in the door and shouted again and again. "*Voy-a! Voy-a!*"

It might have been just a few minutes, though it felt much longer, before Sammy noticed a shadow approaching the crypt. She tensed as the momentary thought flashed by: *Who would be opening that door? The lady or the tiger?*

"Sammy? Are you okay? Wait, I'll get you out."

Alex. Her sigh of relief lasted only a moment. *Which one was he? The one who had locked me in there? If so, why?*

The doors opened and Alex's worried expression morphed into a genuine smile. "Sammy! What were you doing in that crypt? The cemetery closed an hour ago. I thought you'd gone to the taverna with the funeral party."

Did he see me come here? "I know, but...I realized I must have dropped my glasses at the graveside." To verify her story, she pulled her sunglass case from her purse. "Can't wear my contacts this long with dry eyes." She flashed an innocent smile. "On my way back I saw this beautiful crypt. I just had to go inside and look."

Pausing, she faced Alex with narrowed eyes. "Somebody must have a weird sense of humor with such a prank. Or else," she pointed to the Greek name carved in the marble. "Mr. Xadjopoulos doesn't like uninvited guests."

"Indeed," replied Alex, as he picked up his attache case and waved for Sammy to follow him down the path towards the front gate. "Mr. Hadjimanolis was renowned for his successful business deals, but not for his humanity." A pause. "Most of us strive for both."

As they arrived at the exit, Alex turned to Sammy and added, "By the way, though I fervently hope you will not need to use it again during your visit to our country, the word for 'help' in Greek is 'voh-ee-thee-a'."

"Well, thanks for getting me out of there. Wouldn't be the most comfortable place to spend the night." *So maybe he didn't trap me in the crypt, but...* She leveled a questioning glance his way. "Why were *you* hanging around here so long?"

Alex pursed his lips and tapped the attache case. "My father. He passed on almost a year ago. I had to, er, renegotiate his resting place with the cemetery's administration."

Seeing confusion on Sammy's face, he continued. "As I'm sure you saw when you flew into Athens, space in the city is at a premium. In cemeteries, even more so. Most Athenians rent a gravesite for only a year or two. Then, the, er, bones, are collected and placed in a small funerary recess with a marble plaque to commemorate the deceased." Alex cleared his throat. "I would prefer that my father remain undisturbed."

"Oh. Of course." Sammy looked back up at the hill. "I'd have done the same for Bubbe Rose. But I saw a lot of mausoleums up there, ten to twenty years old or more."

"Everything comes at a price," Alex muttered, as they spied the taverna. "I was able to talk the cemetery director down to five thousand Euros a year, and free passes to the museum for her family. In Greece, resting in peace can be quite expensive." The wake party's laughter was loud enough to hear from a block away. "Well, I see that Professor Lambros is being idealized by his colleagues."

"You didn't like him much, did you?"

"I respected his scientific ability." Alex picked up his pace. "I can smell the fragrance of roast lamb, but I expect very few appetizers remain. Fortunately, you still have time to enjoy a classic Greek delicacy."

CHAPTER TWENTY-THREE

S ammy observed that her taverna chair next to Pappajohn had been co-opted by Despina Katsoulis. She nodded for Alex to take a seat across from Professor Roussos and aimed for the last empty chair at the far end of the VIP table.

"Ilan," said the dark-haired muscular guest next to her as he rose and pulled out the seat for her. "And you are?"

"Sammy. Sammy Greene." She raised an eyebrow. "I hear an American accent. Brooklyn maybe. Are you from the City?"

Ilan laughed. "Not anymore. I made *Aliyah* after Uni—I mean, college." He produced a friendly smile as he sat down. "I'm a curator for the Israel Museum in Jerusalem now. Kiki and Alex Matsas visited us last year. I was hoping we could arrange for our museum to display the *Apocalypsi* treasures down the road. Are you a fan of ancient art?"

Kiki and Alex Matsas? Sounded like they were still a couple, despite their divorce. Is that why Alex was staring so intently at Kiki and Loukas Doxiadis giggling over a private joke? Sammy shook her head and smiled back at Ilan. "Hardly. I'm afraid my knowledge of ancient art is limited to a Campbell's soup can. And not Warhol-sized either. I'm here to support some good friends." She pointed towards Pappajohn and Eleni who had paused their meal to comfort Daphne once more. "It's sad. And I understand the Professor was about to announce a big discovery."

"Yes, Professor Roussos was convinced that the Apocalypsi finds were the remains of a sculpture of the Virgin Mary and

Jesus commissioned during the Justinian Dynasty. We have a wonderful display of centuries of Byzantine coins at the museum that we were able to convince Assad to relinquish. You have to come see it the next time you're in town."

"Actually, I've never been to Israel."

Ilan looked genuinely surprised. "Well then, you must visit. Not only Jerusalem, but Tel Aviv, the crystal waters of Haifa, the nightlife on Dizengoff Street." He paused and flashed another grin. "If you let me know when you're coming, I'd be happy to arrange a personal tour."

Sammy felt her cheeks redden. Ilan was a handsome man with no rings or other visible attachments. And, his did seem to be a genuine invitation. Maybe it wouldn't be such a bad idea to spend a few days around the Mediterranean relaxing with a hot guide. Alex was clearly otherwise engaged. Reed was certainly not sitting by the phone.

The first bite of the warm lamb was delicious. Maybe Pappajohn was right. This trip was the perfect place to try something new. She looked up at Ilan and nodded, raising her glass of red wine. "*L'chaim.* To life."

"There's one more piece of *spanakopita.*" Pappajohn put the almost empty plate in front of Alex, drawing his attention. "I'll get the waiter so you can order."

"This is enough, thank you," Alex said. "I'm not very hungry."

"I am, but my reflux says otherwise." Pappajohn pushed the half-eaten lamb and orzo away. "Too old to really enjoy this delicious food." A sigh. "Speaking of old, can you read *katharevousa?*"

"Of course." Alex swallowed a small bite of the flaky appetizer. "It is a necessity in my field. Why do you ask?"

Pappajohn scratched his chin. "We found a photo of a religious document in Lambros' office. Tasos wanted me to run it by Father Mihalis after dinner."

A raised eyebrow. "I would be happy to look at it."

Pappajohn reached for his briefcase. "Here, let me just pull it out and —"

Alex laid a hand on his and winked. "Why don't we go inside?"

Nodding at their other tablemates, they stood and walked towards the kitchen. An old woman in a black dress, her gray hair peeking out from under a black scarf, sat at an inside table eating leftovers from the evening meal service. She barely acknowledged Pappajohn's "*Geia sas*".

Alex sought some privacy at a wooden table as far from her as possible.

After sitting with a grunt, Pappajohn opened his briefcase and fished inside for the photo. "Tasos noticed the word *Parthena*, virgin, so is it about the Virgin Mary?"

"Could be. Or...Alex peeked into the open briefcase. "What's the book in there?"

Pappajohn shrugged. "Just an old Bible."

"Can I see it?"

"Sure." Pappajohn laid it on the table. You think it might be one of those museum books? A codex?" He opened the Bible to the midsection, cracking the spine. "Lambros made some penciled notes on a few of the pages."

Alex winced, then took a clean napkin and gingerly ran it across the inked pages.

"See here," Pappajohn pointed. "I'm not good at Greek script, but I think Lambros scribbled Julian, Honorius, Flavius, Constantius."

"Roman Emperors in Byzantium." Alex squinted as he studied the calligraphy. "No, sorry, not a codex. It's a palimpsest." He turned the paper towards the light. "A palimpsest is a document in which the original writing has been erased and new text has been written over it. If you look carefully you can see traces of the writing under the biblical verses."

"Wow. Yeah. Can you make it out?"

"A little. The pages appear to be only a few centuries old, but the language is ancient Greek, not *katharevousa*. I doubt Father Mihalis would be able to decode it."

"No," said Pappajohn. "I mean can you read the hidden stuff?"

"Only bits and pieces. I believe these words you can just barely see here are from one of the Homeric Hymns." Alex pointed to faded lettering visible between several lines of the text.

"Like the Iliad and the Odyssey?"

"No, the Homeric Hymns are religious poetry. Attributed to Homer, but," Alex chuckled, "like his famous epics, perhaps written by others. There are several schools of thought about 'Homer', you know. Was he a person, the blind bard of Ionia? Or an oral tradition, the accumulated efforts of poets and bards, documented over generations by scribes? The name Ὅμηρος, Homer in Greek, generally means hostage, but could also be a master in a trade."

"Kind of like Shakespeare, right? Effie—my wife—was an English teacher. She told me Shakespeare may really have been a writer named Bacon," Pappajohn said.

"More likely Christopher Marlowe, but, yes, like that." Alex squinted at the text. "I think I see the letters *'allasa'*."

"Which means?"

"It's not an ancient Greek word, per se. It could be 'thallassa' which means 'sea'. But that would have two sigmas." A pause. "Words were written running together back then, without spaces in between. It could also be Π Α Λ Λ Α Σ Α. Pallas Athena?" He shook his head. "I think we need to find a way to safely dissolve the layers of scripture to get a better view of the underlying text."

"Well, then, I've come to the right place. Your museum?"

Alex hesitated. "Of course. But we have hundreds of documents waiting in the queue to be studied. I doubt we could demand a restoration for months at best. Unless the police do some arm-twisting."

Pappajohn shot a quick glance at the table outdoors. Despina Katsoulis seemed focused on her menu. He moved his chair to ensure he remained out of her line of sight.

Alex lowered his voice. "The Captain?"

Pappajohn frowned. "It's Daphne's legal property now, but I don't trust that our watchful friend Katsoulis will see it that way."

Alex nodded. "I do have an idea. We work with a number of antique dealers in town. Why don't I check in with one of our assessor colleagues in Monastiraki tomorrow and see if the text is legitimate. If it is, I'll see if I can fast-track a restoration somewhere—discreetly."

Pappajohn hesitated to hand over the palimpsest. "It's not mine. I'd have to check with Daphne or Tasos. But, here's the photo at least. If you could translate the *katharevousa*, I'm sure they won't mind."

Alex raised a hand before accepting the photo. "I under-stand. Listen, why don't you and Lambros' cousin meet me at half eight in Monastiraki for breakfast tomorrow morning and we can research the palimpsest together? Meanwhile, I'll translate this photo for you tonight."

"Sounds good. I'll ask Tasos to come. Daphne hasn't slept in days," admitted Pappajohn, "so it'll be just us."

Alex stood and slid his chair under the table, before turn-ing back to Pappajohn. "And, say, if you trust her, why don't you invite your friend Sammy, too?"

Pappajohn chuckled. "There are very few people I trust more. We'll see you tomorrow at eight-thirty." He rose slowly, guarding his sore knees, picked up his briefcase and started off for the patio tables. He noticed 'Muscles' Ilan leaning against a wall a few feet away, saying "Yeah" or "Ja" periodically to the speaker on his mobile phone. Passing him, Pappajohn waved. Ilan acknowledged him with a nod. How long had he been there, Pappajohn wondered, and did he hear anything he and Alex had said?

A few minutes earlier, Ilan's cell phone had buzzed, and, apologizing, he'd told Sammy he had to take the call. Smiling, he'd stood and strolled into the kitchen area, the phone pressed to his ear.

Sammy took a few more bites of her dinner and looked around the table for Pappajohn.

"Hello, again, Sammy." Loukas Doxiadis eased himself into Ilan's chair. "I'll move when he gets back, but I wanted to catch you for a minute. Harris' cousin told me you were out yesterday evening and I only got the young boy on the phone this morning. You've been busy busy."

"Well, you know," Sammy said. "Lots to do after someone passes. Funeral arrangements, the will… It's been difficult for the family." She pursed her lips. "Sorry. I'm sure it's been hard on you too. I mean losing a colleague."

"Yes." He sighed. "Roman philosopher Seneca was wise to say, 'The day which we fear as our last is but the birthday of eternity.' I tell you what. Sounds like we both need a break. How about if tomorrow I pick you up and show you a brighter side of Greece? We can visit the Acropolis, have lunch in a sidewalk cafe in Monastiraki. There's a wonderful flea market that sells everything money can buy."

"That does sound appealing. Let me check with Gus and Eleni. See if I have other obligations. If not, shopping it is!"

"Great. I'll give you a call tonight to confirm," Doxiadis said, getting up to let Ilan take his place.

"Everything okay?" Sammy asked a sober looking Ilan.

"I hope so," he replied after a moment's hesitation. "In the world of art, when opportunity strikes, you've got to be ready."

Chapter Twenty-Four

Two hours later, Tasos marshaled his fatigued wife and children into the police car for the drive home. Gus, Eleni, and Sammy grabbed the third in a queue of taxis tipped off by the taverna owner to be ready for pickups.

"Kiki, wait!" Alex shouted to his ex who was just getting into her raven-colored Mercedes E300. Hurrying to the front passenger side, he opened the door and sat down.

"I'm assuming you're not coming home with me," Kiki said as he shut the door.

"No. Just wanted to bring you up to speed. I'm going to Monastiraki tomorrow with Kostas and that policeman Tasos. I'd like to run our discoveries and questions by him. I think he and Tasos are a safer bet to help us investigate than Katsoulis. We can take the files to her after we ask for his expert advice."

"For once, I can't disagree," she said. "I've spent all day going through Harris' police reports, autopsies, photos, and financial transactions. Just the ones in English and Greek. I speak four languages, but none that use the Cyrillic alphabet."

"Well, there's enough there in English and Greek that we can start from. How about I lay it out for Kostas tomorrow and update you over lunch?"

"It's a date." With a teasing smile she added, "For lunch. With a colleague and ally."

"With a friend," he said, as he exited the car.

It seemed as if everyone else in Daphne's household had gone to bed and succumbed to exhaustion, but Sammy lay on her cot struggling with insomnia. More than jet lag, the whirlwind events of the past two days had left her head spinning. Murder, lost computer files, ancient dials. Of course, Lambros' death was tragic, but she had to admit - a part of her was glad she could team up once more with Gus Pappajohn to solve this mystery.

And then there were the three young men who, unbeknownst to them, were also helping to distract her from thoughts of Reed Wyndham and any lingering regrets about not following him to Boston as his fiancée — or wife.

Alex Matsas. Divorced, but obviously still with feelings for Kiki. Sammy had the sense that most people saw him as a shy and soft-spoken academic. Yet on their drive from the airport she'd had a chance to see a tougher side of this personable Army vet. He'd insisted he wasn't the target of the shooter on the motorcycle. *But did he ever file that police report?* And earlier tonight he'd been arguing with that monk who hid something in the crypt. Nothing absolute she could put her finger on, but something was lurking, hidden by his innocent mien. Although she wanted to believe his explanation for why he'd been in the cemetery so late, Sammy had enough suspicions about his honesty to keep from opening up to him about their investigation. Of course, she hadn't told Gus everything either. He trusted Alex, and Gus had a good gut. But *her* gut told her it was best not to share her doubts until she knew more.

Loukas Doxiadis. While she welcomed the opportunity to sightsee tomorrow, his invitation seemed to come out of the blue. Yes, they been on the *Apocalypsi* together. Another tragedy. He'd been kind to her then. Perhaps his offer today was a mere recognition that she needed some respite from the sadness that had rained on her hosts. Besides, he was considerably more handsome than she remembered from six years ago. The gray in his hair and trimmed beard flattered him. She'd surmised he'd be in his mid-thirties now, and the salt and pepper made him look distinguished rather than old. Definitely an eight. He seemed a little put off when she'd called to let him know she had a breakfast commitment at Monastiraki with Pappajohn and Tasos in the morning, but he quickly offered to meet her at the entrance to the Acropolis at noon and give her an informative tour.

And then there was Ilan Einav. With the Brooklyn accent. Trim and muscular at almost six feet, he didn't have a trace of the New York 'nerd' in his demeanor. *He* was a ten. Like Alex, Ilan had served in the military. For Israel. But Ilan's tour, he'd said, had been extended and he'd seen "action" in Gaza that he preferred not to relive over their dinner.

The fact that Ilan was a member of her tribe was intriguing. Bubbe Rose had taken her to synagogue when she was younger, but neither religion nor traditions had resonated beyond her teens As a feminist, she resented the orthodoxy that declared women separate from men, whether in houses or worship or corporate boardrooms. Perhaps that's what had drawn her to journalism. The wave of young women in the field that raced into the fire side by side with their male colleagues. Ilan had assured her she'd find modern Israel quite different from the patriarchy. After all he said, wasn't it one of the few countries in the world that practiced equal rights by conscripting women as well as men? The invitation to visit his new homeland had seemed sincere. She'd given him her number. If he didn't call, she just might.

Sammy's eyelids grew heavy as she daydreamed. Could any of these three be something more than a distraction? Maybe. She did know that in a year she'd be turning thirty. Time was slipping away…

Eleni, asleep in the next bed, rolled on her back and began snoring quietly. The rhythm of Pappajohn's sister's breathing lulled Sammy, gentle waves lapping at her ears, until finally the sandman arrived.

CHAPTER TWENTY-FIVE

Saturday, June 7th
The next morning.

Tasos, Pappajohn, and Sammy rode up the crowded escalator single file and exited the Athens Metro station at the busy Monastiraki plaza. Pappajohn was pleased Sammy and Tasos could join him and Alex at the renowned flea market for breakfast before going to consult with Alex's antique experts. After that, Sammy could break away for her date with Loukas Doxiadis.

Tasos and Pappajohn both yawned as they looked around the busy square.

"I thought I was the only one who didn't get much sleep," Sammy teased.

"We stayed up going over Lambros' bank records," Pappajohn explained. A nod at Tasos. "At least I did."

"Hey, Maths always puts me to sleep." Another yawn from Tasos.

Anticipating Sammy's question, Pappajohn said, "No, nothing new. Didn't see any revenue from his Porsche deposited, and the Fiat was bought used. Five thousand Euros. There were a few deductions for gas, food, etc. The only interesting numbers were three ten thousand Euro cash withdrawals over the past year. But, being cash, we don't know where the money went.

"Purchasing the dials in the photos, I'd guess," said Tasos. "Question is, where are the dials? The police don't have them either."

"You think the scratches on the locks at Lambros' office mean someone got to them first?" suggested Sammy.

Tasos shrugged. "Could be."

Before Sammy could speak, Pappajohn interjected. "Taso, you can check the fingerprint reports, but I'm sure he or she wore gloves. We may just have to keep working with the photos we have of the dials. The fact that they're digital gives us good resolution."

As they walked along a cobblestone pedestrian avenue, dodging tourists, Pappajohn added, "Let's see what Alex has come up with on the document photo we found in Lambros' office. Maybe he'll be willing to help with the dial pictures, too."

Pappajohn filled them in on his conversation with Alex the night before about the *katharevousa* photo and the ancient Bible. "He told me this shop owner may be able to advise us about how to read the palimpsest. Alex is a player in the market for antiquities. Apparently museum life is not just about art and science, but business," Papajohn mused.

"*Everything* seems to be about business," Sammy said. "That's why liberal voices are so critical on the radio."

"Glad *your* voice hasn't been silenced," Pappajohn echoed. "Thanks to this Radio USA. Even when I don't agree with you, which is often, I agree with your right of free speech."

Sammy laughed. "I've got plenty of that. And Radio USA will have an outlet in Boston, so you can disagree with me even more." To Tasos: "Anything from your forensic folks about the missing file? Minerva, was it?"

Tasos shook his head. "Nope. It's gone. Now they're working on the photos we copied from Harris' camera. Maybe in a few weeks. What about your friend in America, Kosta?"

"I called Keith this morning," Pappajohn said. "They've made some progress. The 'Minerva' file contained a few subfiles, also erased. But, they were able to see fragments of each of the files on the disk. You know file data isn't all stored together. Depending on when it's saved, it can be scattered all over a hard disk." He shrugged. "So, it takes time."

"Well, what *do* they know?" Sammy asked.

"Keith said they found three subfolders. 'Minerva', of course was the master folder. One of the subfolders Lambros called 'Monastiraki'. The other two he labeled 'Masada' and 'Makronissos'."

"Makronissos is where my father found our dial," said Tasos. "And we are here in Monastiraki. But what is this Masada?"

"Well, that's one *I* know," Sammy said. "Thanks to my history classes at Ellsford University. Masada was the site of a mass suicide of Jewish rebels during a Roman Empire attack in the first century. The people chose death rather than slavery. But, the Roman Siege of Masada was in southern Judea. I don't think it had anything to do with Greece."

"We'll have to wait and see," Pappajohn admitted. "Anyway, Keith did find some sections of a PowerPoint presentation. Something about a heretic emperor, a murdered philosopher, and a statue of Athena." Pappajohn pointed up towards the hill behind them. "The Parthenon was built to honor the goddess Athena, you know."

Sammy turned to follow his gaze and spied the edge of the Acropolis ruins grandly overlooking the square.

"Oh, my God," she marveled, "It's awesome. I can't believe something so delicate and beautiful is still standing after all these years."

"Two and a half millennia," said Alex as he approached from behind. "Athena was the daughter of Zeus, King of the Olympic Gods. One day he woke with a bad headache and

Athena popped out from his forehead in her full supernatural glory."

To cover concern that Alex might have overheard their discussion of the files, Pappajohn laughed heartily. "Now *that* must've been some migraine."

"Mythology, like religion, thrives on imagination," Alex said. "During the Byzantine period, the building functioned as a Greek Orthodox church, dedicated to the Virgin Mary."

"Aha. Only the names have been changed, like they say on TV." Sammy laughed, as Pappajohn frowned.

"A pagan wouldn't see it that way, I'm afraid," Alex said. "In any case, Christians almost lost the Parthenon, too, under the Ottoman occupation. Not like Haghia Sophia, which is now a mosque. The Ottomans stored gunpowder in the Parthenon's atrium and the gunpowder exploded under Venetian fire during the fifth, no, the sixth, Ottoman-Venetian war. Goodbye, roof."

He shook his head. "So many wars. Lord Wellington announced that in the nineteenth century his ancestor, the Earl of Elgin, arranged for the transport and, er, safekeeping of the Parthenon marbles - the friezes above the entrance - to London. He pointed to scaffolding surrounding the structure. "The restoration you're seeing now has been going on for the last thirty years. After the Olympics next year when we open our new museum, we hope to return the marbles to their home."

"Wishful thinking," muttered Pappajohn. "The British Museum won't give them up. Two centuries." A snort. "Why don't *we* 'borrow' Big Ben for 'safekeeping'?"

Alex chuckled. "One would hope that membership of all our countries in the European Union will encourage collaboration rather than conflicts in the future. Glad to see that even Turkey is interested in joining the EU."

"Then maybe we could resettle Constantinople," said Pappajohn. "My family were refugees from the Catastrophe of 1922 in Anatolia."

"I am sorry. So many have suffered from war," Alex agreed, his tone more serious. "So many refugees, so many hostages, so many victims, so few survivors." He cleared his throat. "Let's eat and hit the bazaar before the midday crowds pack the streets."

The sidewalk cafe was filled with tourists, but Alex spied a table indoors near the restrooms. "It'll be quieter here, and we'll be out of the sun."

Sammy nodded. "Not even nine and it's already hot."

"Supposed to go up to forty degrees again today," grumbled Tasos.

"I wish," said Sammy, and raised a hand. "Yes, I know. Forty Celsius. I don't want to even think about what that is in Fahrenheit."

"A hundred and f—" teased Pappajohn.

"Don't say it!" Sammy covered her ears.

The server handed out coffee-stained menus and the group ordered a varied selection of egg dishes. "I want mine cooked well," Sammy said. "Especially seeing as they leave their eggs sitting out of the refrigerator there on the shelf."

"You refrigerate your eggs?" asked Tasos, surprised. "We're not supposed to. We vaccinate our chickens against Salmonella instead."

"American eggs are washed and sprayed with chlorine mist, but we still get infected," said Pappajohn. "Here, I actually feel comfortable ordering mine over easy." He grabbed a slice of bread. "So, Professor, do you have a translation of the photo I gave you?"

Alex brought out the photo of the document from Lambros' office and handed it back to Pappajohn. "It's interesting.

The language is not *katharevousa*. It's a much earlier version of Greek. I was able to trace the passage on the Internet to John, Bishop of Nikiu, from his Chronicle. It seems to describe an event that happened at the turn of the fifth century in Alexandria, Egypt. Alexandria was a center of Hellenic science, literature, and philosophy. A cadre of believers in Jesus Christ attacked the brilliant female philosopher Hypatia as a pagan. dragged her through the streets until she died, then burned her body and celebrated the victory over what they called idolatry." A sigh. "The Biblical Jesus preached peace, but young Christianity, like other young movements and religions, inspired crusaders rather than evangelists."

"Yes." Sammy told them of Bubbe Rose's three sisters, none of whom had made it out of Europe alive during World War II.

Glancing at Sammy, Alex's voice grew softer. "As archaeologists, it sobers us to see how little man has changed over the centuries. Violence may be embedded in our DNA but, thank God, heroism is seeded in our souls."

"Here are your eggs," said the server, as he arrived at the table, balancing four plates on his arms and shoulders. "Enjoy."

After breakfast the group headed for the shop of Alex's friend. The narrow road was barely wide enough for Pappajohn, Tasos, and Sammy to walk three abreast. Alex took the lead, stepping confidently on the curved stones that paved the alleyway, dodging camera-laden visitors carrying packages and snacks from the adjacent shops and stands.

Sammy marveled at the bazaar's diversity. Goods from Africa and China were being hawked next to souvenirs of ancient Greek memorabilia. Loukas was right, she could spend days and many dollars shopping in the quaint and cute shops. The one suitcase she'd brought was definitely a good preventive measure. The last thing she needed was to wipe out her transition budget before even moving to New York.

Picking up her pace, she sped ahead of her friends, almost colliding with a bearded monk in a hooded black robe who turned into an alley to her left and disappeared into a graffiti covered wooden doorway behind one of the antique shops. Sammy paused for a moment, wondering if he could be the monk she'd seen in the cemetery.

"Better keep up or we'll catch up with you," Pappajohn teased as he plodded by her, trailing Alex and Tasos. "Miles to go before we sleep."

"Kilometers, Gus, kilometers," she replied, slowing down to walk beside him.

The diversity of visitors thronging the narrow streets was a veritable United Nations. Couples, families, teens and young adults, "mature" travelers on a day pass from cruise ships docked at a nearby port walked among groups of robed monks. The chatter was a jumble of languages - Chinese, Spanish, Russian, German, Greek. Recognizable words here and there in English, but was the accent Irish, South African, or Australian?

Reveling in the spectacle, Sammy missed the baseball-capped man with a salt and pepper beard who watched them from the doorstep of a store a few yards ahead. Alex had stopped a few feet away at a shop displaying worry beads, curly haired plaster busts, and colorful dishes with hand-painted angles of the Acropolis and its Parthenon.

"Sammy, Kosta. In here!" Alex directed over the din.

Sammy was helping Pappajohn make his way down the slippery worn marble steps into the store's basement, so she didn't see the second man, trim and muscular, who had also been following them. As Sammy's group entered the shop, the man continued past the basement entrance down the street, blending in with a tour group as he passed.

The elderly shopkeeper's eyes lit up when shown the weathered Bible. He laid it gingerly on a crocheted tablecloth for a better view. After studying a few pages, he spoke in Greek, "The calligraphy in this Bible is definitely post-Byzantine. I'd say mid-Ottoman Empire." He brought out a UV light and shone it over the page where Alex had noted the writing.

"One would need to work carefully to remove the surface text, but I can make out several lines here. You are right, dear Alex, it seems to be a Homeric Hymn. I believe number twelve – no, eleven." He closed his eyes and began reciting from distant memory:

I begin to sing of Pallas Athena, the dread Protectress of the city, who with Ares looks after matters of war, the plundering of cities, the battle-cry and the fray.
It is She who protects the people, wherever they might come or go.
Hail, Goddess, and give us good spirits and blessed favor!

Opening his eyes, he said, "Mount Athos, likely, is the source of this text. To have survived the Ottoman invasion…" He shook his head. "I would return it there and seek their aid to uncover the truth about its origin. Our friend, Bishop Theosophos, is now residing at the monastery of Aghios Apostolos. He can help you. Where was it found?"

Alex hesitated. "A…friend purchased it. He also bought some dials that seem to be a part of the *Apocalypsi* device."

"Ah," said the shopkeeper. "From Makronissos, yes?"

Tasos nodded, but said nothing about his father.

"The island has been deserted since the end of the junta in '74. A convenient place to store and transport Middle Eastern wares, is it not? I have even heard that some of the *Apocalypsi* treasures may have been 'claimed' from the nearby waters by Mt. Athos ascetics who enjoy deep sea diving." He coughed. "Bishop Theosophos chooses to believe in the holy goodness of the monastic life and its acolytes. Those of us living here in purgatory know that Satan can penetrate the highest walls into a willing soul," he added, curiously.

The shopkeeper closed the Bible and handed it back to Alex. Alex gave it to Pappajohn, who placed it back in his briefcase, as the shopkeeper made the sign of the cross on his chest.

"*Efharisto*, Phillippos," Alex said.

The shopkeeper nodded. "Make an appointment with Bishop Theosophos. Tell him I sent you and give him my regards. And be careful. God's lair can also be the devil's den."

Hiding in one of the shops nearby, the monk fished his cell phone from his satchel, flipped it open and dialed his contact. He quickly apprised him of the morning's assignment. "He was always with the girl and the old man. Or with that big cop. Never alone....Unfortunately, yes. I think she recognized me....when?...okay, got it. Then we can focus on the rest."

Hanging up, he slipped off his robes and rolled them in a tight ball to fit in his satchel. He tied his long hair into a man bun and picked up his motorcycle helmet from a table of artifacts, then slipped out the back door toward the street where he'd parked his bike.

CHAPTER TWENTY-SIX

"So, we go to Mount Athos, yes?" Tasos asked after translating everything he'd learned from the shopkeeper.

"I'm in. What's Mount Athos?" Sammy asked.

"It's a mountain and peninsula near Thessaloniki in Northern Greece. There are over a dozen monasteries there serving the Patriarch of Eastern Orthodoxy in Constantinople," Alex explained. "It's a country within a country, semi-independent, like the Vatican." He gave Sammy a pointed look. "But women are not allowed. In the past, the monks didn't even allow boys in until they were old enough to grow a beard, so women couldn't pretend to be men."

Sammy grumbled. "Like Yentl?" recalling the movie where Barbra Streisand dressed in her father's clothing to live as Anshel and study in a Yeshiva. "Come *on*. This is the twenty-first century."

"Not in the 'Holy Mountain'. You can't get in without an entry permit." Alex shrugged.

Sammy glanced at Pappajohn, who shook his head.

"However—I have an idea," said Alex, "Thessaloniki is a beautiful city. Why don't you come with us and spend the day sightseeing until we come back from the monasteries. We can fill you in on our meeting with the Bishop. You can visit the Jewish Museum of Thessaloniki which honors the long history of Sephardic Jewry in Northern Greece. There's also an exhibit on the Thessaloniki Shoah. Did you know that almost fifty-thousand Jews were deported to Auschwitz and Bergen-Belsen during the Nazi occupation?"

"No, I didn't."

"Many more survivors were taken in by Greek families and hidden from Nazi soldiers. The Archbishop of Greece actively opposed the deportation, ordered monasteries to shelter Jews, and provided tens of thousands of false identity papers to safeguard as many." Alex expelled a deep breath. "The Nazi General who was sent to Greece from Warsaw threatened to shoot the Archbishop in a firing squad."

"Did he?" asked Pappajohn.

"No, the Archbishop survived. But, sadly, most of those deported never returned."

A long moment of silence was broken when Tasos raised a hand. "I am so sorry. It's almost eleven. I'm on duty at noon, so I must run and catch the Metro. Work out the trip details with Kosta and we'll go to the Holy Mountain this weekend."

Pappajohn and Sammy waved as Tasos jogged off. Sammy turned to her companions and said, "Okay, I'll go with you. To Thessaloniki." An innocent smile. "But the shop guy also mentioned the exile island where Tasos' father found the disk. Do you think we might find more disks or helpful clues there?"

"Makronissos," Alex said. "It's possible. The shipwreck was close by."

"What did your friend mean about the island? It didn't sound political," Pappajohn wondered.

Alex frowned. "I'm not certain. But, it's not news that there's a worldwide black market in artifacts and treasures of value. Even museum curators have sometimes been tempted by the opportunity to purchase a piece to complete a collection or market a new exhibit. And of course, some private collectors who wish to buy a particular item will donate ill-gotten gains to museums for…applause. Others may hoard their possessions until their deaths, after which their estates often reach out to black marketeers to re-sell the items at an inflated price."

Alex took a deep breath. "I think Phillippos was implying that Makronissos might be a base of operations for one of these black market cells. It's been deserted for years and is perhaps more inviting now because of the nearby *Apocalypsi* find."

"So, maybe we should pay Makronissos a visit, too." Pappajohn narrowed his eyes, "Sammy, did you see anything funny ashore there when you were on the *Thesaurus?*"

Sammy shook her head. "It was stormy, cloudy, raining. So foggy, I couldn't see much of the island at all. And, after Ollie... I wasn't watching anything except Father Mihalis giving last rites."

Pappajohn wrinkled his brow. "Father Mihalis was on the *Thesaurus*, too?"

Sammy nodded.

"The Greek government works closely with the Orthodox Church," Alex said. "A representative to oversee the collection of religious artifacts is not uncommon. St. Therapon is right next to the University. Roussos spent hours with Mihalis vetting the display of the Virgin Mary statue at this week's exhibit."

Sammy glanced at her watch. "Oh dear, eleven-thirty. I promised to meet Loukas at noon on the steps of the Acropolis." To Alex: "Is there a train I can take?"

A wince crossed Alex's face. "Actually, it's a fairly short walk from here," he offered. "Just on the south side of the Acropolis. We can escort you there."

"Um, twenty-first century, remember? No, I'll go alone."

"My knees thank you," said Pappajohn.

"Well then, Kosta, may I treat you to a latte at Starbucks around the corner? " Alex asked. "We can plan our trip and see if we can scope out any more hidden text from Lambros' Bible."

"I still can't get used to paying so much for a cup of coffee," grumbled Pappajohn as they sat at a table inside the Starbucks coffee shop.

Alex smiled. "It's a grande."

"A grande rip-off," agreed Pappajohn, taking a sip. "Gotta say, it tastes good though." He laid his briefcase under the table next to the wall and brought out the Bible.

Alex pulled out a small camera from the pocket of his khaki trousers and began taking photos of the palimpsest.

"What are you doing?"

"I want pictures of every page where Lambros made notes. If the Bible was stolen from Mt. Athos, they may want to keep it. This little tool is our museum's new high resolution camera. This way I'll have a record to study, just in case."

Pappajohn was on his second cup of coffee when Alex looked up from his task.

"By the way, I need *your* help," Alex said, resting the camera next to his empty coffee cup.

"Me? I can't read ancient Greek."

"No, but you can read police reports, autopsy reports, financial statements."

Pappajohn arched an eyebrow.

"A couple of days before Harris died, he sent me and Kiki a few files," Alex began.

Up went the other eyebrow.

Alex continued. "Minerva."

Pappajohn's eyes lit up. "The deleted file!"

"Shhh." Alex put a finger to his lips. "I need *your* help, not everyone in this café."

"Sorry." He lowered his voice. "What did you see?"

"There was a half-finished PowerPoint in the Minerva file and three subfolders," Alex whispered. "Monastiraki, Masada, and Makronissos."

Pappajohn kept his expression neutral. "So what was in them?"

"Harris seemed convinced that the *Apocalypsi* was a fifth century vessel, not a seventh century one. Carbon dating can only be done on, well, carbon. And most of the recovered items were either metal or petrified wood. The team did pick up a few bones, but there was no usable marrow for us to do proper dating."

"So how could Lambros be sure?"

"No one can be sure, but an archaeologist must be a detective. We too use inferences, circumstantial evidence. The artifacts discovered can be analyzed for style, materials, etc. But the farther back you go, the more difficult it is to determine exactly when an item was created."

"I'm not an archaeologist, but, having worked at a university in the United States, I'm aware such differences provide fertile ground for academic debates. Answer me this: are two centuries different enough to take a man's life?"

"Good question," Alex said. "I can tell you that those two centuries cemented Christianity as the religion of Byzantium. As the text in your photo revealed, conflicts between pagans and crusading Christians were prevalent and violent in the early days of Byzantium. In the mid-fourth century, Emperor Julian paid lip service to Christianity, but continued to support and even promote pagan beliefs and traditions across the eastern Roman empire. That's why he was known as Julian the Apostate. I suspect that Hypatia's brutal assassination may have been a warning bell for pagan advocates around the Mediterranean."

"What did Lambros think?"

"Based on the half-finished PowerPoint and some of the other documents we reviewed, he believed that the *Apocalypsi* was not carrying a Justinian Dynasty sculpture of the Virgin Mary and Jesus, but a statue of Athena. Or should I say, *the* statue of Athena, which was reportedly removed from the Parthenon in the fifth century."

"No kidding!" Pappajohn shouted.

A glare from Alex and he lowered his voice again. " Oh, yes—sorry. Why would they put the statue of Athena on the *Apocalypsi?*"

"There are some reports that the Athena statue was seen in Constantinople, the center of the Byzantine Empire, in the tenth century. Perhaps they did it to save it from destruction in Athens by the same fanatics who inspired Hypatia's murder. If the pagans were trying to ship Athena to the capital to keep her safe, Harris may have been trying to prove that she never arrived, but instead drowned in the waters off Exile Island." Alex finished his coffee. "Perhaps we can see if the palimpsest provides support for his conjectures." He tapped the bible with his index finger.

Pappajohn nodded. "But before we do, I have to excuse myself. My bladder has become as useless as my knees. Back in a couple. Watch my things." Pappajohn placed his BlackBerry next to Alex's camera, then stood and ambled stiffly towards the W.C. on the other side of the Starbucks.

CHAPTER TWENTY-SEVEN

S ammy extended her hand to greet Loukas Doxiadis who was waiting on the stone patio at the base of the Acropolis steps. Doxiadis took her hand in both of his and pulled her into a friendly hug along with the standard greeting of a double-cheek air kiss.

"Wonderful to see you." He pointed at the ruins behind her. "Have you seen anything more fantastic?"

This view of the Parthenon was majestic, Sammy had to agree. She also had a clear view of the Erechtheion, whose marble roof was held up by the beautiful sculpted heads of the Karyatides. At the base of the mountain to the east, Sammy could see the partially reconstructed walls of the Odeon of Herodes Atticus.

"I saw Placido Domingo there just a few years ago. An unparalleled experience. I shall check the programmes to see if we can find a performance for us to share." Doxiadis handed a ticket to Sammy. "For our entry." He reached for her elbow, and started to guide her towards the entrance.

His smile seemed genuine, but Sammy's gut had an un-welcome twinge. Doxiadis seemed almost too eager, just as he had last night. She pulled her arm away and quickened her pace to the checkpoint.

"Your pocketbook, Miss," said the guard. He glanced through it, and handed it back to her with a nod and a smile.

Sammy breathed a sigh of relief. After the tragedy of 9/11, security was the order of the day.

Doxiadis flipped off his cap and showed his otherwise empty hands. He was waved through and sped up to catch Sammy who had already reached the first steps to the elevated ruins.

"Last one up is a rotten egg!" Sammy teased, as she trotted up the marble stairs.

"Careful," Loukas warned, climbing up the steps two by two. "Marble is slippery." He tripped midway up, catching himself with his hands. An embarrassed laugh. "See?"

The uniformed doorman at the luxurious Atheneum Inter-Continental hotel off Syngrou Boulevard waved over a Mercedes taxi as soon as Lord Wellington exited the revolving door. Wellington handed the doorman a five Euro note and smiled. "Taking my little yacht out for a couple of days."

After helping the elderly English visitor into the rear seat, the doorman leaned into the taxi and instructed in Greek, "Piraeus". As the car drove off, the hotel valet drew close and whispered, "Little yacht? Eighty meters and sixty million Euros. Ant1 News did a story on it. More suites than our concierge floor. I'm in the wrong business."

The doorman put a finger to his nose. "So is he."

As the taxi turned the corner, a Smart Car drove out of the underground parking lot and waited a few moments before following the cab. Its driver rested a muscled arm out of the open window and adjusted the left side mirror before zooming off after his prey.

Sammy had to admit that Doxiadis was an excellent tour guide, supplementing her History 101 memories with facts and statistics about the surviving monuments from the days of Greater Hellas. He waved a hand at the east entrance of the Parthenon, which was blocked by construction scaffolding. "We used to think it was designed according to the golden ratio, the divine proportion used for many works of art and architecture, but our recent renovations have shown us the true ratio used throughout was four to nine."

Sammy nodded, pretending to understand.

"Let me show you inside," Doxiadis said.

"Can we do that? It looks all blocked off."

Doxiadis pulled out his wallet. "In addition to my University ID, I have a special pass for research. Without archaeologists, there would be no renovation."

Standing inside the spacious atrium of the Parthenon, Doxiadis described modern understanding of how the temple appeared in the Golden Age of Pericles, with Athena's gold and ivory statue nested in its center.

"The statue displayed Athena in victory. In her left hand, she held a shield representing the war against the Amazons. In her right, a model of Nike, the Goddess of—"

"Sneakers," Sammy interjected, grinning.

Doxiadis ignored the joke. "Victory. We're not entirely certain where she held her spear. Perhaps near the elbow of her right arm. The full statue with its base was twelve metres tall. About forty feet," he added for Sammy's benefit.

Sammy looked up at the sky far above her five foot height. "I can't even begin to imagine." She looked down at the marble columns and floor. "Was it marble, too?"

"No. Actually, its core was made of wood and covered with bronze plates. Then a layer of gold plates for the body and ivory for the face and arms. Quite a treasure chest for the city-state of Athens. One that was sometimes scavenged to fund battles against attacking armies. See this area that's been cut out here?" Doxiadis pointed to a rectangular depression in the marble floor.

Sammy nodded.

"This was a small pool of water right here in front of the statue. It would reflect the sunlight and make Athena's gold glisten."

"No wonder invaders were attracted. Ivory and gold," Sammy mused. "I would have liked to see the statue in its glory."

"You can. More easily than I," he added.

"In the Acropolis museum?" She pointed at the museum entrance a few yards beyond the Parthenon.

"No, it disappeared in the fifth century. However, a replica of the Parthenon was built in Nashville, a city in your state of Tennessee, around nineteen hundred. Inside is a reconstruction of the statue of Athena, right down to the winged Nike in her bent right hand."

"Nashville? No kidding!" Sammy laughed. "I have a co-worker, a friend, who's there right now, visiting family. I'll have to call him and tell him to pay old Athena a visit."

Doxiadis smiled. "Say hello to her from Greece. Now, why don't we walk over to the Acropolis museum through the columns here. Mind the step. We don't need any other falls today. The museum is partially underground, built into the mountaintop in the late nineteenth century, but it's now too old and too small. We're going to open a new museum, much bigger, much better, and much safer for the ancient art, however, down near the Dionysos restaurant where I've made reservations for supper." He paused. "Let me show you."

They walked carefully over gravel, dirt and rocks towards the edge of the Acropolis development to a two foot stone wall that surrounded the plateau. From that location, Sammy could look down upon the odeon and stage of the Herodes Atticus theater across the eastern expanse of Athens, with its sea of white apartment buildings nestled between green trees. Her view extended all the way to the mountain of Hymettus miles to the north and to the turquoise waters of the Bay of Saronikos to the south.

"This is why this holy mount was chosen," said Doxiadis.

"Breathtaking," Sammy agreed, as she climbed up onto the stone ledge for a better view.

Doxiadis drew closer. "Don't do that. It's not safe. The stones may crumble."

As Doxiadis approached, a cry from their left startled Sammy. "*Thanatos stous airetikous!*"

Sammy turned, losing her balance for a moment as she realized what was happening. And *who - the* hooded monk. He was running towards them, swinging his murse like a lasso at a rodeo. *Oh my God!* He was aiming directly for *her*. She stumbled as she pulled back. Frantic, she flapped her hands to try to keep from falling.

CHAPTER TWENTY-EIGHT

For a split second, Doxiadis stood frozen. Then he dove at the monk, grabbing the shoulder bag before it hit Sammy and leaping to tackle the attacker with a cry of "*Me!*"

Doxiadis' heroic deflection gave Sammy a chance to find her footing. She jumped off the ledge onto the dirt ground and moved toward Doxiadis who was now in a tug of war with the monk. Doxiadis held an end of the bag and the monk was gripping the strap. Each was shouting at the other in Greek. Before she could reach the men, the strap on the murse snapped as the monk gave a sharp pull. The inertia pitched the monk over the edge of the parapet and down onto the rocks dozens of feet below.

Doxiadis and Sammy ran to the wall and peeked over. The monk's body had bounced off the sharp boulders on the steep hill and lay splayed on the bushes at the base of the mountain, contorted and still.

"Oh, my God!" Sammy's hug wasn't forced. "Thank you, Loukas. You saved my life."

It took Pappajohn longer than a few minutes to return from the WC. After washing his hands, he strolled back into the coffee shop and headed for their table. *What the hell?* A young couple was seated there. And no sign of Alex.

Frowning, Pappajohn approached the twenty-somethings speaking French. "Um, *excusez-moi*, but this may have been my table. I left my briefcase, a book, my phone."

The young man made a big show of exploring the table surface, and the area under the table and chairs. He sat up and shrugged. The young woman shook her head. "*Non. Rien du tout.*"

Pappajohn frowned and grunted. "Did you see a brown-haired guy, medium height sitting here?"

Two heads shaking. "*Non.* No."

What the— Were the tourists hoping to score a valuable BlackBerry? And where was Alex—and the Bible? Pappajohn scanned the café, hoping for a glimpse of Alex. *Rien.* He nodded at the couple and muttered, "Okay, thank you. *Merci.*"

"Kosta, come on! Quickly! I have a taxi."

Pappajohn turned to see Alex's head pop into the café doorway. *What the—* Pappajohn hobbled over and followed Alex out the door and into a yellow taxi idling at the curb, relieved to see his briefcase between them on the back seat. "What happened? Where are we going?"

Alex handed back the BlackBerry he'd answered when it rang in Pappajohn's briefcase. "Your cousin Tasos called. We have to hurry! He heard it on his police radios. There's been a death at the Acropolis. Someone fell over the edge!"

With the Olympics a year away, Despina Katsoulis knew that visitors would stay away in droves if they perceived sightseeing in the capital might be dangerous. A fatal assault at the Acropolis was one of the worst scenarios she could imagine. Blue light on its roof still flashing, her car squealed to a stop behind a couple of blue and white police vehicles already parked on the dirt-covered driveway behind the Herodes Atticus theater. Several officers had sealed off the area around the fallen victim with red and white police tape. A second contingent was visible above the rocks and grass at the stone ledge of the Acropolis plateau.

Hands on hips, Katsoulis surveyed the scene with scornful eyes. The bearded corpse's lifeless gaze at the blue sky betrayed a frozen expression of horror. The Captain squinted into the sun above. *What the devil?* The woman up there — she looked like that reporter friend of Kostas'. Could it be?

Another police car skidded onto the dirt road, lights blazing, and, with the engine running, Tasos jumped out. "Is she all right?" he cried, as he ran towards Katsoulis.

Frowning, Katsoulis pointed up to the overhang where Sammy was gesturing to an officer as if she were reenacting the scene.

"Thank God. I heard the call on the radio and I knew she'd be here, and..."

"Tasos!" Alex waved from the taxi stopped on the paved road below. He sprinted up the hill towards the crime scene. "Is it Sammy?" Far behind him, a worried looking Pappajohn paid the driver and started huffing and puffing along the steep incline as he tried to slip his wallet back into his pocket.

Tasos shook his head and nodded at the corpse. "No, it's a monk of all things." He looked up at the wall again, but Sammy and the officer were gone.

Alex glanced at the monk, and his face turned ashen. He closed his eyes for a second and took a deep breath. "Er...er...so, she's okay, yes? Sammy?" he asked Tasos.

"Yes, I am, Alex. Thanks to Loukas," Sammy responded as she climbed down a rocky pathway to the dirt road, hand in hand with Doxiadis. Her face was flushed and she was hyperventilating. Seeing Katsoulis, she said, "Gave a full report to your officer up there. That monk almost killed me." Shivering, she patted Tasos' arm and walked by him for a better peek at the body. As she caught a glimpse of the monk's features, she gasped. "Wait, isn't that—"

"Sammy, thank God you're not hurt. What happened?" Pappajohn clasped her to his chest in a paternal hug, pulling her away from the disturbing sight.

"That's what I'd like to know!" Sammy said, stepping back from Pappajohn and turning to Alex. "That's the monk you were arguing with at the funeral yesterday. I *knew* I saw him at the flea market. Was he following me or you? You thinnk he might have been the biker who shot at our car on the drive from the airport?"

"Seemed to me that the chap was just mad, shouting and swinging his satchel," offered Doxiadis, making a circuling gesture next to his temple. "Crazy eyes."

"Who did *what?*" Pappajohn said turning towards Alex. "You never told me you were shot at. I trusted you to..."

Katsoulis stepped in, raising a hand. "Stop." She glared at Alex. "I think we need to hear from all of you. The whole story this time." Waving to Tasos. "Take Kosta and the Professor to headquarters in your car now. I'll meet you there." She grabbed Alex by the elbow and motioned to Sammy to follow. "You two are coming with me."

CHAPTER TWENTY-NINE

Back at the police station, Captain Katsoulis spent the next few hours interrogating the group that had been at the scene of the monk's death, starting with Sammy and Alex.

"Let me get this straight," she demanded of Alex. "You knew the victim?"

"Not exactly…" He began to describe his encounter with the man on the motorcycle two days earlier. "I didn't get the licence plate," Alex admitted. "I honestly thought it was all a mistake."

"He shot at you and you thought it was a mistake?" Katsoulis' tone was incredulous.

"Alex told me these kind of ambushes target politicians. That he wasn't the target." Sammy explained.

"That so?" Katsoulis leveled a stern look at Alex and shook her head. "You know you should have made a report."

Sammy turned to Alex, surprised. "I thought you said you'd talk to Tasos."

An embarrased shrug. "By the time I finished the inventory, Tasos had already picked you up." To Katsoulis: "I'll fill you in on all the details now."

"The man shouted something about death to unbelievers," Sammy added. "I thought the monk said the same thing at the Acropolis, too."

"Heretics. Death to Heretics," corrected Alex. "Neither of which apply to us."

"Did you see his face?" Katsoulis asked.

"No," Alex said. "He was wearing a helmet and visor down to his beard. But I did see a symbol on the back. Here, I can draw it. Paper and pencil?"

Katsoulis pushed a pad of paper and a pen at Alex who pondered a few minutes before creating a rough drawing.

$$\text{IC} \mid \text{XC}$$
$$\overline{\text{NI} \mid \text{KA}}$$

"A Byzantine Christian symbol?" Katsoulis asked.

Alex nodded. For Sammy: "Jesus Christ conquers."

"I never saw the cyclist's face either," said Sammy. "But he had long hair. I saw it blowing around in the breeze."

"Monks in Greece don't cut their hair or their beard," Alex told Sammy.

"So is that why you went after him at the funeral?" Sammy asked. "That *was* the monk who tried to knock me off the ledge, right? The one you were arguing with."

Alex sighed. "I'm afraid so. But I didn't know he was the one who shot at us. We were sitting in the church waiting for the service to start. Kiki got up to speak to Professor Roussos and Professor Doxiadis who were standing in the aisle beyond the cameras. I saw the monk come out of the altar, through the side door, and approach the group. He had a satchel of some kind that he was tapping with his hand."

"We call that a kind of man-purse, a murse," Sammy muttered. "Although the way he swung it at me, I'd call it a hammer throw." To Katsoulis: "That's where an athlete throws a metal ball on a string. Track and field."

Alex sighed. "By the time I'd walked up to them, the monk had moved on. I followed him out and demanded to see what was in his...murse. He didn't like that. I tried to grab the bag, but he started yelling and threatening me. Quite un-monk-like behavior, I'd say. That's when I caught a glimpse of his hair sticking out of his hood, and it somehow reminded me of the motorcycle chap. If he had a gun in that satchel, I wasn't going to give him a chance to shoot at me again. So, I went back to the church." A shrug. "And that's it."

"Was there a gun in his murse?" Sammy asked Katsoulis.

The Captain raised her eyebrows to indicate "no". "Forensics is going over it, but all we've found are some crumbs and some rusted metal flakes."

"He had a package in there," said Sammy.

Alex and Katsoulis turned towards her.

"When you all went to the gravesite, I saw him heading down another path. He stopped at that crypt, pulled it out of his bag, and left it inside." To Katsoulis: "That's when you and Gus called me to catch up. I didn't have time to go explore what it was."

Alex raised an eyebrow. "Aha. So *that's* what you were doing in that crypt. I had to rescue her when she got locked inside."

"Probably by the monk or his target," Sammy surmised.

"So, then, what was in the package?" inquired Katsoulis.

Sammy shrugged. "When I got inside the crypt, the package was gone." She shared a look with Alex. "And, thankfully, so was the monk."

Katsoulis spent only a few minutes interviewing Doxiadis. He insisted that he'd never seen the monk before and refused to accept the role of hero - despite his many scratches and a few blooming bruises. "Honestly, it was sheer reflex. I didn't have time to think."

"And Sammy Greene. Do you know her well?"

"No, but I'd like to," he admitted. "You do know we were both on the *Thesaurus* six years ago, but I only met her again at Harris' office the day after he…passed."

Katsoulis leaned in. "What? What was she doing in there?"

"Harris' cousin, the policeman, said he was looking for Harris' will. Sammy was there with the American cop. Apparently, their keys didn't work." Doxiadis shrugged. "I offered to get a master from the office; they said they'd look elsewhere and left."

Katsoulis kept her expression neutral, but instinct had her stroking her chin. "I see."

"Anyway, I saw Sammy at the funeral, and thought I'd ask her out during the mercy meal."

"Hmm. Nice of you to take her sightseeing." Katsoulis produced a half-smile.

Doxiadis sighed. "I wanted to get her away from all this..." he waved his hand around the interrogation room. "Instead I almost lost her."

Katsoulis rose, indicating the session was over. "Well, thank you for your time. I assume I can find you at the university if we have more questions."

"Yes, of course. I have to prepare a final examination. I'd hoped to invite Sammy to dinner, but..."

"Not tonight," Katsoulis nodded.

Katsoulis moved from one windowless interview room to another where she'd asked Pappajohn and Tasos to wait.

"Well, we've been busy little bees, haven't we?" Her words dripped with sarcasm.

She scrutinized the two men like a grade school principal. "Just had a very helpful conversation with Professor Doxiadis. Seems he ran into you at his university. I wonder why? Ah, yes. Your cousin, Tasos, Lambros. He has an office there, no?"

Tasos cleared his throat and looked down at his shoes.

Pappajohn stepped in. "All right, Despina. Clearly Doxiadis told you we tried to visit Lambros' office. We were hoping to find his will before the funeral, but we couldn't get in. We got it at his lawyer's the next day."

Katsoulis' steely gaze focused on Tasos. "And what else did you find in the office?"

"As he said, Daphne's keys didn't work." Tasos' voice cracked. "Nothing." With more confidence. "Besides, there was no police tape or anything…"

"No, you are correct, Officer. Entry was not forbidden yet, though unwise." She leaned back in her chair and eyed the pair. Then she nodded in the direction of the camera perched on a tripod in the corner of the room. "Now I know as experienced police officers both you would turn in any evidence you found that could possibly be useful in the Lambros murder case. That's so, is it not?"

The door opened and a uniformed policeman stuck his head into the room. "Sorry, Captain," he interrupted in Greek. "We have an ID on the victim.

Katsoulis waved him in. "It's okay. Who was he?"

"A monk from a skete in Mt. Athos. Palaia Panaghia. His name was Vasilis Oikonomou. Only twenty-six years old."

Katsoulis nodded. "I saw Father Mihalis come in earlier. He knew him?"

The policeman nodded. "Yes, unfortunately. The monk was Father Mihalis' son."

The group was silent for a moment. Katsoulis finally spoke up. "Thank you, Officer Glezos." After he exited, she turned back to the men. "Any more surprises?"

With a sigh, Pappajohn lifted his briefcase onto the table. "We didn't think this was of any value, but we found this photo of a document in Lambros' office. Some poems in ancient Greek." He handed the codex photo to her. "None of us can read it, so I was going to ask Alex…"

She motioned with her hand. "What else do you have in there?"

Pappajohn shook his head. "Nothing. Just an old Bible. It's Daphne's. We left Lambros' camera in his apartment, so you have that, right? Ever find his phone?"

Katsoulis sighed. "No. Probably smashed in a sewer by now. But OTE did give me his phone records." She relented. "Nothing unusual, except for three numbers. Called two a few times in his last few days. Kiki Matsas." She glared at Pappajohn. "Alex Matsas. And the last one, several calls, including the day of his death. "

"Let me guess," Pappajohn said. "Burner phone."

"Burner phone."

CHAPTER THIRTY

It was dark when Katsoulis released Alex and Sammy. She had a raft of additional questions, mostly for Alex, about his relationship with Professor Lambros. Suddenly the detective's focus had changed from Sammy's trauma and the death of the monk to the professor's murder.

"Lambros called you several times the week before he died, no?" Katsoulis probed.

Alex was unfazed. "Yes. And I finally stopped answering. He wanted us—Kiki and me—to let him present his theory about the *Apocalypsi* findings. Kiki didn't think it was the right occasion. Annoyingly persistent chap, God forgive his soul."

"Pappioannou and his Boston friend have made some progress in uncovering Lambros' theory from the deleted file. Did he mention it to you?"

Alex hesitated. "Well, Lambros did think Roussos was off by two centuries on his dates. And if Roussos was wrong about that, maybe he was wrong about the treasure itself…"

"Minerva was the name of the file," Katsoulis said. "And there were subfiles, but we don't have the content yet, just the names. Monastiraki, Masada, and Makronissos. Did he ever say what they meant? I know Minerva is the Latin for Athena."

Alex glanced at Sammy for a moment. "He did send me some things, but I haven't had time to review them. How about I look them over and get back to you?"

"How about I get a warrant to search your office and home and get back to *you*?"

Alex pursed his lips. "Of course. I'll email you what I have tonight. But, it's from a few days ago, and it isn't complete. I was hoping to study the files so I could be of help."

"I won't stop you, Dr. Matsas. As long as you send me the copies ASAP. And, by the way, if you run into any more 'guns', you call me immediately. Clear?"

Katsoulis let the two leave the station an hour after Tasos and Pappajohn had gone home. Alex drove Sammy to Daphne and Tasos' apartment in Moschato and insisted on walking her inside.

Opening the door, Pappajohn's smile morphed to a frown when he saw Sammy's escort.

Alex raised a hand. "I know, I know. I'm truly sorry. But, things were so upside down that morning, and then, afterwards, especially since we were fine, I just put it out of my mind. I had other things to think about..."

Pappajohn tsked. "If anything had happened to Sammy..."

"Alex got us away and saved my life, Gus. Anyway, the monk was after *me* today, not Alex. I just can't understand why."

"Maybe he spotted you watching him put the package in the crypt," Pappajohn suggested. "He might have waited for an opportunity to catch you alone."

"That doesn't make sense," Sammy insisted. "There was no way I could really identify him from those brief glimpses."

"The Captain told us there were metal filings in the monk's bag. What if it contained the stolen dial?" Alex proposed.

Pappajohn walked them over to the dining room table where he'd laid out the printed pictures and pointed to one. "These are the four dials that were in the museum. Do you know which one was taken?"

"Harris asked me to let him take some photos, yes. Let me look." Alex studied the photo. "This one, with the Zodiac symbols."

"Zodiac symbols?" asked Sammy. "I thought the Greeks were into astronomy, not astrology."

"A little of both," Alex said. "The ancient Greeks adapted Sumerian and Babylonian myths and applied them to the constellations they identified, the ones we know today." He smiled. "They also seemed to believe in voodoo and curses and the evil eye."

"Like the necklace Daphne is wearing," Pappajohn said.

Daphne stroked her blue, white, and black circular pendant. "Keeps away bad luck."

Tasos rolled his eyes. "If only..."

"Anyway," Alex continued, "I doubt we can tell if the metal flakes came from the stolen dial. The device could have had as many as ten or fifteen dials or gears, each with a different purpose. These photos would only tell us half the story."

"But you'll stay for coffee and baklava and help us discover what we can, won't you?" Pappajohn asked.

"Greek coffee, yes. Thick enough to slice." Alex pulled out his phone and started inching towards the bedrooms. "Just need to make a phone call first."

"Where the hell have you been? Didn't we agree to meet over lunch and work on these files together?" Kiki's voice was loud enough to make Alex move the phone away from his ear.

"There was an incident at the Acropolis..."

"You mean the monk who fell? I saw it on the news. What did that have to do with you?"

Alex explained that he'd been with Pappajohn that morning checking out the Bible at Phillipos' shop in Monastiraki when Tasos called to say that Sammy might be in trouble.

"The redhead?"

"Yes. Loukas had taken her to the Acropolis for sightseeing and that monk tried to attack her with his satchel. Of all people, Loukas jumped in and fought the monk who ended up falling off the ledge. Can hardly believe it myself, but I'm glad she's safe."

"I'll bet you are."

Imagining the smirk on Kiki's face, Alex winced, "It's just professional, like you and me."

She laughed. "Okay, okay, Alex. You still could've called me."

"This is my first private moment since the morning," Alex explained. "Katsoulis detoured us to her police station."

"Dammit! And you caved, right?"

"I did my best," he defended. He shared what Katsoulis knew and what he'd been able to keep from her. "I didn't mention you or tell her that Harris had sent the files to you as well."

"Well, that's something. So who was this monk and why was he after Miss Red?"

"Katsoulis says he's the son of Father Mihalis."

"*Our* Father Mihalis? No shit. Now that you mention it, I did see Father Mihalis behind us in the altar talking to a monk. Was that his kid? He walked right by us. With a brown satchel, I think."

"Yeah. Him. I'm guessing he had a dial in there. Sammy saw him put something in a crypt after the service."

"Not the Zodiac dial. How would he get it? Unless..."

"What?"

"I've been looking at the Makronissos file Harris sent us. Apparently, he suspected the island could serve as a way station for illegal trade in artifacts. Like a global art pawn shop."

"That's what Phillipos implied, too. The monk could have connected with the Makronissos dealers somehow. It's worth checking out. I'll give my friend Malcolm a call and see if I can use his motorboat to go there tomorrow."

"Good. Only this time, don't wait a year to give me a call."

"Tomorrow evening, I promise. *Geia.*"

Alex clicked off and rejoined Sammy, Tasos, and Eleni at the dining room table. Daphne brought him a cup of coffee and a fresh piece of baklava.

"I just spoke with Kiki. She thinks our best bet to learn more about the mystery of the dials is to follow up on Phillipos' lead. Anyone want to join me for a daytime cruise tomorrow?" he asked.

"Me," Pappajohn said, reaching for another piece of the sweet pastry, ignoring his sister's silent rebuke.

Tasos sighed. "I'm on duty all day. And Daphne has to take the kids to school. Eleni?"

She shook her head. "Doctor's appointment. Sammy, you should go with Gus."

"Honestly, I'm not a great sailor. Besides, today was more than a little exciting."

Alex took a sip of coffee, then produced a sincere smile. "The weatherman is predicting smooth sailing tomorrow. Trust me. You'll be fine."

Sammy let out a deep breath. And then another. Finally she nodded. "Okay. Guess I'm in too."

CHAPTER THIRTY-ONE

Sunday, June 8, 2003

The taxi driver chose the brand new superhighway north of Athens, avoiding southern coastal highway commuter traffic. Alex's Smart Car could only hold two, so Pappajohn and Sammy had agreed to meet him at their destination. The trip to the port of Lavrium took only an hour as most Athens commuters were going in the opposite direction *into* the capital.

Sammy had few memories of the town of Lavrio from her last visit escorting Ollie's body back to *terra firma*. The grey mist surrounding them then had revealed little of the village; what she could see through her tears had been blurred by the fog. The *Thesaurus* had sailed past the town's old abandoned mine, its ghostly towers poking holes in the dark clouds above the whistling wind.

"Did you know," stated the taxi driver in broken English, "that Lavrio has the oldest theater in Greece? And the mines there, they built the temple of Poseidonas, at Cape Sounion. You must go to Sounio at sunset," he insisted as he drove past a roundabout into the center of the town square. "Only ten minutes from here."

In the bright morning light the city's main street looked charming to Sammy. Colorful restaurants and cafes lined the busy sidewalks where chefs and waiters were putting out chairs for the midday tourist wave. A few blocks beyond was a modern shopping center. The road ended at a crowded marina, the gateway to the shimmering Aegean sea.

As the taxi rolled to a stop before a freshly-painted two story building the color of sunshine, Sammy read the sign on the portico. Ελληνική Αστυνομία Hellenic Police. When they'd trudged in the rain to file their witness reports six years ago, the headquarters' stucco walls had been stained, chipped, and covered with graffiti, and the polished bronze front door was tarnished. Sammy stopped and stared at the door, wondering if the Captain had had time to check on Ollie's camera.

"Sammy, Kosta!" Alex shouted from the pier. "Over here."

Alex introduced the pair to his "mate" Malcolm, who pulled a small motorboat closer to the dock. It was a sleek single-decked open-hull runabout with the console in the center so as many as four people could walk all around from stem to stern with ease. The name "BRAVEHEART " in red and black letters was printed on the hull.

"You mean the *first* mate, right?" Sammy couldn't resist saying, "And I didn't know Malcolm was a Greek name?"

"Wick, Scotland," Malcolm corrected with a charming burr. "Alex and I shared quarters at Oxford. But, no. Today I am entrusting my *"Braveheart"* to Alex." He helped Sammy into the runabout before supporting an unsteady Pappajohn, laboring to balance by bending his knees as the boat rocked with each step. Alex tossed in his rucksack and hopped in behind them.

His friend climbed out. "There's a life jacket for each of you. Tank is full of petrol. Should easily get you there and back. Remember, T-bone the waves."

Alex nodded and followed Malcolm's instructions to start the motor. Malcolm released the anchored rope and tossed it into the boat. The runabout rocked and yawed for the first few yards forward, but Alex soon pointed it to the expanse of open sea beyond the marina and set off smoothly with a thumbs up sign.

The calmness of the water in the marina was comforting to Sammy. She took a seat behind Pappajohn while Alex sat at the helm. It was a crystal clear day and she could see their destination looming in the distance. *Good, it doesn't look too far away.* But, once past the shelter of the cove, the waves and current picked up, and, to her dismay, the boat started rocking.

She leaned over to shout to Alex. "What did Malcolm mean 'T-bone the waves'?"

"I should hit the waves at ninety degrees. Keeps us from tipping over," Alex replied.

"Tipping over?" Sammy forced a weak smile. "Hey, look at that sailboat over there. It looks like it's going to fall into the water!"

Pappajohn laughed. "Landlubber. It's supposed to do that. Sailboats lean into the wind to get speed and zigzag along the water. Watch, he's going to tack in a minute and tip over the other way."

Sammy watched the sailboat shift its sail and, yes, tip to the water level on the other side. She pointed at the dozen or so sailboats taking advantage of the clear weather and brisk breeze in the strait. "I can't believe all these people out here actually enjoy doing that." Shivering, she clutched her chest and lifejacket tightly.

Alex laughed. "I'm not much for sailing either. I'd have opted for a ferry if they had one to Makronissos. After Exile Island was last used for prisoners of the Generals' Junta in the early seventies, the government has declared it a national preserve and discourages tourism."

Sammy stood to grab a pair of binoculars off the floor and scanned the island. "Lots of abandoned buildings. Now, that's interesting. There are a few with colorful graffiti. And rugs covering the doorways..."

"Squatters," said Alex. "Coast Guard usually ignores them. They'll probably clear them out before the Olympics, though."

"Is that where we're going? Oh…" The boat lurched and Sammy fell back onto her seat.

"Wake," Alex said, pointing to a passing boat. "That was what they call a cuddy cabin boat. It has a closed deck. Motor leaves a big wake. Especially going that fast." He steered the boat to port. "Anyway, no. Kiki found a couple of photos in the Makronissos file that correspond to a hidden cove along the island's northern coast with a couple of cave entrances. The island is full of caves."

"Yes, I can see them," Sammy said, distracting herself with her shoregazing. "But we seem to be leaving the abandoned buildings. Wouldn't that be where we should go?"

"The coves to the north are more sheltered and private, because the nearby ferries from Lavrio to Kea go south around Makronissos. We can drop anchor there without being seen. Based on one of the diagrams in my Makronissos file, one of the abandoned buildings we passed may connect through the cave tunnels. If that's true, we can use that route to discreetly explore for signs of a lair. Better than trying a full frontal attack," he half-joked.

"Which reminds me," Pappajohn said. "I talked to Keith before we left Athens this morning. No luck on the subfolders yet, but he was able to retrieve the PowerPoint. There were over thirty slides, and Keith thinks it was pretty complete. He'll email it to me and I'll share it with you and Kiki."

Alex's expression brightened. "Did he find anything new?"

"Actually, yes. Lambros did advocate that the *Apocalypsi* was carrying the golden statue of Athena from Athens to Constantinople for safekeeping, for fear that Christian crusaders would raid and destroy the statue."

"Gold is used in icons as well as pagan statues," Alex admitted. "And Hagia Sophia needed thousands of tons of gold. A wise decision, if true."

"Lambros believed the ship was attacked as it sailed past Makronissos. He wasn't sure if the attack was land-based from outposts on the island or sea-based from the lee side of the island between Makronissos and Kea. Makronissos' proximity to the ancient port of Lavrio, as well as to the Poseidon temple at Cape Sounio would make it ideal for military operations under Emperor Theodosios as well as rogue piracy".

"How did Lambros learn about this place?" Sammy asked.

"Everyone in Greece knows about the tragic history of Makronissos as an island of exile and imprisonment," explained Alex. But, if Lambros bought artifacts, including dials, he may have journeyed here to find them or to pick them up. Same for the unfortunate monk. Actually, it could be a very convenient hiding place for products from around the Mediterranean on their way to Athens and beyond. Treasures stolen from monasteries like Mt. Athos or from countries around the Aegean like Turkey and the Middle East could be stashed here until they're shipped to their buyers in Europe or overseas."

"It's also possible that Makronissos could have been the Athena statue's final destination," Pappajohn suggested.

Alex nodded. "If Lambros is right, in a way, it was."

"Wow! Look at that!" Sammy pointed to an enormous yacht anchored just beyond a cove around a curve in the island's shore. A snort. "I bet I could enjoy a sea cruise on that floating hotel."

Alex's eyes narrowed. "She's a beauty. But I know I've seen her somewhere before." As he swung around the yacht, allowing his passengers to ooh and aah, he noted the name of the vessel on the attached dinghy. "Of course. The *WELLESLEY*. She belongs to Lord Wellington."

"The old billionaire art dealer we saw at the gala?" asked Pappajohn.

"Yes, indeed."

Pappajohn nodded, adding. "Then I suggest we resume our course post haste. Wouldn't want to draw his attention."

"Your gut telling you something, Gus?" Sammy asked.

"Yup. Vamanos."

Chapter Thirty-Two

As soon as the runabout disappeared around the coast, the yacht yeoman pulled the dinghy towards the collapsible ladder. Jean Dumas stepped out onto the deck, followed by his model *du jour*, who slipped off her bikini top and slithered her well-oiled body towards a sun-drenched lounge chair. Wellington followed and clapped Dumas on the shoulders with the hand not holding his martini.

"Ring me when you seal the deal." A chuckle. "And I shall get the price cut in half."

"You have ze French in you, Wellington. I call you soon."

Dumas climbed down the ladder and into the dinghy after the yeoman. The yeoman released the rope and started the motor. He pointed the dinghy toward the no longer deserted cove where a monk stood in the cave entrance waving.

"I think we can anchor here," Alex said, eyeing the sandy beach. There was only one other boat bobbing in the water.

"That looks like the wave-maker we passed a while back," Sammy said. "A cuddle boat?"

Alex laughed. "Cuddy cabin. The cabin looks empty from here and I see a tent up the beach a bit, flapping in the wind. A few do like to come to these quiet shores and 'cuddle', you know."

"Don't you want to get closer in?" interrupted Pappajohn "We're ten yards from the sand."

"I told you to wear shorts, Kosta. Roll up those trousers." Alex swung his rucksack onto his back. "At least you wore your *sayonares*."

Pappajohn shook his head and, kicking off his flip-flops, bent over to reach his cuffs with a grunt. Sammy hiked up her shorts to mid-thigh and, holding her sandals, followed Alex into the warm water, which lapped at her knees. "Hey, it's pretty shallow."

"Can't risk running aground. Do you need help, Kosta?"

Pappajohn swung his legs over the end of the boat and slid into the water with a splash, wetting his pants up to his belt, and almost losing the flip-flops in his hands. His *Ghamo to* was unsurprisingly loud.

The trio plodded down the shore, dodging rocks breaking through the sand. Alex took the lead, following a copy of one of the map drawings he'd printed from his Makronissos file. He stopped at the entrance to a large cave and peered into the darkness.

"You do have flashlights?" Pappajohn asked.

Alex reached into his rucksack and brought them out. "Torches for everyone. One, two, three, and a spare. I have extra batteries on the boat."

"I'll bet you were an Eagle Scout," Sammy teased.

"A Venture Scout, yes. But the Army prepares you even better. Now we should be quiet after we enter the cave. Sounds will echo and might be transmitted farther than we want."

Pappajohn and Sammy nodded and followed Alex into the cool, dark hole.

CHAPTER THIRTY-THREE

Kiki didn't look up from her computer when the door to her office opened. "I'm busy."

"So am I," said a gravelly voice Kiki immediately recognized.

"Good morning, Captain." Kiki offered Katsoulis a polite smile.

"Your husband emailed me Lambros' files last night."

"Ex." *Sure, good going, Alex.*

"So, let's take a few minutes together and use our expertise to figure out what Lambros had found that got him killed."

Kiki almost gagged. "But, I..."

Patronizing. "If he sent them to Alex, he sent them to you." Katsoulis pulled up a chair. "So, the statue of Athena, hmm?"

At yet another fork in the path, Alex checked his map. "This way." He pointed Sammy and Pappajohn towards the right.

Sammy took a moment to absorb the beauty of the cave atrium. Colorful stalactites touched the tips of stalagmite 'fingers' like humans striving for the hand of God.

"Come on," urged Alex. "There are better caves I can show you in Athens near the new airport. Let's not waste time now."

"Yes, I'm freezing in here." Pappajohn looked down at his wet clothing.

"We don't have much longer to go. We're taking the hypotenuse," Alex said. "We should end up right under the Delta battalion officers' quarters."

Ten minutes later, the trio arrived at a hollowed out chamber.

Alex aimed his flashlight at a twenty foot ladder that led to a metal door above. "Wait here." He scrambled up the ladder and lifted the metal door. As it opened, the loud squeak echoed in the chamber below and down a darkened hallway in the building.

Alex peered down at the pair. "Thankfully, it looks empty. Come up and then we'll recon."

Sammy helped Pappajohn crawl up, spotting him from behind. "How are your knees holding out?"

"Climbing with my hands, Sammy. Knees gave out a long time ago."

The building had no visible power and hanging ceiling lights were bereft of bulbs. Most of the windows were cracked or broken, admitting jagged rays of sunlight that created irregular shadows in every room. Several of the windows had bars, and one large room had remnants of handcuffs and chains bolted to the wall. Few doors remained along their journey. Most were either missing or off of their hinges, wood rotting or metal rusted, leaning against graffitied plasterboard. Alex led them down the hallway toward another wing which seemed only a little less abandoned.

"Was that a thing crawling on my feet?" asked Sammy, her voice reflecting anxiety.

"Place is full of insects and small mammals. Just don't look down. They're more afraid of you," said Alex.

"I don't think so," said Sammy. "Are you sure anyone's here?"

"Shh." Alex shone his flashlight into the distance. "There should be a stairwell a few more yards forward there going down to a cellar. But we have to stay quiet."

The hallway ended in a cinderblock wall with a stairwell to the left. Alex motioned for them to follow him down one story of steps. At the landing they spotted a wooden door that seemed much more modern than the relics upstairs. Slivers of artificial light framed the polished wood and shining lock. Alex put a finger to his lips and slowly pulled off his rucksack to reach inside. This time he brought out a can of WD 40.

Alex quietly oiled the hinges on the wooden door and its handle, then popped the tin back into his bag.

"What else do you have in there?" Sammy asked.

Finger to his lips again, Alex slowly opened the wooden door a slit and peeked into the next room. Widening his view a little more revealed a large auditorium lit by fluorescent fixtures. Folding tables and chairs were set up randomly around the room. At the far end, several modern doors opened to yet another room where stacked cartons and boxes were piled between a broader staircase leading back up to the ground floor.

Several monks, wearing habits similar to Mihalis' son's, were bringing in boxes on carts and loading paintings, icons, statues, vases, and sculptures onto some of the tables. Alex smiled. "Must be an elevator back there," he whispered.

At a far table, a monk stood with a toupeed man dressed in a lightweight leisure suit. They both had their backs to the trio, but they could see the monk laying out a few items - dishes, bowls, jewelry, coins.

"Hey, that's a mezuzah," Sammy said *sotto voce*.

Alex nodded.

The monk pointed to several vases, swords, and shields at the adjacent table. The man shook his head and made a round shape with his hands. Turning toward another table, he momentarily exposed his face.

Alex took a sharp intake of breath. He quickly closed the door and pulled Sammy and Pappajohn back into the landing. "My God."

"What?" asked Pappajohn, a worried look on his face.

"That's Jean Dumas. He came to our gala. The art dealer from Paris."

Pappajohn raised an eyebrow. "Yes, I remember. French playboy. I think he was talking to the Greek Orthodox priest." A frown. "So, he's dirty. Surprise, surprise."

Alex rubbed his chin. "We need to see what's in there. What's on display. A few of those artifacts look quite like *Apocalypsi* finds.."

Pappajohn rolled his eyes. "Why don't we just stroll in and ask them to show us? We look like art dealers, huh?" He shook his head. "My advice? How about we sneak back to the cove, get on our boat, sail to Captain Katsoulis and tell her what we've seen. Let her team coordinate a sting operation or a SWAT rescue."

"No." Alex reached into his backpack again.

"Wrong answer," muttered Pappajohn, who looked up to see a gun handle pointed at his chest.

"Take it. I brought one for me too. Just in case." Alex removed a second pistol from his backpack and tucked it into the back of his shorts. "I assumed you don't know how to shoot," he added to Sammy.

Sammy stood frozen and managed to sputter out a "N-no. What are you going to do?"

Pappajohn was aghast. "Are you kidding?"

One more dive into the rucksack and Alex brought out three small Israeli civilian gas masks and a canister of tear gas. "I'm prepared. I don't want to hurt anyone. It's just to keep us safe. Go down one more story to the bottom floor of the building, put on your mask, and wait in the landing below. I'll toss in the tear gas up here and join you. When they run outside, we can do a quick scan of what's there — and what, if anything, we need to 'borrow'. Nobody gets hurt. And *then* we go to Katsoulis."

CHAPTER THIRTY-FOUR

Katsoulis lit her fourth cigarette and offered one to Kiki. She emptied the ashtray into Kiki's rubbish bin and leaned back in her chair. "So, here's what we've got, right?" She drew in a deep puff. "Lambros thinks the *Apocalypsi* is a fifth century war ship. It's not taking the Virgin Mary to Haghia Sophia, it's taking Athena to Constantinople where she can be stored for safekeeping by the supporters of Julian the Apostate, yes?"

Kiki nodded.

"Something — enemies, a storm, who knows — capsizes the ship off of Makronissos and Athena never gets there. A millennium and a half later, all that's left of her is a bronze 'skeleton'. Which, after a little polishing, will be put somewhere in some Athens museum that no one watching MTV will go see." Another puff. "What I *don't* see, is a motive for murder. A spirited debate in Archaeology journals perhaps, but not murder."

"You didn't know Harris," Kiki admitted. "But, you're right. He would likely have gone through channels to publicly embarrass Roussos and Roussos would fight back with the University governing board." A sigh. "Murder would be at least a few years down the road."

"So," Katsoulis continued. "It has to be something else."

"We don't have his complete presentation."

"Not yet. I will have to have Kosta arm-twist Boston. But we do have the three subfiles. What do they tell us?"

Kiki frowned. "Monastiraki is the bazaar, but it's also a retail outlet for antiques and artifacts. Harris scanned receipts from several shops for a variety of antique items. Coins, documents, books. A few of the shopkeepers have police records."

Katsoulis nodded. "They also have friends in the government. Go on."

"Makronissos seems to be another place that's selling or trading in artifacts. Maybe the *Thesaurus* didn't collect all of the *Apocalypsi's* treasures. Fortune hunters may have established a base on the island to do their own diving and collection. No matter which century the ship was built, its remnants would bring a great price on the open market. Or the black one."

"Okay, so they collect *Apocalypsi* treasures and provide some to buyers at Makronissos and some at Monastiraki. But what about Masada?"

"I've been stuck on that one," Kiki said. "I do know that there was a big exhibit at the Jerusalem Museum in Israel about Masada last year. I heard something about a few pieces missing. But, the museum visitor who came to the gala -what was his name? Ilan? He was pretty close-mouthed about that. 'Ongoing investigation', and all..." She flipped a yellowed Rolodex. "I had an old classmate who's working in Jerusalem now. Why don't I try to call him? See if he can tell us something more."

Once Sammy and Pappajohn were safely hidden a floor below, Alex slipped on his mask, reopened the door and tossed in the tear gas canister. The room quickly filled with tear gas, followed by the monks' shouts in Greek, a few Slavic-sounding languages, and a cry of help in French. As Alex had hoped, there was a rapid rush for the larger set of doors and stairs on the opposite side of the room. Two monks grabbed the stumbling Jean Dumas under each arm and carried him out with his legs wagging.

As soon as the room cleared, Alex waved for Sammy and Pappajohn to follow him inside. Alex took one side of the room, Pappajohn took the opposite, while Sammy started searching tables with unopened boxes. One box Sammy opened had a number of Greek icons displaying various Orthodox saints. Some boxes had crosses and chalices decorated in gold and silver and bejeweled with rubies and emeralds. Another box labeled CODEX had books and bound documents, some in plastic bags.

As Pappajohn whistled and waved, Alex picked up a jeweled knife and a small urn and added them to his rucksack. Pappajohn pointed to a few bronze struts on the table before him, a few tarnished coins, and a rusted dial. Alex grabbed the dial and stashed it in his bag just as a shout came from the floor above at the top of the stairs. Alex and Pappajohn both pulled out their pistols, and motioned for Sammy to aim for the entrance.

Closing the door behind them, Alex could hear the monks racing down the stairs and the clatter of the elevator door opening beyond. He and Sammy stood a chance of outrunning the monks, but Kosta? Pappajohn was already short of breath climbing one flight.

Alex paused to pull out a second canister from his rucksack. He'd use it if he had to, but it was his last. Like the guns, it was a souvenir of his Army days. Better to make the monks cry than die. "Come on, Kosta, you can go faster."

"I can," Pappajohn puffed, "but my knees can't." He waved at Sammy who'd entered the first wing already. "Go with her and get help. Keep her safe!"

Alex could hear the monks shouting in Greek that the display room was empty. He heard, "This door. They went out this door!" He placed an arm around Pappajohn for support. By the time they reached the first hallway, Sammy had arrived at the end. She opened the metal door with the ladder leading to the chamber.

"I'll go down!" she cried. "I'll try to hold Gus for the first few feet and then maybe we can jump."

"Go down all the way. I'll spot Gus from up here. You can try to support him if he slides down." The open door was tempting, but Alex could see that some of the monks who'd been in the display room were now tracking their path from outside of the abandoned wing. He heard the monks' footsteps moving up the stairs inside the far wing. It wouldn't be long before they'd reach them. Thank God, they'd at least made it to the ladder.

Pappajohn turned and grunted as he lowered himself onto the ladder with Alex's help. Each step was obviously painful and slow. Alex had no choice. Out came the second canister, ready to toss. "Go!" he yelled.

Pappajohn took the last ten feet of the slide with his hands, his hard landing somewhat cushioned by Sammy's grip under his arms. The monks had made it to the first wing and were approaching at top speed from inside and out.

Alex tossed the second canister, shut the metal door, and did a one hand slide down the ladder, landing on buckled knees. "Move. We only have a few minutes."

Though his own knees and ankles were sore, Alex put an arm under Pappajohn's shoulders and helped him hobble toward the cave entrance. Sammy jogged ahead and returned to advise Alex that, after traversing the two cave tunnel forks, their exit and the cove remained clear, except for the still-flapping tent and the bobbing cuddy boat.

An echo of the squeaking metal door from far behind signaled that some monks were soon to follow. Fortunately, the last kilometer to the cave entrance was under a large hill, which meant the monks outside would have a tough climb up and down to reach the cove where the *Braveheart* was anchored.

This time, Pappajohn didn't bother to roll up his trousers. Tearing off his mask, he plunged full force into the warm water, using his arms as oars to propel himself towards the runabout.

Sammy pushed through the water behind him towards the boat. She tossed her mask onto the next to Alex's and helped Pappajohn climb on deck as Alex started the motor. Sammy pulled the anchor while Alex throttled up, and, with all aboard, spun the boat around leaving a circular wake that crested on the sandy beach just as the monks arrived at the cave entrance.

A bullet whizzed by Pappajohn's head as the boat raced out into the strait. He pulled out his gun, aimed, and fired at the sand, intentionally missing the monks. "Step on it, Alex!" he shouted. "I don't want to hurt anyone either."

Kiki hung up with a warm thank you. She turned to Captain Katsoulis. "My colleague confirmed the Masada theft. There's an active search still ongoing."

Katsoulis stubbed out another cigarette and stood. "I'll give the Culture Minister and Interpol a call and arrange for a team to go to Makronissos and investigate. Meanwhile, you and Alex should sit on this information so we don't tip our hand."

"Uh, I'm afraid it might be too late."

Katsoulis' mouth set in a tight, grim line. "Alex? Don't tell me he went there today."

Kiki hesitated. "He said he was thinking about it. I'm not sure…"

Katsoulis didn't wait to hear more. Pulling out her cell phone, she dialed her station, at the same time heading for her car. Kiki only heard, "Get a team to Lavrio right away!"

CHAPTER THIRTY-FIVE

T he runabout managed to sail beyond the range of the bullets on the beach, but Alex hadn't counted on a few monks jumping into their own boats and giving chase from coves on both sides of the tip of the island. Their so-called "fishing vessels" seemed to have souped-up engines that outpaced the Braveheart's top speed.

"The better to avoid the Coast Guard," Pappajohn grumbled as Alex maximized his power, leading the runabout's motor to complain with a high pitched whine. "We won't be able to outrun them at this rate." A frown. "How much ammo did you bring?"

"Three cartridges each." Alex looked at the three boats gaining on them and shook his head. "Guess I should have listened to your advice."

A rifle bullet whizzed past as Alex zigzagged across the strait.

Sammy ducked onto her seat. "That was too close."

Alex turned the wheel at the sound of another rifle shot. This one caromed off the hull of the roundabout only centimetres from Pappajohn. Pappajohn spun astern and fired a volley of bullets into the water ahead of the pursuing boats.

They slowed for a moment, then sped up again. "We don't have enough ammo for me to keep them back, Alex," Pappajohn said. He shook his head. "May God forgive me if I kill a monk."

Another bullet hit its target this time. The motor of the Braveheart. The engine sparked and sputtered, flaming out.

"They'll blow us up!" cried Sammy, as Pappajohn reloaded his gun.

"I'm going to hell, but I'll do my best," Pappajohn announced, lifting his gun and aiming for the monk with the rifle.

A loud roar. The *Braveheart* rocked as the cuddy cabin boat sped between the runabout and the monks' vessels. Automatic weapon fire from the hidden cabin blew holes in the hulls of the fishing vessels and drew a few mis-aimed shots in return from the monks who were now desperately bailing or steering. The monks' boats were taking on water and soon switched direction to return to shore. The cuddy cabin boat fired at each of the monks' boat propellers, stalling the sinking boats before they could reach the beach, but out of range of the motorboat. The cuddy cabin boat then swung around and drew up alongside the bobbing *Braveheart*.

A head popped out of the cabin.

Sammy gasped. "Ilan!"

Ilan nodded and waved to them. "Hop in. I'll give you a tow to Lavrium. Hurry. I've called the Coast Guard. Don't want to be around when they pick up our fallen friends."

Sammy jumped onto Ilan's boat and helped Pappajohn steady himself as he navigated the moving gap.

Relieved, though equally annoyed and embarrassed, Alex tossed the *Braveheart*'s rope to Sammy who tied the motorboat to the stern of the cuddy cabin boat. Alex threw his backpack over into their boat, keeping his pistol — just in case.

"I'll stay here and steer," Alex announced, muttering, "Malcolm's going to be livid."

Pappajohn nodded as Sammy helped him into the cuddy cabin.

"Thank God you came, Ilan," Sammy said. "I thought we were done for."

"What were you doing at Makronissos anyway?" Pappajohn asked.

Ilan shrugged. "Same as you. Investigating. Only a little more discreetly."

"You were in that tent?" said Sammy.

"Yup." He winked at her. "Chilly in there all by yourself at night."

Sammy blushed. "Well if there's any good news in all this - today's adventure has cured my seasickness."

Pappajohn looked out behind him at the bouncing *Braveheart*. "Poor Alex looks a little green in Ilan's wake."

CHAPTER THIRTY-SIX

The cuddy cabin boat dropped off the *Braveheart* near its berth in the marina and sailed on to its dock. Alex glided the runabout into its berth. He tied the rope to the post and stuck his gun in the back of his trousers, covering it with his shirt until he could hide it in his car. Sighing, he examined the port hull, noting the five centimeter bullet track and then turned to gaze at the engine in the stern, which, he despaired, would be a total loss. Of course he would offer to pay Malcolm, but perhaps in installments...

"Hey, Poseidon."

Alex froze. Katsoulis' voice? Yes, there she was on the dock, hands on hips, obviously in none too fine a mood.

He feigned a sincere expression. "Just taking my friend's boat out for a spin."

Katsoulis' frown deepened. "The Coast Guard has just arrested a dozen monks — *with* firearms."

"Firearms?" Alex was glad the bullet's damage to the hull was on the opposite side of the runabout.

"The radio hasn't stopped for the last half hour. Interpol and EKAM teams are on their way to Makronissos right now. You weren't near there, were you?"

"No, no, just up the coast here. I..."

"Come on there, Matsas!" Ilan shouted from the pier behind Katsoulis. He pointed to Sammy and Pappajohn who stood near him. "We've been waiting for a half hour. I can't drink any more Greek coffee. Time to eat."

Alex saw that Ilan was carrying his rucksack.

"So, you gonna buy her?" asked Ilan.

Alex hopped onto the pier, making sure his back didn't face Katsoulis. "No. I don't think so. Too much money for my budget." He smiled at Katsoulis and opened his palms. "Do we have a table?"

Katsoulis glared at Alex, then at Sammy and Pappajohn, each of whom displayed their best expression of innocence.

Ilan leaned his T-shirted chest against a lamppost as Alex sidled towards him, affecting a convincing fifties' Marlon Brando. "If you hurry. They'll hold it for another ten minutes."

Katsoulis shook her head. "I just came from Kiki's office."

Alex froze for a moment, but Sammy walked back to where Katsoulis stood. "Captain. Your ring. It's so unique. Is that the evil eye I've heard about?"

As Katsoulis gazed down at her finger, Alex slipped his gun to Pappajohn who slid it into the backpack Ilan was carrying. "Yes. I wear it for good luck. My husband was killed while on duty and now I'm my son's only parent. Anything to help make sure he's not orphaned." She quickly looked back at the men, all three of whom stood together radiating sympathy.

Alex broke first. He threw up his hands and said, "Okay, Captain, Kiki probably told you I might have planned a trip to Makronissos, but I never even got close. I…"

"Look there," interrupted Ilan, "I believe that's Lord Wellington's yacht sailing into port. I saw it last year at the Tel Aviv Marina. It's huge."

"Yes, the TV said they have to berth it in an old ferry berth at the Port of Piraeus because of its size," Katsoulis admitted. "The Coast Guard has temporarily closed the straits on both sides of Makronissos for the criminal investigation, so I guess the *Wellesley* will have to wait here until they're reopened."

"Glad I didn't make it out that far then," Alex said. "Boy, am I hungry. Do you want to join us for a late lunch, Captain?"

Ilan swallowed a smile as he started inching away, followed by Sammy and Pappajohn.

"No thank you. I see the EKAM team is arriving. I need to arrange for the Coast Guard to ferry them out to the island and find out when we can expect Interpol." Her eyes narrowed again. "Let the police handle the investigations, Matsas. Understand?"

Alex nodded and headed toward the restaurant. As soon as Katsoulis was out of sight, the group detoured to Alex's parked Smart Car a block away. Alex opened the trunk and motioned for Ilan to give him the backpack. Instead, Ilan pulled out a tiny camera from his pocket and fished into the bag.

"I don't want anyone to know I have these guns," Alex protested.

Ilan scoffed as he removed the dial along with the other artifacts, laying them in the trunk so he could take quick photos. "No problem, Doc. We're both on the same team." He smiled at Alex. "Aren't we?"

Placing the items back in the backpack, Ilan closed the trunk with a slam. Giving the others a crisp salute, he set off in the direction of his cuddy cabin berth.

CHAPTER THIRTY-SEVEN

"Oh, my God," cried Daphne, as Sammy and Pappajohn arrived at her apartment. "We were so worried."

"It's all over the news," Georgie announced. "They caught the bad guys."

"That they did," said Pappajohn. "Though I expect God will be more forgiving of sinning monks than Despina Katsoulis will."

"I tried to warn you she was on her way," said Tasos.

"No cell towers on Makronissos," explained Pappajohn. "And, unfortunately, my BlackBerry is a bit waterlogged."

"We can dry it out with a little rice," Sammy suggested. "Do you have some?"

"Rice? In a Greek home?" Daphne laughed. "I'll get it right away."

"Did Alex come back with you?" Tasos asked Pappajohn.

"No, we took a taxi. Alex drove to the museum to see Ms. Matsas, and, um, go over what happened."

"Tell us everything," Eleni insisted. "Come, eat and share what you found."

Sammy and Pappajohn related a sanitized story of their adventure, omitting the reclamation of the illegal artifacts and the gun battle during their departure. "Alex tried to call Father Mihalis from Lavrio," said Pappajohn, "but his phone is out of service. The secretary at St. Therapon said he left for Mount Athos this morning."

"Alex wants to go to Mount Athos tomorrow," Sammy said.

"It usually takes a few weeks, but he said he can arrange for an entry pass for you and me, Tasos," Pappajohn said. "We can catch the seven A.M. flight on Attica Air tomorrow morning and make the nine forty-five ferry from Ouranopoli."

Tasos tsked. "I do wish I could go, but I'm on duty tomorrow, too. And with all the chaos after today's bust, I might get stuck with more than one shift."

"Overtime," nudged Daphne, as Tasos sighed.

"I can get us plane tickets online and fly up with you and Alex, Gus," Sammy volunteered. "I'd love to tour Thessaloniki. You think Bishop Theosophos can help us – you — talk to Father Mihalis? We can try to find out how his son got mixed up in all this."

Pappajohn nodded. "Alex thinks so."

She pulled out her cell phone. "I'll just give Alex a call and get things rolling."

"Oh, yes. I forgot," said Daphne. "There's been someone special calling for you all midday." She looked like the cat that swallowed the canary. When Sammy didn't bite, Daphne continued, "Professor Doxiadis. He would like to invite you to the cinema tonight. Either the nine or eleven show."

Sammy swallowed her yawn, stood and flipped open her phone. "That's so nice, but, tell you the truth, after all this, I'm exhausted. I think I'll go to bed early, and, for a change, sleep well tonight." She smiled at Daphne. "If the Professor calls again, just ask him for a raincheck after we get back from Thessaloniki, okay?

"Yes, Alex," Sammy whispered from the bathroom. "You, Gus, and Tasos. Just have your friend meet us at…um…yes, that's it. Ouranopoli…Greek ID or passport, I'll tell them. Our plane should arrive at eight…. Tasos will take a later flight and catch the noon speedboat…just leave his pass with Athos Sea Cruises, he said….Of course I'm coming. I'd love to see Thessaloniki and visit the Jewish Museum. You'll be back by evening, right?…I'll make our reservations now."

After booking tickets for herself and Pappajohn on the seven A.M Attica Airlines shuttle, Sammy gave in to fatigue and nestled herself in her cot in Eleni and Maria's room. She'd have to get up at least an hour before Pappajohn to be at the airport by five-thirty and she needed the quiet time to do what she had to do. Fortunately, Georgie had agreed to lend her his backpack, emblazoned with the green trefoil logo of Athens' primary soccer team, Panathinaikos, so she wouldn't have to pack her things for the trip into her pink carry-on. Even more fortunately, Georgie was nearing her five foot height, so his Sunday suit and his dress shoes, borrowed for a couple of days, would be a good fit.

"They're very likely from the *Apocalypsi*," Kiki agreed as Alex showed her the artifacts he had rescued from Makronissos. "Let me see the dial."

Kiki nodded as she inspected the rusty plate and its gears. "Needs work, of course. But, it seems comparable. I'll show Director Tountas tomorrow. Did you take a photo?"

"Yes, I have photos of nine dials now. My plane leaves tonight at eleven, but let's sit down and see if the additional dials help us scope out more about the device."

"By the way, I've put in a call to our colleagues across town who have been studying the Antikythera mechanism," Kiki said. "Our device looks a little more advanced than theirs, C.E. versus B.C.E., but it might have some functions in common."

"Imagine," Alex said. "The second analogue computer. What a tragedy that such technology was lost for more than a millennium." He shook his head. "Wish we could recover the 'owner's manual.'"

Kiki laughed. "Come on, that would be too easy."

Alex stroked his chin. "You know, we really should share these latest discoveries with the University at some point. Especially with Professor Roussos. He was so meticulous about categorizing every amphora and vase."

"Or at least dumping the task onto junior faculty like Doxiadis."

"I wonder how he's going to take the PowerPoint Kosta's friend was able to recover."

Kiki huffed. "He'll demand proof and keep arguing his perspective. Roussos isn't the type to back down."

"In any case, we'll need at least the summer to sort through all the new finds and update our exhibit. Are you planning to reschedule the gala and presentation before next autumn?" Alex asked.

"If we're ready. Tountas and I will work with the Ministry of Culture to ensure we get the *Apocalypsi* finds, but that could take months, *after* the police investigation. So we have time. Roussos always goes to St. Therapon with his wife for Sunday services. Maybe I'll get up early and go this week and give him a heads up." She sighed, adding, "I can't help but feel sorry about what happened to Father Mihalis' son. Mental health issues are so hard to deal with. I haven't heard anything about a funeral, but I'll bet Father Mihalis won't be there this Sunday."

"I doubt it, too. I called St. Therapon yesterday and the staff person said he had left for Mt. Athos," related Alex. "The funeral may be up there. Away from all the press. I'll find out tomorrow when we visit the Bishop and let you know."

The burner phone buzzed without caller ID. Father Mihalis' deep voice responded in Greek. "What do you want?"

"My condolences."

The priest muttered a curse.

"Now now. I just thought you should know. They are coming to Athos, too. Tomorrow morning. You may want to make yourself hard to find."

The other burner phone hung up before Mihalis could reply.

CHAPTER THIRTY-EIGHT

O ne hundred twenty nautical miles left. Ilan nudged the cuddy cabin boat to over ten knots, grateful that the wind had died down for the night and an almost full moon guided his path in the darkness. If all went well, he'd arrive before dawn, drop anchor south of the Russian Orthodox St. Panteleimon monastery and swim to shore just north of St. Demetrios. A recon to Panteleimon would have to wait, but time was of the essence at Demetrios, the home base of the Eastern European Orthodox monks arrested on Makronissos.

Inside his waterproof backpack was the equipment he needed, including the pilgrim robes. He'd climb to the monastery before dawn, make his way in, and get the ledgers and some video evidence before the monks returned from morning services. He'd memorized the list of treasures he was eager to document before they were hidden by the monks or confiscated by an Interpol or Greek police team. Time was running out. Wellington and Dumas would be leaving soon, as the temperature in Athens was steadily rising.

Sammy's phone vibrated at three-thirty A.M. A stream of moonlight snuck through an opening in the drapes. She quickly turned off the alarm and glanced around to ensure her roommates were still asleep. Tiptoeing into the hall, she paused to listen for snoring at Daphne and Tasos' bedroom. Daphne was curled up, purring along with her dreams, but Tasos' breathing was irregular, occasionally gasping. *Sounds like sleep apnea.* Better lay off Daphne's high-calorie cooking, Sammy thought.

On the nightstand next to Tasos' lanyard with his police ID lay his leather wallet. Sammy tiptoed over to the table and picked it up. A gasp from Tasos almost made her lose her grip. Thankfully, he quickly fell back into slumber. Sammy took a deep breath to calm her shaking hands.

Inside the wallet, behind his credit cards, Sammy located Tasos' Driving Licence and Greek national ID card. *That's what I need.* She eased it out of the slot and slipped it into her jeans pocket. Closing the wallet, she replaced it on the nightstand and tiptoed out of the room.

Back in her cot, Sammy put the ID in Georgie's backpack and reset her alarm for half past four.

CHAPTER THIRTY-NINE

Monday, June 8th

Sammy clutched both armrests as the A319 gunned down the runway and took off almost vertically. "Boy," she complained, "these hot-shot pilots fly like they drive."

"It's only a half hour," Pappajohn said. "Here, eat some bread rusks. Biscotti. Help settle your stomach."

Sammy forced a smile and bit into the hard toast. Twenty-eight and a half minutes and counting.

At the airport, Alex surprised Sammy and Pappajohn by the Attica Airlines counter. "Glad you made it safely."

"So am I," said Sammy. "Some vehicles stop on a dime. These planes stop on a drachma!"

Alex laughed. "It's kind of a macho thing for the pilots. Relax. I hired a car for us and I will drive sanely this time. Not a Smart Car, by the way."

Pappajohn and Sammy both smiled as they entered the Citroen, Sammy enjoying the room in the back seat.

"We're running a bit behind," said Alex to Sammy, "so let's head straight to Ouranopoli, and I can loan you the car to return to Thessaloniki."

"Don't I need an international license?"

"Theoretically. But no one ever checks. Your American one is fine. Anyway, the trip back should be shorter, less than an hour. And even better tonight. We'll call your mobile to pick us up at the end of the day."

"Do they allow cell phones up there?" Sammy asked.

"Yes, though reception isn't always great. And not in the churches. But we can ring you when we return to Ouranopoli or—"

"I can just spring for a taxi back and we'll meet you at the museum. Just enjoy the day at one of Greece's most beautiful cities, Sammy," Pappajohn interjected. "And the weather is perfect. Not as hot as Athens."

"So, what did you and Kiki think about our discoveries?" asked Sammy.

"Apocalypsi finds, we're pretty sure. Including the additional dial. When we return, we should all put our heads together and see if we can figure out about how the device was used, now that we have more pieces of the puzzle."

"I suggest we also invite Despina. Boy, look at this traffic," said Pappajohn. "Are we going to miss the ferry?"

"I hope not. Mt. Athos is one of Greece's top tourist destinations," Alex said. "We'd have had to wait for weeks to get in if it weren't for my friend. Many Orthodox Christians make pilgrimages to live and worship with the monks for a few days. Britain's Prince Charles has come more than once to find a spiritual home."

Sammy smiled, "It's like the Wailing Wall in Jerusalem."

"More like the Hajj in Saudi Arabia, but yes," said Alex.

"Wow, amazing," was Sammy's only comment, as she added, "You know, something I've been meaning to ask. How is the water in Greece so blue?"

Pappajohn frowned as Alex parried. "Because Poseidon, the God of the Sea, has borrowed the color from the God of the Sky, Uranus."

"Glad you didn't pronounce it the American way," Pappajohn added.

At nine-thirty they arrived at the ferry dock where paasengers were already boarding. Sammy helped Pappajohn out of the car. "It's a trek to the boat, Gus. Go ahead and get started. Alex can get your bag and catch up."

Grumbling, Pappajohn started trudging towards the gate. "At least there's a ramp."

Alex opened the trunk and gestured toward the next pier. "Athos Cruises is over there. I can run there and drop off Tasos' entry permit if you take the bags to Kosta."

"Don't worry," Sammy said. "Give me his permit. I'll drive over and drop it off before I return to Thessaloniki." She gave Alex's shoulder a squeeze as he handed her the pass. "Have a great trip. See you tonight!"

Alex carried his rucksack and Pappajohn's bag on the other shoulder and hurried off toward Pappajohn who was nearing the ramp. Sammy stood by the car, waving occasionally. Once they'd both boarded, she got in the car and drove over to the Athos Cruises offices downstream. Parking outside the offices selling tickets for the speedboat, she remained in the Citroen until the ferry left the dock. She'd return for her noon reservation after she was ready. She didn't want anyone to recognize her from her appearance now.

"What is it, Kosta? You've been frowning for the last hour. I thought you'd enjoy the beautiful sea and the awe-inspiring view."

"I am, Alex. It's not that." He shook his head. "It's Sammy."

Alex sighed. "I wish she could have joined us. Perhaps EU pressure will change things some day."

"No, I mean it's not like Sammy to give up so easily. Not one feminist comment on our whole drive. Nothing about unfairness, discrimination, equality. That's not the Sammy I know." A deep breath. "I just hope I'm wrong, but..."

"She seemed really excited to visit Thessaloniki and the Jewish museum," Alex said. "I wouldn't worry about her,

Kosta. You can spend a week in Thessaloniki and not run out of things to do."

"I hope you're right, Alex. I pray you are. " Pappajohn forced a smile.

CHAPTER FORTY

S ammy parked on a side street in Ouranopoli and strode
towards her destination. Along the route, she passed several
souvenir shops, some of which displayed fake moustaches and
beards. She considered that choice momentarily, but felt those
costumes would be easily spotted. *Nope, stick with Plan A.*

The hair salon was not busy at this early morning hour and
Sammy was quickly assigned to a female stylist. Sammy had
printed a sixties picture of a mini-skirted Twiggy from the
Internet. She pulled it out and pointed to the hairdo she
wanted. "And make the color *kaffey*," she said, trying to
remember the Greek word for brown.

"But that will be too short for your face," the stylist protested in fair English. "And your red curls are so pretty."

"It's so hot in the summer," Sammy said. "Besides, I'm
tired of dyeing it red," she lied. "I prefer my natural brown,
okay?" *The better to look like Tasos' picture on the ID, my dear.*

The stylist shrugged and shuffled off to mix the dye.
"Whatever you say."

After a leisurely cruise on the west flank of the peninsula, the
ferry docked at the port of Dafni, the main entryway to the
mountain and monasteries. The voyagers lined up to show their
entry passes for admission to the base of the mountain range.
From there a stone and dirt path wound from the sea to the
aeries.

Pappajohn snorted. "It's like the TSA here. Are they worried about terrorists?"

Alex nodded. "A little. They're more worried about women. They believe the presence of a woman will dishonor the Virgin Mary. Mt. Athos doesn't even allow female animals, cows, goats..."

"Passes," announced the bureaucrat manning the station.

Both men handed their passes and were asked to show IDs. Pappajohn pulled out his passport. Alex offered his laminated teal Greek national ID. After a few seconds, the guard waved them in and they began the uphill trek a kilometer southeast to the monastery of Aghios Apostolos where Bishop Theosophos had agreed to meet them at noon.

Pappajohn made slow progress, breathing heavily and speaking only to complain about his knees. "We'd better get there soon. For me, once up, once down. That's it."

CHAPTER FORTY-ONE

S ammy allowed herself no more than a moment of regret as she studied her altered reflection in the salon's mirror. Gone was her natural red color along with her curls. The stylist had a point. But, the new pixie hairdo gave Sammy the boyish appearance she required for her plan.

Noting the cigarette pack in her stylist's apron pocket, she offered the hairdresser a sizable tip and, after paying, asked if she could bum a cigarette. "Take two," said the stylist, smiling, and proffered her pack of Camels and a lighter.

Sammy puffed on the first cigarette and labored not to cough. She waved good-bye and dashed out the door to her car, coughing all the way. Perfect. Exactly what she needed. By the time the cigarette had burned close to the filter, Sammy's voice was scratchy and hoarse.

She kept the lit stub for one more task. Inside the car, she pulled out the laminated Greek ID card with Tasos' fuzzy picture and applied the lighted end of the cigarette over the last two digits of the printed birth year and the digit past the comma under height. The cigarette burned through the laminate and charred the numbers. Anastasios Kapsis would now be fourteen years old and one and a half meters tall.

With a fine pen, Sammy added a loop to the six on the handwritten entry pass birthdate and changed it from 1969 to 1989. One last task - putting on Georgie's suit in the back seat of the rental car - and Sammy would give Yentl a run for her money. Thank heavens they weren't enforcing the 'beard rule' anymore.

Still, Sammy couldn't contain her anxiety when she boarded the speedboat. Her hand shook as she showed her entry pass with her thumb over the birthdate on the ID. The bored greeter waved her on and she settled in for the short ride to the gates of Mt. Athos. *So far so good.*

The rocky coastline and towering green mountain range framed by azure waters was impressive. What a wonderful place to meditate and seek solace. Too bad this beautiful land had been co-opted by the patriarchy who were allowed to practice gender apartheid and discrimination. Sammy recalled a trip to synagogue as a young child with her mother and father before their divorce. The Orthodox temple seated women apart from men. Angry that her family couldn't be together, Sammy asked her mother why. "Tradition" was her mother's answer. "That's the way it is." Sammy refused to go back. And, as she grew, she resolved to change *that's the way it is* to *this is how it should be.*

The loudspeaker on the speedboat was delivering a lecture on the monasteries of Mt. Athos in Greek. Fortunately, there were brochures in a rack on the ship. *Greek, Bulgarian, Romanian, Russian?* She found one in English and skimmed the information provided. Disappointing. Nothing more than she had learned on the Internet last night. The mountain was huge. Where to begin her investigation?

Going to the Aghios Apostolos monastery Phillipos had suggested seemed the wisest course of action, but was guaranteed to bring her right to Alex and Pappajohn. Scratch that. She didn't have time to trek to all the monasteries one by one. Better to try to find Father Mihalis and see how much he knew about why his son did what he did. Perhaps if she asked about Mihalis when she arrived at the entry port, someone could direct her to the monastery where his son had taken his vows. Vows that surely did not include attempted murder.

It was almost one thirty when the speedboat docked at the busy port of Dafni. Hoping to pass as a teen, Sammy disembarked with a group of elderly pilgrims. The strategy almost worked, but this time, the bureaucrat greeting visitors was more diligent. After checking her entry pass, he asked to see the ID card, frowning as he studied the burns over the date and height. What was taking him so long?

"Cigarette," she blurted with a low cracking voice, trying to mimic a Greek accent. *Plan B.* She broke into a spasm of coughing and croaked, "Water." The guard returned the ID card and pass and waved towards a food stand twenty yards up the path. "*Ekei exoune. Pighene.*" Pretending to understand, she tucked the ID's into her suit pocket and hurried towards the stand, hacking loudly.

Once there she pointed to a bottle of water, paid, and drank several sips. Whispering, she asked the vendor, "Speak English?"

"Yes. Many *touristes.* You want food? I have *tiropites* and *spanakopites.*"

"No. Thank you. By the way, you wouldn't happen to know a Father Mihalis?"

"Yes. Three." Annoyed at not making another sale, he turned to a bearded tourist who had approached the stand. "*Tiropites?*"

Sammy dug into her backpack and brought out a two Euro coin. "Give me one of those cheese pies. Six feet tall, gray hair, gray long beard?"

The vendor handed her a lukewarm *tiropita.* "I tell you already. I know three. All three have the gray and the..." He made a gesture by his chin.

Frustrated by her inability to make herself understood, Sammy rolled her eyes and decided to continue on the steep path up the mountain. A young monk ran up to her as she mounted the stairs. "Psst, boy. Father Mihalis of Aghion Therapon?" he asked in broken English.

"I think so," Sammy said. "A church in Athens, near the University."

"Yes. He is visit some time in the Palaia Skete where is his son. Northwest near monasteries Aghios Panteleimon and Aghios Demetrios. Dimitar in the Bulgarian. I take you?"

Sammy nodded and offered him her uneaten cheese pie. "For you. Thank you."

The young monk accepted the treat with a small bow. He devoured it quickly as they set off together. The paths were mostly dirt roads, occasionally sprinkled with pebbles or rocks, and lined by thick green vegetation stretching westward to the blue sea below. As they passed individual monasteries, ancient stone buildings nestled at cliff's edge, some nearby roads were paved with cobblestones. "Slip much in snow in winter," observed the young monk. "You stay for pilgrim?"

Another nod.

"You come to Aghios Pantokratoras. Mine. We have bed."

Sammy smiled and lowered her voice's register. "Yes. Maybe. After I see Father Mihalis."

It took almost an hour to reach a more modern settlement buried in a gully in the mountain and overlooking the sea below. "Here is skete." The monk pointed to the stone steps leading to the monastic house. "You come next time to my. We pray you me."

"Thank you," Sammy said, as she set off down the steep steps, trying not to lose her footing.

"Alexander Matsas!" Bishop Theosophos greeted the curator warmly with a double cheek air kiss.

"My friend, Kostas Pappaioannou," said Alex, introducing Pappajohn in Greek.

Pappajohn leaned forward and took the Bishop's hand, kissing it lightly.

"You were at Professor Lambros' funeral, next to the cousin, yes?" the Bishop asked.

Pappajohn nodded. "You were talking to Father Mihalis and his son in the altar."

The Bishop seemed startled for a minute. "Yes, yes. Was that his son? The one who fell at the Acropolis. *Theos xoresto'ne,* God forgive his soul. What a tragedy."

"We heard Father Mihalis was coming to Mount Athos, maybe to bury his son here."

Sighing, the Bishop said, "I have not seen Father Mihalis, nor heard from him. But, a burial on Mt. Athos will guarantee his son a place in heaven. That may be some solace for a bereaved father. I shall endeavor to minister to the Father." He looked up at Alex. "And what can I do for you? Your call seemed so urgent."

"Philippos suggested we contact you. Professor Lambros had been researching the objects found on the sunken ship *Apocalypsi.*"

"Yes, I attended the gala," the Bishop said. "I cannot forget how Lambros' killer defiled the recovered bronze skeleton of the Panaghia statue with his victim's body. As Ioannis Chrisostomos said, 'We are commanded to have only one enemy, the devil. With him never be reconciled.'"

"Professor Lambros believed the statue may have been of Athena, not the Virgin Mary," Pappajohn said.

The Bishop narrowed his eyes. "That seems unlikely. I prefer to pray that we have been blessed with a glimpse at the consecration of Aghia Panaghia and Issous in the remnants of the statue that have survived."

"Phillipos said we should ask you about this palimpsest," said Alex, as Pappajohn pulled the antique Bible from his bag. "He suspects it may be from a Mt. Athos archive or library."

Alex opened the book to several pages on which Lambros had penciled notes in the margins. "The writing under the Biblical text here is a Homeric Hymn about Pallas Athena. Lambros made notes that he was able to read sections about the Spring equinox and the change of seasons. On this page, he also jotted down *Kairos* and *Astrolabe*. And on this page, *golden ratio*. Finally, here, 'sea voyage to her new home.'"

Theosophos paged through the palimpsest, noting Lambros' comments and occasionally moving his desk lamp's strong light over a magnifying glass to determine a correlation. "I do not believe this book, this palimpsest, came from Aghios Apostolos monastery, though we do have similar documents in our library that have not been overwritten. If you would entrust the Bible to me, I can have our librarians attempt to reproduce more of the underlying writing for you." He pursed his lips. "But, as you know, such work takes time. Months at the very least."

Alex nodded. "Your library has a wealth of information from the days of Emperor Constantine's reign. If we can access historical documents from the fourth and fifth centuries? We were also hoping to locate the source of a photo of a codex Professor Lambros had in his files."

"Of course. We can walk to the library and I will ask Abbot Bartholomeos to allow you to search the stacks. He is very knowledgeable about the planning and construction and of Haghia Sophia in the sixth century as well and provided valuable counsel to Professor Roussos."

Alex smiled. "I understand. Thank you."

As they set off, Pappajohn asked the Bishop, "You've heard about the arrests on Makronissos yesterday? The news is saying the monks are from Mount Athos."

Another sigh. "Chrisostomos also said, 'For a brother, never be at enmity in thy heart.' We must forgive those who stray from the Word of God and Christ and offer them the hope of confession and repentance. Frankly, I myself am not convinced these men are from our monasteries and sketes. It is easy to don the robes; much harder to reject one's vows."

"But there will be an investigation," Pappajohn said. "The police may not be as forgiving."

"What matters is the judgment of God," said the Bishop. "Nevertheless, the Patriarch will be arriving tomorrow and the Archbishop and I have meetings scheduled all day with the Minister of Culture, the Prime Minister, and senior officers in EKAM and Interpol." He led them into the library, where the Abbot was waiting to greet them. "For that reason, I shall leave you here in the able hands of Abbot Bartholomeos to continue your research and I shall return to the business of ensuring the continuation of our globally honored and respected evangelical ministry." His tone was firm, but held a hint of anger.

"Thank you, Bishop," said Alex. "We are very grateful. If our friend Anastasios Kapsis comes to your office, please send him to us, yes?"

The Bishop nodded. "I shall. May God bless you both."

As soon as the Bishop departed, Pappajohn spun on his heels and faced Alex. "What did you say about Tasos?"

CHAPTER FORTY-TWO

"Reservation?" asked an older monk as Sammy reached the highest level of buildings in Palaia Skete.

"No. I am looking for Father Mihalis."

"He died."

Sammy didn't know what to say. "I'm sorry. How?"

"Fell off the Acropolis. Vasilis."

The son? "No, no. I'm looking for his father. Mihalis."

"At Aghios Demetrios. Dimitar. No reservation here, you go now." The monk turned away.

Sammy realized Demetrios was the monastery they'd passed a few minutes before. Sighing, she jogged back up the steps and headed south.

Unlike the skete she'd just left, Aghios Demetrios was the size of a small village. A group of male tourists were strolling down the cobblestone streets and eyeing the colorful two story stone buildings. The monks here paid little attention to Sammy as they strode toward a church in the center square, its Byzantine domes topped by crosses. The ringing bells were beckoning the faithful to worship. Sammy could smell the bitter incense pervading the atmosphere from a block away.

Surely the church would know where Mihalis was, Sammy surmised, so she made her way to the entrance. The air inside was chill and damp, reminding her of the cemetery crypt. She drew a long breath to calm herself and followed a group of tourists into the lobby where long, thin white candles were being sold for one to ten Euros apiece. The visitors in the long queue each dropped coins and bills into a box before taking a candle.

Walking over to a votive stand filled with sand, they lit their candles, and dug the unlit side into the sandbox. Each visitor then stepped over to a gilded icon, made a sign of the cross on their forehead and chest, and air-kissed the icon. Sammy crinkled her face, watching some worshippers actually touch the icon with their lips. As they entered the main auditorium, a monk handed each worshipper a program.

An ornately clad priest walked by as Sammy was approaching the front of the line. "Excuse me," she said, injecting the gravel in her voice more easily as her throat became irritated by the incense in and around the church. "I'm looking for Father Mihalis."

The bearded priest stopped and stared at her intently.

She looked down, hoping he would focus on the hair on her head and not the lack of it on the lower half of her face.

"He is at the library. Three blocks south." The priest walked off, looking miffed.

"You didn't kiss his hand," said an older visitor with an Australian accent. He handed her a candle. "Here. The light is there." He pointed to the stand.

Sammy tried to appear confident as she lit and placed the candle in the sand. Walking over to the icon, she noted that the devout crossed themselves with their three fingers together, like a Girl Schout sign, instead of the open hand Ollie had used before his dive. Leaning into the icon, she attempted to mimic Ollie's cross, but with three fingers bunched, before taking a program and sidling out the exit door.

"Please follow me," said Abbot Bartholomeos in Greek before Alex could respond to Pappajohn. He led them into a massive atrium with hundreds of thousands of books and papers lining rows upon rows of shelves. Around the sides of the room were smaller discrete libraries, many of which displayed ancient texts on tables behind glass windows and doors. In some of the rooms and aisles, monks and civilians were poring over books, jotting down the wisdom in the ancient pages.

"Temperature-controlled, environment controlled," said the Abbot, gesturing at the array of rooms. Our goal is to preserve and protect the knowledge and literature of ancient religious elders and saints. Some of our texts date back to the earliest days of Christianity and the beginning of Constantine's reign in the fourth century Anno Domini."

Alex took a deep breath. Though he had visited Mt. Athos before, this was the first time he could access such a library, such a treasure trove of religious history. Grinning like a child with an ice cream treat, he said, "With your blessing, I shall be a frequent visitor. But, today we are looking for texts relating to the death of Hypatia in Egypt in the year 415. Anything in that time frame in Athens, Attica, or Constantinople."

The Abbot nodded and escorted them to a glass-walled room towards the rear of the atrium. He unlocked the door to a smaller room filled with bound parchments, papers, and manuscripts. "The Julian era of Apostasy." Waving them in," he said, "I must attend to a few urgent events for a few hours, but please make yourselves at home. As you know, we do not allow photos here. However, there are pads on which you can make notes." Nodding, he closed the door and walked back into the atrium.

Pappajohn waited for the Abbot to move out of sight before repeating his question. "Why did you say Tasos was going to join us?"

Frowning, Alex put a finger to his lips. "Please. Whisper. It's a library." Shrugging. "Because he is. Sammy told me he had to work and wouldn't be able to fly out til noon."

"*Ghamo to!* I knew it!" Pappajohn exclaimed.

Alex winced. "Please, Kosta. We're in a monastery." He looked puzzled. "*What* did you know?"

"Tasos had to work today. *All* day. He wanted to come with us, but said he couldn't."

Understanding flickered across Alex's face as the penny dropped. "Oh no."

"You gave her the entry pass, didn't you?"

"Afraid so," he admitted.

"I asked her why she was taking Georgie's backpack, but she said her carry-on was too bulky. Why did *I* believe her?" Pappajohn threw up his hands.

"Listen, there have only been a few women who have penetrated the Mount," Alex said. "We shouldn't worry. Even if Sammy tries, the entry staff will catch her. She'll just be put back on the ferry to return to Ouranopoli. It's been attempted before. The guards know how to look for fake beards and mustaches. Besides, I don't think they sell those in red."

"You don't know Sammy," Pappajohn moaned. "We have to find her before she gets herself arrested." He pulled out his cell and started to dial her number.

Alex shook his head. "Impossible. Mount Athos is hectares and hectares. How would we do that? Where would we go?" He sighed. "I hope that we—you—are mistaken. But, if not, and she is here and she's caught, I still have my friend. I can try at least to ask that they forgive her and let her go without charges."

Pappajohn grunted, as he tried to dial Sammy's phone again and again. "I can't get a signal."

"No signal on my phone either. We'll have to wait." Alex patted Pappajohn's shoulder. "Mt. Athos hosts monks, not murderers. The women who have come to the peninsula in the past have been handled with care. Sammy will be safe, don't worry. We have our job to do and too few hours to do it. Let's begin with the texts here on Julian the Apostate."

CHAPTER FORTY-THREE

Hurrying down the cobblestone streets of the Saint Demetrios monastery, Sammy arrived at the library sometime after six P.M. Adopting a confident stride, she entered the lobby. A monk sitting at the front desk seemed rapt in Bible study. As she approached, she noted this Bible was written in the Cyrillic alphabet.

"Excuse me. I'm looking for Father Mihalis. He was supposed to meet me here."

"You are late. He is in with Abbot Teodor. Go." The monk pointed to a hallway beyond. "Left, right, left, number thirty-three."

Sammy nodded, and set off at a brisk pace down the polished marble hallway. She marveled at the richness of the stained wood, the lushness of the crystal chandeliers, and the variety of the icons and artwork lining the hall and the open rooms filled with bookcases. Taking a moment to pop into one of the empty rooms, she skimmed the titles of books that had survived since the empire of Byzantium.

A lifetime of treasures to study here, would that I could return.

With a sigh, she continued per the monk's instructions and approached room thirty-three. Even from a few feet away, she could hear voices arguing behind the closed wooden door.

The sounds weren't clear, but the language seemed to be mostly English, with perhaps some Greek words. She recognized Father Mihalis' voice from the *Thesaurus* as soon as he cried, "He is murdered!" The priest seemed to be lashing out about his son's death.

"His passion was your fault. You Greeks give up your pragmatism for your faith. That is foolish," said the other speaker in an Eastern European accent. Was that the Abbot talking?

"And you give up your faith for your…"

"For our survival!" shouted the Abbot. "The only words our leaders understand are Euros and dollars. If the spigot dries up, so do we. Now your son's death has loosed the lions and the vultures upon the stronghold it took us years to build. How long will it be before Interpol is at our gates?"

"The Greek government will protect you and Aghios Demetrios. And the others. Our country and Orthodoxy are one."

"You fool yourself, Mihalis. We have hours, perhaps a day or two, before the *gendarmes* arrive. The PASOK party and their Prime Minister Simitis will not fall on their swords for us. They are socialists, and worse, they are secular."

"For that my son gave his life. To keep the pagans and the humanists from our doors. PASOK has forced the civil marriage. They want to burn the dead body like an animal. Will the Olympics next year celebrate Christ? Or Athena? Because of my son, it will be Christ!"

As the argument continued back and forth in the same vein, Sammy tiptoed to the end of the hallway to see what was behind the two large doors framing the wall. Opening one required her full strength. Luckily, the noise of her efforts was masked by the shouting. She slipped into the large room. It was lit only by the afternoon sun streaming from tall windows that stretched from her waist to the wooden beams above. A huge bookcase filled one entire wall.

Sammy crept closer and saw hundreds more ancient and old texts. Surprisingly, many shelves were sitting empty. On the floor were boxes, some filled with books, others with art treasures and icons. Another box had liturgical vestments, crosses, and chalices. Tablets of paper were scattered around the room, documenting and archiving the contents of the boxes, and the intended destination for their safekeeping.

On some of the tables were dusty books. The first Sammy saw was in Cyrillic lettering. She slowly sounded out the words, using the alphabet she'd tried to memorize for her trip to Greece. *Codex Athous Dimitriou.* A second text was in Greek. Sammy recognized the name Archimedes, and a name that she deciphered as Conon. *Conon, the Barbarian?* Swallowing a giggle, Sammy opened the book and saw what appeared to be pages and pages of incomprehensible mathematical calculations and diagrams.

Getting an idea, Sammy pulled out the cell phone she'd bought at the airport Germanos store a few days ago from her suit pocket. Might it have a photo option like Tasos'? *Yes, that looks like a camera lens, and a viewfinder—bingo! Kudos to the EU!* Grateful for the more advanced tech, Sammy started taking photos of some of the most intriguing designs, including a drawing that appeared to depict a spiral snail's shell.

Another book, also written in the Greek alphabet, lay closed on the next table. Sammy was able to make out the words *Hipparchos* and *Korinthos* on the cover. The only word that resonated there was *Korinthos.* She'd seen a city called Corinth south of Athens on the map.

Several pages in this text were filled with drawings of a device that had multiple gears. Some appeared to be simpler, but a few looked like the photos Pappajohn had of the *Apocalypsi* gears and dials, with phases of the sun, moon, and stars. Perhaps these designs could provide more clues as to how the museum's *Apocalypsi* device actually worked. With her cell, she began snapping shots of the drawings and lettering on page after page, faster and faster.

"I'm afraid you'll have to translate the ancient Greek and *katharevousa* for me, Alex. I didn't learn either in Greek School," admitted Pappajohn.

Alex laid down his pencil and smiled at Pappajohn. "Of course. Most of what we have found so far are historical texts and codices that outline the history of the Byzantine Roman Empire from the days of Emperor Constantine in the fourth century ACE. Constantine legalized Christianity and identified Constantinople as the Empire's capital under Greek culture. Emperor Theodosius made Orthodox Christianity the state religion at the end of the fourth century and began banning other faiths.

"Emperor Julian ruled over the Western Provinces during the fourth century and was the last non-Christian ruler of the Roman empire. He encouraged traditional Roman religious practices rather than Christianity to keep the empire together and forbade Christian teachings. So the Church called him Julian the Apostate. His influence remained until Emperor Justinian who was a passionate advocate and supporter of Christianity. Justinian funded the reconstruction of Haghia Sophia as the consummate symbol of Orthodoxy."

Alex pulled over a document to show to Pappajohn. "Here, I did find another reference to the murder of Hypatia in March of 415 CE. Apparently, her death struck fear into the hearts of pagan supporters in the Roman empire, and, I would assume, pagan priests."

"Did you find anything about the *Apocalypsi*, a shipwreck, or the statue being sailed to Constantinople?" Pappajohn asked.

"No, but shipwrecks were common. Remember, only *we* call the ship the *Apocalypsi*, the uncovering. I doubt she even had a name in ancient times. Anyway, if the Athena statue never made it to the capital, her fate would likely not have been recorded by Christian scribes in the Byzantine history texts." Alex scratched his head. "Something puzzles me, though.

Athena would certainly be physically safer in Constantinople, like your friends Keith and Lambros said. I can't help but wonder — with growing anti-pagan sentiments — if nesting her somewhere on Makronissos may not actually have been the safest choice to protect her from the Christian crusaders. Perhaps the shipwreck was in fact caused by the weather and prevented Athena from reaching her intended home on Exile Island. Or…"

Alex leaned back in his chair and, lost in thought, gazed out the room's glass windows.

Pappajohn followed his gaze. Next to the window, a monk was using a manual wheel and pulley system that elevated a platform to the highest shelves of the library atrium in order to reach his desired book. He pointed. "That monk looks like a window-washer. Never been much for heights myself. I always wondered how they dare get up there every day."

Alex sat up in his chair and clapped Pappajohn on his back. "That's it! Kosta, you are a genius!"

Pappajohn looked at him, startled. "What?"

"A lift," Alex said. "They used a lift."

"Okay, now I'm totally lost."

"When we get back to the museum, I'll show you. Archimedes created the first elevator in the third century BCE. It was based on pulleys, winches, and levers. They wound a rope around a wheel operated by slaves. The Colosseum in Rome had multiple lifts that could go up and down all the storeys in seconds. What if the 'statue of Athena' on the *Apocalypsi* wasn't the *real* Athena at all? What if the safest place for the real Athena was her home in the Acropolis instead?"

"And they lifted her with one of those contraptions? A forty foot statue?" Pappajohn was incredulous. "Not very far up, I'd guess."

Alex shook his head. "What goes up, can go down. Say they learned of the turn of events all throughout the Mediterranean.

They must have had a plan in place to protect the most sacred pagan artifacts, including the Athena statue, from the Crusaders." Alex pointed towards the floor. "Down. Deep in the mountain under the Acropolis. A vertical tunnel could have been built over a hundred years — or less. Especially if there were already unexplored caves under the ground, as we've seen throughout mountainous Greece. When the alert finally came, Athena, Protectress of Athens, could have been lowered into the mountain and, in turn, be protected by her subjects."

Pappajohn scoffed. "Quite a leap there, though I suppose it's possible. But if that's the case, then who or what was the statue on the *Apocalypsi*?"

"An excellent question, Kosta. An excellent question indeed."

CHAPTER FORTY-FOUR

A scream from the other side of the wooden doors startled Sammy. Slipping her phone into her pocket, she hid behind a table until she thought it safe to tiptoe over to the double doors and peek into the hall. At least a dozen monks were running toward room thirty-three, chattering in Greek and Eastern European languages.

The door to that room opened. The Abbot stepped out, his mauve robe splattered with specks of black. The monks stood in a semicircle around the Abbot, staring. He spoke in the Eastern European language first, and then in Greek, and, one by one, the monks began to step away. "Return to your tasks." were the only words Sammy heard in English, before the Abbot reentered the room and slammed the door shut.

After the hall emptied, and silence returned, Sammy snuck out and ran towards the front entrance. Whatever had happened in room thirty-three, she didn't want to be around to find out. Or get involved. She hadn't gotten a look inside, but she was sure she didn't see Father Mihalis exit. That didn't bode well. *Time to scram.*

Determined to escape, she tiptoed toward the lobby. Luckily, the monk at the main desk was still immersed in his reading.

Just as she reached the front door, a group of older monks entered. Sammy recognized one of them as the monk who'd handed her a program before she'd snuck out of the church a few hours before.

"Impostor!" he shouted, pointing to her.

Trying to maintain some semblance of control, Sammy began protesting in the deepest possible voice when two monks grabbed her upper arms in a firm grip and walked her back toward the front desk. She was glad she'd removed her bra while putting on Georgie's suit. And, for the first time in her life, she was grateful she was blessed with A-cup breasts. She hoped Georgie's tight suit jacket buttons would keep 'the girls' hidden enough not to divulge her true gender.

"Call the Abbot," one of her captors ordered the monk at the front desk.

The monk dialed a number on his console phone and spoke briefly in a Slavic tongue. Sammy thought she heard the word *Politsya*. Police.

It didn't take long for the Abbot to march down the hallway to the lobby. He was still dressed in mauve robes, but these were not stained. No sign of the black splatter Sammy had seen ten minutes earlier. "What is the emergency?" he demanded in Greek and English.

"This boy," said the church monk, "is an impostor. He does not know how to cross himself. He did it Catholic, not Orthodox. Forehead, left first, and then right, instead of right first and then left. What is he doing here?"

"Being a rebel again," said a voice from the door. A deep voice with a New York accent. *Ilan? Impossible*, Sammy thought.

But it was. Dressed in a long robe, Ilan's face sported a two-day growth of hair. "Teenagers. I'm afraid my son likes to 'poke the bears'," Ilan said. "I brought him here to teach the value of the Orthodox faith and the worship of Christ our God." He shook his finger at Sammy. "You have not learned the lessons I taught. You are not ready to honor our history and culture."

Ilan turned to the Abbot and the other monks. "I truly apologize for my son's poor behavior. I will instruct him better before we return again. Thank you for your understanding."

The Abbot nodded and the monks released Sammy, who slipped next to Ilan. Ilan took Sammy by the ear and made a show of dragging her out of the library lobby.

"Ow, that hurt," Sammy complained as they turned the corner and Ilan led them to the monastery village entrance. She rubbed her ear and tried to kick him in the shins in revenge.

"The proper response is 'thank you'. If the police had arrived, you would have been arrested. Fines, prison, deportation. All of the above."

"I would've talked my way out of it," she muttered as they left the monastery. "Begged them to let me go. Escaped before cops could get here. Something."

"Say again?" Ilan pointed north up the dirt road, where blinking blue lights visible in the twilight were approaching from the distance. "Hurry it up, run."

"That's not for me, is it?" Sammy said, shivering, as she broke into a trot. "Do you know where you're going?"

"Yes. Just keep up. And no, that's not for you. That's for Father Mihalis. And his murder."

CHAPTER FORTY-FIVE

I t was close to eight P.M. when Pappajohn raised his head and looked around. "Do you hear that?"

Alex nodded. "Sirens?"

"Police."

Together they said, "Sammy!"

Without a word Alex tore his note sheets from the tablet and folded them into his pocket while Pappajohn closed the books and replaced them on the shelves in the study. They hurried out of the room and across the atrium floor, ignoring frowns from the researching monks. As they opened the door to the lobby, they ran into Abbot Bartholomeos.

"I was coming to see if you were finished. Did you find what you were were looking for?"

"Yes," said Alex, "thank you. More than you know. But we must be off now, thank you again."

Pappajohn was already nearing the exit door when Bishop Theosophos raced in. "I'm sorry but all visitors have to leave. The boats will gather everyone to depart right away."

"What happened?" asked the Abbot.

"A death at Saint Demetrios! I just got the news.

Pappajohn turned white. "Not...?"

"Yes," said the Bishop. "Father Mihalis is dead."

Sammy and Ilan hiked through the pine forests and skidded down the hill to the beach where Ilan had anchored his boat. The blue lights from the police cars cast an eerie flickering glow on the horizon, framing the demeritorious monastery of St. Demetrios with an azure halo.

Ilan slipped off his robe to reveal bathing trunks. He folded the robe and placed it in his rucksack.

Sammy felt her heart beating faster. Not even Reed had six-pack abs.

"ID's, phone, shoes, jacket, that football backpack. Stuff everything in here. Roll up those trousers and your blouse sleeves," he instructed Sammy. "Hurry." Zipping up the bag, he stepped into the warm water. "Come on."

"Whoa," Sammy said. "I thought you had a boat."

"I do. And Mt. Athos has a shore patrol." He pointed to the cuddy cabin, bobbing in the distance. "You swim, don't you?"

"Um, laps in a pool in LA - breaststroke, with my head out of the water. I don't know if I can make it that far. And the water, now that the sun's setting, it's so black."

"Well, if you don't want us to get caught, start doing a doggie paddle. I'll swim out to the boat and throw you a life-preserver. You can kick while I tow you in. If you get tired, turn and rest on your back. The salt will keep you afloat. Hurry." He dove into the sea ahead of her and began a rapid and smooth crawl stroke.

"Does Greece have sharks?" Sammy asked, but Ilan was too far ahead to hear. She began doggie paddling towards the cuddy cabin boat.

True to his word, at the halfway mark, Ilan swum back to her and helped tow her with the life preserver the rest of the way, and then gave her a lift onto the boat. He handed her a fresh towel before ducking into the cabin. "Back in a minute."

When he returned, he was dressed in a short-sleeved tee and tan shorts looking none the worse for wear. On the other hand, Sammy's pixie hairdo was plastered to her forehead.

"Your turn." He handed Sammy Georgie's backpack, along with her phone and ID, and directed her to the cuddy cabin. His eyes briefly focused on Tasos' ID, and Sammy spotted a hint of a smile.

Below decks, Sammy changed back into her own garb, shaking her head. Georgie's clothing was drenched and muddy. She'd have to buy the boy another suit, perhaps a bigger one, as he would soon grow as tall as his dad.

Back on deck, she offered Ilan a belated thank you.

"You're welcome. But can I now ask what possessed you to sneak onto the mountain? Obviously you know they don't allow women there." He acknowledged her masquerade with a flourish of his hand and a teasing grin. "Not that you don't make a fine looking young man. If that's what floats your boat," he added, winking.

"I was hoping to find Father Mihalis and figure out why his son tried to murder me — us." She pursed her lips. "He was fighting with the Abbot about his son and the other monks, so I thought I'd explore a little while I waited for them to finish. There was this one giant empty room that had tons of old books, artwork, artifacts, etc. Boxes and ledgers all around. Looked like they were trying to pack things up. Then I heard a scream and the Abbot came out of the room. His robes, well I think that splatter could've been blood. I hope..I hope Father Mihalis is okay…"

"Save your breath, Sammy." Ilan started the engine and steered the boat away from the harbor.

"Mihalis really was murdered?"

"Yes. But, I'm sure the Abbot will argue self-defense. He's had time to arrange the scene and none of the monks will dare defy him." Ilan retrieved a small video camera from his pocket and handed it to Sammy. "However, this little item will tell the real story. I installed it on the windowsill outside Teodor's office while they all attended the dawn service this morning.

The Abbot also had a lot more informative ledgers inside his office tracking sales and shipments to and from Athos, Makronissos, and parts beyond, that I was able to photograph. I would have rescued you sooner, but I had to undo the installation first."

Sammy studied the tiny camera. "Impressive," she admitted. "In fact, if I didn't know better, I'd suspect you aren't a museum curator, but some kind of secret agent."

"Moi? Nah, a secret agent wouldn't know an amphora from an athame," he said, as he swung the boat towards Ouranopoli. "But the information I've collected will allow Captain Katsoulis and her team to help our museum reclaim the items that we want to bring home."

The crowds at Dafni filled the entry area as passengers were herded onto a variety of boats and ferries for the trip back to Ouranopoli. Rumors about the reason for this exodus were rampant, and Pappajohn was relieved that the name "Sammy Greene" hadn't cropped up. Still, Anastasios and Tasos were both common names in Greece, and they recurred among the murmurs, shouts, and greetings in the crowd enough to worry Pappajohn.

He tried to catch a signal to call Sammy's cell, but, still no luck. Frustrated, he inched over to one of the entrance staff and brought out the old badge he still carried in his back pocket. "Has anyone been arrested?"

Most ignored him, but one harassed staffer shouted, "We are a polity, and your badge does not mean anything here. Our rulers are God, Christ, and the Holy Spirit.

Pappajohn was ready with a retort, but Alex pulled him away. "Kosta, forget it. There's nothing we can learn or do here. Let's go back to Ouranopoli and, if Sammy isn't waiting for us, we can try to call her from there. Please. If she's in trouble, I will call my friend."

Pappajohn shook his head and trudged onto the ferry, his face drawn.

As they sat on a bench on the boat, Alex whispered into Pappajohn's ear. "You are not worried that she...that she is hurt, too?"

"No. Not Sammy. But I should have known. I could have stopped her."

CHAPTER FORTY-SIX

I lan docked his boat next to the pier.

As Sammy hopped off, he handed her her backpack.

"You're not coming up?"

He shook his head. "No. I have some tasks waiting for me in Athens." He smiled. "Now, if you want to come with me…?"

Sammy grinned. "Rain check, okay? Gus and Alex will worry if I'm not here to pick them up."

"Okay, rain check. Perhaps not too far in the future we can sail together. How about from Cyprus to Haifa?" With a hearty wave, Ilan swung the cuddy cabin boat around and sped off into the darkness of the sea off the coast of Halkidiki.

After waving back, Sammy jogged over to where she'd parked her car. She tossed the moist backpack into the trunk knowing she'd likely have some 'splaining to do'. Somehow, she'd have to slip Tasos' ID back into his wallet tonight. Hopefully, a new suit for Georgie, and a Nintendo DS game as a bribe, could keep the pre-teen from asking too many questions.

She drove the Citroen to the parking lot where a line of vehicles waited for returning pilgrims. As she stepped from the car, she spotted a packed ferry approaching. It was almost ten P.M. Perfect. Pappajohn and Alex should be onboard if they wanted to make the midnight flight.

Sure enough, Pappajohn was among the first travelers off the ferry. As he walked down the ramp he leaned on Alex. Sammy waved but realized that, with only a quarter moon, they probably wouldn't recognize her with the new hair color and pixie cut. She waited until they got closer and yelled, "Alex, Gus, over here!"

Alex appeared startled. "Is that you, Sammy?" he asked as they approached the car. "Wow. Nice haircut."

Pappajohn looked at Sammy and shook his head. "So how *was* the Jewish museum?"

Sammy chose to ignore his obvious sarcasm. "I decided on a spa day instead, Gus. Don't you like my new 'do'? Got tired of all the curls in this weather. It was so cheap. Only thirty Euros for the cut and dye." She did a dance turn to show off her new style.

Pappajohn seemed both angry and relieved. "Kicked you out of Mt. Athos, didn't they?" He resisted her offer to help him into the car. "You're lucky they didn't arrest you. We were very worried. Especially when the police arrived."

"Police?"

"There was a death," Alex informed her. He opened the driver's side and stepped in.

Sammy feigned surprise as she took her seat in the back. "Oh, no. What happened? Were you there?"

"No," Alex said, "we were at a different monastery. It happened at Saint Demetrios. Father Mihalis."

"Father Mihalis? You're kidding." *Sell it, sell it, Sammy.* "How did he die?"

"We're not sure," Alex replied, as he started the car and drove off towards Thessaloniki. "There's been a clampdown on any communications. They're moving all the visitors off the island, too." He glanced at Pappajohn. "Kosta may be able to learn something from Captain Katsoulis in a day or two."

Sammy met Pappajohn's narrowed eyes in the car's side view mirror. If he'd sucked on a lemon, Pappajohn's expression couldn't have been more sour. Sammy hoped it was because of Alex's comment, and nothing more.

CHAPTER FORTY-SEVEN

I t was well after midnight when a taxi returned Sammy and Pappajohn from Venizelos airport to Moschato, weary and somber. The two hadn't spoken since Alex left them at the arrivals gate. Pappajohn unlocked the door to Tasos' and Daphne's apartment. More silence. Apparently the family was asleep.

"Okay, I know you're mad, Gus," Sammy whispered, hoping to break the ice. "But I'm not sorry I did what I did."

"I thought I heard the door," Daphne said, coming out of her bedroom clad in a cotton robe.

"What did you...." she stared at Sammy. "Your hair! It's adorable! I'm sure it will be so easy to take care of. I wish I could cut mine short like that, but Tasos would have a fit."

Sammy shrugged. "One advantage to not having a boy-friend."

Pappajohn frowned. "Why don't you tell Daphne *why* you cut your hair?"

An eye roll. *Should I spill the beans?* Why not? "I tried to sneak onto Mt. Athos. I thought this haircut would make me look more like a boy."

Daphne raised an eyebrow as she pointed to Sammy's jean shorts, T-shirt and sandals. "Dressed like that?"

Sammy hesitated. "Georgie lent me his backpack and I, uh, borrowed his clothes." Sammy opened the bag. "I do have to apologize to him and to you. I, uh, fell, and I'm afraid his suit is ruined. I'll buy him a new one tomorrow, I promise." She handed Daphne the damp jacket and shirt.

"Nonsense, Georgie is growing out of his clothes so fast, I wouldn't be surprised if these don't even fit him any more." She laughed. "Besides, Mt. Athos needs to join the twenty-first century. Good for you for trying to sneak in."

Pappajohn shook his head. "We were very worried. She could have been arrested. Or worse."

"But she wasn't, right? And *we* were worried about you and Alex. The news came on about a death on the island, but they didn't tell us who. Tasos finally called around and learned it was an old priest."

"Father Mihalis," Pappajohn said.

"Oh, my God. The priest whose son was killed at the Acropolis?"

"Yes."

"Goodness." Daphne said, shaking her head, "Look, you've both had a hard day. How about we all have a cup of chamomile before bed?"

"That would be great," Sammy said. "Gus?" She offered him a warm smile.

Pappajohn inhaled a deep breath. He looked at Sammy, and sighed. "I won't say I approve of what you did, but I can say I'm glad you're okay. That we're all okay. Because you never know…" He didn't have to finish his sentence.

"What the hell time is it?" It was clear from Kiki's voice that she'd been asleep when her phone rang.

"You told me to call," Alex said.

"At two in the morning? I'm not a party girl any more."

"Couldn't wait. I had to tell you what we found."

"Okay, I'm sitting up. What did you find?"

"Texts corroborating Harris' theory that Parthenon officials wanted to protect the Athena statue from Crusaders.

Harris thought these pagan priests sent her to a new home in Constantinople in the Constantinian dynasty, but I believe he was wrong."

"That would certainly make Roussos happy. So it really *was* the Virgin Mary then?"

"I don't think so. What if the statue of Athena or whoever on the *Apocalypsi* was just a decoy?"

"Of Athena? Then where did the real one go?"

"Still at the Parthenon." Alex ventured.

Kiki scoffed, "Covered with an invisibility cloak?"

"No, Kiki. Covered with pebbles and rocks. Lowered by a lift into the Acropolis mountain."

"Tell me *you're* asleep and you're just talking in your dreams."

"We'll come in and meet you in the office tomorrow. Give me a chance and I'll show you how it could have worked."

"Okay, Alex. I'll just pretend I'm dreaming then and Roussos had it right all along. See you tomorrow, *Geia.*"

Sammy forced herself to stay awake until she was sure everyone was fast asleep. Thankful that Daphne had been so understanding about Georgie's clothes, she was less sure that Tasos would appreciate what she'd done to his ID. Tiptoeing into the master bedroom, she carefully placed the card back in Tasos' wallet. Hopefully, it would be a long time before he pulled it out and noticed the cigarette burns on its face.

Creeping back into her own room, she settled onto the cot and fell asleep the moment her head hit the pillow. Still, she couldn't keep mayhem, monks, and murder out of her dreams.

CHAPTER FORTY-EIGHT

Tuesday, June 10ᵗʰ, 2003

"Ah, my colleague from Mossad. Have you been enjoying Greece, Mr. Einav? " Captain Katsoulis asked as Ilan entered her office and took a seat opposite her desk.

"Just arrived back at Piraeus," he said, stretching his arms and legs. "As I expect you're aware."

Katsoulis adopted a poker face.

"Nice try. I'd do the same thing if you came to Israel," Ilan admitted. "Anyway, I've been trying to get the proof we've needed on our black marketeers, Lord Wellington and his buddy Monsieur Dumas. I've heard buzz that their yacht may be leaving Lavrium for Monaco instead of Piraeus today. Your raid on Makronissos has cast a pall on their little vaca-holiday."

"None of the monks have given up their buyers," Katsoulis complained. "Not one word about Wellington or Dumas. And the monks' records and transaction ledgers are all in code. I have nothing that allows me to legally stop the *Wellesley* from leaving Greek waters."

"You do now." Ilan brought out a USB cord and asked to upload the photos and videos from his tiny cameras. "As a vacationing camper on the northwest shores of Makronissos for a day or so, I was a tourist just hiking and bird-watching. And look at the vultures my camera happened to catch."

Over the next half hour, he uploaded a day's worth of photos of stolen artifacts, ledgers and receipts as well as videos. These showed Jean Dumas and the monks negotiating at

Makronissos, then delivering their black market purchases by dinghy to Lord Wellington who waited on the yacht. "It's all yours, Captain. In exchange we get the Masada artifacts back by next year, yes?"

Katsoulis nodded as she dialed her phone and gave orders in Greek. "Send Antonis and his unit to the pier and hold the *Wellesley*. I'll be out there with the warrants as soon as I can."

She stood and offered a handshake. "Thank you, Mr. Einav. I am truly grateful. Now I need to see the judge and meet with the Coast Guard. We'll keep you apprised about the Makronissos finds. You'll get them back right after the trials."

"Wait. I do have one more item I've uploaded."

"Maybe some other time. I'm in a hurry."

But Ilan had already started the recording. "You'll want to see this. Abbot Teodor and Father Mihalis at Saint Demetrios monastery last night. I placed a video camera in the ringleader's office to catch any Makronissos follow-up after the arrests."

Katsoulis' eyes narrowed. She sat down again and focused on the screen, turning up the volume to hear traces of the argument between the clergymen.

"Fast forward to the end," Ilan instructed. "Play there."

Almost an hour into the video, a cursing Father Mihalis could be seen aiming a fist at the Abbot's chin, blaming him for his son's death, threatening to turn him in to the police. Teodor backed away and grabbed an ornate knife he used as a letter opener — an athame, Ilan explained. Lunging at Mihalis, the Abbot stabbed Mihalis repeatedly in the chest and abdomen. It took several minutes before the priest's screams faded into silence.

Katsoulis stared at the screen as the video wrapped up with Teodor wiping the blood off his hands and exiting into the hall. She exhaled a deep breath after the movie ended. "So it was Teodor who got Mihalis' son involved in his black market trade. We've been trying to catch these rogue monks for years, but they've always been one step ahead. I need to call Thessaloniki right away." A hint of a smile. "Thank you…"

"Sorry I didn't get there in time to stop them, but the video is yours." As he stood, Ilan spied a large, bulky film camera lying on the floor on the other side of Katsoulis' desk. He pointed and tsked. "Couldn't afford anything more modern?"

"What? Oh, that. No, it's not ours. It's an old Nikonos camera from CNN. I got it from Lavrium the other day. Belonged to a CNN reporter who died years ago during a dive off the *Thesaurus*. We haven't had a chance to check the film yet, probably waterlogged. Forensics is a little backed up after the last two days, if you can't guess."

"We can help, if you want. Avram has been docked at Piraeus with the mobile lab. We can get it back to you this afternoon."

Pursing her lips she considered the offer, and finally said, "Yes, take it. Go."

By noon, Pappajohn and Alex had laid out all the materials they'd collected on a large table in a conference room at the Hellenic Archaeological Museum. On one end were some of the new artifacts Alex, Sammy, and Gus had taken from Makronissos. Photos of the palimpsest pages with Lambros' notes, the photo of his codex, and Alex's notes from Mt. Athos lay in the middle. Facing across, were the printed dial photos from Harris Lambros' and Georgie's cameras. They'd been enlarged to life-size on Alex's computer. Beside these was the reconstructed Apocalypsi device Alex had reclaimed from Makronissos. He'd placed the rusty dial and gear behind the three polished ones. At the very end of the table were copies of museum exhibit guides on Archimedes' elevator as well as engineering specs for the Roman Colosseum elevators.

Alex took the lead, walking Kiki, Sammy, and Pappajohn through the collected evidence. "Harris' codex photo from his office here records a report of the murder of Hypatia in 415 CE and the increased aggression of the new crusaders," Alex lectured. "At Mt. Athos yesterday, we found several documents from the fifth and sixth centuries that refer to this event as a turning point that struck fear in the hearts of pagans throughout the Roman empire." He handed his notes to Kiki, who began scanning them.

"Lambros' Bible palimpsest overwrote Homeric Hymns, which described Pallas Athena as the protector of Athens, her namesake city. Harris made some notes in the margins of several pages," Alex said, pointing to the photos. "These indicate that the guardians of Athena were deeply concerned about preserving the embodiment of their goddess. Harris believed they hoped this burst of Christian violence would fade in the future with a return to co-existence, as promoted by the pragmatic Emperor Julian. Bishop Theosophos promised to have his librarians work on the actual palimpsest to identify as much of the underwriting as possible. But that may take months."

Sammy asked, "So you're saying they moved the statue onto the warship in the fifth century, and sent it to…?"

"Constantinople," Pappajohn jumped in. "Or Makronissos, like Lambros suggested in his PowerPoint, and like you suggested yesterday, Alex. But now you don't agree. Why do you think the statue is still at the Acropolis?"

"Emperor Flavius Theodosius was not an apostate. He was influenced by his sister Pulcheria to become a fanatic Christian. Based on the texts we reviewed in the Aghios Apostolos library, Theodosius went to war against the king of the Sassanids who was persecuting Christians. He also collected all the laws made since the reign of Constantine I, published as the Codex Theodosianus. With his navy patrolling the Aegean Sea, a trireme with the pagan statue would be an inviting target for attack by Christian sailors. A gilded statue would be destroyed without qualms to provide the tons of gold needed for the decoration of the Haghia Sophia."

Kiki nodded. "Even getting to Makronissos would be a challenge, considering all the traffic of the period in these straits. But if they were transporting the Virgin Mary…? They could wrap the statue in cloth, make part of it look like Panaghia for any curious inspectors and get a free pass to Makronissos or Constantinople." She frowned. "When was Hypatia killed?

"March 415 CE," said Alex.

"Then the weather could be the cause of the shipwreck," Kiki suggested. "November through March in the Med is *Mare Clausum*."

"The seas are closed," Alex translated. "But, that's the point. Not a decoy Virgin Mary, but a decoy Athena, with a bronze skeleton covered with cloth, on a ship that is accidentally or intentionally capsized…? The Crusaders will be convinced that Athena rests at the bottom of the sea. When they reach the Parthenon, they will no longer aim to desecrate Athena. God and Christ will have already done it for them, so to speak."

"And, in either case, the *Apocalypsi* sailors could swim to Makronissos and catch a boat home," Pappajohn suggested.

"Let's say you're right, Alex. What do you think they did with the real statue?" asked Sammy.

Alex walked over to the end of the table with the elevator diagrams. "Take a look at the designs for these lifts, centuries before the year 415 CE. The artisans who built the Parthenon, the Erechtheum, and the Theseum had the technology to build a functioning manual elevator and shaft. Instead of risking the real Athena on a perilous sea voyage, they could lower her into the ground to keep her safe until the Crusaders receded."

"Assuming that's so, where would she be then?" asked Kiki.

"Occam's Razor. The most obvious explanation is usually the whole picture."

"And that is…? Kiki urged.

"In the Acropolis itself. Removing the marble blocks on the floor of the Parthenon and lowering the statue into a pre-dug shaft in the mountain is easier than trying to move it somewhere else under the eyes of approaching fanatic Christians and their spies."

Pappajohn shook his head. "Still sounds like science fiction to me. Though if it was technically possible, I guess it makes sense."

Sammy scratched her chin. "The Christians never left Athens, right?"

"Right," said Alex. "But, over almost two millennia, Christianity evolved. Mature religions tend to be less prone to consider or embrace violence. Perhaps Athena could have risen again to find a place in a more diverse and tolerant society such as modern Greece. Unfortunately, before such a Rennaissance, the Byzantine Empire fell to Ottoman conquest, followed by centuries of war. That's a likely reason why Athena has not returned for over fifteen hundred years." Smiling, Alex added, "I posit the statue is nested below the Parthenon, and if we look in the right place, we will find her."

CHAPTER FORTY-NINE

I lan watched Avram gingerly remove the film from the CNN camera and begin the restoration process.

"There's some aging," Avram said in Hebrew, "but it's salvageable. The compartment was waterproof. Look at the etching inside here. I think this camera may have been the reporter's, not CNN's."

Ilan leaned in to see the faint scratches which read Oliver Haines. Ollie? Sammy's Ollie? "How long do you think it'll take?"

"I should have it by this afternoon. Go back to your hotel and take a nap and a shower. I'll call you if anything comes up sooner."

"Okay," Kiki said after considering Alex's theory. "If you're correct, exactly where is the statue?"

"The obvious answer seems to be where it stood in the Parthenon," Alex said. "Thankfully, there are a number of surviving texts and drawings that show the location of Athena in ancient times in the center of the temple, facing east. In fact, I'm told our museum was contacted in 1982 for specs and information, when the Athena statue was commissioned for the Parthenon in Nashville, Tennessee."

Sammy's ears perked up. "You know, Jim Lodge, my radio producer slash engineer, is in Nashville now. His brother is playing in the Grand Ole Opry."

"There's a Parthenon in Nashville?" Pappajohn asked.

"It was built years ago," Sammy said. "Loukas Doxiadis told me they've made it look exactly like the one in Athens. With copies of the Elgin Marbles and all the original colors. It's an art museum now."

Kiki's look was withering. "We may agree to support the marketing of our culture, but we vehemently oppose its Disneyfication. At least they have finally added the gilding of the statue in the style of Phidias' plans." She turned to Alex. "Well, if you are correct, it would either be where the statue originally stood or not. Didn't the renovation team do a ground penetration radar study of the Parthenon a few years ago?"

Alex nodded. "I pulled the report. There's a network of small caves and tunnels identified in the mountain, but none of them large enough to hold Athena. And, no, the rest of the mountain was read as layers of stone. Nothing about a shaft or a statue."

Kiki shrugged. "Well then."

Alex raised a hand. "Wait. The radar picked up bands of stone and the cave hollows, none greater than two metres. But, what if Athena had been lowered deep into the mountain, and then stones were placed around and above her to fill up the shaft? The report does note layers of stone across the mountain down to twenty meters, some of which have changed direction and angles due to repeated earthquakes. They weren't able to go deeper because the stones absorbed the sound waves. You can ask Elias at the Acropolis Museum if their team would be willing to do another ground radar run."

Kiki sighed. "I can *ask*. But what if his findings are the same as before? That is, nothing."

"Then we would have to explore below the floor of the Parthenon manually, meter by meter."

Kiki shook her head. "Somehow I can't see Elias and the Acropolis Museum excavation team buying into that option."

"No, I wouldn't expect you to do that. Our first step would be to try to define exactly where we need to dig."

"Oh, that's all. Okay, how do you propose to do that?" Kiki asked, unconvinced, continuing the sarcasm. "I vote for the site where the statue stood."

"Actually, Loukas showed me where that was," Sammy said. "There was a reflecting pool in front of the statue and you can still see where the marble was cut."

Kiki's smile was patronizing. "The floor of the Parthenon has multiple cuts and erosions. And there was a votive room and storage area enclosed by columns behind Athena which has not yet been restored.

"Kiki's right," Alex said. "Right under the statue would be difficult. How do you dig a shaft when the statue sits over the opening? Remember, the shaft construction, like Rome itself, was not built in a day." He walked over to the enlarged photos of the dials laid out along the table. "No, I expect that the shaft was in a different location, but likely nearby." Smiling, he looked at the others one by one. "We've focused on the statue and the arguments between Roussos and Lambros. We've investigated the illegal trading in artifacts, amphorae, solidi, codices. But, we've glossed over the *Apocalypsi* device itself."

"I thought your display said it was like a compass. Or something like that. They used it to navigate the ship, right?" said Pappajohn.

"An astrolabe," Alex offered. "Yes, we believe so. But it could have had other functions, too. Think of the Antikythera mechanism, found over a hundred years ago off the Greek island whose name it bears. It's believed to be the first analogue computer, using the methods of Hipparchus, built somewhere near or around Rhodes or Korinthos, Corinth."

"Corinthos?" Sammy sat up in her chair. "Wait a minute." She flipped open her phone and scrolled through the stored photos she'd taken. "Here. And you said Hipparchus, too, right?"

Alex frowned and walked over to see what she had.

"There was a codex, stolen from the Library of Pergamon. I took some pictures with this *schnazzy* Europhone. There were drawings of a device that resembled ours, only it was older, and had a lot more dials and gears. Some of the dials do look similar, and there's writing in Ancient Greek next to each sketch. If we can print these out and blow them up, too, you might be able to read them."

Alex's face was a chaos of emotions. "Yes. Kiki, can you upload these? Then we can enlarge them and bring them in here to study. I recognize similar dials from the Antikythera mechanism in some of these designs." To Sammy: "Where did you find these?"

Sammy quickly glanced at Pappajohn. *Was that a look of surprise or suspicion? Oh well.* "In the library of the monastery of St. Demetrios."

CHAPTER FIFTY

T he phone's vibration woke Ilan. Opening one eye, he checked his watch. Three P.M. *Well, a couple hours of sleep was better than nothing.*

"Good morning," he said in Hebrew.

"Not so good," returned Avram. "Come see the film."

Twenty minutes later, Ilan boarded Avram's boat and joined his colleague in its laboratory. "I converted the film to an MPEG-4 file so we can keep a copy." He handed Ilan several flash drives. "And one for you." He stored the developed film in a sealed tin and rested it on Ilan's lap. "For your police friend. Now watch."

"I am fast forwarding through a lot of what the media people call B-roll. Shots of the ship and the *Thesaurus* expedition team."

Ilan burst out laughing when he spotted a younger Roussos sporting a pencil-thin mustache and sideburns. And Doxiadis - hair down to his shoulders and a beard to match. Pretty Sammy with her red curls. The expression on her face suggested she wasn't enjoying the ship's rocking. Poor Lambros, waddling on the deck, resembled a quacking puffer fish among the scuba divers and other archaeologists.

"It's a ways in. Just a lot of chattering scientists and some views of Makronissos rising into the rain and fog. Now the dive."

The next section showed a different universe, dark and peaceful. Ilan was a capable scuba diver, but Ollie was clearly a

265

professional underwater photographer, beautifully capturing the colorful mystery and danger of the dimly lit floor of the strait where the *Apocalypsi* had ultimately lain to rest.

"Here," Avram said.

Ilan studied the video. The film shook as Ollie tried to lift something from the sandy floor. Good, he got it — wait, it looked like one of the dials and gears from the Apocalypsi device. Ilan tapped Avram on the shoulder. "Give me a close-up of that, will you?"

Alex squinted as he focused. The dial showed Roman lettering that read Quintilis and Sextilis. A Julian calendar, perhaps?

Avram hit PLAY and the video began again. Agitation and thrashing. Ollie had aimed the camera to show that his fin was caught. More shaking made it difficult to see details until a second diver came into view and disconnected Ollie's oxygen and grabbed what looked like a dial from his vest pocket. Amazingly, the camera had continued to film. The last shot on the reel was of the killer reattaching Ollie's oxygen and releasing his body so it could rise to the surface. At that moment, Ilan got a glimpse of the features of the murderous diver, stretched behind the mask. Damn if he didn't look like the monk who died at the Acropolis.

Captain Katsoulis had just returned from Lavrium and was not pleased to see Ilan at her door holding Ollie's camera. "Nothing, huh?"

Ilan handed her the camera. "I don't think this is CNN's. My guess, it belongs to the murder victim."

Katsoulis froze. "Did you say murder victim?"

Ilan pulled the film tin from his pocket and handed it to her, along with one of Avram's flash drives. "The last five minutes. But I don't think you'll have to worry about a prosecution. Not in this world, anyway."

Pappajohn sat back in his chair with a huff. "*Ghamo to!*"

Alex pursed his lips, and Kiki burst out laughing.

"Dammit, girl," Kiki said. "You've got testicles, going into Mt. Athos."

"Well, that would've helped," Sammy joked. "Come on, guys, it's not the end of the world. Without civil disobedience in the United States, we'd still have Jim Crow."

Kiki and Alex looked at each other, puzzled.

"This is Greece, Sammy. Not America," Pappajohn snapped.

"Without *me*, she'd have been deported back to America by now," said a Brooklyn-accented voice from the door. "Fortunately, they believed she was my son." Ilan entered the room and walked around the table, nodding with an occasional "hmm". "Looks like you're making some progress here." He handed a flash drive to Sammy. "Just came to drop this off. It's a copy of the film from your colleague Ollie's camera."

Sammy's expression sobered quickly. "Wow. How did you get it?"

"Captain Katsoulis. But I suggest you don't watch it until you're ready. Even *with* balls, it's horrible to watch a good man die." Ilan paused at the section of the table with the photos of the dials. "Hmmm. Where did you get this photo?" He picked up a picture of one of the dials with carved lettering of the Julian calendar months.

Pappajohn looked at the photo. "From Lambros' camera in his apartment. But we never found the actual dial. Why?"

Ilan turned to Sammy. "Because a very bad person, who is now dead, stole it from your friend Ollie, and maybe again from Lambros as well." He focused on the flash drive gripped in Sammy's hand. "Only when you're ready. There is nothing that can be done any more."

Ilan walked to the door and turned to address the group. "The Captain informed me that her team has recovered the stolen artifacts from our Masada exhibition. We'll have them back by next year." He smiled, adding, "So, I'll be leaving for home soon. I'm glad everything turned out for the best." He nodded at the display on the table, then waved. "Hope your research goes well, too. *Geia*!"

"Ilan, wait," Sammy cried, jumping up from her seat and following him out the door. "You telling me the camera caught Ollie's death?"

Ilan stood in the hallway, his face a mask of pity. "No, Sammy. I'm sorry to say that the camera caught your colleague's murder."

As Alex and Pappajohn waited for Kiki and Sammy to return, Alex tried to answer Pappajohn's questions about the Antikythera mechanism.

"Hipparchus was the theorist, but the manufacture of these devices took place in Rhodes. What we know so far about the mechanism is that the ancients moved or turned each dial to manipulate each parameter, just as today we enter data into a computer via a keyboard. The gears between the dials aligned each dial with the others to perform a calculation and produce a result. Think of an abacus or a slide rule, in which the data entry is manual, but the ratio or relationships for each data point are predetermined."

"You'll note the dials in the photos are of different sizes," he continued. "Some have writing, some have Greek numbers, some have holes, and some have etched arrows. We have the three dials and the gears the thief left in the display case right here on the table as well." He pointed to the device with three restored dials and their gears connected and a rusty dial and gear at the end. "Fortunately, the night of the gala, our thief ignored three out of the four dials, the ones which displayed Greek numbers, and took only the Zodiac dial, with the ornate etchings of the constellations." Alex suddenly stopped talking, a frown dawning on his face.

"What?" asked Pappajohn.

"Peculiar. The Zodiac dial is an impressive work of art, but I would think someone eager to solve the mystery of Athena would grab all the tools available. And that includes all the dials and all the gears."

"Maybe he didn't have time," Pappajohn offered.

"True. But the murderer did take the time to stage Lambros' body in the statue…"

"Or, maybe he couldn't carry them out during the gala without getting caught," Pappajohn suggested. "Especially in a tuxedo."

"Good points," Alex acknowledged. "Let's see what, if anything, these other dials tell us."

They both paused as Sammy trudged in, looking pale and disheartened.

"Our monk killed Ollie," she muttered. "I just can't believe it." She pointed to the photo of a dial with the names of the Latin months. "For that dial."

"Your monk?" asked Pappajohn. "What? You mean the one who tried to assaulted you at the Acropolis?"

Sammy nodded.

"Oh, my God" was all Alex could say.

"Wait a minute," said Pappajohn. "That has to mean this dial, these dials, are critically important. If they're motive for murder. Mur*ders*."

Alex took a deep breath before agreeing. "And we only have four of them here. We still don't have in hand the Zodiac dial, the months, the moon, the winds, or the Kairos dial. Just their photos." He glanced at the device next to the picture. "All we have are three dials and gears with Greek numbers, and the dial from Makronissos showing the movement of the sun."

"We'll have to make do with what we have, Alex," said Pappajohn. "Detectives don't always have all the clues when they start an investigation. We work with what we've got, and, if we're lucky, those clues put us on the right path and lead to others." He eyed the built device. "For example, I see that all four of the dials there are different sizes, from smaller to larger. That makes sense, if you want to read the results. You wouldn't want a big dial to hide a little one, right?"

Alex nodded. "So let's see the sizes of photos we have. Starting from the back, we have the largest one, the Zodiac dial, the one stolen from the back of the device on the night of the murder. In the photo, you can see etchings of all the constellations and Zodiac symbols around the perimeter of the dial. For example, today is 22 May, so we could turn it to Gemini."

"Gregorian or Julian calendar?" asked Kiki, as she walked in and laid down the enlargements from Sammy's phone camera above the dial photos on the table.

"You're right." Alex tapped his temple with a finger. To Sammy and Pappajohn: "We use the Gregorian calendar nowadays. It's more accurate than the Roman Julian calendar. But in the first century, it would have been Julian. It changed in 1582 in much of Europe, but in Greece, in 1923, dropping thirteen days." He turned the dial again. "So, that would make it 9 May, and Taurus, the Bull."

"Bull. That's what it is." A laugh escaped from Kiki.

Alex gave her an icy glare.

"Now the next dial would probably be your colleague's. Ollie's." Alex said to Sammy. "It has the names of the months etched in Latin. After that, maybe the one with the phases of the moon and its position in the sky, the photo here. Then, the phases of the sun, at the back of our device, thank you, Kiki and your reconstruction team. Next, maybe the one with twelve radial lines and Greek numbers. There are a few letters under each Greek letter number, *Απαρκτιας, Βορεας, Καικιας.* I believe this is a classic twelve wind rose. A Greek wind compass."

"Ah, *that* was the twelve Georgie counted," Sammy said. "What *is* a wind compass?"

"Well, Thales and Socrates experimented with the properties of magnetic lodestones," said Alex, "but the magnetic compass arrived in Europe in the Middle Ages. It's possible that some traders might have brought magnetic compasses to Eastern Europe through Persia or India from China even before the Silk Road, but most Greek and Roman sailors used an eight point or twelve point compass based on the direction of the winds to navigate. For example, *Aparctias* was a north wind, and *Voreas* was NNE." Alex grabbed a piece of paper to sketch what he'd just explained.

"Interesting," said Pappajohn as he studied the drawing.

Kiki pointed to some of Sammy's photos. "You got earlier versions of these dials, Zodiac, sun, moon, winds, four, eight, twelve. And a series of columns of Greek numbers. An amazing discovery." She looked at Sammy and produced a genuine smile. "Your photos will help us understand more about how the Antikythera mechanism and the *Apocalypsi* device were used. May I share these with our colleagues at the Athens

Archaeological Museum? I'm sure they'll be visiting St. Demetrios' library ASAP."

"If the books are still there," Sammy warned. "I saw the monks packing things up. My guess - to get them out of the monastery."

Pappajohn interjected. "They won't get far. Not with Despina and Interpol on their trail."

"I'll call our colleagues today, as soon as we're done," Kiki said. "Alex, aside from showing us how the sailors navigated their ships back then, I can't see how this information helps us find Athena on dry land in Athens. Unfortunately, without the attached gears, we can't incorporate the dials in the photos into the device we've reconstructed. We can only tell what they were measuring, but not how they were connected together."

Alex sighed. "I know. We'll have to work with the four dials we have connected." He nodded at Pappajohn. "And see if they lead us to the path to Athena."

"What about the Kairos dial? Did it work with the winds to help determine the weather? Or was it some kind of clock to go with the sun, the moon, and the stars?" Pappajohn asked Alex.

"You're right, Kosta. *Kairos* means weather in modern Greek, but in ancient Greek, it meant 'time'. Not necessarily time of day. More like time to grab an opportunity or make a decision."

Pappajohn nodded. "So what do these concentric letters say in ancient Greek?"

"Other than the word *Kairos* on one side of the dial, the letters on the other side circle around the dial, in a Mycenean style of writing." Alex squinted to read the faint, sandblasted letters. "*If you are a friend, you will find what you seek*," he translated from the ancient Greek.

"Oh, that's clear as mud," said Pappajohn. "I just got a hankering for Chinese food."

"I thought the numbers on the other three dials would be harder to decode," Alex agreed, staring at the device.

"Come on numbers, be my friends," said Sammy. "Math and I never had an amicable relationship," she admitted, pointing to the device "Gus, you're a computer guy. Doesn't this early computer resonate for you? No pun intended," Sammy added, recalling their jeopardy three years before in Los Angeles, when malware had infected a computerized safety system, making buildings resonate *with* earthquakes and sway *more* rather than less.

Pappajohn shrugged. "Let's see." To Alex: "How does it operate?"

"There was probably a handle, which we haven't found yet, but, if I turn the front dial, the gears in between the next two dials make those turn, too."

"Okay, one thing I see," said Pappajohn, "is that the numbers align in a predictable sequence."

Alex nodded. "Shall we plot them out?"

"There are more than a hundred combinations," Pappajohn observed. "This could take forever." He checked his watch. "It's a little after nine A.M. in Boston." He nodded at the phone console at one end of the conference room table. "Mind if I call Keith?"

CHAPTER FIFTY-ONE

"If the gears are connected, three hundred sixty to be exact. A circle is three hundred sixty degrees," Keith explained through the speaker. "Each point can be thought of as one degree."

"Instead of degrees, the ancient Greeks used fractions of pi," Alex explained. "You got the measurements, right?"

"And the gear ratios, thank you," said Keith. "I'm sitting here at my PowerMac G4, and running the photos of the device you emailed me. I'm able to create a model of each dial and gear. If we need to, I can even print them out in 3-D."

"I've heard about this type of printing," Kiki exclaimed. "Can you create a 3-D model of the dials we don't have?"

"Well, we're still in beta, but yes. Problem is…"

"We're not sure what size they're supposed to be," interrupted Alex. "If only Lambros had familiar objects we could compare in his photos. But, you have all the specs now, yes?"

"Yes, running the program now. Three columns of numbers from the dials and from Sammy's codex photos. I'm plotting a graph with the data as well." Hmmm. "Sending you a diagram. Tell me what you think."

Kiki checked her laptop. "Got it. Opening." The others gathered around to see the model Keith had sent.

"Gee, that looks like those snail drawings I shot at the monastery," Sammy said.

"Snail drawings? Let me see," said Alex.

Sammy leaned over and selected a photo from Kiki's pile. "That one."

Alex considered it for a moment before his expression brightened. "Sammy, that's not a snail. It's a spiral. Archimedes' Spiral, if I'm not mistaken."

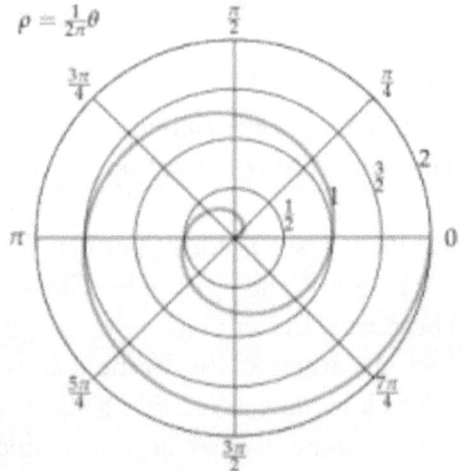

"I think you're right," Keith said. "These numbers do form an Archimedean spiral. Each radial line represents a fraction of the mathematical constant known as pi."

"Archimedes?" Sammy asked. "I'm pretty sure his name was written in Greek on the cover of the book I found in the monastery's library. Along with Conan the Barbarian."

"It's actually Conon the Mathematician, Sammy," Alex laughed. "But that could mean we're on the right track."

"Is this spiral the same as the Golden Ratio Spiral that Loukas mentioned at the Acropolis?" Sammy asked.

"No," said Keith. "The Golden Spiral of Phidias is a logarithmic spiral based on the Golden Ratio. In other words, the points on the spiral change with the constant Phi.

"Phi, Phidias. I can remember that. But what's different about ours?"

"Different formula," Keith explained. "The points on the spiral move away from the start with a constant speed and rotational angular velocity."

"That, I can't remember. Glad one of us can," Sammy said, tapping her temple.

"What is it, Alex?" asked Kiki, as Alex buried his nose on the device.

"Anybody have great eyes?"

"Don't look at me," said Pappajohn.

"I do. So far," said Sammy. "What do you want me to look at?"

"These dials. Do you see anything peculiar?"

"Yes," said Sammy, "The dials. The Greek letters which are numbers. The device. Everything."

Eye rolls from the others. "No. *On* these disks," said Alex.

Sammy took a closer look at the first dial. "This tiny hole?"

Alex nodded. Sammy looked at the second and third. There's a hole like that on the other two disks, too."

"Line them up, Alex," said Pappajohn. "Let's see if we get anything."

Alex turned the dials. "Sigma Kappa… Keith, here are the numbers in English. What does that alignment show?"

"Hold…okay, if I draw a radius from the start to where it intersects the spiral, it's one number on the spiral line. Two hundred twenty."

"Then that's it," cried Alex. "We found it!"

"Right on," said Pappajohn. "X marks the spot. Or r for radius."

"Wait a minute, guys," Sammy interjected, as she looked at the graph Keith had just sent them. "I see what you did. Okay. But, you have this spiral turning in one direction Can't it go the other way? Then two hundred twenty would be on the opposite side, right? And where is the starting point in the

Parthenon? If you start at the edge of the Parthenon, can't you end up on the gravel or over the ledge?"

"You're right, Sammy, "Alex admitted. "Depending on where you start and which way you point the spiral you could place the two hundred twenty point somewhere on the entire floor."

"So we're back at point zero," Pappajohn groaned.

"No, I have an idea," Alex said. "We do have that dial of the sun. Likely used to predict eclipses. Sammy, do you see any dots on this one?"

Sammy examined the rusted dial and gear. "Hard to tell with all that gunk on it. Can your renovation team clean it up?"

Alex looked at Kiki. She sighed and nodded. "Give us a day. It won't be complete, but I'll see if we can clean over the etchings of the sun near the rim. Alex, take the device over to Varvara and ask her to do her magic. Meanwhile, I'll give Elias at the Acropolis a call and see if he'll run another ground penetrating radar survey tomorrow. Maybe he can locate something that makes all this" — she waved a hand across the table — "moot."

"Keith," Pappajohn said to the speaker. "Thank you. This is a great start. We'll call you in the evening, and send you a cleaner photo of the sun dial as soon as it's ready."

As Sammy and Pappajohn were walking out, Sammy's phone vibrated. Checking the caller ID, she sighed when she saw it was Doxiadis. She'd promised to have dinner with him during her trip. And it would be nice to get away from the intensity of the puzzle solving *and* forget, for a while, her sadness about Ollie's murder. She clicked to answer the phone and responded, "Where would you like to meet?"

Chapter Fifty-Two

"Where are we going?" Sammy asked Doxiadis as she squeezed into his Smart Car. *Dang, doesn't anyone here drive a Mercedes?*

"Vouliagmeni. We'll drive past the old airport and take the coastal highway to the peninsula. No better place to enjoy the sunset. There's a beautiful lake there with warm water weaving through a series of caves. If it was earlier in the day, I'd have suggested you bring a bathing suit and we could explore the caves together."

"Thanks, but I'm not much of a swimmer," Sammy admitted. "I prefer to sit in the sun and get skin cancer, I mean, a tan. But, you're right, this is a pretty stretch. Kind of like Beverly Hills."

"Glyfada, Voula, and Vouliagmeni are the Greek Riviera. I think it's prettier than Monaco, but then again, I'm partisan. I've never been to Beverly Hills."

"Well, you'll have to visit Los Angeles some day. If I ever go back there, I'll let you know and you can get my twenty-Euro tour."

"Have you finished your schoolwork?" Katsoulis said in Greek, sounding like an interrogator.

"Almost," replied her son. "I just need a break. Can I use the computer?"

"No video games until everything is finished. You know the rules."

The teen shuffled back into his room, grumbling.

Katsoulis inserted the flash drive into her USB slot and began playing the video. As Ilan had suggested, she fast forwarded through the ship scenes and sped to the underwater murder.

Watching the cameraman fighting for his life was heartbreaking. Her husband Spiros' death, thank God, had been mercifully swift, the bullet in the heart had found its target. Wiping away a tear, she gasped when she recognized the face in the scuba mask at the end of the reel - the same murderous monk who had tried to kill Sammy.

The lakeside restaurant had a beautiful view of both the water and the surrounding rocky hills, which were sprinkled with cave entrances lit by yellow spotlights. Softer light from candles tickled by the breeze twinkled over their white tablecloth on which a bottle of Greek rosé lay half-finished.

"This is really beautiful, Loukas."

Doxiadis raised his glass. "A beautiful haven for a beautiful woman."

Sammy clinked hers to his. "Skinny Asses."

Doxiadis looked shocked. "What?"

Sammy laughed. "Gus tried to teach me a little Greek. He gave a toast and it sounded like Skinny Asses. So, that's what I say now and it works."

The smile returned. "*Steen eeghia sas.* It means 'to your health'. Try it, just separate the words. *Steen*—"

"Oh, look." Sammy changed the subject. "Our dinner is here. What did you order for us?"

The waiter answered in English. "Our finest roast lamb and potatoes with lemon. May I take your salad?"

Sammy nodded, and picked up her dinner fork, poking the meat, which melted softly onto the plate. "Mmm, this looks good."

"And so does your new hairstyle. Very cutting edge."

Sammy chuckled. "Yes, I cut a lot of edges."

"You did not like it long?"

Sammy was about to tell him about her adventure on Mount Athos, but decided not to risk spoiling the evening with another dose of male disapproval. "Not in this summer heat. I'll grow it out when I get to New York in the fall."

"Not Los Angeles?"

She shook her head and explained that she had been hired as an on-air host for Radio USA. The new network was due to launch its programming at the end of the summer.

Doxiadis listened with interest and suggested that she spend her vacation in Greece relaxing and enjoying Greece's museums, archaeological sites, and picturesque islands. "I would love to give *you* a personal tour, but," he said with a frown, "I'm still teaching classes through the rest of June."

"I can relate. I've been kind of working, too. Trying to help Alex with some museum finds. My friend Gus, the ex-cop, is working with Captain Katsoulis to investigate Professor Lambros' murder, and to figure out why the monk attacked us. I've been checking in with them to see if they've solved the case – or rather, cases."

"And have they?" Doxiadis asked.

"Not so far. I did hear that the monk who fell off the Acropolis was the son of Lambros' priest, Father Mihalis. Imagine that." She swallowed a bite of the delicious lamb. "Loukas, I'm so grateful you were there. If it weren't for you, I wouldn't be here tonight."

Doxiadis patted her hand. "I couldn't let anyone hurt you. Still, I wish the young monk had survived. Then at least the one mystery would be solved and perhaps even Harris Lambros' death as well."

"You think the monk murdered Professor Lambros?"

"Captain Katsoulis said Harris had bought some black market artifacts. Perhaps the monk was part of the rogue outpost trading from Makronissos I saw on the news." Doxiadis shook his head. "We have an expression in Greek, 'don't get mixed up in the birdseed or the chickens will eat you'."

Sammy laughed, "Or, as we say, 'if you lie down with dogs, you'll get up with fleas'."

"Elias agreed to redo the radar in the morning," Kiki said to Alex after thanking Varvara for working on the Makronissos dial into the night. "Alex, go home and let Varvara finish. It will take hours before the dial is ready."

Alex nodded. "I will. Soon."

"Uh-huh. All right. I'll see you in the morning. I'll stop by and check if Elias found anything first."

"*Geia*, Kiki. And, thank you." Alex drowned his yawn with a smile.

"Why are we stopping here?" asked Sammy, as Doxiadis squeezed his tiny car onto a crowded parking lot on the sandy beach.

"No trip to Athens is complete if you don't have a drink at one of our hopping discos." He opened the doors and they stretched to get out.

The boom-boom-boom of the beat reverberated across the crowded cove filled with twenty- and thirty-somethings drinking and dancing under strobe lights beside clear lapping water. Doxiadis led Sammy toward one of several bars and ordered them both a clear drink in a shot glass.

Sammy grimaced as he handed one to her. "I can smell the alcohol from here. Licorice or something."

"It's ouzo. Take a big gulp. Don't worry."

She swallowed the drink which burned her mouth and throat. "God, Loukas, is this drain cleaner?"

"No, it's *brain* cleaner," he returned. "One more and you'll feel like dancing."

CHAPTER FIFTY-THREE

Wednesday, June 11ᵗʰ, 2003

S ammy opened her eyes, but recognized nothing in the bare space. She was lying on a cot, an IV running a clear liquid into her left elbow crease. Alarmed, she sat up, but wished she hadn't. The entire room - white everywhere she could see - swam around her. Overcome by a wave of nausea, she laid back down.

"You're awake," said Pappajohn, pulling a folding chair to sit beside her cot. He looked up at the IV bag. "Nurse is hydrating you. Professor Doxiadis told me you passed out after your third ouzo shot. He brought you here."

"Ohhh, my head...I don't remember a thing," Sammy said. "Where is here?"

"It's a tent set up to help revelers who've had too much to drink."

"Oh, great. A drunk tank. Where is Loukas? We were dancing and talking and drinking that poison, and then..."

"He stayed with you for a few hours, but called me to babysit early this morning. He has a class to teach. He told me he didn't realize that the ouzo would affect you like that." Pappajohn shook his head. "Guess he's never dated a five foot woman before."

The nurse walked in and checked the IV. "Almost done. You'll be right to go in a few minutes, ducks," she said with an English accent. "You should see this tent when it's World Cup. Brits here and Frogs over there."

"That so. How much do we owe you?" Pappajohn asked as he stood.

"Thirty Euros," said the nurse.

"Is that all?"

"All covered under National Health," the nurse explained, winking. "But I won't turn down a fiver for me."

CHAPTER FIFTY-FOUR

Thursday, June 12, 2003

Alex didn't look much better than Sammy when she and Pappajohn were dropped off by taxi at the museum at dawn the next morning. *Had he slept at all?*

To Sammy's dismay, Kiki appeared chipper. *How does she do it?*

"Elias is starting the ground radar sweep now."

"Anything on the sun dial?" Papajohn asked Kiki.

"Yes, Varvara found three tiny dots."

"I'll call Keith," said Pappajohn, already dialing. A moment later his IT partner was on the line. "Hi. You still up?"

"Waiting for you," Keith said. "Just got the photo file on the sun dial, thanks, Kiki. Yes, I see the dots. Three, right?"

"Yes," said Alex.

"Kiki, I got the Parthenon floor plan, but can you send me the alignment on the Acropolis?"

"Coming," Kiki typed on her laptop keyboard and hit SEND. "Athena was the center rectangle, facing east."

"I blew up the photos of the other dials you sent," Keith said. "Difficult to see, but there's a dot on each dial, except for one. Didn't find a dot on the months. However, there is one right between Aries and Pisces on the Zodiac photo. I'd say March 21. The vernal equinox. Apartias on the winds, due north, and a quarter moon for the moon. Now, looking at the sun…"

The conference room was still.

"This is interesting," said Keith. "I ran one trial with the center of the spiral smack in the center of where the Athena statue once stood. Depending on how the spiral opens, the two hundred twenty point on each side puts the targets just inside the columns of the Acropolis and the columns dividing the atrium from the storage room. That's convenient."

"Yes," Alex agreed. "Easy to dig behind that barrier without drawing too much attention. But which side?"

"I'm plotting the position of the sun at the three points where the dots are." Laughter. "Very clever, those Greeks."

"What?" asked Pappajohn.

"The first dot is the sun's position in winter. The third dot is the sun's position in spring. Right in the middle, the Vernal Equinox. And a straight line right to the center of where Athena used to stand."

"So we start the spiral there at the center," piped in Alex.

"Yes, open to the right as you face Athena. The right is north. The spiral moves clockwise, in the direction of the moving sun from winter to spring. And in that case, the two hundred twenty intersection comes out on the left, according to the floor plan, exactly where the storage room corner used to be."

Alex was grinning from ear to ear. "Houston, we have a location!" He shared a high five with both Pappajohn and Sammy.

Kiki was already on the phone with Elias, directing them to pay special attention to the area Keith had suggested.

A few hours later, after a quick lunch at the museum cafe, the group reconvened in Kiki's office.

"Elias and his team just called," Kiki said. "They ran the ground radar again over the area where Keith's calculations directed. But the radar still shows nothing. All the way down thirty meters."

Alex's disappointment was clear.

"They also checked the area around where the statue used to be, the area under the reflecting pool, and both sides of the storage room site." She shook her head. "Just a few small caves and layers of stone and rock. I'm sorry, Alex."

Alex sat with his head in his hands. "I was certain we had her. Certain."

Pappajohn clapped him on the shoulders, with an encouraging, "You tried."

"Look," Kiki sighed. "I've still got a little capital with Elias, if you know what I mean. You did say that the stones and rocks could possibly hide a statue from the radar. If you really think she's down there, maybe, maybe I can convince Elias to let his excavation team do a focused dig. But you'd better be damned sure that you're right."

"Kosta, let's run the numbers again with Keith. If we get the same results, I'll stake my career on it."

CHAPTER FIFTY-FIVE

Saturday, June 14, 2003

The crowd that gathered at the Acropolis on the sunny morning numbered in the thousands. Kiki's knack for public relations was on full display. TV vans lined the dirt roads leading to the Acropolis walls. Satellite dishes stretched into the sky for a peek at the ledge and the Parthenon above. Reporters were allowed access into the Parthenon for the first time since the renovation for the Olympics had begun.

Sammy stood beside Eleni and Pappajohn watching the flow of people, lights, and cameras. Construction equipment was in place, ready to remove the Parthenon's marble blocks from the ground and begin digging below to locate the shaft where Alex expected to find the Athena statue. He had run the programs over and over with Keith. Each time, the Archimedean spiral calculations were pointing to the same position, the same number. Two hundred twenty on the southeast corner of the storage room.

Sammy could tell that Alex was anxious. Pacing back and forth, trying to ensure that the workmen implemented his instructions exactly. It didn't help that Professor Roussos stood a few feet away, arms crossed, twirling his mustache and rocking back and forth on his Bruno Maglis. Or that Loukas Doxiadis seemed bored, leaning against a restored column and trying to catch Sammy's eye. Kiki floated between a frowning Director Tountas and the reporters, ensuring that "Hellenic

Archaeological Museum" would be in everyone's story — and that Tountas would know she was the source.

Digging out the rock under the marble floor was a more difficult task; the sounds of the jackhammers, sledge hammers, and shovels made conversation impossible. Workmen came and collected each piece of stone removed and placed it into a labeled wheelbarrow for study and eventual replacement. Several viewers stepped out of the atrium, annoyed by the dust and noise. Eleni stayed focused on the dig, but Pappajohn was an early escapee, choosing to amble over to the craft table, where seats and water were available. Sammy was surprised to see Captain Katsoulis stub out a cigarette and sit down next to him, pulling out a pad and sharing her notes. Pappajohn's resuscitated BlackBerry made a quick appearance as well. Sammy wondered if the two police officers were discussing the murder of Professor Lambros that had led them on a jagged path to the Acropolis today.

Two hours later, a ten by ten hole had been dug down to twenty feet. The Acropolis team looked for an opening through which they might thread a camera to search for a shaft or a statue below, but the rock remained solid without a hint of previous excavations.

The Acropolis team approached Alex with looks of concern. Alex shook his head and gestured at the hole, and the workmen resumed digging. By two P.M., the hole had been excavated to sixty feet. Layers of stone and rock were all that could be seen and removed. A small hole in the roof of a cave hollow allowed a flexible line with a camera to be threaded through, but its path showed only more rock and a small tunnel of less than six inches that may have been bored by an animal or water many years before.

The sides of the pit were inspected by the University's geologist. No trace of gold, bronze, ivory, rotted or petrified wood, or any man-made substance were identified by visual inspection. The geologist returned to examining the stones stored in the wheelbarrows for any signs of ancient artifacts or construction.

Finally, at seven P.M., the head of the Acropolis team called a halt to the digging at over one hundred feet. "There is nothing there. Finis!" He waved to the workers to stop and announced to the remaining visitors that the inside of the Parthenon would once again be closed, in the hopes that repairs from this "wasted" effort could be performed in a timely manner.

Alex protested, but his words were in vain. As the construction team placed safety barriers around the pit, he stood looking down into it, shaking his head. "I was certain. It had to be."

Sammy wasn't entirely sure that the trickles of sweat down his face didn't include a few tears.

Roussos, laughing, clapped a smirking Doxiadis on the back, and aimed for the TV cameras to re-pitch his version of the *Apocalypsi* story and deride the fantasy of Drs. Lambros and Matsas.

Kiki raced after him, hoping to salvage everyone's reputations with the right angle of spin.

Tountas' frown deepened as Elias, his counterpart from the Acropolis museum, approached and began mentioning the financial contribution he was expecting from the Hellenic Archaeological Museum to repair the damage from today's dig.

Doxiadis sidled over to Sammy and said, "I expect there won't be a celebration tonight. Would you accept my invitation to show you the Port of Piraeus and treat you to a fresh seafood dinner? I promise that this time I won't offer you anything stronger than wine."

"That's kind of you, Loukas. Maybe in a couple of days. I think we'll be needed here this evening for moral support."

Doxiadis nodded and smiled. "I'll hold you to that, you know."

Sammy returned a thinner smile. "Yes. I know."

"Alex, wait. Where are you going?" Sammy ran up to him as he stepped into his Smart Car and started the engine. She knocked on his window until he rolled it down. "I know the reception was canceled, but you're still invited for dinner. Daphne's food can cheer anyone up."

"I'm not exactly in the mood for a celebration, Sammy. Sorry. Please give Daphne and Tasos my regrets."

Sammy hurried over to the passenger side and hopped into the car with him. "Maybe it's best if you had some company."

Without responding, Alex drove off as she buckled her seatbelt. A few kilometers northwest of the Acropolis, he maneuvered the car into a tiny parking space, and turned to her, mumbling, "I just needed a quiet place to take stock."

He switched off the engine. Sammy followed his lead out of the car. He locked it, pocketed the keys, and set off down the block with Sammy at his side.

At a fenced building on Melidoni Street, Alex stopped to stare at a building with Hebrew lettering. It obviously was being renovated. "The Ioanniotiki Synagogue. Suffered a lot of damage in the 1999 earthquake. Hopefully it will reopen soon. There may be only thirty-five hundred of us in Athens today, but we need our own place to worship."

"Us?" Sammy's wrinkled brow reflected confusion. "I don't understand."

"My mother was a Romaniote Jew," Alex said. "My people have lived in Greece and the neighboring Eastern Mediterranean countries for over two thousand years. That makes us the oldest Jewish community in the Eastern continent."

"Wow, I've never heard of them," Sammy admitted.

Alex took a deep breath. "Unfortunately a majority of the Jewish population in Greece were killed in the Holocaust. My mother's parents were lucky. They were shielded in Thessaloniki by a Greek Orthodox Bishop they had once befriended. After the war, most of the survivors of the concentration camps left for Israel, America and Western Europe."

Sammy grinned. "So you and I are are landsmen, as my grandmother Rose would say."

Alex returned the smile. "Yes. Like you, I'm not very religious, but I do find Friday night services comforting sometimes." He pointed to a large stately building with marble walls and columns across the street. "Temple Beth Shalom. It's Sfardi, following the tradition of the Spanish Jews who fled here 1492, but the sunset *mincha* is quite nice. Want to join me?"

Sammy nodded. "It's been a long time since I've been to synagogue, but, why not?"

CHAPTER FIFTY-SIX

Sunday, June 15ᵗʰ, 2003

"What the hell happened?" An angry Ilan stormed into Katsoulis' office. "Who dropped Wellington's charges?"

Katsoulis sighed. "Take it up with your intelligence colleagues. Apparently the CIA and MI6 don't want us interfering with their undercover operations."

"Wellington?" Ilan slapped his hands on his thighs. "That's bullshit! If he's a spy, I'm a *schmuck*."

"If I understand the meaning of the word — Yiddish, isn't it? — it looks like you are. And me, too. Unfortunately, unless we keep the military and intelligence support of the British and the Americans, we won't have an Olympics next year," she muttered. "There *is* a bit of good news, however. The French have denied all ties with Monsieur Dumas. He will go to trial here in a few months, thanks to your videos at Makronissos. Even better, we've arrested Abbot Teodor and his henchmen from St. Dimitar. They'd tried to escape to Aghion Panteleimon, but we got to them first. We salvaged the books and treasures they were trying to hide and are cataloguing them now. We should be able to return the stolen Masada artifacts to you by this time next year." A smile. "Mission accomplished, no?"

Ilan had continued to curse under his breath. Throwing up his hands, he stormed out of Katsoulis' office with an emphatic "No!".

Alex thanked Daphne and Eleni for the luncheon and nodded to the somber group. "It'll be okay. As I say too often, Rome wasn't built in a day."

"You're lucky they don't sentence you to die in the gladiator ring nowadays," said Pappajohn.

"Actually, I have an appointment at six to meet with a formidable opponent," Alex admitted. "Kiki wants to see me at the museum this afternoon." He couldn't hide his concern.

Sammy's tone was earnest. "If you want, we can all put in a good word for you. How hard you worked to find the answer. She should understand that. You're friends."

Alex scoffed. "Friends. After this debacle, I bet *she* won't be my friend any more. So much for our amicable divorce." He sat staring at the floor, lost in thought. "Amicable. Pfft." He looked up, his expression brightening. "Sammy, you're a genius!"

Sammy was surprised. "My professors didn't think so."

"No, an amicable 'friend'."

"Well, yeah, sure. You're my friend, too."

"No — I mean, yes — but that's not what I mean. In the phrase, the clue was the 'friend' part. Not us. The numbers! The amicable numbers!"

"The what?" said Sammy and Pappajohn in unison.

"Of course!" Alex continued, oblivious. "Friendly, amicable numbers. That's it!"

Sammy shook her head. "*What's* it?"

Think about this. If we were able to figure it out where Athena was hidden, wouldn't some Crusaders be able to as well? That's why they added that additional clue. Kosta, can you call Keith?"

"Now? Two thirty P.M. here…Seven thirty A.M. there…" Pappajohn sighed. "For a good reason?"

Alex nodded.

Pappajohn dialed from his cell and tapped on his speaker.

"Keith, it's Alex."

"Hey, Alex. Really, sorry, my friend. Heard on the news that the dig went bust. I still think we had the right spiral and intersection point, though, based on what you gave me."

"We did, sort of. But two hundred twenty wasn't the correct number after all," Alex said. "I missed a very important clue. The phrase on the Kairos dial."

"The cookie fortune?" Pappajohn interjected. "If you're a friend, you'll find Athena or something?"

Alex nodded. "'Friend' was the key. The phrase was referring to a friendly or amicable *number*."

Explosive laughter on the speaker phone. "Amicable numbers! Of course! Damn, those Greeks are clever."

Sammy looked at Pappajohn, who shook his head. "Gus and I still don't know what you're all talking about," Sammy complained.

"Amicable numbers are two different numbers for which the sum of the divisors of each number is equal to the other number," Alex explained. "So, for our calculations, we don't use two hundred and twenty, we look for two hundred and twenty's friend. That's two hundred and eighty four. And that plots out to a different location…the north side of the Parthenon, behind the statue, just off center before the storage room wall.

"Keith, I'm sending you the spiral and the locations of the points at two hundred twenty and two hundred eighty four. Hell of a lot easier to move the statue to a shaft in the atrium, rather than behind those columns, I'd say."

Sammy and Pappajohn looked at each other, eyebrows raised.

Alex couldn't contain his excitement. "Send your analysis to my email address, Keith, thanks. I'll go over it on my computer at home this midday before I meet with Kiki."

He bolted out the door with a warm *efharisto* to Daphne and her family.

Pappajohn was about to wrap up their call when he had another thought. "Keith, do you have a minute to hold on?"

"Of course. Just running the new numbers again, to be certain."

"What is it, Kosta?" asked Eleni, noting his furrowed brow.

He waved a hand. "Sammy, is your friend Jim still in Nashville?"

Sammy nodded. "Yes, I think so. What's up?"

"Can you ask him to do us a favor?"

"Sure." She flipped open her phone and dialed Jim's cell. "Hey, it's Sammy. How's the Opry?"

"My bro Harvard killed it last night," Jim Lodge grumbled, "We didn't get back until the crack of dawn. Which it still is here, dammit."

"Sorry. Go back to sleep. I just wanted to ask a favor."

"I'm awake enough now. What can I do you for?"

"It's for Gus. Remember him? Here." She handed the phone to Pappajohn.

After a quick hello, Pappajohn explained finding the Apocalypsi device dials and Alex's attempt to locate the Athena statue's shaft. "We dug over a hundred feet down. Nothing. Apparently Alex is *persona non grata* at the Acropolis. They won't let him try again. So we thought maybe you could do a beta test at the Parthenon in Nashville. If it works, maybe he can convince the Acropolis folks to change their minds."

"Sure, tell me what to do and I'll try it as soon as the place opens. How's your family, by the way?"

"All good, Jim, thanks. We'll catch up when I get back to the States. My boss Keith MacKay will call you on your cell with the instructions, okay?"

"You got it, brother. 'Bye."

"Keith?" Pappajohn returned to his phone. "I'll bet your numbers will work out, but how about we do a beta test in Nashville."

By eight thirty A.M. in Tennessee, Jim stood inside the Parthenon replica. He dialed Keith's number, ignoring the 'phones forbidden' sign. "Yep, the exact spot," he whispered. "Behind and to the north. I took a few pictures around the site. Boy, is she one mother of a statue, by the way. Forty feet. How wide was the hole?"

"Gus told me it was five by five meters and a hundred feet deep," Keith said.

"Looks like you all missed it by just a few yards. Where'd you get your numbers?"

"From the Apocalypsi device dials. Input date, time, location, direction, depth. A remarkable analog computer from the fifth century."

"No shit. So, glad I could help. I'm going back to bed now."

"Wait. I just want to double-check something. Let's run the spiral from end to start, too, and see where it goes."

"Okay, give me the steps again and I'll try it."

Holding his phone to his ear, Jim started walking back along the path of the circle as Keith guided.

"Excuse me."

Jim stopped and turned to face a museum guard.

"May I ask what y'all are doin'?" The guard's tone wasn't friendly. "Not allowed to make calls in here."

Guess I should've changed my wrinkled clothes, Jim admitted to himself. He could see his reflection in the Athena statue's gilding a few feet in front of him. *Homeless chic*. He turned off the phone. "Oh, sorry, didn't know that. Won't do it again."

The guard stood there, watching as Jim held his position. "May I help you with something?" the guard asked, finally.

"Nah. I'm good. Just admiring Athena's, um, butt." A broad smile.

The guard frowned and was about to respond when a family of tourists lost control of a young child who made a beeline for a sculpture of Athena's sacred owl, shouting "Harry Potter"! The guard ran off, hoping to stave off sticky fingers from petting the owl.

Jim quickly dialed Keith back. "Hurry up, I don't want to get arrested here. I'm carrying."

"A gun?"

"No, man, a joint."

Keith laughed. "Gus told me about you. Now go forward two steps, right one step, and…" Keith continued his instructions.

"Hey, Keith. I can't."

"The guard?"

"No, the statue. I'm right in front of her. I'd need to pass through her. Your destination is right in the middle of her base." He saw the guard approaching again. "Guard's coming back and I'm getting out. Did you get what you need?" he asked as he started jogging towards the exit.

"You bet," Keith said. "Now get clear before they cast you in Midnight Express."

CHAPTER FIFTY-SEVEN

Monday, June 16ᵗʰ

Alex dreaded the confrontation he was expecting with Kiki. His failure Saturday would no doubt have a damaging impact on her career and ambitions. He'd had such faith in his analysis, had been so certain he'd find the statue, that he never considered any negative consequences - however unintended. But, certainly once they heard about his error, and received the correct location, they'd be willing to try again. The Athena statue was Archaeology's Holy Grail. And now he had the right answer.

Entering the museum office, he felt a punch in the gut as he saw Tountas seated beside Kiki. Working at the Hellenic Archaeological Museum had been his dream come true as a freshly-minted PhD. Without Kiki's influence, he'd have had to apply for a position at one of the new community colleges cropping up in Athens in the past decade. She'd been so grateful for his tutelage as they worked together on their PhDs that she'd advocated for them to be hired as a team. But, losing players don't stay in the line-up. He had to convince her – them - that his theory was still valid and, with the correct numbers they'd recalculated, he could lead them to this Holy Grail.

Kiki's face was stiff and stolid. Her eyes, however, despite her make-up, had a hint of redness.

Fighting to maintain a calm expression, Alex took a chair opposite them and began with an apology. Flushed with enthusiasm, he presented the graphs he'd printed from Keith's files showing the original location on the Archimedean spiral, explaining how the duplicate meaning of the word φιλικός, 'friendly' and 'amicable', on the Kairos disk had led them astray. But now the new calculations were done. The Acropolis Team could re-do the measurements in an hour. In fact, Keith was running a beta test this morning at the Parthenon model in Tennessee to confirm that the new numbers matched.

Out of breath, he sat back and hoped they would share his enthusiasm. The tears welling in Kiki's eyes didn't bode well, and, with his disappointment and dread growing, he waited for the hammer to fall.

"We have the paperwork ready," Tountas began in Greek after a few minutes of painful silence. "We will accept your resignation today. Kiki has found some funds in our budget to cover the expenses of yesterday's debacle, so you will not need to pay for the useless excavation. Please sign here." He pushed the papers across the table, along with a pen.

A long silence, then Alex's voice cracked. "Thank you," he said, looking at both Tountas and Kiki, who stared down at her clasped hands. Clenching his jaw, he picked up the pen and signed the paperwork without reading it, and slid it back to the Director. "My deepest apologies, and my deepest gratitude to you both for allowing me the opportunity to serve the museum for these few years."

Without another word, he stood and walked out. It wasn't until he was locked inside his Smart Car, that Alex felt it was okay to weep.

At the station, Captain Katsoulis scrolled over pages and pages of microfiche, studying the records of two men she'd identified from Ollie's video.

Vasilis Oikonomou, Father Mihalis' son, certainly fit the profile of a juvenile delinquent. Three arrests for breaking and entering, marijuana sales, and heroin possession before he was eighteen. Then at twenty, intoxicated, he hit a pedestrian while riding his motorcycle, paralyzing the victim.

Katsoulis shook her head. Son of a protopresbyter. No doubt the archpriest arranged for his entry into the monastery rather than a jail cell. A snort. "Every parent's nightmare. Oh, Spiro, how I wish you were still here."

The second man didn't have an official record, so Katsoulis left the microfiche and moved back over to her computer. The biography on his university department webpage listed his PhD, the subject of his thesis and current research, and the classes he was assigned to teach. Unfortunately, no under-graduate studies were listed. Katsoulis did a manual search of the graduation lists of the three Greek Orthodox seminaries. At the last site, the Aristotelian school of Theology in Thessaloni-ki, she found the name that explained the hand signal she'd seen on Ollie's video. Worried, she picked up the phone and dialed a fellow captain of the Thessaloniki police.

That sucks royally, thought Ilan, as he settled in for his last night in the cuddy cabin boat at Piraeus. All that work and Wellington walks off scot-free. Tomorrow he had to leave for Beirut for his next assignment. *But, Lord Wellington, we'll duel again. Count on it.*

Wasn't as bad as what that poor Alex must be going through, though. National laughingstock. Humiliated on global television. Fired from his job. Will probably never work in this town again, as the saying goes. Yeah, Wellington sucks, but Mossad will see this as a win. Could have been worse.

He scratched his nascent beard, made a cup of palatable instant coffee, and opened up his laptop on the small table. Inserting the flash drive, he started the MPEG-4 file from the beginning, sipping coffee as he watched the *Thesaurus* team rocking and rolling during the rough autumn weather. He was going to miss Sammy. *Hope she takes me up on my invite to Israel.*

There was no way he would watch Ollie's death another time. As a fellow diver, Ilan had vividly imagined how the cameraman must have felt as his life was slipping away. But, he did want to see if he could identify the monk before his dive. Had he swum from the island, or was he already on board the *Thesaurus* as part of their diving team?

The answer was revealed when he saw the monk in a wet suit, sans mask and tank, approach his father, Father Mihalis. The film hadn't picked up sound, but the two seemed to be having a spirited exchange, with a back and forth dance of gestures. Neither seemed pleased at the end of the discussion. The monk then disappeared from view and Ollie's camera followed Lambros as he staggered on deck and opted to "go below". There was Sammy again, full of "spunk". *Hope she grows out her hair again.* Doxiadis, on the other hand, looks better with *his* hair cut. A second later, the camera showed Sammy heading below.

Ollie obviously had stayed on deck to continue filming. Thank goodness, because there was the monk again. He had a mask on the top of his head, and was walking toward the gate in the boat's railing where oxygen tanks were stored. Along the way he stopped to talk to Doxiadis, of all people. Man, they seemed to be talking a long time. A lot of mirroring, too. And was that some kind of a sign gesture as they parted? He rewound the file. The monk seemed to make a hand sign with his third finger and thumb. And Doxiadis? That looked like the Boy Scout salute. Ilan shook his head and stopped the video. Even with the coffee, he was getting sleepy. Better to be well rested for his voyage tomorrow.

Sammy took a taxi over to Alex's apartment after he called her with the news. He sounded so discouraged that she cancelled her evening plans with Doxiadis. Piraeus would be there tomorrow.

Alex's studio apartment was spare and professional. A futon, a desk with a CRT monitor, a small table with papers in piles, and a large bookcase filled with textbooks, scholarly works, classic literature, and modern publications on philosophy, psychology, archaeology, and history.

Alex sat on his futon, hands between his knees, and offered Sammy a cup of tea.

"I'll make it." She walked to the kitchenette and set up the teapot. "Which cabinet — oh, okay, I found it."

The cups of tea were soothing to both, and they sat in silence for a few minutes sipping. Alex took a deep breath. "I understand faculty positions in Classics and Archaeology are even more rare in the United States than in Europe."

Sammy shrugged. "Journalism isn't the easiest field either. I just got canned – sacked —from my job. Again."

"But you have another in New York in September, no? Changing jobs is common in show business."

"I wouldn't exactly say I'm in show business, but, yes, everybody gets fired occasionally. You just have to tell yourself 'it's their loss', pick yourself up, and move on."

"You make it sound so easy."

"No, Alex, it's never easy. Not ever. But you know something? I'd much rather try something I care about, even if it doesn't work, than decide to take a safe road just to avoid risks and failure." Sammy regarded him for a long beat. "Life means passion, *demands* passion. Otherwise, we're not living, we're just pre-dead." She looked into his eyes and offered a genuine smile.

"Well then, for life." He leaned forward and lightly kissed her on the lips.

No rejection. Instead, his kiss was returned warmly.

Teacups were rested on the table as Alex and Sammy embraced.

Katsoulis hung up the phone and sat back in her chair, putting her fingertips together. Her counterpart in Thessaloniki had reached the Dean of the Theology School and Seminary. The Dean did remember his former student. Very well. The young man had wanted to be a priest, but was declared unfit. Rabidly devout, but not grounded or pragmatic. Priests needed to be guided by faith, not obsession. He didn't take well to the recommendation that he consider graduate school instead instead of the clergy. God and Christ had told him to become a crusader for Orthodoxy in these times when secularism and Western values were holding sway. It would be his mission, even if he *was* never accepted as a priest.

Katsoulis shook her head. Nine-eleven had shown the world what fanatic religiosity could lead to. She had to make sure there would be no such victims here in Greece.

CHAPTER FIFTY-EIGHT

Tuesday, June 17ᵗʰ, 2003

Sammy's phone vibrated. She turned to pick it up before it woke Alex. Glad he was finally able to get some sleep. Tiptoeing out of the bedroom, she whispered into the receiver, "Hey, Gus. What time is it?"

"Nine thirty AM. I wanted to check if I was needed for a tent run at the disco again?"

Sammy laughed. "Nope. Fool me once, etc. Quite sober."

"Should I ask where you've been all night?" Pappajohn ventured.

"Who is it, Sammy?" asked Alex, walking into the room in his boxers.

A chuckle from the receiver. "Never mind," said Pappajohn. "*Mazel tov!*"

After a quick shower at Daphne and Tasos', Sammy left for her luncheon appointment.

"I was surprised when I got your call, but I'm glad we could meet before I return home tonight," Ilan told Sammy as they sat in the open air café of the renowned Dionysos restaurant in downtown Athens. "My work here is done."

Sammy glanced at the Acropolis beyond towering over the picturesque neighborhood. The Parthenon faced the restaurant, serving as a magnificent reminder of the Goddess it honored - her mission to serve and protect the people of Athens - people like Alex.

Where were you, Athena, when Alex needed you?

Sammy smiled at Ilan. "The missing Masada pieces?"

Ilan nodded. "We'll get them back after the trial of Jean Dumas."

"And Wellington?"

Ilan tsked. "He lives to fight again. Life isn't always fair, as we know."

A sigh. "Yeah. They fired Alex last night. Kiki and her boss Tountas."

"I know. CNN ran the story," Ilan responded. "I am sorry. I was honestly surprised the dig didn't succeed. Alex is a careful archaeologist."

"His analysis seemed perfect. But we never considered that the message itself was in code. It wasn't *Athena's* friends we had to identify, it was the *numbers'* friends. Amicable numbers."

"You're kidding." Ilan wrinkled his brow.

"You know what they are?"

"Yes. Read — studied engineering at Uni. Among other things," Ilan admitted.

The waiter served them a large dish of Greek appetizers. "Enjoy," he said in English.

"*Efharisto*," they responded in unison, and broke into laughter, when they both added, "Jinx."

"So what were you saying about amicable numbers?" Ilan asked, shifting a *dolmas* onto her plate.

"That's what made the difference. We tested the calculations with the amicable number at the Nashville Parthenon and it worked. Thirty feet behind the statue, near the north side, not the south."

"'For want of a nail,'" Ilan quoted the proverb he'd heard in childhood. "So, Alex will try to dig there then?"

"Unfortunately not. As far as the Acropolis is concerned, it's one and done."

"Politics trumps evidence, I'm sorry to say." Ilan regarded the Acropolis for a few minutes. "Maybe with time he'll be able to convince them."

Sammy followed his gaze. Doing so, she spotted something on the side of the mountain, beyond the rear of the Parthenon and the Atticus theater. "Hey Ilan, do you see those openings? In the rocks. What are they?" She pointed to what looked like two adjacent dark rectangles framed in white, high above the ground.

"Never been there, but they look like they could be entry-ways into the mountain below the Acropolis. Probably maintenance tunnels or vents for the museum's physical plant. Or more caves, hills here are full of them," he said, biting into a *spanakopita*.

"Yeah," said Sammy, not quite there.

Ilan gave her a dubious look. "Hey, don't even think about it. Besides, it's at least three stories up. How would you get there? You're not a rock climber, are you?"

"Of course not," said Sammy, swallowing a bite of *tiropita*. She manufactured a playful grin. "I'm afraid of heights, remember?"

As soon as Sammy and Ilan parted, with promises to keep in touch, Sammy took a cab to Alex's apartment. She spent the next half hour explaining her brainstorm. "It looks like there's a small ledge on the frame of the openings. So all we have to do is go up to the Acropolis, drop a rope from the parapet behind the Parthenon, and slide down."

Alex shook his head. "After this week, they won't let me in the Acropolis at all. You know that. Nice try."

"They haven't banned me. I can get in and drop you a rope from the ledge and you can climb up from the hill below."

"You realize that if they see us we could be arrested. The Acropolis has more guards than Mt. Athos."

"They won't. I'll do it at night. Tonight. The security checkpoint is at the Acropolis stairs on the other side. I'll put a rope in Georgie's backpack and play Acropolis tourist before hiding out in the restroom at the Acropolis museum. After they close, I'll sneak to the back and drop the rope down. Once I'm on the ledge, I'll lower the rope and you can climb up with the equipment. You can sneak into the grounds in the evening and hide in the bushes til dark. No one will see us."

"And how exactly am I supposed to get in? Er, I don't know if you've noticed, but there's an iron fence entrenched all around the ruins. With spikes atop." Alex frowned. "Even wire cutters won't stand a chance."

"They would where I was this morning."

Alex looked confused.

"See, with all this terrific Greek food I've been enjoying, I decided to get some exercise, burn off a few calories before my lunch date. So, I jogged around the perimeter of the Acropolis grounds. Amazing what you can see on foot, if you ignore all the No Trespassing signs. Wouldn't you know, there's an alleyway on the north side. It leads to a hidden gate and a dirt path near a row of trash bins. I'm guessing that's where construction equipment is guided through for the ongoing renovations. Anyway, no one's bothered to replace the iron fence in that section. There's just a wire fence with a simple lock on the gate that only digs about an inch into the mud. You can cut the fence or the gate lock, or dig a trench and crawl in—under the wire, so to speak."

"You're mad, you know."

"You'll be mad if you let them stop you from the discovery of the millennium."

"Okay, say I—*we*—make it in. Then what?" Alex shook his head.

"Those openings on the side of the mountain are big. We can take the tunnels or vents or whatever they are to under the museum. Based on your new calculations, that's only a few yards from under the Parthenon itself, right?"

Alex rolled his eyes. "A few yards of limestone at best. There's not going to be a red carpet to guide our way to Athena from there."

"Okay, so bring a couple of pickaxes?"

"Good idea, Sammy. And a month later we might be able to finish digging our own tunnel."

"What about a jackhammer then? Do they make them portable?"

"Possibly. But portable is relative. Especially when you're climbing up a rope."

Sammy scrunched her face. "Any way we can blow a hole open to help us out?"

"Sure. And that's what will happen - literally. We'll be blown *out* of the mountain." A sigh. And then a raised hand. "Wait, I must be losing my mind, but there may be another option. I don't know…"

"Let's hear it."

"Our artifact restorers use a number of materials to clean finds. It's delicate work, but sometimes we have to burn off layers of lime or sandstone to even get to the object."

"With a blowtorch?"

"No, with *Acidum Salis*. Spirits of salt. Hydrochloric acid. Or actually an older version of it that was called muriatic acid."

"Never heard of that. Hydrochloric acid I know. We used it in a chemistry class I took at Ellsford. Pretty harsh stuff."

Alex nodded. "One needs a mask and hazmat suit in a closed space." He stroked his chin. "I can't believe I'm saying this, but we could get the acid, the sprayer, and the outfit at Praktiker. That's a German hardware store a few kilometers from here. I can even hang a couple of light pickaxes from my belt. One for me, one for you. But, one revision. We'll need a rope ladder, not just a rope. I'm ten years past my Army days, and I'll be carrying too much gear. Just give me an hour to rerun my calculations, and let's go shopping."

"Does that mean you're in?"

Alex sighed again. "Yes, Sammy. IN-sane."

CHAPTER FIFTY-NINE

Tuesday, June 17ᵗʰ, 2003

S ammy aimed to enter the Acropolis at six P.M. When she'd visited with Doxiadis a few days earlier, the entry guards had searched her purse, so she had no doubt Georgie's now dry backpack would be targeted by screeners. Alex would have to wear the necessary protective gear and carry the sprayer and axes on a tool belt as he climbed up. Finding a sturdy enough rope ladder was going to be the biggest challenge. The nearby hardware store only had standard rope ladders, five meters long, which used thin plastic or wood cylinders as steps. The ladder had to be easily hidden on Sammy, who would have to drop it down from the parapet of the Acropolis above. *Yes, Mr. Guard, I always travel with a ladder—it's my good luck charm.* Packing the equipment into the tiny trunk of the Smart Car, Sammy admitted her enthusiasm was running out of steam. *Perhaps this was an impossible dream after all.*

But Alex's spirits were unfazed. He drove the Smart Car to an industrial neighborhood west of the Acropolis, parked it at a ninety degree angle in a tiny space, and turned to Sammy, "Wait here. I have a friend who can help us. Be right back."

Fifteen minutes later Alex returned with a satchel. "Forget the backpack," he said, handing it to Sammy. "Carry this."

She opened it carefully and found a green, scrunched up ladder.

"It's two Yates Gear, Ultralite, Urban Assault Ladders, ten meters each. Made of Kevlar. My army buddy, Manolis, kept a few things from his tour of duty, too. We tied them together. You climb down and I'll climb up."

Sammy pulled it out. "Wow, it's compact and really light. But, they'll get suspicious if they see these at the checkpoint. They do look like ladders, you know." She thought for a moment before brightening. "Or not. I have an idea." Stepping out of the car, she collapsed and twisted the ladders into a makeshift belt, which she wrapped around her mid-section several times like a waist-cinching corset. "Ta da. New fashion. Or, better yet, a back brace."

Grinning, Alex fished two small grappling hooks from his pocket, each with a ring attached. "You'll also need these grappling hooks. Titanium Gravity XLs. There's no metal detector and I doubt they'll pat you down. Put them in the satchel."

"Your, um, friend sure has some good equipment." She examined the small hooks. "Hope they hold." Her eyes narrowed. "Nah, it's better to bluff than to hide." She slipped off her pierced stud earrings, and threaded a ring through each ear. "Dangling earrings. Who says I don't have style?" Along with her cell phone, she stuffed one of Alex's new flashlights, a bottle of water, and her jacket into the satchel. "You never know, it might get cold tonight."

Alex nodded. "I hope not. We lost the first round of hide and seek with Athena this week. Let's pray our new approach will be a lot warmer."

As planned, Sammy approached the Acropolis entry point two hours before the ruins closed for the night. She would hide in the museum restroom until the sun set around nine. Then, after dark, she'd make her way to the parapet and try to spot Alex waiting below.

Striding with false confidence up to the security guards, she showed the ticket she'd just purchased.

One guard yawned and balanced his half-smoked cigarette on the edge of the counter next to his chair. "We close at twenty hundred," he muttered, as he tore the ticket in half. "And not one minute later."

It took Sammy a moment to figure out that he meant eight PM. She smiled and balled the stub in her fist. "Thank you. I'm just taking a few pictures. I'll be out way before then." Sammy started to step away, trying to ignore the other guard who was staring at her waist.

"One moment, Miss, we check your bag."

Sammy froze.

The second guard waved her back, his eyes still focused on the waist 'brace'. "You have the spine problem, yes."

Sammy tried not to stutter. "Yes, curvy spine," she nodded as the guard began rifling through the satchel.

"My daughter, too. Scoliosis. She hates brace." The guard pulled out Sammy's water bottle and her jacket. He then tested her phone by flipping it open so it would light up before replacing the items.

Sammy felt a drop of perspiration fall on her chest. "Yeah, so do I. Makes me sweat. What price beauty, eh?"

Nodding, the guard waved her through.

Sammy took her time walking up the steps. *Stay calm, stay calm.* Atop the Acropolis, she paused to breathe, and to take in the three hundred sixty degree panorama of the thriving city below. Her tour of the ruins with Loukas Doxiadis a few days ago had been cut short by that murderous monk's assault. Sammy shivered a she passed the ledge where the monk had fallen to his death. She'd barely caught her balance at the last minute, thanks to Loukas' intervention. And in a few hours she would have to climb over the edge of the Acropolis, with only a thin ladder between her and the rocks below.

"I've come back here several times myself," said a voice behind her. "Trying to assuage the guilt. Could I have saved both your life *and* his?"

Loukas Doxiadis! What was he doing here?

Sammy spun around and forced a smile. "You shouldn't blame yourself. *He* attacked us." She patted him on the arm. "There's nothing we can do now to change things."

"No, there isn't. You're right." He shrugged. "We were on our way to see the Acropolis museum that day. Now that we're both here, how about we continue our tour there this evening?"

Sammy tried not to appear dismayed. "Of course, Loukas. Why not? We have a couple of hours before they close."

"Eight o'clock already. Where did the two hours go?" said Doxiadis. "We've only seen half the museum."

Sammy sighed. "Ah well. Thank you for the fascinating lectures, Professor."

"My pleasure. May I give you a ride home?"

She raised a hand. "No thanks. This was wonderful, but I'll just take the subway back."

"I won't hear of it," Doxiadis said. "It's not so safe after dark. Come. Or at least let me get you a taxi."

"No, thank you, Loukas. Please. I can get my own cab. I kinda have to use the, um, loo, so don't wait for me." She kissed him lightly on the cheek. "Don't worry. Thank you and have a good evening."

Doxidis shuffled towards the door, waiting for her to near the WC. At the restroom door, she waved, and the professor left. Finally.

The restroom was empty. Sammy entered an open stall, locked it, and climbed onto the toilet seat, crouching with her feet straddling the opening until the museum's lights went out a few minutes later.

Sammy sat in the darkened bathroom, watching the time until her watch read eight thirty. At that exact moment she felt the building jiggle from the massive front doors closing. If she'd still been in Los Angeles, she'd have guessed that shake was a two point five on the Richter scale. Just enough to make one wonder if a heavy truck had rolled down the street.

She cautiously opened the restroom door and peeked out into the darkness. The coast was clear, so she tiptoed towards the entrance. Good news - no chains or double locks. Not so good news - an alarm pad next to the door was blinking.

Damn, the whole building must be wired. Okay, let them focus on a burglary in the museum.

Grabbing an armful of flyers and brochures on a display by the door, Sammy scattered them around the front rooms of the museum. Her intent was to make a paper trail leading away from the entrance while she took a path in the opposite direction. Hopefully, this would give her the few minutes she needed to get down off the Acropolis and out of any guards' reach.

As she pushed open the front doors, her footsteps were drowned out by the blaring of the alarm. Heart beating wildly, she jogged and hopped over the gravel and rocks until she reached the rear northwest edge of the Acropolis. Stopping to catch her breath, she slipped off her "earrings", attaching them first to the Kevlar ladders and then over the top of the stone parapet that separated her from the ground forty feet below. As she'd planned, the Acropolis guards on duty had run toward the museum. She smiled now, imagining them trying to figure out if the "break-in" had been accomplished by a burglar or a litterbug prankster.

Sammy slipped the satchel over both shoulders like a backpack. Trying not to look down, she swung her legs over the edge and began her descent. Without a wooden bar at the top to keep the ladder steps from curling and the handles apart, each step required her to place one foot behind the other and balance as the ladder swayed left and right. Halfway down, her foot slipped off the Kevlar, and she felt herself sliding down several steps of the ladder before she was able to catch herself. Only ten more feet to go, and she'd be at the ledge where the "holes" opened.

Her progress was slower than she'd hoped, but she didn't dare move faster, or turn to look behind her to see if Alex was waiting below. As she neared the openings, she saw that the ladder had shifted away by at least two feet from the side of the openings. Could she make it to the ledge? Worried that an attempt to swing the ladder closer might dislodge the grappling hooks above, Sammy stretched a leg as far as she could and reached the ledge with her right toes. *Good.* Inch by inch, she pulled herself closer so that she could leap onto the ledge. She'd have to risk that inertia wouldn't send her off the other side. One, two, three, jump.

That jump landed her at the opposite end of the ledge. She clutched at the rim to keep herself from falling as she rolled onto her side and curled up into a ball. She could feel her rapid heartbeat slowly returning to normal as she caught her breath. *Made it!*

After sitting on her hands for a few moments to stop the adrenaline shakes, she inched forward and peeked over the ledge to see if Alex was there. Spotting the light of his flashlight waving from below, she pulled out her own flashlight and waved back. *So far so good.*

Alex was more adept at scaling the ladder, though, laden with his tools, he struggled with its swaying as well. Fortunately, the sun had set, and neither of them would be easily visible from prying eyes above or below. She could no longer hear the guards' voices above from her post. Perhaps they were still in the museum trying to find the intruder and assess the 'damage'. *Hurry, Alex, before they start searching the rest of the compound.*

In five slow minutes, Alex's longer and sturdy legs mounted the ledge. Despite being decked in muddy overalls and headgear, and carrying a large backpack crammed with equipment, he was able to remain standing as he landed by her side and helped her to her feet. Alex waited until they had both entered the "cave" before enfolding her in a warm hug with an enthusiastic "Brava!"

"What's that?" Sammy asked, as Alex pulled out an iPod-sized device from his belt. Its cord was connected to a mike that was now playing static. "Cave karaoke?"

Alex chuckled. "No, another of Manolis' little army toys. A Geiger counter. It's possible the basalt is a little radioactive." They started walking from the entrance down a man-made tunnel paved with scratched and stained marble stones. A stream of foul air greeted them as they entered. It seemed to originate from a a concrete tunnel to their left which paralleled the side of the mountain. Sammy could hear a humming noise from its distant darkness.

"I expect that *that* road not taken would lead us to the heating, ventilation, and air conditioning rooms in the basement of the museum," said Alex. "We should head for the unknown beyond this door over here." Removing a small kit from his toolbelt, Alex pointed to a rusted metal door that blocked the pathway to the right. A faded sign on its face read NO ENTRY in English and Greek.

"Let me try," Sammy offered, holding out a hand for the lockpicking tools. "I learned a few tricks growing up on the Lower East Side. Hope it isn't alarmed." Within a few moments, she opened the door with a loud squeak, revealing a musty, unlit concrete tunnel turning southwest.

"Just old," Sammy exhaled and waved a hand. "Looks like it's been awhile since they've had guests. After you."

"Unfinished," Alex observed, after about ten yards as the paving ended and transitioned into a small tunnel of stone. "We're now in a natural cave. That's a good sign." He pointed the device ahead of them. "This gadget will be useful to tell us if we're getting warmer or colder in our little adventure."

"Couldn't we have used that upstairs?" She gestured at the cave wall overhead as they ventured forward.

"I did. Nothing. There are three meters of stone above us, so I'm not surprised."

"And *when* was the last earthquake?" Sammy didn't sound relaxed.

"Cave roof is getting smaller. We'll have to crouch a bit."

"Speak for yourself, Alex."

Another chuckle. After a few minutes along the cave path, they arrived at an open area with several branches of natural tunnels. Alex waved the Geiger counter in all directions, but there was no guiding sound. Two of the tunnels had collapsed, and were filled with boulders. "That earthquake? 1999."

"So what now?"

Alex shook his head. "If I've calculated my steps correctly, based on Keith's graphs and the radar map of these pathways, we should be under the southeast corner of the Parthenon right now." He pointed to one of the collapsed tunnels. "That one fits the calculations, but..." He tried to dislodge the boulders with both arms to no avail.

"The pickaxe?"

"No, I wouldn't dare. It's clearly unstable. We'll have to use the tunnel next to it and hope it takes us fairly close to our goal." He nodded towards the next tunnel, which was five feet high and open. "We may have to try all of them, one by one. Let's go."

"Are you sure your calculations are right? These caves seem too accessible to me, even with those two blocked."

"I expect the ancients had a back door allowing them to check in on Athena, at least until the Ottoman conquest of the Acropolis. The 1687 armament explosion might also have caused the collapses we saw. I bet some of the caves behind us were used for storage when they expanded the Acropolis museum in the fifties. Had they known what we surmise…"

They continued walking guided by flashlight as Alex counted under his breath. "One hundred and forty. The number of steps of the hypotenuse. Ten more to go. We've curved a bit east, but we still should be close."

He aimed his light beam into the distance, but all Sammy could see all around was a smooth cave wall. "I think we've hit a dead end," she said. "No exit. So we go back and try another one."

Alex shook his head. "No, it should be here." He tried the Geiger counter again, this time producing a weak signal. "Aha!" He edged closer to the wall, took out the pickaxe, and started chipping away at the cave wall to the west. "Limestone."

"I hope to God they can't hear us upstairs," Sammy whispered, as Alex continued his rhythmic attack. "Are you sure we're in the right place?"

"We'll find out soon enough. Go back a few yards where we came from. I'm going to try to spray the wall with the acid and you need to be out of the way."

"Won't argue with that. Be careful."

Sammy watched Alex pull his hood, mask, and goggles over his face, remove the spray gun from his gear kit, and fill it with the clear liquid from a two liter plastic jar. The fumes drove her back along the path, but she could hear the rush of the spray as it burned a hole into the cave wall. The task seemed to take forever; sitting with her back to the cave tunnel wall, she closed her eyes for a moment's rest.

Startled by a nudge on her shoulder Sammy looked up to see a hoodless Alex standing above her, pickaxe in hand and a smile on his face. She jumped up.

"Come and see what we've found."

"Is that what I think it is?" Sammy asked when they'd returned to the excavation site.

A three-foot hole had been carved several feet into the cave wall, and Alex's pickaxe had knocked off enough of the remaining stone to allow human passage.

"Yes. A man-made stone wall. Look at the masonry. Beautiful, but definitely not modern. Here, take this spare pickaxe and start chopping. Careful, though. Don't want to scratch Athena if she's there."

"I'll be as gentle as a sculptor, Alex."

For another hour, they picked and hacked until enough of the masonry had been chipped off to allow a peek into a dark chamber. Alex directed his light into the space.

"What do you see?" asked Sammy.

"Blocks of sandstone and pumice. About ten meters beyond, it looks like marble again. Unpolished, rectangular blocks." The excitement in this voice was obvious. "Sammy, I think we may have found a shaft."

"See any ropes or pulleys?"

"No. Ropes would never have survived the centuries. Winches might have fallen into the shaft when the ropes disintegrated. We'll need to take more of these stones out so we can go into the shaft ourselves." He checked his watch. "Three AM. The sun rises at six. We'd better hurry."

They removed more of the man-made stone wall piece by piece, until the opening allowed passage of one person at a time. "I'll go first," said Alex. "I can toss out some of the pumice to create a space for us to stand."

"Maybe I should, being smaller and lighter," Sammy countered. "Let me do it. You won't lose your chivalry points."

"All right. But be careful. I brought a rope. I'll hold onto this end, so I can pull you up if you fall."

Sammy climbed through and landed on the sandstone. After passing some of the pumice stones in the shaft to Alex, she tested a few more steps across the shaft, holding onto the rope. "Seems solid enough, Alex." She jumped up and down.

"Hey, what are you doing?"

"Making sure it's safe for you. And me. Together. Come in."

Alex tied the end of the rope to a robust stalagmite and made his way in as well. He glanced around the shaft. "Four walls of marble. Layers of sandstone packing the shaft. The size seems to fit our Goddess friend."

"Well, where is she? We're only twenty feet up and she's forty feet tall, right?"

"Nothing prevents a deeper shaft. I grabbed the ladder at the end of the mountain path. There's another thirty feet down below that's at least to the level of the Herodes Atticus Theatre and Dionysos restaurant. But, we might be closer than we think. Look at the boulders to your right. That looks like it was a passageway that could have allowed Athena's acolytes to check in on her discreetly every so often and not be seen."

"Okay, now what do you suggest?"

"Let's try to remove a little more of this shale and build our own cave. Here, support this big piece on each side with these stones to make a kind of bridge over us."

"Hope that slab holds up, Alex. Here, buttress it on three sides."

An hour later, they began lifting up the next layers of shalestone below. The air in the shaft was musty and little circulation from the tunnel could get through the one-person opening. Sammy and Alex were both sweating, and Sammy's arms ached from the effort of moving the stones.

"I don't know if I can do this much longer, Alex," Sammy said, her voice weak. "And we're out of the water I brought."

"One more layer. We're so close. Just one more."

Sammy grunted and pulled off a few loose pieces of pumice and shale. She gasped. Below the stone she held in her hands, was a helmet with a sphinx in the center, and below a few pumice rocks, a griffin on each side. "Oh, my God."

Alex stood staring at the find, his eyes welling up with tears.

Sammy laid the stone down and reached over to give Alex a hug and a kiss. "We found her!"

"Athena lives again!" Alex returned the hug, until another voice filled the room.

"But not for long."

Alex and Sammy pulled apart and spun around to see a man with a trimmed beard and salt and pepper hair standing in the opening of the shaft, holding both ends of Alex's rope. Loukas Doxiadis!

CHAPTER SIXTY

Wednesday, before dawn, June 18ᵗʰ, 2003

"Loukas! What are you doing here?" cried Sammy. This visage did not resemble the friendly one she had seen just a few hours ago above ground. Doxiadis' eyes radiated both anger and ice, his mouth was set, his jaw clenched.

"Vasilis and I had been following you two for the last week, Sammy. Among your many unwise decisions, you shouldn't have left the ladder hanging from the Acropolis ledge."

"Vasilis? You mean the monk that attacked us? I don't understand. You saved me."

Doxiadis snorted. "I couldn't let him kill you before I found out what happened at Monastiraki. We needed time to learn what you'd discovered. Thankfully, it only took you a few extra-strength shots of ouzo to disclose the details of your little adventures at the nightclub." He shook his head. "Vasilis was not supposed to die. That his strap broke was God's will."

"Why are you doing this, Loukas? We've never hurt you."

"You are hurting Christ our Lord. It is my God-given mission to protect Christianity from those who wish to undermine our hard-won victories of centuries. Pagans, atheists, and infidels. Like Harris Lambros *and* the two of you!"

"Doxiadis, stop this nonsense and get down off that opening," Alex said. "You'll knock pieces of the shaft wall into the shaft."

"Shut up!" Doxiadis shouted. "This is all your fault. You and your *Apocalypsi* discoveries. An insult to Christ. And your little girlfriend there, dishonoring our faith and our sanctuary at Mt. Athos. Yes," he said, glaring at Sammy. "You told me all about it at the disco." A loud scoff. "Our monasteries are starving, literally starving. No money, no resources. Our priests are sidelined in our schools. Our churches are empty, except for the old. Thanks to the rise of secularism and heresy from 'scientists' like you, Matsas. You are heretics and deserve to die."

"Um, Alex," Sammy whispered. "I think he actually means it."

"Yes, damn you," Doxiadis yelled. "I warned Harris, but did he listen? Even after I'd convinced that fool Roussos that the statue was the Virgin Mary, Lambros kept pushing Athena. Athena, Athena, Athena! After he called me that night, I knew everyone would come to our country to gawk at the pagan *Apocalypsi* finds and not to worship Panaghia. I had to kill him—it was the only way to stop him. Just like I have to kill you."

Alex spoke into Sammy's ear. "You grab the rope when I rush him."

"Stay back." Doxiadis reached into his pocket and pulled out a gun, pointing it at Sammy. "The punishment for heretics, including Athena, is death. You will all face that justice."

"What does he mean by that?" Sammy mumbled.

Alex shook his head.

"All three of you will be buried in Athena's grave." Doxiadis' face grew redder and redder. "When I close up this wall again, nobody will ever know this was your gateway to the devil in Hell."

"If he closes the wall," Alex whispered to Sammy, "we'll only have a few hours of air. I'll try to knock him down and get his gun. You make a run for it and get help..."

Sammy looked at Alex, stricken. "He'll shoot you," she whispered back. "Please, don't."

He ignored her. "Get ready."

Sammy shook her head, and mouthed the word, "No".

"But," Doxiadis continued, oblivious, "Because I'm a good Christian, I won't torture you. To show my compassion, I will execute you each with a simple gunshot to the heart and leave your corpses to rot on Athena's crown. Sammy, you first. It will hurt Matsas more to see you die. Close your eyes. There will only be a second of pain. But it will be nothing compared to the fires of Hell."

As Doxiadis raised and cocked his gun, Sammy reached for Alex's hand and shut her eyes.

The sound of a gunshot echoed through the shaft.

CHAPTER SIXTY-ONE

Wednesday morning, just before dawn, June 18th

Pappajohn's phone rang, waking him from a fitful sleep. Georgie, with the gift of youth, slept through without a stir.

I hope that's Sammy. And that she's with Alex and not in trouble. Sammy was still out when he gave up and went to bed. His heart sank when he heard Katsoulis say hello. *Oh, my God. What else could it be at this hour?*

"Sorry to wake you, Kosta, but, I wasn't able to reach Sammy. Is she there with you?"

Pappajohn sat up on his roll-away. "I don't think so. Let me check." He rose and peeked into her room. The cot was empty. "No, not here. She was spending the afternoon with Alex. I thought maybe... Is she okay?"

"I hope so. One of my men saw her this evening at the Acropolis museum with Loukas Doxiadis."

"The professor who saved her life? Well, then, she should be all right."

"No, Kosta." Katsoulis related what she'd discovered about Doxiadis' academic and personal history. "I'm worried. I had my team run a trace on his licence plate. His Smart Car is still parked a block from the Acropolis. The place closes at eight and Doxiadis doesn't live nearby. Wait, I'm getting a call on the other line from the officer I sent to the Acropolis."

Pappajohn returned to his room and grabbed his clothes to be ready to go when Katsoulis came back on the line. "What is it?"

"Security cameras did pick up Sammy going into the Acropolis around six P.M."

"With Doxiadis?"

"No, alone. She was wearing a T-shirt, jeans, huge dangling earrings, and this strange belt around her waist. About five minutes later, Doxiadis walked through. He looked nervous and agitated."

"You don't think he would try to hurt her, Despina? He just saved her life last week."

"I looked up the records of the monk's accident and read the officers' reports. Apparently some witnesses heard the fighting duo shouting in Greek."

"Death to the heretics?"

"Yes, from the monk. And '*me, me*' from Doxiadis."

"I remember. He was trying to pull the monk away from Sammy."

The American tourists thought he was deflecting the attack to himself, too. But one Greek witness heard Doxiadis shout '*Mi, Mi, oxi akoma!*'"

"Don't, don't, not yet," returned Pappajohn, translating— and now really worried.

"Exactly. Wait, I'm getting another call. Please hold."

"Katsoulis came back on the line more quickly this time. We did a perimeter check. Above and below. No bodies, thank God. However, it looks like someone dug a ditch under a construction fence and broke onto the grounds with an Army crawl. And they did find two ten meter Kevlar ladders tied together next to the side entry leading to the museum ventilation shafts toward the back of the Acropolis. I'd better send a car to pick you up."

"No, I'm downstairs already haling a cab. I'll meet you on the ground there."

Sammy's eyes flew open to see Doxiadis fall from the opening above onto the excavated helmet of the Athena statue. The sphinx atop the helmet pierced his chest through and through. As he lay face down at their feet, his blood dripped onto the pumice and sandstone, dyeing it red.

Sammy and Alex both looked up to see another man standing in the opening.

"Ilan!" Sammy let out her breath. "My God, thank you!"

"From me, as well," added Alex. "Efharisto."

Sammy frowned. "But, wait, weren't you supposed to be long gone?"

"Remember, I told you not to do this, Sammy. But after getting to know you, I guessed you might anyway. So I figured I could leave in the morning, which," he looked at his watch, "it almost is. Gave me time to keep an eye on you, just in case." He peeked into the shaft, and smiled. "Well, you did it. You found her. Congratulations!" Eyeing Doxiadis' prone body, pierced by the helmet, he added. "I don't believe in the Olympic gods, but I do believe in karma. Let me tie this rope back and I'll help you all climb out."

"And Doxiadis?" Alex asked.

"His body will be in good hands in a few hours." He took a deep breath. "I can't say the same for his soul."

When they arrived back at the cave entrance, the Kevlar ladders were gone, replaced by a fire truck whose ladder was extended and stretched to reach the openings' ledge. Parked close by was an ambulance, police cars, and a very anxious-looking Katsoulis and Pappajohn.

"Well, isn't that nice of them," Ilan said, sliding down. He hopped off the truck and saluted Katsoulis.

Alex came down next, offering to spot Sammy as they both slowly descended. Ilan helped them off the fire truck.

Pappajohn wrapped his arm around Sammy's shoulders. "We were so worried."

Katsoulis' tone was harsh. "What the hell were you doing in there?"

Alex stepped in. "Captain, we found her. Athena. She's there, under the stone. We uncovered her helmet."

"You could've been killed," scolded Pappajohn, as he glanced up at the entrance.

"We almost were, Gus. Loukas tried to kill us. If it wasn't for Ilan…"

"His body is in the lift shaft," Ilan said. "No need for the ambulance. Just the coroner. A thirty-eight caliber slug right through the heart. I'll come down to the station and give a full report."

Sammy turned to Katsoulis. "Please don't arrest him. He saved our lives. I'd be dead now if he hadn't shot Loukas."

She spun back to Ilan. "How did you know about Doxiadis?"

"Your cameraman friend's tape. Ollie shot a lot of video on the *Thesaurus* prior to his murder. Some of the footage was on the deck. The monk was there, arguing with his father. Then he chatted for quite a while with Mr. Doxiadis. Just before the monk walked over to pick up his mask and oxygen tank, he and Doxiadis parted with some hand signals. I looked them up online. The monk's was the sign of Jesus Christ, and Doxiadis' was…"

"The Sign of Benediction. A blessing," interrupted Katsoulis.

At the police station, Pappajohn, Katsoulis, and Ilan shared one interrogation room, while Sammy and Alex sat in another. The glass window between the rooms allowed Alex and Sammy to watch the other group, but not to hear their conversation. Katsoulis had agreed to question Ilan first, as he insisted he needed to leave for Israel as soon as possible. Declining to be videotaped, Ilan wrote and signed a written statement of the night's events.

After a half hour, they all stood. Ilan shook hands with Katsoulis and Pappajohn. Pappajohn nodded and clapped him on the back.

Sammy, observing, said, "I think he's saying thank you for saving us. Well, I'm glad he wasn't arrested. I thought handguns were illegal in Greece."

"They are," Alex said, looking pensive. "He could only have a handgun here if he was a Greek cop," explained Alex, one eyebrow raised.

"But he's not a cop, is he?" Sammy asked as Ilan left the other room.

Ilan opened the door to their interrogation room before Alex could respond. "On my way," he said, entering. "Just wanted to say goodbye before I set sail."

"The man of a thousand skills, I thank you," said Sammy. "You must have a great army in Israel to teach you all that."

"Well, yes, we do. But there are other places to learn those skills as well." Smiling, Ilan put a finger up beside his nose.

Sammy's jaw dropped. "Wait. No. You told me a spy couldn't tell the difference between an amphora and, what was the other one — an athame?"

"I must have meant the spy who doesn't do his homework." Laughing, he saluted Alex, and took Sammy's right hand in both of his. "Katsoulis knows how to reach me. If you ever decide to visit — or apply to Mossad for a job."

With a warm wave, Ilan ducked out of the room.

"Damn," said Sammy to Alex.

"Well said."

CHAPTER SIXTY-TWO

S ammy and Pappajohn returned to the Moschato apartment just in time for the midday dinner. The Kapsis family gathered around them, eager for updates.

"Everyone was talking about it at church this morning!" said Daphne.

"And I wore my new suit," added Georgie. "Thank you, Sammy."

"It's all over the news," Eleni said. "The *anastasis*, the resurrection, of the ancient statue of Goddess Athena!" She pointed to the TV. "Look!"

"But that poor Professor, the one who liked you so much. Slipping and falling on Athena's helmet..." Daphne shook her head. "He was so handsome," she added, as the broadcast showed his university website photo with his captioned name. "What a shame."

Sammy shared a glance with Pappajohn. Clearly Katsoulis and her team had scrubbed Ilan from their adventure. The TV cameras must have arrived after they'd left the scene, because only crime scene tape, police and their cars, and the coroner's van were on the B-roll loop the news station kept replaying. And Katsoulis apparently wasn't eager to have the public learn that the Acropolis was the site of a second attempted murder in one week. She and Gus would have to tell Tasos and Daphne what really happened after the kids had gone to bed.

Sammy's phone vibrated. She flipped it open to talk to Alex. "Yes...I'm seeing it...I know...well, it'd blow his cover…no kidding! Let me put you on speaker. Folks, it's Alex."

"Hello, all. I was telling Sammy that they found our museum's missing Zodiac dial at Doxiadis' flat. He also had several gears, the two dials Harris bought, plus your dial, Tasos. It's evidence now, but I'm sure you'll get it back soon."

Tasos and Daphne looked at each other. "Maybe we can lend it to the museum exhibit for for a while, to help complete the Apocalypsi device," Tasos said as his wife nodded.

"That would be wonderful. We could put a nameplate on it saying 'on loan from the collection of Yiorgos and Anastasios Kapsis.'" Daphne giggled, clapping her hands. "You'll talk to Kiki Matsas?"

"Yes," he said. "When it's time. It will take months for the Acropolis archaeologists to safely raise the statue. Perhaps it can be displayed in time for the Olympics next summer."

"We will all be invited to the gala then won't we?" asked Daphne.

Tasos rolled his eyes, and Sammy and Pappajohn laughed, as Alex added, "Of course."

Thursday, June 19th

At nine A.M. the next morning Sammy stumbled into Daphne's kitchen still rubbing her eyes. Pappajohn, Eleni and Daphne were sitting at the table finishing breakfast.

"Well, Sleeping Beauty awakens. Was it Alex's kiss?" Pappajohn bantered.

"That's tonight. I needed a good night's sleep first…except for a middle-of-the-night phone call from Jim Lodge. He sends regards, by the way."

"I'll have to invite him to Boston and Eleni can cook us a Greek dinner," Pappajohn said.

Eleni smiled. "Yes, you're all welcome to visit as soon as I find a new place there." To Sammy: "I sold our house in Somerville when I married Big George."

"You're going to stay at my house," Pappajohn insisted. "Even with Ana and Teddy there, we still have an extra bedroom."

"Oh, Gus. I couldn't impose…"

He raised a hand. "I won't hear of any objections." he told his sister. "It's our family's home and you're family. And, Sammy, whenever you're up our way, you're family, too."

"Aw, thanks. And, ditto. I can't promise you a guest bedroom in a New York City studio apartment, but I'll take the sleeping bag when you visit." She accepted a cup of Greek coffee from Daphne with thanks and joined them at the table. "So, Gus, I heard you have a date with Despina?"

A frown. "Who told you that?"

"I told her you were going to have dinner together this evening," admitted Daphne

Pappajohn scoffed. "Just a chance for two colleagues to go over the Lambros case."

"Uh-huh. Sure. Don't tell me she isn't just a little bit attractive." Sammy teased.

Daphne giggled. 'Shhh."

"Goodness, Gus, you're blushing," Eleni said.

Pappajohn fanned his face with a hand. "It's just the heat. It's summer."

"Okay. But I think you two make a great team, really." Sammy took another sip of her coffee.

Daphne shook her head. "I still can't believe Loukas Doxiadis killed Lambros…."

"He fooled us all. Who could have known he was really a zealot masquerading as an open-minded academic?"

"Self-appointed judge, jury, and executioner," said Sammy.

"Well, I'm glad he missed on that last one," Pappajohn said, as Daphne and Eleni nodded.

Sammy smiled. "So am I, Gus, so am I."

CHAPTER SIXTY-THREE

Friday evening, June 20th

As the sun was drifting below the horizon, Alex and Sammy
sat at a seaside restaurant in Piraeus sharing a fresh-grilled
fish.

"The phone hasn't stopped ringing," Alex complained.
"I just had to get away." An embarrassed chuckle. "Well, I
didn't mean it like that."

Sammy smiled. "No, I know what you meant. But, this is
your moment. Yours and Professor Lambros'. You deserve all
the press coverage and accolades."

"Pity Harris isn't here to enjoy them. He reveled in this
sort of circus. As does Kiki."

"She's been on all the Greek stations, CNN, and the BBC,
talking up your museum Looks like she's back on track for the
Director job when the old guy retires."

"I wouldn't be surprised. But it's not my museum any
more. Despite what Kiki implies."

"They offered you your job back, didn't they?"

Alex nodded. "And I turned them down."

Sammy looked genuinely surprised. "Wow. No kidding."

"I have a better offer I'm considering. From Aristotle
Vandis. And the Vandis Foundation."

"The airline billionaire?"

Another nod. "He's asked me to take on the Directorship
of the Vandis International Foundation for Hellenic Arts and
Culture."

"That's quite an honor," Sammy said. "Congratulations! Here in Athens?"

Alex broke into a wide grin. "In New York, New York."

Grinning from ear to ear, Sammy leaned in and gave Alex a warm hug and kiss.

EPILOGUE

August, 2004

"Hurry up," Daphne urged her family. "We don't want to be late."

"Relax, sugar," Tasos responded, as he put on his cummerbund. "I can always put the blue light on the roof of our car."

"Okay, Mr. Detective," said Daphne, giving Tasos a quick kiss on the cheek. "I love this new formal you bought me." She twirled around to show off the dress.

"You should, at the price I had to pay. Almost all of Katsoulis' bonus."

Maria glided in wearing a little black dress that ended mid-thigh.

"What, they ran out of material?" Tasos grumbled.

"Oh, Baba. Yanni will meet me – us — at the Acropolis. He just got his driving licence and wants to drive me to the opening this afternoon at the Olympic Stadium."

"Tell your boyfriend to remember that detectives still carry their guns, okay?" half-joked Tasos.

"I'm ready," said a voice that ranged from gravel to squeak. "But my new suit is already too small," complained Georgie who had sprouted a few more centimeters in the past six months.

"Alex and Sammy just left the InterContinental," Daphne announced. "Let's go."

The scaffolding around the Parthenon had been shifted so that the invited guests could walk the red carpet from the marble stairs directly into the temple's atrium. Beyond the rows of folding chairs, at the center of the building, rose the forty foot statue of Pallas Athena, the Goddess and Protectress of Athens. Home again.

The Kapsis family and Maria's plus one stopped to gaze in awe at the imposing statue before heading to their reserved seats in the front row. Sammy, her red hair and curls framing her smiling face, jumped up to great them all with hugs and double cheek air kisses.

"Georgie," she announced. "You won. Three inches taller than me now and, unlike me, you're still growing." She winked. "Hey, Alex," she called. "Come and see who's here."

Alex said a quick good-bye to the dignitaries with whom he was chatting and strode over to greet the Kapsis family. "Did you come with Despina and Gus?" he asked.

"They haven't seen us for two weeks," Pappajohn boomed, with a twinkle, as he and Captain Katsoulis walked up from the side aisle. "Despina why are you keeping Tasos so busy?"

Katsoulis, dressed in a fashionable blue and white dress, rolled her eyes. "If you want to take some of Tasos' shifts…?"

Pappajohn laughed and shook his head. "No thanks. I'm busy enough being a consultant for you and for Keith. By the way, Keith says hi to you all. Remotely, over a VPN, of course. And Eleni will be arriving with Ana and Teddy tomorrow, and can't wait to see you."

Kiki Matsas appeared at the dais with Elias, the Director of the Acropolis Museum. She tapped the microphone, and asked for everyone to sit. The murmurs of conversation died down as the attendees took their seats.

Elias stepped to the microphone and welcomed the audience to the Acropolis and the Parthenon. "Today's celebration would not have been possible," he continued, "without the tireless efforts of…"

As Elias took a breath, Sammy smiled at Alex.

"…Dr. Angeliki Matsas, Director of the Hellenic Archaeological Museum." Elias leaned over, took both of Kiki's hands in his and gave her a double-cheek kiss that lingered for more than a few seconds.

Sammy and Alex looked at each other and swallowed their laughter. "They make a good couple," Sammy whispered.

"…and I would also like to thank my colleague," Kiki continued, "the Director of the Aristotle Vandis International Foundation for Hellenic Arts and Culture, Dr. Alexander Matsas, who flew in from New York to celebrate with us today. Alex, could you please stand."

Looking embarrassed, Alex started to rise. Sammy squeezed his hand, and, in a moment of joy, he returned the squeeze and guided her up on her feet as well. As the crowd applauded, Alex raised his and Sammy's arm in a cheer. They both looked briefly at each other, and, facing the imposing goddess, shouted together, "Welcome Home!".

THE END

ACKNOWLEDGMENTS

We would like to express our thanks to Dr. Anastasios Chassiakos, mathematician and engineer, whose expertise was instrumental (no pun intended) in developing realistic calculations for our fictional ancient device that led our protagonists to uncover the Athena statue.

Thanks as well to our early readers, consultants, and "editors", Joan Cochran, Alice Suna, Paul Willand, Jim Reynolds, EG Stassinopoulos, Paul Scotton, and Sharon Gerstel. Their critical and helpful eyes were most appreciated.

Thanks also go to Torsten Muller who designed a new cover for our re-release!

Finally, thanks to our spouses, Joel Shlian and Anastasios Chassiakos, for their unfailing love and support.

- Deborah Shlian and Linda Reid

ABOUT THE AUTHORS

Deborah Shlian is a physician, healthcare consultant and author of numerous nonfiction articles and books as well as seven award-winning medical mystery/thrillers including the Florida Book Award for Rabbit in the Moon and three in the Sammy Greene series. Deborah moved from Los Angeles to Boca Raton where she lives with her husband. Learn more about her on her website www.shlian.com

Linda Reid is a physician and journalist who has written for the Washington Post, the Baltimore Sun, and the Los Angeles Times, as well as a broadcaster and commercial actor on radio and TV. She has co-edited two textbooks on Health Administration with Dr. Louis Rubino, and co-authored three mystery/thrillers and one short story in the award-winning Sammy Greene series, with Dr. Deborah Shlian. As Y. S. Pascal, she co-authored the mash-up novel, Elementary, My Dear Spock, with Mary W. Matthews; and authored the award-winning science fiction novels Renegades, Redemption, and Rebirth in the Zygan Emprise series. She is currently a Clinical Assistant Professor of Pediatrics at the David Geffen School of Medicine, UCLA, and a Fellow of the American Academy of Pediatrics and the American College of Physicians. Linda and her husband spend their vacations enjoying visits with her children and extended family in Los Angeles, New York City, Washington DC, and Athens, Greece.

WOULD YOU DO US A FAVOR?

We hope you enjoyed reading *Deep Waters* as much as we enjoyed writing it. If so, would you write an honest review of our book? Let us know if the story touched you in any special way.

Your review doesn't have to be long. Just a sentence or two will be great.

Your feedback is so appreciated.

Thanks so much for your kindness and generosity.

We look forward to hearing from you!

And, we hope you enjoy Books 1 and 2 in the Sammy Greene Thriller Series—*Dead Air* and *Devil Wind*.

Available on Kindle, Amazon, and, Audible.

www.ingramcontent.com/pod-product-compliance
Lightning Source LLC
Chambersburg PA
CBHW031608100726
47898CB00006B/1703